At the Moment of Victory

At the Moment of Victory

Catherine Louisa Pirkis

MINT EDITIONS

At the Moment of Victory was first published in 1889.

This edition published by Mint Editions 2021.

ISBN 9781513272016 | E-ISBN 9781513277011

Published by Mint Editions®

minteditionbooks.com

Publishing Director: Jennifer Newens
Design & Production: Rachel Lopez Metzger
Project Manager: Micaela Clark
Typesetting: Westchester Publishing Services

Contents

Prologue

The hush of twilight was falling upon the rugged mountains and deep ravines of Santa Maura, a lonely hamlet on the Corsican coast; bird-notes were dying under it; the whirr and stir of summer insect life growing faint; even the wash and swirl of the Mediterranean sounded dreamy and far away under the spell of the "silent-footed Angel-herald of the night." He beckoned to the great, gloomy forests of pine and cork, and they sent forth their shadows in troops and squadrons; laid his soft, dull hand on the heavy odours of magnolia and myrtle, and they poised in mid-air, knowing that heaven's gates were shut against them; he drew his veil of mist from east to west across the stormily-purple sky, and the smirch of tawny orange, which marked where a great, golden sun had blazed itself out, was seen no more; touched with his finger of mystery the figure of a woman descending a mountain path straight into the heart of a ravine, and lo! she stood transfigured into the likeness of a ghostly visitant from the kingdom of Hades.

That woman might have been Astarte herself for the silent grace of her movements and the dead whiteness of her face, which showed as if moon-washed from out the surrounding dimness.

In the ravine into which she was descending, Night was following hard and fast on the "angel-herald's" step to claim his own. The mountains rose gaunter, more drear, more black with every downward step the woman took, until, at length, they seemed literally to pierce the vaporous gray sky with their peaks and turrets.

High over one of the highest of these peaks there shone out through the vapour one star of intense metallic brightness; at the immediate base of this rock, bowered amid olives and vines, stood a small country house, a stone-built chalet, surrounded by a narrow strip of garden.

The woman was making her way straight for this chalet. At its garden-gate she paused for a moment, looking right and left and in all directions, as if to make sure that her movements were unseen. Unheard they must, have been; not ghostly fingers themselves could have unlatched that gate more noiselessly, nor ghostly feet have trodden with a lighter footfall that garden path, which, winding in and out among arbutus-trees and myrtles, led to the creeper-covered porch of the house. Under this porch had been placed a small table and a rustic reclining seat. On this seat lay a man, locked in heavy slumber.

He was about thirty years of age, and of remarkably handsome appearance, swarthy, mustachioed, and with waves of black, curly hair sweeping across his forehead. His arm pillowed his head. On the ground at his feet, as if carelessly tossed on one side, lay a broad-brimmed hat. On the small table beside, him stood a glass about three-parts filled with wine.

This way, that way, all ways the woman looked hurriedly, furtively, with every step she took. Not a sound broke the stillness; not a leaf rustled, nor belated insect flitted. She stood within a hand's breadth of the man now; she held in her breath; then, slowly, cautiously drawing from beneath her cloak a small phial, she poured its contents noiselessly into the glass of wine. As she drained the last drop into the glass, she chanced to lift her eyes to the door of the house. It stood wide open, disclosing a stove-place filled with flowering plants, over which, against the wall, hung a large, square mirror.

In that mirror, as the woman lifted her eyes, she could see darkly reflected the whole shadowy garden-picture. She could see, also, her own white face, and white hand which held the small phial.

I

When I marry again," said young Mrs. Cohen, with cheeks something the color of field poppies, and eyes that flashed like diamonds under lamplight, "I shall marry a boy—years younger than I!"

"Quite so," assented her companion, a young man who leaned over the piano at which she was seated; "it is absurd for women to marry men older than themselves!"

"And it is very ridiculous of you," continued the lady, "to imagine because I like to—to—"

"Squabble?" suggested the gentleman.

"Have a little fun with you now and then, that, therefore, I am willing to marry you."

"My dear Madge, I never for a moment imagined anything of the sort. I took your last 'No' as final six months ago."

"Everyone knows that you are years—years—years too old for me."

"Oh yes, years, years, years too old. I am the whole of three years and three-quarters older than you are."

"Everyone knows that we haven't the faintest liking for each other."

"Exactly. Everyone knows," mimicked the young man, "that we can't be ten minutes in the same room without quarrelling."

"In fact," continued the lady with heightening voice as well as colour, "we are getting positively to detest each other."

"The wonder is that we are ever to be found in each other's company."

"I am positive," cried Mrs. Cohen, jumping up from her music-stool, "that it was you who said that 'the library was getting confoundedly hot;' yes, those were your very words, and you must 'get out of it.'"

"I am confident it was you who looked over your shoulder—at me—and said, 'I am going into the music-room to practise, and—'"

"Yes," interrupted the lady, "that was because I saw Sir Peter looking at me, and I knew how delighted he would be if we crept out of the room together for all the world as if we—"

"Were bent on spooning?"

"And it's of no use your standing: there agreeing with me, as if I didn't know what I was talking about or didn't mean what I said. I repeat, when I marry again, I will marry a boy if I like."

"Why not? How would you like a nice little middy, about fourteen?"

"He shan't be a day over twenty at any rate, and he shall be obedient and tractable, and I'll call him 'my child.'"

"Ah, he'll like that!"

"And I'll tell him where to get his clothes and what cigars to buy!"

"He'll be sure to buy them, won't he? Look here, Madge, let's give over squabbling, and strike a bargain. I'll engage to look out for this amiable young gentleman, who'll buy his clothes and cigars where his wife tells him, if you'll undertake to marry him as soon as he's found. I can't say more, can I?"

Madge made no reply. She seated herself at the piano once more, struck a chord, ran off a little prelude, and then commenced singing her scales at a very high pitch.

Her voice was a mezzo-soprano, and her high A was a very high A indeed.

Here is the portrait of Mrs. Cohen as she sits at her piano.

Age, twenty-four years. Figure, small and slight. Eyes, hazel-green and deep-seated. Eye-brows, dark and arched—the best feature in her face. Nose, inclined to the classic, but nothing remarkable. Mouth, small and sensitive. Complexion, decidedly sallow, but flushing readily under excitement. Hair, dark brown, cut short, thick and curly.

"Young Mrs. Cohen would be nothing without her curls," once Madge had heard a dowager say as she left a ballroom. Since then she had diligently cultivated her curls as her one strong weapon in her armoury of charms—an armoury, by the way, of which she had not a very exalted opinion.

"I think you are a remarkably plain young woman. It is a positive trial to be confronted with you so many times a day," she was in the habit of saying when she looked at herself in her mirror.

And here is the portrait of Lancelot Clive, the young man who stood for a moment listening to the scales and then walked away saying to himself: "Not 'soft, gentle, and low,' today, at any rate!"

Age, close upon eight-and-twenty. Good height, well-developed chest. Eyes, bright blue, sparkling and fun-loving. Hair, golden brown, irrepressibly curly, no matter how short it might be cropped, and a complexion bronzed by constant out-door exercise.

Madge half-turned her head as her companion left the room; but she in no wise lowered the pitch of her A. Madge's vocal scales were a wonderful outlet for her superfluous energy. She had recommenced taking singing lessons within a week of her marriage with old David Cohen, the retired diamond merchant; had dropped them in the early days of her widowhood, but had resumed them with surprising-vigour during the present year, when she had once more taken up her abode in the home of her girlhood.

"Selling herself for a diamond necklace," had been Lance's summing up of the marriage, to which he had received a hasty summons, while pursuing his studies at Oxford. A summons, by the way, to which he did not see fit to respond.

"Doing what is expected of me as Sir Peter's *protégé*—keeping Lance from making himself ridiculous and blighting his prospects in life," had been Madge's version of the case to her own heart, as she stood before the altar vowing to "love, honor, and obey" a man old enough to be her grandfather, and whose highest conception of happiness was an interval of freedom from gout, which enabled him to "read, mark, learn, and inwardly digest" the money article in the daily paper.

Madge was in the very middle of a voluminous shake on her high A when the door behind her opened, and admitted a small, plump old gentleman, who looked as if he were in a very great hurry indeed.

There was something in the mere turn of the handle which made Madge say to herself: "It's Sir Peter," and stop her singing at once.

"Madge," said the old-gentleman, "where is Lady Judith?" But he did not wait for an answer. He had crossed the room and had gone out by another door before Madge could open her lips.

She did not, however, recommence her singing; she knew by experience that he would soon come back again with possibly another question.

He did so come back; this time entering by one of the long French windows of the room, and his question now was:

"Where is Lance?—can't find anybody this morning, and I've so many things to get through, I don't know which way to turn;" and then he disappeared again.

This small, plump old gentleman was Sir Peter Critchett, sixth Baronet of that name, of Upton Castle, in the County of Cumberland. His plumpness was a remarkable fact if the extraordinary activity of his habits were taken into account. Except at mealtimes, he was never still.

"He's a fortune to me in boots," Sir Peter's London bootmaker was wont to affirm, as he packed up the last of the twenty-five pairs, he was in the habit of sending yearly to Upton Castle.

And "He pays the salary of my head man in the carpets he wears out," said the upholsterer, recollecting the number of times that he had been called upon to renew the library carpet in Sir Peter's town and country houses.

Cruikshank would have delighted in sketching Sir Peter's plump, placid face, separated from his bald head by a ridge of stiff, grayish hair, which radiated in hard lines backward from his temples.

Lance had often tried to rival Cruikshank on the backs of old envelopes and magazine covers. Once, in the very middle of dressing for dinner, he had snatched up his hair-brush, and with pen and ink had sketched on its ivory back two very round eyes over-arched by two very astonished-looking eyebrows, a short nose—a mark of exclamation expressed it exactly—an innocent-looking little mouth, and no chin to speak of. Then, holding the brush sideways to his view, he had discovered what had inspired the idea, namely, the long, stiff hair-bristles which framed the portrait precisely as the stiff, radiating lines of grayish hair framed the original.

By that perverse ruling of fate which so frequently sends people on the scene at the exact moment that their presence is least welcome, Sir Peter had entered Lance's dressing-room just as he had laid down his hairbrush.

"What's this—a picture?" asked the old gentleman, taking up the brush and holding it this way, that way, all ways, so as to get a good view of the sketch.

Lance's presence of mind did not desert him. "It's a kindergarten brush," he replied without moving a muscle. "It's intended to make children—boys that is—fond of brushing their hair. You can get lots of them at the corner of Oxford Street."

Not alone in face and feature was Sir Peter remarkable. Fancy a child, with its insatiable love of new toys, its perpetual rebellion against "routine," its hatred of instruction, and lack of experience, suddenly transferred from pinafore to coat-tails, and transported from its nursery to the society of grown-up men and women! Such an one might have figured as Sir Peter's prototype in Nature's workshop.

"He is the Prince of Pierrots," someone with an eye for character had once said of him. "His *protégés* and his schemes of benevolence are marbles and peg-tops to him."

Sir Peter rejoiced in an extensive and well-earned reputation for philanthropy.

People were in the habit of coming from all parts of the country to lay before him their divers' schemes of charity, and to beseech his patronage for them.

It must be admitted, however, that such beneficent schemes as succeeded in winning his favourable notice, occasionally went into his hands very big and came out of them very small. For instance, a gigantic plan for rescuing from the gutter every little street Arab in London would result in the importation into the Castle gardens or stables of some unkempt, untaught little urchin, who, in the process of his civilisation, would drive head-gardener or groom nearly frantic. And a big scheme for educating the orphan daughters of clergymen of the Established Church re-solved itself, in the person of Madge Cohen—then Madge Grant—into the transference of one little forlorn maiden from a scene of poverty into the luxurious home-circle of Upton Castle.

The forlorn little orphan was now a rich woman, thanks to her marriage with old David Cohen. She had her town house, and her country house, her horses, and her diamonds. But for all that Sir Peter did not feel inclined to wash his hands of her. No! Just as he had chosen her first husband for her, so was he now desirous of choosing her second; and it seemed to him, that a better could not be found than Lancelot Clive, the son of his old friend, Colonel Clive, and his own adopted son and reputed heir.

Among his many schemes of benevolence, this held the first place; and from morning till night his energies were concentrated upon the endeavor to bring about a marriage between these young people, an event which there was every reason to believe would have come about in the natural order of things, if he could but have been content to let matters take their course.

"If he would but let us alone," Madge sighed, as now for the third time Sir Peter entered the room, and paraphrased his former question somewhat as follows:

"What is Lance thinking of, eh, Madge, to leave you to your own devices in this fashion? Has Lady Judith carried him off to her farm to help her count her latest brood of Brahmapootras—eh?"

Madge, not having yet got her breath back after her late passage-of-arms with Lance, would have liked to answer:

"I haven't the remotest notion where Lance is, and he never comes near me again to the end of time pence-halfpenny."

That she did not so answer was entirely owing to the fact that whatever else she might forget, one thing she always re-membered, namely, that once she had been Madge Grant, a poor little waif, and dependent upon Sir Peter's bounty.

So, she answered composedly, as if she enjoyed being catechised in this personal fashion:

"Lance is, I dare say, in the gun-room, looking over his fowling-pieces, and Lady Judith not at her farm. I heard her half an hour ago tell your new secretary that she wished to speak to him in the morning-room."

And then she went back to her scales, sighing once more:

"If he would but believe that the world could get on without him!"

By coincidence, the very same words were at that moment on Lady Judith's lips as she sat in her pretty morning-room, engaged in conversation with the gentleman who had only the day before been installed as private secretary to Sir Peter.

Yet, conversation is scarcely the proper word to denote talk in which, as the Irish-man said, "the reciprocity was all on one side." For Lady Judith was all but stone deaf, and the private secretary, after one or two vain efforts at assent or demur, had yielded to circumstances, and now stood a patient listener to her energetic harangue.

Lady Judith was a woman of between fifty and sixty years of age, and her gait and dress expressed every one of those years in uncompromising severity. She had a supreme contempt for those who sought by the arts of the toilet or graces of manner to negotiate a truce between middle life and old age. Her one pleasure in life was the management of her home farm, her one duty—from her point of view that is—to play the part of cog to the household wheels which Sir Peter kept in perpetual motion. In fact, she was florid and large-featured; in figure, tall and stout. She towered a good three inches over the person she was addressing—a small, spare man of about fifty, gray-haired and whiskerless, with expressionless features and eyes that looked out of such narrow slits that it was impossible to tell what colour they were.

She had risen from her chair in the course of her oration, and now, fan in hand, stood rounding her periods with sustained vigour.

Her fan was an absolute necessity to her; once set upon "conversation" she never failed to talk herself hot and red in the face. She wielded that fan in no dainty, coquettish fashion. In her hands it suggested the whirring arms of a windmill on a breezy height.

"I suffer so from the heat," she parenthetically informed the private secretary, announcing a fact that must have been evident to the most careless observer.

Then she went back to the main subject of her discourse.

"This talk between us is entirely confidential, Mr. Stubbs," she said, speaking in a high key as if she were addressing someone on top of a church steeple. "Sir Peter has the kindest heart in the world, and a very wide reputation for benevolence. *Entre nous*, I should not be at all sorry if his reputation could be curtailed—this is quite in confidence, you understand—and it occurs to me that by the exercise of a little judgment and discretion on your part—an occasional word put in now and then, do you see—the multitudinous outlets for his benevolence might be reduced in number. Of course, you will have to use great tact; *entre nous*, Mr. Stubbs, Sir Peter is a trifle obstinate when once he takes a thing into his head. Your predecessor was a man without tact, and a little too fond of hearing himself talk; and, of course, quickly got his dismissal. Well, as I was saying, Mr. Stubbs—but this is quite confidential—Sir Peter has the kindest heart imaginable, but if he could only be made to understand that the world could get on without him—" she broke off abruptly, asking the question:

"What is the matter—toothache?" as an expression of agony passed over Mr. Stubbs's face.

It was not to be wondered at that Mr. Stubbs should have exhibited a change of feature, for, all unknown to the lady, the door behind her had opened, and Sir Peter himself had entered the room, and stood listening to her discourse.

It was matter for congratulation that at that moment a diversion was affected by Lance dashing into the room in hot haste and whispering something into Sir Peter's ear with many a furtive look at Lady Judith.

Mr. Stubbs, being blessed with quick hearing, caught the words:

"Accident on the rails below Lower Upton! Come along at once! I've had the cart brought round. There'll be lots for you to do."

II

Upton Castle stood high among the Cumberland hills, some nine hundred feet above the sea level. Above its gray stone walls the Cuddaw Fell rose in sharp grandeur another nine hundred feet, belittling with its sweeping curves and massive crags the strong-hold beneath, which once had held its own with the best of border fortresses, and which successive masters with big purses and luxurious tastes had adapted to the exigencies of modern requirements.

"The mountain belongs to us," Lance used occasionally to say, looking upward with a measuring eye from the top of Sir Peter's bald head to the cloud-capped Fell. "Or we belong to it," he would add as an afterthought. "I'm not quite sure that isn't a better way of putting it."

Had any one asked Lancelot Clive, at this period of his career, to put his notions concerning the whole duty of man into a nutshell, he would have replied without a moment's hesitation, "Get as much fun out of everything as you possibly can."

He had a free and easy way of treating the elderly Sir Peter, which at times Madge wondered over, and at times she envied. But then he was a *protégé* of a different stamp to what she had been. His mother, who had died at his birth, had been a Critchett, and his father had been Sick Peter's oldest friend. When Colonel Clive had died suddenly of fever in India, it seemed the most natural thing in the world for Sir Peter to continue the orphan lad's education, and, when Eton and Oxford were said good-bye to, to install him at Upton as his adopted son and heir.

"The young fellow was born to good luck," everybody said, although at the same time they were willing enough to admit that things must have been very different with him had Gervase Critchett lived or had a son.

Gervase Critchett had been Sir Peter's only brother, who, as a young man, had been seized with a sudden desire for wildlife in the West. In pursuance of this idea he had gone out to Mexico, had bought a ranche there and had been killed, there was every reason to believe, in one of the numerous, unreasoning insurrections which the history of that country records.

Lance was a thoroughly genial, good-hearted young fellow. He had a lofty way of patronising everybody and everything that came in his way which might have been irritating or amusing, as the case might be, if it had been less genially or unconsciously extended. "Uncle Punch and Aunt Judy" had been his schoolboy nicknames for Sir Peter and Lady Judith—herself, by the way, an Earl's daughter.

It was a misfortune for Sir Peter that his wife owned to the Christian name of Judith, it so forcibly suggested the characteristic sobriquet for her husband.

In the same lofty, patronising fashion. Lance would speak of the old Castle as "the dungeon," or "the jail," or more frequently still as the "whited sepulchre," "tolerable for three weeks at a time, in-supportable for a fourth."

It was the gray of the mountainside which suggested the last unfortunate simile. Seen in the glint and glare of a noonday sun on a summer's day, the old Castle stood out in hard, staring whiteness against the graduated gray of the rocks so tenderly laid on by Nature's practised hand.

But when the summer's sun had sunk behind the Cuddaws, and the red, sunset flames had died out of its windows, the old house seemed to shrink into the mountainside and become part and parcel of the shadowy crags. Purple then became the keynote of colour of the whole landscape.

An artist sketching it might have done without his reds and yellows, but his purple he must have had, or his picture would have lacked that subtle yet everywhere-present charm of mystery, which only the shadowy purple could impart. There it was, deepening the gray of the mountain, the silver of the overhanging mist, flashing darkly out of the sheen of the distant lake, clouding the blue of the thickset pine-wood, and finding; its focus in the foreground of the picture in the luxurious heather which spread itself in straggling patches over hillside and valley.

That valley seemed to stretch away into a limitless distance, until it kissed the horizon. Lower Upton, with its new railway station and few scattered cottages, lay hidden somewhere among its copses.

Lower Upton was about seven miles distant from the Castle "as the crow flies," but a good nine miles if the windings of a steep, rocky road be considered. That was a nasty bit of road, especially at midday' under a scorching sun, with Uncle Peter "in good form," as Lance was apt to phrase it, on the box seat.

"Uncle Peter" was in uncommonly "good form" on the morning when he and Lance set off together for the scene of the railway disaster; that is to say, he made the nasty bit of road seem double its length with an incessant flow of interruptions, or rather what would have been such if Lance had not been wary.

"Lance," said the old gentleman so soon as they were outside the Castle gates, "it has only just struck me that we might have sent a man on to Carstairs to tell the doctors there. Of course, old Broughton will be on the spot, but he may want additional help. We had better turn back and leave a message."

"All right!" said Lance, touching up his horses, not turning their heads, "we'll leave a message for Aunt Judy at the keeper's cottage as we go along."

A message was left at the keeper's cottage, and Lance rattled along over the flinty road for another half-mile. Then a second idea "struck" Sir Peter.

"It has just occurred to me, Lance." he said, with a sudden start that would have shaken the nerves of a timorous "whip," "that it would have been as well to have left word for the wagonette to be sent down after us; it might serve instead of an ambulance. Just turn the horses' heads. It's only a question of a quarter of an hour."

"Ah, that will do at the next cottage—Turvey, the mole-catchers. We'll send a message back by one of his small boys," answered Lance calmly as before, and again whipping up his horses.

Then Sir Peter had cramp first in one leg, then in the other, and insisted upon getting down to "walk it off."

Finally, within half a mile of Lower Upton, his third and last "idea" struck him.

"I do think, Lance," he said, getting more and more cheery as they neared the scone where he supposed his energies would be called into requisition, "it would have been a good idea to have told them to send down with the wagonette something that could be converted into an ambulance—wonder it didn't occur to you when you left the message at Turvey's. The sufferers may be too much injured to stand the jolting of—"

Here Lance pulled up sharply. "Ho, there!" he shouted to a man who chanced to be coming along with a cart of hay.

"Who-a, my lass," said the man to his horse, and stood at attention.

"You're going up the Cuddaw Road, I suppose?" queried Lance. "Well, you'll meet Sir Peter's wagonette coming down. Tell the man to turn back, take the doors off the stables, and bring them along with him—they're wanted for ambulances."

"No, no!" shouted Sir Peter. "There are plenty of hurdles down at the farm. Are you out of your mind, Lance! Do you hear, my man, hurdles from the farm?"

But it was exceedingly doubtful whether the man heard him, for Lance had once more touched up his horses, vowing that unless they put speed on, they might as well turn back at once. Then he drew a fancy picture of the scene of disaster, which, possibly, the railway station presented; of wrecked carriages lying along the line, sufferers in various stages of mutilation stretched on the platform awaiting succor.

Sir Peter subsided into tranquility, as Lance knew he would, before the prospect of so vast a field for his energies. He buttoned up his coat, so as to be tight and trim, and ready for action.

"If I were you, I would let your shirt sleeves alone," said Lance, noticing a side glance which the old gentleman gave to his wristbands.

Sir Peter looked like a naughty child forestalled in some mischievous idea.

"But we'll take our rugs with us, Lance," he said, "they'll be sure to come in useful one way or another."

But alas for Sir Peter s forethought and prognostication! The little railway station presented its usual picture of rustic quietude as Lance drew rein at it.

The station-master came forward to reply to Sir Peter's queries. The accident, he explained, had occurred five miles down the line. A number of coal trucks had been overturned through the breaking of some coupling irons, and, as the line could not be cleared before night, all traffic through Lower Upton was stopped for that day.

"The worst damage," he went on to say, "was the inconvenience that passengers travelling North had been put to. They had been compelled to alight at Lower Upton and had had the choice offered them of remaining there for another twenty-four hours, or, of travelling back twenty-five miles of their road to Carstairs, whence they could travel North by various routes. Most of the passengers had adopted the latter course—all in fact except one—a young lady," here he glanced towards the waiting-room of the station, "who appeared to be greatly annoyed at the delay to her journey, and who seemed unable to make up her mind what to do. She spoke with a foreign accent," the man farther stated, "and he was not sure whether she thoroughly understood his explanation of how easily her journey might be continued by travelling back twenty-five miles."

"Capital!" said Lance, "there's something for you to do after all, Uncle Peter. Of course, we're bound to offer our services to the young lady. We can drive her anywhere she would like within twenty miles or take her to the Castle for the night and bring her back in the mornings: when the line's clear. 'Greatly annoyed,' 'foreign accent.' Why, I'm beginning to feel like Don Quixote already? Come along."

They went into the waiting-room to see a tall, slight young lady standing there with a small portmanteau at her feet. She wore a long gray travelling cloak which reached to the hem of her dress, a gray beaver hat, and gray gossamer veil which entirely hid her features.

III

The hot afternoon began to wane. Lady Judith and Madge drank their tea out of doors under a spreading cedar, which made a shady nook on the lawn. Madge brought out a writing-folio with her, thinking it possible that Lady Judith might fan herself to sleep, as she often did on a summer's afternoon, and thus give her the opportunity of getting through a little of her correspondence.

Lady Judith, however, was not disposed for sleep, but for "conversation," in her sense of the word, that is. The number and variety of topics she touched upon while she and Madge stirred their tea, suggested a comprehensiveness of knowledge that would have done credit to the compiler of "Enquire Within Upon Everything."

Madge, a well-seasoned listener, leaned back in her rocking-chair, indulging in her own train of thought under cover of an occasional sympathetic remark, which Lady Judith as often as not did not hear.

Sir Peter and his fads, as might be expected, received the lion's share of the lady's criticism; thus:

"My dear, if it had not been for me the Castle would long ago have been turned into an orphanage or almshouse, or perhaps into a lunatic asylum—though, for the matter of that, it's half-way on the road to one now at times, with the queer sorts of people he brings into it." And so forth for a good twenty minutes, with brief interludes for fan or tea-cup.

Lance and his misdoings next received, as it were, a passing glance.

"Where is the use," she queried, pathetically, "of my saying to him as I do every day of my life, 'Lance, do your best to keep Sir Peter from making himself ridiculous'? Or of his saying to me, as he does every day of his life, 'Aunt Judith, I go to bed at nights with Uncle Peter on my mind, I get up in the morning with him on my mind, and he is on my mind all day long'? when he never so much as lifts a little finger to keep him out of mischief. My dear, it's my belief that that young man looks upon life as nothing more than a big jest from year's end to year's end. He'd sell his soul any day of the week, and think himself well paid if only he could get a laugh out of the bargain."

The mere mention of Sir Peter's name had been guaranteeing to Madge of close upon half an hour for uninterrupted indulgence of thought. During the recapitulation of his offences she had been mentally concocting an answer to a letter received from her lawyers that morning, asking for instructions on certain matters connected with the Cohen property.

"Dear sirs," she had been writing in intent, "I wish the bonds and deeds you speak of were at the bottom of the sea. Do just whatever you like about them. And as for the house at Redesdale, it may be unlet to the end of time for anything I care—"

She had got so far, when Lance's name high over her head, in Lady Judith's falsetto, brought her letter-writing to a halt. For once in her life her ideas were in unison with Lady Judith's.

"Sell his soul for a laugh—yes, that was Lance to the backbone," she said to herself a little bitterly. "From morning till night playing at life instead of living it. Never in earnest—never even seeming in earnest. If he had only seemed ever so little in earnest six months back when he had made her his offer of marriage, how gladly she would have said 'Yes' to it, instead of meeting it with the indignant exclamation, 'Sir Peter told you to ask me.'" Then she drifted into cloudland again, picturing a series of pleasant possibilities, if Lance, for once in his life in downright solemn earnest, were to come to her and say: "Madge, I forgive you for doing what you were bidden and marrying money-bags. I loved you then, I love you now, I'll love you always." Ah! how gladly would she pour out those money-bags at his feet! What a heart's delight the counting of her gold, the management of the Cohen property, would be to her then.

And as for lawyers' letters, they might come every day of her life, and be welcome as love-letters, if only she had the privilege of tossing them over to Lance, and saying:

"You'll settle all that, won't you?"

When her wing wearied and she came down from cloudland, Lady Judith had taken Mr. Stubbs, the new secretary, for her text, and was descanting upon his qualifications, or otherwise, for his duties.

"It's my belief, my dear," she was saying when Madge's sense of hearing came back to her, "that Sir Peter only engaged him because he heard from the people who recommended him at Carstairs—I forget their name—that he had been unfortunate in business matters all his life through. He has been twice through the Bankruptcy Court; at one time he was a stockbroker; then he turned lawyer's clerk; then he went into a newspaper office at Liverpool; after that into an auctioneer's office; and after that—after that," this repeated with a contemptuous emphasis, "he comes to Upton Castle, and acts as private secretary to

Sir Peter!" Here Lady Judith paused to fan herself, and to get breath to go on again.

"He wouldn't be so bad-looking if only he would open his eyes wider," said Madge, feeling she was expected to say something. "As it is, it makes me sleepy to look at him."

Lady Judith only caught part of her sentence, and characteristically understood to refer to Sir Peter.

"Open his eyes little wider" she exclaimed, shrilly. "I wish to goodness he would! He would see then how people impose upon him, and lay traps for him to walk into, and then make fun of him behind his back. But there—one might as well tell a blind man not to run his head against a post as tell Sir Peter to open his eyes and look an inch in front of him."

They had now travelled in a circle back to their starting point—Sir Peter, and his delinquencies. Madge mechanically returned to her unanswered lawyers' letter. "I don't care two straws," her thoughts resumed, "whether the house at Redesdale is let or unlet, or whether the farmers are paying half-rents or whole rents—" She had got so far when the sound of wheels coming slowly up the steep drive, which led through the grounds to the Castle, made her look up, to see Lance in the distance, waving to her from his high dog-cart.

She looked and looked again. Was that Sir Peter seated behind? Where was the groom, then, and who was that, all in gray, seated beside Lance on the box-seat? Were the questions which rapidly presented themselves to her for an answer.

Evidently, they suggested themselves to Lady Judith also, for she broke off abruptly, shaded her eyes with her hands, and inquired: "Whom have they brought back with them? Can you see, my dear?

Madge shook her head. "Another *protégé*, I dare say," she answered. But the way in which she spoke the word "*protégé*" was a protest against her use of it. The emphasis she laid on "another" seemed to say: "I least of any one in the world ought to throw stones from out my glass-house."

Sir Peter, in spite of his short legs, was out of the cart before Lance. He crossed the lawn towards the ladies in a very great hurry, while Lance followed at a more leisurely pace, accompanied by the young lady in gray—Madge could see that she was young, by the slimness of her figure, and the grace of her walk.

He came up looking hot, and a little out of breath. "My dear," he said, addressing his wife, "you heard of the accident at Lower Upton. The young lady we have brought back with us had no chance of continuing her journey to the North for another twenty-four hours; so, I told her you would be delighted to receive her till—"

Lady Judith arose from her seat erect and stately.

"I want to know," she said in an authoritative voice, "whether there are any more coming. I heard that the wagonette had been ordered to follow."

Evidently, she had had visions of the wagonette returning packed with lame, maimed, halt, or otherwise injured individuals.

"No, no, no," and Sir Peter shook his head vigorously to emphasize his noes; "only this young lady, I give you my word. Let me introduce her to you."

A few steps behind him. Lance was presenting the lady in gray to Madge.

Madge had left her rocking chair and the shade of the spreading cedar and stood in the glare of the sunlight on the lawn. Lance stood facing her, with the glint of the sunshine on his curly hair, and its gleam in his bright blue eye. Between them stood the young lady, tall and shadowy in her gray garments.

"She came like a shadow between us; I felt my blood chilled," was the description Madge gave of this meeting in after days.

At the moment, however, she merely thought to herself: "Why doesn't she lift her veil? Does she intend suddenly to startle us with a blaze of beauty? or is it perhaps because, like me, she isn't proud of her face, and prefers keeping it hidden as much as possible?"

As if conscious of Madge's thought, the young lady at that moment raised her veil, and dared the unshadowed light of the blazing summer sun.

Madge stood looking at her wonderingly. The face that fronted her, albeit one likely to attract an artist's pencil, was not of a type easy to class. The features—so far as nose, mouth, and chin went—though fairly regular, were unpronounced; the complexion was of a dead, unvarying white, which was doubly accentuated, first by coral-red lips, next by black, straight bars—not arches—of eyebrows, and a thick band of black hair drawn straight across her forehead. The eyes Madge could not see, for the young lady kept her full white lids downcast. It was a face which might attract, and a face which might repulse, according to circumstances; but whatever it might be, it was not a face to be seen one moment and forgotten the next.

"What a peculiar-looking young woman," thought Lady Judith, putting up her eyeglass and staring at her uncompromisingly.

"Eh, I had no idea she was half so handsome behind her veil," thought Sir Peter, taking a steady survey.

"She would make a grand Cleopatra if her eyes are as black as her brows," thought Lance.

"She might sit for the portrait of Jael, who drove the tent-peg through tired Sisera's forehead," said Madge to herself, as far off as ever from answering her own question as to the young lady's beauty. Evidently she did not mind being looked at, for her face showed not the faintest sign of embarrassment.

But, whether intentionally or otherwise, she avenged herself for Lady Judith's eye-glass.

"Is that your housekeeper?" she asked, turning to Madge, and speaking in a slow, deep voice, with an unmistakably foreign accent.

As she spoke, she lifted her full white lids, and Lance saw not the black eyes her hair gave promise of, but large dark-gray ones.

How Sir Peter, at that moment, thanked Heaven for his wife's deafness!

"That is Lady Judith Critchett," answered Madge, stiffly.

"What does she say?" asked Lady Judith, conscious that she was an object of attention to the young lady.

"That she is delighted to make your acquaintance," said Lance, right into Lady Judith's ear.

"Ah, yes," said Sir Peter, drawing a full breath of relief, "let me present you to my wife. Miss—Miss Rosalie," he began, hesitatingly.

"Jane," corrected the young lady.

The incongruity of the name with the face struck Madge.

"Ah, yes. Miss Jane—Jane?" went on Sir Peter, interrogatively.

"Jane Shore," answered the young lady.

The incongruity of the name seemed to vanish at once.

The dressing bell at that moment rang out its reminder. Madge thought it best to end an ungracious situation graciously. "If you will come with me," she said, addressing Miss Shore, "I will show you to your room, and send my maid to you."

"Thank you," was the reply, in slow, halting phrases, which seemed to imply that the English tongue was scarcely mastered. "I will not trouble you to send a maid. I have been travelling for two whole days. Will you give me a bed? It is that I want, not dinner. I am tired—nearly to death."

And the three last words were spoken in a tone that set Lance's brain wondering, his heart pitying.

IV

How can you let him make himself so ridiculous?" asked Madge of Lance, after dinner that night, as together they stood at one of the long drawing-room windows, watching the crimson after-glow fade from the cloud-mountains in the sky, and the night-blue slowly spreading athwart the valley.

"Him! Who, what?" asked Lance, starting as if suddenly aroused from a reverie.

"Why, Sir Peter, of course. Why did you let him bring an utter stranger into the house in this way? A word from you would often prevent these foolish things, yet you never speak that word," she said, echoing Lady Judith's lament.

She spoke in low tones. That drawing-room owned to four windows and three doors, and there was no knowing but what Sir Peter might enter by one of them at any moment.

Lance shook himself free from his thoughts.

"Now I like that, Madge," he began, laughingly, "You know Uncle Peter as well as I do—when once he has taken a notion into his head, not the Lords, and the Commons, and the whole bench of Bishops combined, would prevent him carrying it out."

It seemed as if the mantle of Lady Judith had temporarily fallen upon Madge's shoulders—she was not to be mollified. Lance's laugh, too, did not mend matters.

"It would be bad enough," she went on, "if you stood by and said nothing; but when you absolutely carry him off to the scene of a railway accident for the whole and sole purpose of—"

"Giving him something to do," finished Lance. "My dear Madge, I wonder how many times in your life you have said to me, 'Give him something to do or he'll drive us all mad.'"

"Yes, but not such a something as this. If you must bring people into the house, bring men whom you can entertain, not women who will be left on our hands."

Lance eyed her curiously. Madge seemed more disturbed than so trifling an incident warranted.

Again, he tried to laugh the matter off.

"You don't mean to say you're hard-hearted enough to wish we had left this poor girl to sleep at the railway station? You know there's not an inn even at Lower Upton at which a lady could put up."

"Why didn't she go on with the other passengers to Carstairs? There were more people than she, I expect, who came down by her train."

"She hadn't made up her mind what to do when Uncle Peter and I drove up on the look-out for—"

"Forlorn, beautiful young women," finished Madge, sarcastically.

"Exactly. And finding what we went out to seek, what could we do but—"

"She is not beautiful," interrupted Madge, vehemently. "Her face has a history written on and not good one."

But even as she said the words the thought in her heart was: "I would give all the Cohen diamonds and every penny have in the world to have such face."

Lance put on seriocomic expression.

"Ah! everyone knows, Madge, that you never mean one-half you say," he said as thoroughly bent on teasing as if he were a schoolboy and Madge a screaming, refractory parrot.

"I mean every word I say; and I repeat, her face is an evil one and repulses me. Somehow it makes me think of midnight bridges and dark rivers, and—"

But at this moment a door opened, and Sir Peter entered. He stood for a moment looking about him.

There was Lady Judith, asleep in a low chair, her head thrown back, her big fan drooping from her hand, her face crimson as usual. Evidently, she had fanned herself into the arms of Morpheus. There were Madge and Lance whispering together in the window recess, for all the world like a pair of lovers.

"Delightful!" thought the kind-hearted old gentleman. "Just as it should be! Capital match I Most suitable in every way!"

And as he could not bring himself to interrupt the lovemaking of the young people, he crossed the room on tiptoes, and went out by the opposite door.

Madge seemed instinctively conscious of Sir Peter's thoughts.

"Why did he run away like that?" she queried, plucking nervously at the posy of yellow roses which she wore in her waistband.

"He'll be back again in another minute," said Lance, composedly.

And sure, enough back again he came.

This time through the window, the third from the one at which Lance and Madge were standing.

"Don't disturb yourselves," he said, standing in front of the two and falling into a backward and forward heel and toe motion he frequently adopted, and which suggested the idea that he had suddenly been put upon rockers. "Don't disturb yourselves. I only came in for a moment to say that—that—"

He paused abruptly. Honestly, he had nothing to say. If he had spoken out his thoughts he would have said: "The house is horribly still; it is time I set someone or something stirring."

"That it was a fine evening" suggested Lance.

"Ah, yes, a fine evening! That was it.

And—and it was a disappointment our guest couldn't sit down to dinner with us." This was a sudden thought and he jumped at it.

Madge here plucked so viciously at her roses that two or three fell to the ground.

Lance picked them up and presented them to her in the most lover-like attitude he could command.

Sir Peter smiled benignly on him. "Ah, 'Gather your rosebuds while ye may.' You know what the old song says, eh?" Here he gave Lance a sly little dig in the ribs, and forthwith vanished by another window.

Madge turned sharply upon Lance.

"Why do you do it?" she queried, hotly.

"Why do you make believe and make him think that—that—"

"That—that—" mimicked Lance.

"My dear Madge, all my telling in the world wouldn't convince Uncle Peter that we were not desperately in love with each other. You try your hand at telling him and see what will come of it."

"You tell him things as if you didn't mean them—you ought to—to make him understand that—that—" Again she broke off, and again Lance mimicked her.

"That—that you haven't the faintest liking in the world for me, that, perhaps, you may marry a chimney-sweep tomorrow; but Lance Olive—never. "Well, I'll do my best to make him understand."

"I never said such a thing; you've no right to put words into my mouth," she cried, vehemently; and then, as if fearful of losing her self-control, she half-hid her face in her yellow roses, and left the room.

"If things could only have been different five years ago!" she said to herself as she closed the door behind her. "If I had but been free, as other girls, to choose or to refuse!"

V

Lance remained standing at the open window. A half-amused expression flitted across his face.

"How ridiculous of Madge," he thought, "to lose her temper over a girl she has only seen once in her life, and whom most probably after tomorrow she'll never see again!"

Presently the half-amused expression on his face gave way to a more thoughtful look.

"In spite of her 'No,' six months ago," he thought, "I believe she has a faint liking for me. I wonder if I asked her a second time what answer I should get!"

The wonder was one to entertain, not to dismiss as a passing thought. So, with a glance at the still peacefully-sleeping Lady Judith, Lance took his cigar-case out of his pocket and strolled through the French window on to the outside terrace. The evening air was cool and balmy. The garden showed weird and mysterious under the long night-shadows which were beginning to troop forth from beneath the trees and Castle walls.

Lance went strolling in leisurely fashion along the dim paths, his thoughts as serene and limpid as the dark stretch of summer sky overhead. It did not require the miserable rushlight of a young man's vanity, nor that stronger light which experience of women's ways gives, to read clearly Madge's apparently capricious conduct, when once a steady attention was accorded to it. She would be wooed for herself, not for her wealth; wooed, too, in downright passionate earnest, not by a lukewarm suitor edged on by a lively guardian. This was what her alternate sweetness and sourness, her petulance and playfulness meant if they meant anything at all.

And after all, so Lance's thoughts ambled, in leisurely time to his leisurely steps, there was no reason why Madge should not be thus wooed. Hers was a sweet and attractive personality when once one had learnt to pierce that outer armour of caprice wherewith temperaments like hers, rendered super-sensitive by circumstances, frequently clothe themselves.

When Sir Peter had brought her, a shy little maiden of twelve, to Upton Castle, Lance had made a fine pet and plaything of her. Later on, as she had developed into the girl in her teens, he had been honestly in love with her. Later on still, when Sir Peter had taken her future in hand and considered he had done a thoroughly good day's work in marrying her to old David Cohen, Lance had seen fit to indulge in the bitterness of a rejected suitor, and to anathematise her for a heartless flirt, although at the same time he had gone out of his way to convince "Uncle Punch and Aunt Judy," and all the world beside, that he and Madge had never been more than brother and sister to each other. During Madge's short married life he had seen next to nothing of her; but when, on the death of her husband, she shut up her town house, let her country house, and came back to the home of her girlhood, he was willing enough to listen to Sir Peter's suggestion that "he and Madge were made for each other," and to do his best to obliterate from his recollection that short period of her wedded life.

Thinking over his offer of marriage now in this dreamy half-light, he said to himself that he did not wonder at the impetuous "No" it had received, considering what a small amount of energy he had displayed in the making of it. Doubtless it would have met with a different reception if Sir Peter had left him alone to make it in his own fashion, instead of jogging his elbow, as it were, morning, noon, and night, to do at a rush a thing which could have been far better accomplished by successive steps.

Lance finished his cigar, but still lingered out there among the shadows and heavy flower-scents, indulging now in this pleasant thought, now in that. The Castle grounds wound downwards with many a steep pathway right into the valley, where, among the stalwart pines and drooping larches, stood the keeper's cottage and the home farm. It occurred to him that there was something he particularly wished to say to the gamekeeper about a bit of land that was to be enclosed for cover that year; so, in spite of the growing dark, he decided to make his way down to the cottage at once, lest tomorrow's occupations might once more sweep the matter from his mind.

The shadows closed around him as he descended the incline. Behind him lights were beginning to show in the Castle frontage through its trellis-screen of sycamore and cedar. Overhead the smirched gray of twilight had given place to the sapphire-blue of a night-sky pierced with a hundred thousand "star windows to let out heaven's light." His downward path showed gray in front of him, dimly tesselated with the faint shadows of the planes and wild plum-trees which grew at intervals on either side. Then for a brief distance the path wound upward again, with a wood on one side, and a high thorn hedge on the other. Beyond this hedge a bare brown upland rose, treeless and shadowless.

A gap in the hedge, where the last hunt had ridden through, framed for Lance a bird's-eye view of this sterile waste. It showed him something else beside the dry stunted turf and a few scurrying rabbits—the figure of a woman sharply outlined against the night-sky. She half-sat, half-crouched, with arms encircling her knees. She wore no hat, her hair was tightly coiled about her head, her face was upturned to the heavens.

Lance was neither poet nor painter; but nevertheless the weirdness and mystic beauty of the scene made itself felt. That crouching sibyl-like attitude, the wildly desolate surroundings, seemed to transport him straight from the Cumberland hillside to classic ground, peopled with the queen-prophetesses of ancient myth. If the woman had suddenly tossed her arms on high, and burst into some wild invocation, it would have seemed all in keeping with the ghostly scene.

But she did nothing of the sort. Instead, as if conscious of his presence, she suddenly turned her face towards him. Then Lance, in utter amazement, recognised, by the light of the stars, the pallid face and jet-black hair of Miss Jane Shore.

He was through the hedge in a moment, and in another was standing beside her on the shadowless waste.

"Miss Shore!" he exclaimed. "What are you—can you be doing out here at this time of night?"

The girl did not start nor move from her crouching attitude. For one instant her large gray eyes were lifted to his face with a hunted, forlorn look in them which made his heart ache for her.

"Looking at the stars," she answered, dreamily, absently. Then she let her gaze sweep the sky once more.

There was no moon; the bare upland on which they stood showed, in the half light made by the summer sky and myriad stars, a ghostly patch from out the surrounding gloom of dense hedges and denser woods. The girl's upturned face seemed more like some marble mask than a thing which had life and could redden and smile; the black sweep of hair across her forehead heightened its pallor into an almost death-like whiteness, while the gray garments which clung to her showed like so much dim shroud-like vapour from which she was just emerging.

An artist seeking an impersonation of a fallen star, looking upward to its lost place in the heavens, might have found his ideal realised here.

Lance, in his young, robust flesh and blood, felt himself in some sort out of keeping with his environment.

For a moment he felt tongue-tied; then, as if to break a spell, he made his voice to be heard.

"If you are fond of star-gazing," he said, "you ought to go to St. Cuthbert's churchyard—it stands on a promontory—you can get a splendid view of the heavens there, right away over the Irish Sea."

Treeless though this upland was, the expanse of sky it commanded was comparatively circumscribed, on one side by the thick wood which stood on yet higher ground, on the other by the majestic crags and headlands of the Cuddaws.

Only the first part of his sentence seemed to catch her ear.

"Fond of star-gazing," she repeated, slowly. "Is one fond of gazing on the faces of one's enemies? The stars are my enemies. I hate—hate them."

The last words were said with a vehemence that left no room for doubt as to their sincerity.

Lance tried to be comfortable and commonplace. "Pardon me," he said, "then why do you come out here with nothing between you and the sky, when you could so easily, by drawing your curtains, shut out the faces of your enemies?"

She answered his question circuitously. "You ask your friend to tell you your fortune; he will say pleasant things to you—he will lie to please you. You ask your enemy; he will speak truth to you—the stars cannot lie."

The effort with which she spoke the English tongue was marked in this sentence.

"For all that, or rather in spite of all that, I don't think I should feel disposed to neglect the society of my friends for that of my enemies," he answered, lightly, but feeling all the time that his light words were strangely out of place.

She turned her large luminous eyes full on him. "What if you have no friends to neglect?" she asked, coldly, stonily, as one might who had long been accustomed to look the fact in the face.

If Lance had been in his usual frame of mind, words would have come trippingly to his tongue at hearing a handsome young woman thus frankly proclaim her friendlessness. That he stood silently gazing at her for a good minute and a half showed that he was undergoing a new experience. Her head drooped, her hands lay limply in her lap.

Seated thus, she gave him the impression of some one half-stunned by some crushing blow, listless and indifferent whether a second would follow.

"I can hardly credit such a thing," he began, hesitatingly.

She did not let him finish his sentence. She rose slowly from her crouching posture.

In the dim light her tall figure seemed to elongate itself beyond its real height.

"Look in mid-heaven!" she said, in the same hard, bitter voice as before.

Lance followed the sweep of her hand to where, under the shadow of the Cuddaw Fell, the old Castle dominated the landscape. High in the heavens, directly over the top-most peak of the Fell, a planet shone out with brilliant, metallic lustre among a thousand stars.

Lance, very hazy in astronomical knowledge, would have liked to ask a thousand questions. What planet was it? Had it a bad character among the planets? And so forth.

But she would not allow one. She drew the hood of her cloak over her head, and so closely round her face that naught but her glittering, forlorn eyes showed beneath it.

"Come, let us go back to the house," she said. "I have seen enough for one night."

VI

Lance, thinking afterwards over his walk back to the Castle in company with Miss Shore, was driven to admit that never before in his life had he spent so silent a quarter of an hour, in solitary company with a handsome young woman.

Lance had something of a reputation for his conversational powers, but now they appeared suddenly and unaccountably to have failed him. Except in the briefest thanks for assistance over stiles or rough pathway, or monosyllabic acquiescence in his remarks about the beauty of the night, he did not hear Miss Shore's voice.

Once or twice, as they walked along the dim lanes, in and out among the treeshadows, he found himself looking at her wonderingly, trying to define, not alone her personality, but what special quality it was in that personality which seemed to attract and repulse him at one and the same moment.

In that bewitching, bewildering half-gloom of the summer's night, she looked, in her long, clinging gray garments, scarcely less shadowy than the shadows among which they walked. In the smooth paths of the Castle gardens her steps became slow and gliding, and he fell a little behind in his walk, asking himself if it were a real living woman he was following, or merely a bloodless shadow which would by-and-by disappear into the mist and vapour out of which it had emerged.

Inside the hall-door, they parted with a brief "Good-night."

"Who was she? what was she? whence had she come? whither was she going?" Lance wondered, gazing dreamily after the tall, slight figure as it glided noiselessly up the broad oak staircase.

Lady Judith's falsetto, in gradual approach from the farther end of the hall, brought him back to commonplace earth once more.

Lady Judith's voice sounded near and nearer. This habit of speaking as she came along was a peculiarity of hers. She was invariably heard before she was seen.

She had her night-lamp in her hand, and, as usual, a fine flow of words on her lips. Madge had gone to bed with a bad headache, and she herself—well, had been a little startled: as she was sitting alone in the drawing-room something had happened which had set her shivering.

Lance's face said, "Fancy! Aunt Judy shivering!"

"If it had happened to any one else," the lady went on serenely, "I should have said that it was a dream; but you know, Lance, I never by any chance indulge in an after-dinner nap."

"No one would ever dare accuse you of such a thing," said Lance, with a double meaning.

"Quite so. I admit that sometimes—sometimes, though rarely—I close my eyes to rest my head; for, what with my farm and Sir Peter, and one thing and another, my brains do get tired at times. Well, I was sitting, as you left me, in the dark corner of the drawing-room—with my eyes shut, perhaps, I'm not sure—when I seemed to hear a rustling at the further end of the room, and, looking up, I saw a tall, gray figure glide, yes—glide is the word—across the room from the door to the open window, where it seemed to disappear. Now, wasn't it uncanny?"

"Tall and gray?" said Lance. "Don't you mean little and gray? And didn't it come back again so soon as it had gone out, and then go out again by another door?"

As if to verify the impromptu sketch which Lance had given of him, the study door opened at this moment and Sir Peter came forth.

"My legs ache with sitting still so long. I've been dictating letters ever since dinner, and yet my table's covered; and Stubbs is still hard at work!" he said, plaintively, as he opened the door which stood opposite the study door, in order that he might have a free line of march.

A sudden thought struck Lance:

"Uncle Peter, can you give me three minutes?" he asked, "I want to speak to you."

Sir Peter was delighted.

"I know, I know," he said, rubbing his hands gleefully and shutting the door briskly on Lady Judith's portly figure mounting the staircase. "My dear boy, I know exactly what you're going to tell me. It's about Madge. You've asked her again, and she has said 'Yes,' and you want to be married at once! It would be a capital idea to make one thing of my birthday festivities and your wedding festivities next month, eh? My dear boy, I'm delighted—delighted! A quarter of an hour's talk will settle—"

"I wish to goodness you'd let me talk," interrupted Lance, brusquely. "I haven't asked Madge, and I haven't the slightest intention of doing so—that he added, correcting himself, "I know if I were to ask her just now I should simply get a 'No' for my pains. Now, will you listen to what I have to say?"

It was evident that he had quite forgotten his pleasant meditation over his leisurely cigar in the earlier part of the evening.

Sir Peter looked towards the corner of the room where Mr. Stubbs sat at a table writing by lamplight, with his back to them. "Is it anything private—strictly private?"

Lance had quite overlooked the secretary. But then he was just the sort of man to be overlooked—one of the kind we may meet every day, and whom we may see a dozen times over, and then come away, and one of us will assert that he's tall, and another that he's short; a third that he's fair, and a fourth that he's dark; while, as a matter of fact, he is most likely none of these things and could best be described by a series of negations.

"No, not exactly private," answered Lance, leading the way, however, to the other end of the room, and speaking in a low voice. "But I know you delight in doing a kind action, and I was going to make a suggestion to you."

Sir Peter was all eager attention at once.

"I hope it covers a wide area," he said, describing a semicircle in the air with his arms. "I dislike wasting time and strength over microscopic schemes."

"I don't think my suggestion can be dignified by the name of 'scheme,' microscopic or otherwise," said Lance. "It's about Miss Shore." Then he hesitated.

Sir Peter was most willing to help him along. "Fine young woman—very," he exclaimed. "Good figure, well dressed. Foreign mother, I suppose—must be. Shore is a Sussex name, isn't it?"

"I was thinking," Lance went on, "that it might be kind to ask her to prolong her stay here for a day or two; she seems very desolate and friendless"

"Eh? what, desolate and friendless?"

And Sir Peter s eye wandered to the writing-table, where a locked drawer held his cheque-book. "Did she tell you so? I didn't hear her say so as we came along, and I think I heard all your conversation."

Of necessity he must have done so, seeing that during the drive home he had leaned forward with folded arms on the box-seat, which Lance and Miss Shore occupied, for the express purpose of so doing.

Lance felt discretion was needed. "I can't say that she told me so, but I inferred as much from—from the fact of her travelling alone, and from the very melancholy look on her face. You may have noticed it."

"Ah, yes, now you speak of it I did notice that she had a peculiarly sad expression of countenance. I'm sure I shall be delighted. Ask her to stay as long as she feels inclined."

"The invitation would come better from the ladies of the family," suggested Lance.

"Ah, yes, of course. Well, you ask Lady Judith to invite her to stay on a bit."

"No; you ask Lady Judith," said Lance. "The suggestion would come better from you."

Sir Peter rubbed his chin thoughtfully.

"Eh? No; I don't think it would. Between you and me, Lance, Lady Judith and I don't hit it off altogether as I could wish sometimes. I don't like to say but don't think she would be at all likely to give Miss Shore a welcome, if she looked upon her as a possible *protégé* of mine."

Lance began a vigorous demur to this.

"Now, Uncle Peter—"

Uncle Peter gave a little jump. "I've got an idea—capital idea! You ask Madge to invite Miss Shore to stay on a day or two, and we'll tell Lady Judith when it's done."

"Ah, capital!" echoed Lance. "You ask Madge, and it's settled at once."

"No, you ask Madge. The suggestion will come better from you, my dear boy."

Lance's face changed. "No, I don't think it would. Between you and me, Uncle Peter, Madge and I don't hit it off altogether as I could wish sometimes. I don't like to say but I don't think she would be at all likely to give Miss Shore welcome she looked upon her as possible *protégé* of mine."

"EH, WHAT! DON'T HIT OFF, you two?" cried Sir Peter. "Don't believe a word of it. You squabble, do you say? Nonsense; what you call squabbling is coquetry on her part, nothing more. Don't get such an idea as that into your head for a moment. Women are born flirts—born. I ought to know, I have had twenty-five years' experience of married life."

How far his married life had helped him in his experience of feminine coquetry it would be impossible to say. One might as well at any time have attempted a flirtation with the Marble Arch in Hyde Park, or the old Cuddaw Fell itself, as with Lady Judith.

Lance backed out of the study before this tirade.

He did not notice that Mr. Stubbs, half-turning his head as he sat, watched him out of the room with a curious look in his narrow eyes.

VII

As a rule, the moral temperature of a household can be more easily taken at the morning than at the evening meal. At the dinner-hour conventionalities are treated with greater respect, and idiosyncrasy is swamped.

Breakfast at the Castle on the morning after Miss Shore's arrival was a typical meal.

Sir Peter ate it walking from room to room.

Lady Judith ate it talking of her farm and her dairy.

Madge ate it reading her letters.

Lance was accustomed to get through breakfast at a fairly brisk pace and then be off to the stables or kennels. On this particular morning, however, he deviated from his usual custom for he ate next to nothing, and then sat still with his empty plate before him watching the door.

It was an odd, jerky sort of breakfast. Food seemed eaten, as it were, in parentheses. Exercise on Sir Peter's part, conversation on Lady Judith's, letter-reading on Madge's, and anything you please on Lance's part, seemed to be the real object of their assembling at nine o'clock in the morning. Lady Judith was in high spirits over a new patent incubator which she had just introduced into use at her home farm. She could talk of nothing else, and imagined that every one at table was addressing inquiries to her respecting it—which inquiries she answered appropriately or otherwise, as the case might be.

For instance, when Madge asked how a new maid, engaged a day or two previously, was doing her work, she got for reply:

"Works magnificently—in an altogether superior fashion. I shall recommend the thing all over the county."

And when Lance chanced to make a remark upon the extraordinary heat of the previous day, the lady broke in with:

"It hatched over ninety chickens yesterday, and no less than one hundred and ten the day before."

The door of the breakfast-room immediately faced the study on the other side of the hall. Both these doors were set wide open; and Sir Peter, oscillating like a pendulum between the two rooms, would be one moment eating a morsel of chicken in the one, and the next dictating a line to Mr. Stubbs, already seated in the study at his writing-table.

"I hardly know which way to turn, my hands are so full," he said to Madge, literally in passing.

To have heard him speak one might have thought at the very least that he was a Cabinet Minister, with the responsibility on his shoulders of keeping even the balance of power in Europe.

Madge, looking furtively at Lance as she got through her correspondence, seemed to read, "Is she coming?" written on his face. "I sent my maid to call Miss Shore," she said, coldly, answering, as she imagined, his unspoken thought. "But she tells me she could get no answer to her knocking; so I suppose the young lady is tired with her long journey."

If she had spoken out all her thoughts she would have added: "Really, I have no interest in the matter beyond the wish that the young lady should save the mid-day train from Lower Upton."

Lance dawdled about the morning and breakfast rooms for half an hour or so, and then disappeared into the gun-room. Sir Peter had eyes and ears only for his correspondence. Lady Judith went trailing through the cornfields, fan in one hand and a big white umbrella in the other, down to her farm.

Madge, feeling that the responsibility of Miss Shore's movements rested on her shoulders, despatched her maid once more with orders to rap louder than ever at the lady's door, and not to come away till she received an assurance that she was heard.

When, however, the maid came back with the same report as before—that, in spite of twenty minutes of rapping at intervals, not a sound was to be heard, Madge made her inhospitable wish give way to a kindlier impulse. It might be as well, she thought, if she herself went up to the young lady's room, in case illness or some accident had befallen her.

So, accordingly, she made her way to the upper quarters, and delivered a series of raps on the closed door.

All the same, never a sound broke the stillness within.

Then Madge thought it was high time that she turned the handle and ascertained for herself the condition of affairs on the other side of the door.

She made as much noise as she could in entering. There was Miss Shore lying on her bed, dressed in her gray cloth travelling-dress of overnight. Her hat was on the floor beside the bed, as if it had been suddenly tossed off; her gray cloak was flung, as if at random, over the face of the toilette-glass.

But was it at random? This was the question Madge asked herself; for there was also the cheval glass pushed into a distant corner of the room, with its face turned to the wall.

With an odd feeling of apprehension, Madge approached the bed and looked down into the sleeper's face.

Her head was thrown back on the pillow, leaving the white, slender pillar of a throat bare to view. Her face was dead white; the bandeau of black hair, which fitted the head like a crown, had slanted forward, overlapping the eyebrows; her lips showed scarcely so coral-red as they had in the sun-light on the lawn; her breathing was low and regular, and there was nothing to give Madge the impression that the sleep was an unnatural one.

Nothing except a glass standing on a little table beside the bed, which might—so Madge conjectured—have been hastily drained and set down before the sleeper had thrown herself back on her pillows.

Madge debated for a moment in her own mind what she should do. Ought she to endeavour to rouse the young lady? Or was she in a condition that required medical aid?

She made the round of the room. She drew up the blind, letting the morning sun fall full on the sleeper's face. It transformed the dull black hair into the glossy black of a raven's wing, marked out line by line every blue vein in all its delicate tracery on cheek and eyelid; but never so much as a fluttering breath showed that the girl was conscious of any disturbing influence.

Then Madge thought it would be as well to take counsel on the matter; so to the gun-room accordingly she went, taking it for granted that she would find Lance there. He was just coming out of the room as she reached it. They took a turn or two in the outside gallery while she detailed to him the state of affairs.

Lance looked disturbed and distressed, she thought; but, for all that he treated the matter lightly.

"Depend upon it, she's worn out with travelling. Didn't she say that she had had two days of it?" he said. "Don't you remember once how sixteen hours after slept right off for heavy day's tramp Leave her to have her sleep out she'll wake right enough later on in the day."

"What about the glass beside the bed?" queried Madge, suspiciously.

"Oh, shouldn't think any more of that, if I were you don't say word about to Sir Peter, or he'll be sending off for a dozen doctors, and as many nurses. Take my word for it, there's nothing to fuss over."

They walked up and down the long gallery for a minute or two in silence. "What do you think about the looking-glasses being hidden and turned to the wall?" presently Madge asked.

Lance laughed.

"Accident—pure accident. The thing was in her way; she pushed it in a corner; she wanted to get rid of her cloak, and by chance threw it over the other. You've made a mountain out of a mole-hill."

"Have I? I'm not so sure of that," answered Madge, slowly. "Being what she is"—here she eyed Lance narrowly—"it is difficult to understand her not wishing to look at herself in the glass. Now, if she were as ugly as I am, the thing could easily enough be understood."

With the first part of her sentence, Lance seemed to be entirely in accord; the latter part he ignored.

"Yes," he said, thoughtfully. "As you say, being what she difficult to understand that she could have the slightest objection to be confronted with her own face in mirror."

Then, as if to end a discussion which was distasteful to him, he made slight excuse, and went back to his guns once more.

Madge, suddenly recollecting that she had on the previous day left her work-basket in little sitting-room off the gallery, turned the handle of the door, to discover, to her amazement, Mr. Stubbs, just within the room, "not a yard from the key-hole," as she said to herself indignantly. He was in standing posture, as if he had retreated before the opening door.

Madge's face showed her astonishment. "I came here to find Lady Judith," he said, a little hurriedly. "I suppose she is down at the home farm?"

Then, without waiting for a reply, he slipped past her out of the room.

The impression left on Madge's mind was that Mr. Stubbs had been an intentional listener to her conversation with Lance.

VIII

Lady Judith spent nearly the whole of that day at her farm; the first half in the dairy, inspecting the working of a new butter-making machine; the second half in the meadows under the trees, among the shorthorns and "black Welsh." The patient, dull-eyed beasts must have thought her a sort of incarnated stormy south-wind as she stood over them, with her big fan, superintending the administration of aconite in soda-water bottles, to those who appeared to be suffering from incipient pleuro-pneumonia.

Sir Peter grew tired of his letter-writing as soon as the morning meal offered him no excuse for incessant perambulations; so he ceased dictating, got into the saddle and rode over the hills to see how the new wing of the parish schools, in which he took a great interest, was progressing. Half-way there he suddenly recollected the existence of Miss Shore as a visitor in the house, galloped back at a tremendous pace, set all the bells ringing and every servant he could seize upon running backwards and forwards with inquiries as to where she was, what she had been doing all the morning, and whether she had got over the fatigue of the previous day.

The replies of the servants were necessarily unsatisfactory, and Sir Peter, catching a glimpse of a pink skirt among the laurels in a shady nook, had Madge suggested to his mind as a more likely source of information.

Madge was stitching in leisurely fashion at a group of yellow marguerites on a brown plush ground. Lance, in gray tweed suit, was leaning over the back of her chair with Roy, a great tawny mastiff, stretched on the ground at his feet with his nose on his master's boot.

Madge had been a little startled to hear Lance's voice over her shoulder, suddenly asking the somewhat eccentric question:

"Madge, if you had had the choice given you, what planet would you have chosen to be born under?"

"Planet—planet!" echoed Madge. "Oh, what planet is supposed to give women beauty and powers of fascination? It must be Venus. Under Venus, of course."

"Yes, it must be Venus," decided Lance. "Well, what are the other planets supposed to do or to give? And what's the name of the one that shows now every night over the Cuddaw Fell?"

Madge laughed outright. "Are you going in for astrology or astronomy—which? Upon my word, I haven't the remotest notion what planets are in the ascendant—is that the phrase?—at the present moment."

"Madge, "said Sir Peter's voice just then, a little jerkily from want of breath, "can you tell me where Miss Shore is, and whether she feeling rested, and she would like letters or telegrams sent away to her friends up in the North or down in the South, wherever they are?"

"She was sound asleep when I came out of the house. I haven't the least idea what her wishes or plans are," answered Madge.

"Asleep! Asleep! At this time of day? Impossible! My dear, she must be ill. We'd better send some one to fetch Broughton—"

"Oh, let her alone, Uncle Peter," interposed Lance. "The poor girl's evidently tired out with a long journey. I dare say she'll wake up right enough a little later on, and tell us what she wants to do or have done."

Lance's words were verified.

Madge's maid, sent up about tea-time, came down saying that Miss Shore had answered her rapping with the intimation that she would come downstairs in the cool of the evening, and the request that yesterday's newspaper might be brought to her.

"Yesterday's newspaper!" repeated Madge. "You had better go to Mr. Stubbs for that; he'll be more likely to have taken possession of one than any one else in the house."

Then, in her own mind, she indulged in free comment on the extraordinary fashion in which this young lady—an utter stranger to them all—had seen fit to conduct herself since she had come into the house. No apology had she offered for her inattention to household hours; no request had she made for means to continue her journey.

"Really," Madge decided, "her beauty may be a matter of dispute; but, as to her breeding, there can be but one opinion."

Madge was not disposed to modify her opinion at any rate, when, later on in the day, as she pinned a bouquet of crimson roses in her dress preparatory to descending to dinner, she caught a glimpse through her muslin window-blind of a picture—a garden idyll it might have been called—which made her flush scarlet, though not with pleasure.

Such a pretty picture, too! A young lady, in pale gray robes, leaning back in a wicker garden-chair; a young man, hat in hand, in the act of presenting her with some flowers.

Madge stood for three minutes watching them. Evidently the lady declined the flowers, for the young man tossed them on one side with a disappointed air.

"Would she like any others?" Madge could fancy he asked, for the young lady shook her head, with a slight movement of her hand as if flowers were distasteful to her.

Then the dinner-bell clanged, and the two turned their faces towards the house.

In the summer it was the custom of Sir Peter and his family to dine in the large inner hall of the Castle, instead of in the dining-room. This hall was palatial in its dimensions, oak-panelled and oak-ceiled. It was hung on one side with ancestral portraits; on the other, Gothic windows looked out into the garden. A wide mantelpiece divided the ancestral portraits right and left. Over this mantel-piece was a long, low mirror, which reflected the pretty picture of waving trees and summer sky that the Gothic windows framed.

As Madge entered by one door, she could hear the footsteps of Lance and Miss Shore crossing the vestibule to enter by another. Lance's voice, too, caught her quick ear in a remark as to the gloominess of the house compared with the outside summer brightness. She heard the words:

"Dismal old hall! Talk about eighteen centuries looking down upon you, it's nothing to compare with eight-and-twenty Critchetts looking down on you as you eat your food."

The last word brought him and his companion into the room.

Lady Judith was on the point of taking her seat at table. She was not in the best of tempers. Sir Peter, overhearing Lance's talk, chanced to remark that, "however gloomy the hall might be, it was nevertheless a pleasant refuge from midday sun—the coolest room in the house, in fact." Lady Judith catching the word "refuge," and nothing more, not unnaturally concluded that another scheme of charity was in progress of development, and immediately became voluble and prophetic on the matter.

With a formal bow she waved Miss Shore to her seat at table. "Refuges, indeed! As if there were not enough and to spare throughout the kingdom!" she declaimed. "Two at Carstairs to my certain knowledge, and a good workhouse with accommodation for fifty men and as many women within three miles outside the town." And again she waved Miss Shore to her seat.

But Miss Shore did not take it. She stood motionless, her head turned from the table, her hand resting on the back of her chair. Madge could see that this was a necessity to her, for she trembled so violently that she needed to support herself with extraneous aid.

"I cannot eat tonight," she said, turning a white face towards Sir Peter. "I will go up to my room."

Madge flashed a glance first to Lance, then to the looking-glass opposite which Miss Shore's chair had been placed.

"Can you eat seated on this side of the table?" she asked, rising and offering her own place.

Miss Shore, with a brief word of thanks, accepted Madge's chair.

"She is ashamed to look herself in the face for some reason or other," was Madge's uncharitable mental comment on the little episode.

IX

Nature is a strict economist in her work, she does not squander her resources. She gives to the "viewless winds" and invisible thunders the blasts of trumpets and crash of artillery; but when she paints the "awful rose of dawn," or the golden glories of sunset, heaven's echoes are mute, and without so much as a muffled whisper, the great cloud pageant issues forth, troops across the sky, and vanishes.

Madge never saw the sun sink behind the Cuddaws, without some such thought as this in her mind.

As she stood on the terrace that evening after dinner, watching the stormily-splendid clouds that, gathering low on the horizon, were slowly quenching the limpid tints of the after-glow, it seemed to her that those sumptuous reds and purples should have come with the crackle of field-pieces and the roar of battle; and that those tender, translucent greens and yellows should have died into the gray with the sounds of softly retreating harps and viols.

Dinner had been a short meal that night, and would have been shorter still could the wishes of three, out of the five seated at table, have been consulted. Miss Shore ate next to nothing, spoke never a word unless pointedly addressed, and then her replies were all but monosyllabic. Lady Judith eyed her keenly at intervals during the long discourse for which the word "refuge" served as text. Sir Peter eyed her benevolently, asked after her health, didn't wait for an answer; asked if she would like telegram or letter sent to her friends anywhere to assure them of her safety, didn't wait for an answer to that, but hoped that she wouldn't feel herself bound to continue her journey on the following day unless she felt disposed so to do.

To all this, Miss Shore replied with a manifest effort: "Let me stay one day more. I won't ask for another—one day more, only that."

The request was put in eccentric fashion, even conceding to the speaker a certain indulgence for her unfamiliarity with the English tongue. This was scarcely the way in which an unexpected guest might be supposed to crave permission to extend a stay in a hospitable house. A criminal at a bar of justice, pleading that his sentence might be deferred for another twenty-four hours, might have done so in much such a voice, with much such a look on his face as Miss Shore had on hers.

Even Sir Peter became dimly conscious that his kindly commonplaces had some- how touched a deep chord, for he stumbled and stammered over his courteous consent to her request.

As for Madge, looking up she caught Lance's eye fixed on Miss Shore's white face with so intensely interested a look in it that the words of kindly courtesy she was about to utter died unspoken on her lips.

It was the recollection of that look which sent her out by herself on to the terrace, to watch the sunset glories instead of the less fascinating spectacle of Lady Judith fanning herself to sleep in her arm-chair.

As for Miss Shore, no sooner had the meal come to an end than she went straight up the stairs to her own room once more.

Presently Lance joined Madge on the terrace.

"There's a storm brewing overhead," he said, by way of beginning conversation.

"Is there?" answered Madge, by way of ending it; for the cloud of undefined annoyance caused by Lance's irrational sympathy for an utter stranger had scarcely passed away.

But, nevertheless, they might soon have drifted into cheerful talk if Sir Peter's short, quick footsteps had not at that moment been heard, followed at an interval by his blithe, cricket-like voice.

"Don't let me disturb you, young people," he chirruped. "This is the time for saying sweet things—blushes are not so conspicuous, eh, Madge?

"So far," said Madge, sententiously, "we've said nothing, beyond a remark as to the possibility of a storm coming on."

"Eh, nothing! Why, Lance, you sly fellow, what has become of all those grand speeches you were so busy concocting at dinner-time, that you hadn't a word to say to anybody?"

"Madge knows all the sweet things I think of her; there is no need for me to say them," answered Lance, in light, complimentary fashion.

"Ah, yes—yes. Very neatly put, 'pon my word. Now, Madge, you must say something equally sweet by way of acknowledgment."

"Lance knows exactly what I think of the sweet things he thinks of me; there is no need for me to say it," answered Madge, solemnly, and not in complimentary fashion.

And her thought, as she said this, was:

"If he would but let us alone! If an attack of gout would but keep him prisoner for a week, everything might come right."

But Sir Peter's persistently optimistic view of the "situation" showed that gout was yet a long way off.

"Ah! that's right, that's right," he said, more blithely than ever. "Where young people so thoroughly understand each other as Lance and you do, long-winded speeches are unnecessary."

And he tripped away lightly once more, no doubt with the sound of wedding-bells in his ears.

"He'll come back again in another minute," said Lance, looking over his shoulder after Sir Peter's retreating figure.

"Come for a row, Madge; there's something I particularly want to say to you tonight."

But, though Madge acquiesced, and, fetching a light shawl, was ready in a moment. Lance evidently found his something hard to say, for they wound along the garden paths in an almost unbroken silence.

The heat seemed to increase upon them as they descended the slope under the overarching boughs. Flower-scents hung heavily in the air. The whirring of gnats and flies was almost intolerable.

Lance, with a visible effort, made a remark which seemed to be suggested by nothing and to lead nowhere. It was:

"Madge, do you know you've a fine reputation for benevolence and Christian charity? I had no idea till the other day, when I was dining at the Brabazons', what a lot people think of you."

It scarcely seemed possible that Madge could know by intuition whither Lance's remark was intended to lead, yet she answered coldly:

"Really, I don't care two straws what people think of me. Please talk about something interesting." She laid marked emphasis on the word "people." "If he has anything nice to say to me, he may as well say it on his own account," was her supplementary thought.

Lance read that thought easily enough, and the desire to tease her immediately became irresistible.

"Oh, of course not; why should you care even one straw? 'People' say pleasant things of you one minute, and disagreeable things the next. That's the way of the world."

"They have no right to say disagreeable things," she answered, sharply. "Not that it matters much—I never listen to gossip, and don't wish to know what any one says of me, whether agreeable or disagreeable."

"Of course not. Envy is at the root of nine out of every ten of the spiteful things women say of each other."

"Women! What women have been running me down?"

"Don't get excited, Madge. It's a tribute to one's breeding to be disparaged by the crowd."

"Disparaged! Who has been disparaging me? Lance, I insist on knowing what was said of me at the Brabazons' the other night!"

Lance laughed outright.

"Ah, now we've got back to the point where we diverged. I was going to tell you what was said of you at the Brabazons' the other night, and you wouldn't listen—here we are at the edge of the stream. Well, Lottie Brabazon said that you were the Lady Bountiful of the county, and put every one else to shame with your generosity to the poor."

With his last word Lance stooped to unmoor the boat.

Here the larches gave place to willows and osiers, and the expanse of running water somewhat cooled the hot air. The clouds hung ominously low, however, with more of black than purple in them now.

This miniature river was formed by the conjunction of two little streams which had been diverted from their course to add to the beauty of the Castle pleasure-grounds, by dividing the flower-garden from the park. It made a pretty little bit of landscape, with its fringe of bulrushes and water-flails on one side, and plantation of aspens and willows on the other.

As Madge stepped into the boat, a sleepy swan sailed majestically from out the shadowy reeds. It headed the boat for a few minutes, showing snow-white against the dark shadows thrown on the water by the inky clouds overhead; then it disappeared into the dimness beyond.

Madge's good-humour came back to her.

"This is heavenly!" she said, taking off her bracelet and paddling with her hand in the cool stream. "I dare say we shall got a good fifteen minutes out here before the storm breaks."

Lance shook his head.

"Ten only," he said, reading the sky with an eye practiced in cloud and mountain presages. "Madge, don't let's squabble for five, at least, out of those ten minutes; there is something I particularly wish to say to you."

He had grown suddenly serious.

Madge grew serious also.

"It's about Miss Shore?" she said, questioning and affirming in a breath.

"Yes; about Miss Shore," he answered, quietly. "Madge, do you know she is very friendless, very desolate, and, I should imagine, only partially recovered from some heavy sorrow."

"She has taken you into her confidence?"

"To a very limited extent," laughed Lance; but his laugh was a little uneasy. "Just before dinner this evening I came upon her in the garden. We talked—no, I suppose I did the greater part of the talking—but, at any rate, somehow or other I elicited the fact that she is homeless and friendless, and it doesn't require a very vigorous stretch of imagination to conclude from those facts that she is moneyless also."

Lance's, "Somehow or other I elicited the fact," can scarcely be said to be a true statement of what had taken place between him and Miss Shore, in that brief five minutes before dinner of which Madge's prejudiced eyes had conveyed so distorted an impression to her brain.

He had found the young lady in the garden, leaning back in her chair with white, inanimate face, like that of one newly recovered from a swoon. The flowers he held in his hand to present to her he had at once tossed on one side, as incongruous with the look of suffering her face wore.

"You are ill," he had said with real concern. "Let me send word to your friends."

"You must find them before you can send to them," had been her brief reply.

Then she had waved him on one side with the impetuous request that he would let her alone—not persecute her with questions.

"I thought she was travelling to friends up in the North when the train broke down. You said so; Sir Peter said so—some one said so, at any rate," said Madge, presently.

"Did some one? I'm not sure. Well, at any rate, from what I got out of her this afternoon it seems as if she hadn't a friend in the world, and, what is more, she appears perfectly callous on the matter, as if the fact were of no importance whatever."

"And you want me to take a vast interest in a matter on which the person most concerned is callous!" exclaimed Madge.

"Well, yes; why not? A man jumps into the water and tries to drown himself, and sometimes he is more than callous on the matter—has, in fact, a very strong objection to being pulled out again; but, for all that, we do our best to save him."

Madge made no reply.

She was a woman of strong prejudices, and those she had conceived against Miss Shore at first sight were stubborn ones; nevertheless, she had been so accustomed all her life long to yield compliance to Lance's wishes, that it was almost easier for her to let go those prejudices than to deny him now.

Lance's manner did not exhibit the uneasiness he had expressed to Sir Peter over-night, respecting Madge's possible reception of a petition from him on Miss Shore's behalf.

He went on composedly as if denial were out of the question.

"I've no doubt I went to work this afternoon in a very bungling fashion—I'm not a particularly good hand at getting people's confidence when they've no mind to give and she was very loth to speak of herself—but dare say, Madge, you were to interest yourself and have a talk with her—"

There came at this moment a flutter and a rustling from among the reeds and osiers at the water's edge.

"What's that?" queried Madge, sharply, turning her head towards the sound.

Lance's look followed hers.

"An otter, I dare say," he answered, quietly. But, nevertheless, he kept steady eye on the spot whence the sound had come.

Madge dealt sharp, though not final, blow to her prejudices. "Yes, I'll try and get tomorrow, and find out if we can help her," she answered slowly. "It's rather difficult to offer people money right out—but perhaps she may be clever at singing, or painting, and may be able to give me a few lessons. At any rate, I'll promise to do what I can." Then she changed the subject abruptly, exclaiming: "How dark it's getting! Hadn't we better think of turning back?" In good truth, she had had enough of Miss Shore and her friendless condition.

Bird-notes had ceased now; only a distant sound of whirring insect life broke the stillness.

Lance looked up at the sky. "We must get back at once, or the storm will be on top of us," he answered. As he finished speaking, there came the low growl of advancing thunder.

Lance plied a swift oar. As they shot past the shadowy nook, whence the rustling sound had come, he peered in curiously among the reeds. The flags waved; the osiers bent and whispered; but it was only the wind rising now.

X

The storm was a dry one; it broke in its full fury almost immediately after Madge and Lance got back to the house. They had scampered up the steep garden paths as if pursued by the storm-fiend himself, and Madge had to stand a good three minutes just within the hall-door to get her breath back.

"Get away from the trees, Madge," he had said, catching her arm and pulling her along at a fine pace.

Well, she could easily understand his anxiety to get her and himself under shelter from the storm. What she could not understand was his haste to rush out into it again. It is true he shouted to her as he disappeared in the outside darkness: "I've forgotten something, I shall be back in a minute." But that something ought to have been of first importance to necessitate such a headlong rush into what threatened to be one of the worst tempests the country-side had known for years.

Lance's seemingly eccentric conduct, however, admitted of an easy explanation. When he had peered among the reeds and water-flags as his boat shot past, he had thought he saw the flutter of a gray skirt, whose wearer it was easy to identify.

Madge had read easily enough the forlornness which Miss Shore's white face and stony manner expressed. Lance had read the forlornness, and something else beside. A mood half-desperate, half-defiant, which might possibly find for itself a desperate means of ending a hopeless life.

It was this thought flashing into his mind as he reached the hall-door, that speeded his feet through the storm to the water's edge once more.

But when he got down there among the sedges and willows, not a soul was to be seen. A startled bird flew from out a marshy hollow with a sharp cry; a solitary frog croaked a dismal note of warning; an ominous breeze, rippling the dark surface of the water, set the reeds bending and whispering together. Other sound there was none.

Something glittering at the bottom of the little boat they had just quitted caught his eye. Picking it up he saw that it was the bracelet which Madge had unclasped as she had paddled in the stream. A brilliant flash of lightning cleft the inky clouds over his head, and for one brief moment the whole night-hidden landscape stood revealed.

Old Cuddaw crowned standing out bold, bleak, and bare against the leaden sky. Below, the Castle showed gray solid block of masonry with every turret and gable sharply defined. Lower still the valley lay, dim expanse of waving, shadowy trees, out of which crept stony path, leading with many to the Fells.

It seemed less like one grand expanse of scenery thus laid bare to view than combination of two landscapes, the one belonging to the sky, the other to the earth beneath.

In that brief, vivid illumination, Lance saw something else beside the sky picture and the dim valley with its upward-winding path—the figure of woman in long flowing cloak in that path, making her way rapidly towards the mountains.

It did not need a second flash of lightning to tell him who that woman was. But what her motive could be in thus daring the storm on those mountain heights was not so easy to discover.

He thought with dismay of the slippery mountain paths, the shelving ledges, the holes, and gaping precipices. He who had known them from boyhood would yet have hesitated to dare their dangers on a moonless night. And there was she—a woman, a stranger, without guide or light—making for them with straight and rapid steps, that implied purpose and design.

His course was clear to him. A shorter way led out of the valley than the one she was following; it intersected the former path at the point where the mountain ascent began. By using his utmost despatch he might intercept her at that point, and succeed in inducing her to take shelter in a sandy hollow beneath the over-arching rocks, which, in his boyish days, had been a favourite play-place for him—his "Crusoe's cave."

It was not possible to make swift headway through the woody moorland which lay between him and this haven of refuge. The darkness was increasing with every step he took. Overhead the thunder crashed with a bewildering rapidity, every peal prolonged to twice its length by the mountain echoes, till from east to west, from west to east, the heavens seemed one vast plain of rolling artillery.

He hailed the bright, scintillating lightnings as he would have hailed a friendly lantern. They showed him the briar and tangle in his path, the big stumbling-blocks of boulders, the pitfalls of disused gravel-pits. They showed him also, when at length he reached the "Crusoe's cave," Miss Shore's slender figure standing about thirty feet above his head on the over-lapping ledge.

Whatever she was or was not, one thing was certain: she must be a practised mountaineer, or she could never have reached even this moderate height in safety.

"How much higher is she going?" thought Lance. Then, making one vigorous effort in the pauses of the thunder, he shouted to her at the top of his voice, calling her by name, entreating her to wait for him, so that he might take her to a place of safety.

There came an awful flash of lightning at this moment, which seemed to spend its fiercest strength on the very ledge of rock on which she stood.

Lance, half-blinded, looking upwards, saw the girl standing motionless, while the lightning seemed literally to smite the ground at her very feet. Then came the terrific, resonant thunder, then the inky, bewildering darkness closed in upon the mountain-side once more.

Half-stunned, as well as half-blinded, Lance made his way up the stony path which lay between him and Miss Shore; his heart, stout as it was, quailing at the thought of the sight that might greet his eyes as the dire result of Nature's cruelly-expended forces.

But no sight more dire than that of Miss Shore leaning against the bulging side of the rock met his view as he rounded the path. She might have been carved out of the rock itself for the motionlessness and rigidity of her outline. The hood of her gray cloak had fallen from her head; her bandeau of black hair had uncoiled, and hung in a long black line on one side of her ashen-white face; her eyes were round and staring.

She did not turn her head at his approach, merely pointed to the ground at her feet, where the quick thunderbolt had literally split the rock and "kissed its burial."

"Did you see that?" she asked, under her breath, in an awe-stricken voice.

"See it!" cried Lance. "Who could help seeing it? Thank Heaven you are safe—don't waste a moment, take my hand, I'll get you down into a place of safety."

But the girl did not stir. "Would that have killed any one else?" she asked, in the same slow, suppressed voice as before.

"Why, of course not, or else it must have killed you," answered Lance, trying to laugh off what seemed to him a stupefying terror on her part. "You see I wasn't far behind you, and I wasn't hurt. Come, make haste into shelter; we don't know what the next flash may do."

His last words were lost in the crash of another peal.

But it was farther off now. The storm had evidently spent the worst of its fury. The dense sky parted; light clouds went travelling across carried by the upper current.

Still the girl did not stir.

"By poison or fire or flood must be—there is no other way," she muttered under her breath, with eyes not looking at Lance, but beyond him.

"Poison, fire, flood!" All in moment there seemed to be revealed to Lance terrible reason for the emptied glass beside the bed, for the crouching figure among the water-reeds, for the bare-headed defiance of the lightning on the mountain.

Debonair and light-hearted to the last degree, it cost him an effort to shut his eyes to the horror of the whole thing, and to say in an easy, commonplace voice: "Never mind about that; the thing is now to get into a place of safety. Come."

She looked at him steadily for a moment.

"Yes, I will come," she said, slowly. "Fate is stronger than I."

She did not take his hand; she walked slowly beside him with head bent, and eyes fixed on the ground.

There was no need to seek the refuge of the "Crusoe's cave." Overhead, the light clouds parting showed a faint rift of light from a young moon; far away in the distance the thunder was dying hard in a succession of low, sonorous growls.

But few words passed between them on their way back. Lance thanked Heaven when they stood within the Castle grounds once more. Miss Shore seemed tired, dazed; her voice was weak, her footsteps dragged.

Lights were more conspicuous in the upper than in the lower rooms as they approached the house. One long French window of the library, left unshuttered and unbarred, gave them easy and unnoticed entrance.

"She ought to be locked in her room at night," thought Lance, as he said his good-night to his companion at the foot of the stairs.

"Oh, Lance," said Madge, coming out of the drawing-room a moment after, "where have you been? How white you look! We were just talking about sending out a party of men with torches and umbrellas in search of you."

Lance tossed her bracelet to her. "A golden reason for risking a wetting," he said, laughingly, and then vanished forth-with, before she had time to frame a second question.

XI

Madge, bent on keeping down the growth of her prejudices, did not forget her promise to Lance, and the morning after the storm saw her seated in Miss Shore's room doing her best to win that young lady's confidence, with the benevolent hope of finding a pretext for inducing her to prolong her stay at the Castle.

It was up-hill work, however. Miss Shore seemed bent on playing the part of a fertilising shower to Madge's prejudices, for rebuff after rebuff did she deal to her kindly overtures.

Miss Shore had not made her appearance at the breakfast-table on the morning after the storm. Her breakfast had been taken to her in her own room, together with the morning's paper, for which she had once more sent down a special request.

"You are interested in politics—in the foreign news?" asked Madge, by way of making a beginning, and noting that Miss Shore had folded the paper with the Continental news uppermost.

She started.

"I care for foreign news! Why should I? It is nothing to me," she answered, almost fiercely.

Madge felt that she had somehow made a wrong start.

"One naturally likes to have news of one's own country when away from it," she said, apologetically.

"Country!" cried Miss Shore, flushing scarlet, "this is my country; I have no other."

Madge felt bewildered.

"But—but," she stammered, "you are not English, surely. Are you not Italian? You gave me the impression of being Italian."

"I am not Italian; I am English. My father was English; I am English. Hear how I speak!"

Evidently she was ignorant how markedly foreign her accent was.

"I am sorry," said Madge, frankly. "I was hoping that you might be Italian, and that—that we might have studied the language together. I am so wishing to be a fluent linguist."

She did not like to say: "I was hoping that you would be able to give me some lessons in Italian, for which I might have paid you a guinea an hour," She could only hope that her meaning would gradually dawn on her languid listener.

The meaning, however, did not seem to dawn, so Madge went on again:

"I am wanting to improve myself in all sorts of ways. I sometimes feel I am very much behind other people in accomplishments. I want to get some good teaching in singing—I am particularly fond of singing. Do you sing?"

"I do not."

"Dear me, this is unpromising," thought Madge. "There's one thing she couldn't give me lessons in—courtesy. What shall I try next? Ah!—Perhaps you play on the piano or on the violin?"

"I do not know a note of music."

"Really?"

There came a long pause.

Miss Shore folded her newspaper with the advertisements outside, but still kept it tightly in her hand.

Madge looked out of the window. The storm of overnight had disturbed the weather; the air was full of a vapoury heaviness through which the mountains showed black against a leaden sky.

Those mountains suggested an idea:

"I do so wish I had devoted more time to art before I married! I would give anything if I could paint those mountains—that sky. Of course you can paint?"

"I can."

Madge's spirits went up.

"How I envy you—" she began, but then stopped.

She did not care, with other interests growing upon her, to volunteer for a long course of painting lessons; that would mean at least three hours daily in Miss Shore's company. As well reside in "thrilling regions of thick-ribbed ice," as that.

Another idea suggested itself.

"I don't mean flower-painting or portrait-painting; I mean can you sketch scenery—mountains, and lakes, and valleys?"

"I hate the mountains," said with slow, suppressed bitterness.

"Hate the mountains! Well, even if you hate them, it needn't prevent your being able to paint them," said Madge, beginning to lose patience a little.

"I can paint them. I have painted mountains grander than these." She broke off a moment, then added, as if she were compelling herself to a course that was advisable rather than attractive: "Do you wish me to paint these mountains for you?"

"That's it—the very thing," cried Madge, drawing a long breath of relief. "I have been wanting, for a long time, to decorate a little room downstairs which I occupy sometimes with a set of water-colour sketches." (This was a fib, but Madge was at her wits' ends.) "It was my boudoir before I married, and now Sir Peter is good enough to have it refurnished for me. If I could get six or eight pictures of Cumberland scenery hung round should feel decorated at once."

"Six or eight! There," thought Madge, "she can take just as long as ever she likes over them, and I'll pay her whatever she asks me for them. And Lance isn't satisfied with my morning's work, I don't know what will please him."

"I will paint them if you wish it," said Miss Shore, and then she looked at the door as she had endured Madge's company long enough.

Madge rose instantly.

"Is your room comfortable? Have you all you want here?" she asked, looking round as she so often did when welcoming Lady Judith's guests to the Castle.

Both looking-glasses were pushed into a corner now, both turned face to the wall. Miss Shore followed Madge's gaze towards that corner.

"They were in my way. I pushed them there," she said, coldly, in a tone that prevented further questioning.

Madge felt that she had earned the thanks which Lance accorded to her, when, later on in the day, she contrived to inform him of her plan to put a little money into Miss Shore's purse.

"I must admit that she is not a taking young woman," she said. "I never felt myself so chilled and repressed in my life before."

The seriousness Lance put into his answer startled her.

"Madge, I do believe," he said, "that that poor girl has had some terrible experience. I never before in my life saw human eyes with such a hunted, desolate look in them."

"It's wonderful," said Sir Peter, coming into the room at that moment, "how much one can get through between sunrise and sundown, if one only sets to work with a will!"

"Wonderful!" echoed Lance, his seriousness gone in a moment, like a ghost at the cock's crow, and getting up and opening a door on the opposite side of the room, in order that Sir Peter might have free egress whenever he felt so disposed.

Sir Peter had been in a particularly lively frame of mind during the past few days, and Mr. Stubbs had had rather a busy time of owing to his patron's wish to remodel every one of the charities on whose committee-list his name figured.

The letter-bag had gone out stuffed every night, yet Sir Peter's brain appeared to be brimming over with ideas.

"I have a splendid scheme on hand just now," he said, thoroughly content now that he had succeeded in breaking the thread of Lance's and Madge's talk, and had concentrated their attention entirely on himself. "A splendid scheme! A little vast—a little vague at present, perhaps."

"Ah," echoed Lance again; "a little vast, a little vague!"

"But what of that? In my schemes I must be vast, or I am nothing. The fault of one-half the schemes of charity submitted to me is that they are microscopic. I say to Stubbs every morning of my life, 'Double, treble, quadruple the proportions of that project, then I will look at it.' But I must have elbow-room—elbow-room in all I undertake." Here he lifted his elbows in the air with an upward, wing-like motion.

"Ah, elbow-room, of course," said Lance, also executing the wing-like movement with his elbows.

Sir Peter made one turn round the room, and came back again.

"The truth of it is," he said, lowering his voice, and looking over his shoulder, "if it were not for Lady Judith I should by this time have won for myself the reputation of an universal—"

"Provider?" suggested Lance.

"Benefactor," finished the old gentleman, not understanding the allusion.

"But, as it is"—here a deep-drawn sigh—"when I would soar on wings like a bird," here he again executed the upward, wing-like movement, "Lady Judith brings me down to earth again, and I feel myself nothing more than a kite with a string attached to it."

Then he pulled out his watch.

"What, half-past twelve is it? And I have had no exercise today. Ah! I must be off for a little stretch in the Park."

"There is a case of foot-and-mouth disease at Lower Upton," said Lady Judith, entering the room by the door by which Sir Peter was about to quit it.

She was fanning herself vigorously. Sir Peter backed into the room before her. Her robust handling of her fan might have conveyed the impression that she had fanned him back again over the threshold. Now that the husband and wife were together in the room, Madge thought it would be a splendid opportunity to get their combined sanction to the little plan she had just been detailing to Lance respecting Miss Shore.

She accordingly, in a key sufficiently high to reach Lady Judith's ear, asked Sir Peter's consent to it.

Sir Peter's face grew rosy with pleasure.

"The very thing! the very thing!" he cried, rubbing his hands gleefully. "I told you, Lance, if Madge were only consulted on the matter, she'd arrange it all easily enough! And you said—"

"No, I didn't," said Lance, apprehensive of what was coming, and not at all pleased that Madge should know that he and Sir Peter had beforehand taken counsel together on the matter.

"Well, I said I have a hundred plans for—"

"Ah! I dare say you said that," interrupted Lance, bent on preventing further disclosures.

Lady Judith unintentionally became his ally.

"Is she to be a permanence in the house? That's what I want to know," she asked in her highest key, her fan once more with its backward motion stirring the air as much for Sir Peter as for herself. "And am I expected to take her in hand, and be a sort of Providence to her?"

Sir Peter slipped behind her, retreating backwards towards the door.

"No, no, my dear, nothing of the sort; don't trouble yourself. Madge will take all responsibility on her own shoulders, I'm sure."

Lady Judith turned on him, executing the double action with her fan once more.

She caught the word responsibility only.

"Yes, it is a responsibility; and I admit that, if I am to have responsibilities, I would sooner they should be of my own choosing. There was the last gardener's boy you sent home—wretched little being! He had lost a thumb, and was horribly bow-legged, and I remember you said to me: 'Nice little fellow! Can't you put him into page's livery, and make something of him?'"

"My dear, I have no wish for you to put Miss Shore into page's livery, I assure you," said Sir Peter, making a feeble effort to render the situation comic, but getting at the same time a step or two nearer the door.

Lady Judith fanned him on another step or two.

"And the last stable-boy you brought home from London had such a diabolical squint, that he could only see the time by turning his back on the clock and getting a glimpse at it over the top of his ear. Yet you said to me: 'First-rate lad that! find him something to do at the farm!'"

But she had fairly fanned Sir Peter on to the door-mat now, and had to appeal to Lance and Madge as audience.

They, however, through long practice, were able to continue undisturbed their own subjects of conversation under the immediate fire of her oratory.

XII

Madge, in a moment of exasperation, had wished that gout would seize Sir Peter and hold him prisoner for a week, while she and Lance arranged their affairs to their own liking. Gout, however, was far too elderly and dignified a complaint to attack one of his essentially juvenile temperament.

A single case of measles occurred to a six-months' old baby in a hamlet about fifteen miles distant. It seemed a perfectly natural dispensation of Providence that Sir Peter should be the second victim.

"Don't know what's the matter with me, Lance," he said pitifully, "I feel as if my legs didn't belong to me."

"Perhaps you've tired them a bit," said Lance, suggesting a far-away possibility.

"I would sooner have it myself twenty times over," said the worthy medical practitioner who was called in; "how on earth we're to keep him in one room without a lock or key is more than I can think."

When by dint of combined effort they succeeded in getting Sir Peter to bed, they could have fancied that his pillow was stuffed with steel springs which sent his head up with a jerk as soon as it was laid upon so perpetually were his eyes and ears on the alert for all that went on around him.

His correspondence was a great anxiety to him.

"You'll see to my letters, Lance, won't you?" he begged, "and"—this added in timorous whisper—"you'll keep my study-door locked and the key in your pocket, won't you?"

"Oh, you mean lock Stubbs in, and not let him out till the letters are all answered," queried Lance.

"No, no, no." Here the whisper grew more confidential still. "I mean keep Lady Judith out, in case—in case she might—you know—you know."

"Oh yes, I know," answered Lance, reassuringly. "I'll look after your letters, never fear, Uncle Peter, and keep down the correspondence right enough."

Lance's idea of "keeping down the correspondence" was simple and effective. He evaded Sir Peter's order to lock the study-door by never going near it at all.

"Bring the letters and pen and ink into the gun-room, Stubbs," he said; "while I overhaul my fishing-tackle, you can read them out to, me, and I'll do a Sir Peter and dictate replies."

To the gun-room the letters were accordingly taken, and Lance, with a cigarette between his teeth and his fishing gear in his hand, quickly disposed of Sir Peter's correspondence.

Mr. Stubbs read the first letter, and then waited in silence for a reply to be forthcoming.

"Go on," said Lance. "We'll read them off half-a-dozen at a time, and then I dare say one answer will do for the lot."

The first half-dozen consisted mainly of appeals for advice on matters concerning the internal working of certain charities of which Sir Peter was president.

"Toss all that lot into the waste-paper basket," said Lance. "They'll answer themselves if they're let alone. If they don't get any advice from Sir Peter, they'll conclude they'll have to do without it. Now we'll go on to the next half-dozen."

They chanced to be appeals for help from various benevolent institutions.

"Ten pounds to each all round for that lot, Stubbs, and tell them not to bother again," said the young man. "And that'll do for this morning—the rest will keep till tomorrow; I'm off to the stables now."

If he had known what letter lay unread in the packet which Mr. Stubbs proceeded to lock up in Sir Peter's secretaire, he would scarcely have decreed in such light-hearted fashion that "the rest would keep" till the morrow.

He detailed to Madge, later on in the day, the easy, comfortable manner in which he had got through his morning's work.

"The truth of its Madge," he said, "half the world fret themselves to fiddle-strings over nothing at all! Rest on your oars and let the wind carry you along whenever you've chance, that's what say."

Madge, drawing conclusions from a contrasting experience, was disposed to contest the matter with him. "What if the wind carries you the wrong way?" she asked.

"Oh, then try your muscles and have a tussle for it." said Lance, half-way up the stairs to Sir Peter's room, in order to explain to him his patent method of disposing of troublesome correspondence.

"Don't, don't," cried Madge, guessing his intention, and following him at express speed. "It will send him into a fever and give him a bad night."

"It'll make him sleep like a top," persisted Lance, and forthwith much to the consternation of the nurse in attendance, he proceeded to recount to the old gentleman his morning's work.

Sir Peter was wrapped up in flannels; his face was very red; his eyes were streaming. His face grew redder still, his eyes streamed worse than ever, as he listened to Lance's description of "the mass of work" he had got through in a quarter of an hour.

"It'll take weeks to undo the mischief you've done," he moaned, and then his cough stopped him.

Lance vanished discreetly before the combined wrath of Madge and the nurse.

Madge volunteered her services in the way of opening and assorting letters.

"I can at least send temporary answers and tell everybody to wait till you're well again," she said, soothingly.

"The very thing, Madge; the very thing," cried Sir Peter, all serenity once more.

"You open my letters—no one else, remember—and tell everyone they shall have my entire—mind, my entire attention so soon as I get about again. Any letters of importance put carefully on one side in the right-hand drawer of my secretaire—lock it up and keep the key yourself."

And then he coughed incessantly again and had to eat black-currant lozenges for the rest of the afternoon.

As Madge crossed the gallery leading from Sir Peter's room, she paused at a big flowering myrtle that nearly filled a window-recess. Letting her eyes wander for one moment to the outside greenery and flower-garden, she was conscious of a sensation as physically painful as the scent of the myrtle was physically pleasant.

Yet it was nothing very much out of the common that met her view—merely Lance arranging sketching stool and easel on the green sward below the terrace, under the shade of a big sycamore, whence a good view could be had of the magnificent sweep of mountain scenery without daring the heat of an afternoon sun.

Now, purely as a matter of commonsense, Madge ought to have been delighted at Miss Shore's promptness in endeavouring to carry out her wishes. And as for Lance, well, she had seen him scores of times performing the same office for the numerous young ladies who had fallen in love with the mountain scenery, and had forthwith conceived the desire to caricature it in wishy-washy colours on a square of paste-board.

Yet, nevertheless, Madge, as she noted the graceful, undulating outline of the dull gray figure against the shining back-ground of a laurel hedge, and the lingering assiduity with which Lance adjusted the easel, had to do battle all over again with the unaccountable prejudices with which the very first sight of a beautiful face had inspired her.

XIII

Madge, true to her promise, seated herself after breakfast next morning at Sir Peter s writing-table, informing Mr. Stubbs of her intention of opening the invalid's letters and dictating their replies.

Mr. Stubbs, all obsequious attention, seated himself in his usual place at a smaller table at her right hand.

Madge's prejudices had made themselves heard respecting Mr. Stubbs as well as Miss Shore. She had conceived for Sir Peter's private secretary an intense dislike, the ground of which did not seem to be covered entirely by the fact of her having discovered him in what appeared to be a listening attitude.

She had tried to imbue Lance with her notions, hoping that from his wider experience of men and their ways she might get wherewithal to substantiate her shadowy repugnance to the man.

"I am sure he is sly and underhand," she had said; "and he looks and looks at me whenever he comes near me, as if he were taking stock of everything I do or say, or think, even."

Lance had characteristically laughed off the idea.

"I never knew any one like you for taking fancies into your head," he had said. "Why, if I lived twenty years in the house with the man, it wouldn't occur to me to notice whether he turned his eyes up or down, this way or that. He writes a good hand, and he does what he's told to do, and what more in reason can be expected of him?"

Madge was not a bad woman of business when she gave her mind to it. She ran over one-half of Sir Peter's correspondence lightly enough, dictating brief and temporary replies; Mr. Stubbs's pen failed to keep pace with her fluent dictating, so, as he wrote, she continued opening the remaining letters, and mastering their contents.

One among those Lance had been too lazy to give his attention to, had an Australian post-mark.

"Dear me! Sir Peter's fame has reached the antipodes," was her mental comment as she broke the seal.

But when her eye had mastered the first few sentences, mental comment she had none to make, for the simple reason that her brain was in a state of chaos.

It was a bulky letter, some two or three sheets in length, but was written in a round, schoolboy's hand, which rendered it easy reading. It was dated from "Rutland Bay Settlement, Western Australia," and ran as follows:

> Sir,
>
> "I must beg your indulgence for the liberty I am taking in thus addressing you. The remarkable circumstances I have to communicate must be my excuse.
>
> "Let me begin by stating that I am a minister of the Wesleyan persuasion, and sole spiritual adviser of the rough but not unkindly miners who constitute the scanty population of this place; also that my statements can be very easily substantiated by reference to some of the leading members of the community, whose names I subjoin.
>
> "Now for my story.
>
> "Sixteen years ago, when this settlement consisted in all of fifty souls, there occurred during the equinoxes a terrible wreck on this coast. A vessel went down with all hands, in the night—at least, so it was supposed from the spars and wreckage washed on shore at daybreak. Something else besides spars and wreckage was washed up with tide—a portion of the mainmast, with a woman and an infant lashed to it. The woman appeared, from her dress, to be a nurse; but she had been so terribly injured during the gale that she died as soon as she was brought to shore. The child was a fine little boy of about a year old, dressed as a gentleman's child. His linen was marked simply with the initials G. C.

"All, this, sir, occurred about ten years before I came to the colony. When I, by the direction of our Conference, took upon myself the office of shepherd to these stray sheep, this infant had grown into a handsome boy, and was of so strikingly-refined an appearance, that so soon as I set eyes on him assisting the miners in the lighter portion of the work, I asked the question:

"'What gentleman's son is that?'

"The miners who had sheltered and brought him up were the roughest set of men I had ever lived among; but, for all that, had treated the boy with the kindliest consideration, had taught him to read and write, and had, on account of the extreme fragility of his health, allowed him to lead an almost idle life, evidently looking upon him as one cast in a different mound to themselves.

"I took the boy in hand immediately on my arrival in the settlement, supplied him with books, and carried his education as forward as possible.

"So much for the boy. Now for the sequel to my story.

"About six months ago a vessel put in here, a Canadian trader, manned by a crew of divers nationalities. One of the seamen, a Scotchman, by name John Rutherford,. had a strange story to tell. He said that sixteen years previously he was serving on board a Mexican passenger-boat, which had been wrecked off this coast. He, with some others, had taken to the boats, and, after many perils, had been picked up by a Canadian schooner. Subsequently, he had joined the Canadian merchant service. He gave full particulars concerning the terrible wreck of the Mexican boat, and the names of the passengers, so far as he could remember them. Among them, he said, was an English gentleman, a Mr. Grevase Critchett, and his wife, a South American lady, and infant boy, who had hurriedly taken flight from La Guaya, North Mexico, on account of an insurrection threatening there. Rutherford spoke of the father's despairing agony at his inability to save his wife and child, of his lashing the nurse and the boy with his own hands to the mast, and of his frantic endeavours to make his wife leap into the boat as it pushed away in the darkness. Rutherford related also, that on the previous night, when the gale had first burst on them, Mr. Critchett had taken him on one side, and, in view of possible danger to himself and the chance of his child being saved, had related various particulars concerning himself—that he was brother to Sir Peter Critchett, of Upton Castle; that his marriage "had been solemnised at the British Consulate at La Guaya, and his boy's birth had been duly registered there—"

"Madge, Madge!"—at this moment said Lance's voice just outside the door—"are you going to shut yourself up with the ink-bottle all the morning? Can't you come for half an hour's canter?"

Madge started. Her thoughts were far away from Upton, among the wild miners of Australia, and yet, if the truth be told, the under-current of those thoughts carried but one name in their depths—Lance's, and Lance's only.

Instinctively she jumped from her chair and met Lance at the door. It would have been too dreadful, it seemed to her, without word of warning or kindly preliminary hint, he had stood behind her and had read over her shoulder the story which gave Sir Peter an heir to his name and to his wealth.

"I can't ride today," she said, steadying her voice as well as she could. "I mean to work all the morning at Sir Peter's letters, and then I have to drive with Lady Judith to Lower Upton."

"How white you look, have you a headache?" interrupted Lance. "Look here, Madge, I want to show you my last new fowling-piece, it came down by the first train this morning." And there and then, outside in the hall, he exhibited his latest acquisition in deadly weapons, unscrewing and putting together again its internal arrangements, descanting meanwhile in enthusiastic fashion on its vast superiority over all others he had ever been possessed of.

Madge's thoughts were in a whirl. It was with difficulty that she managed to keep up a fair show of interest in Lance's talk. She trembled for the safety of the letter, which, in her haste to intercept Lance, she had thrown open on the writing-table.

She went back in five minutes' time to the study to find the letter folded neatly in half with a paperweight on top of it.

She flashed an inquiring glance at Mr. Stubbs, who sat, pen in hand, waiting for further instructions.

"The wind fluttered it off the table," he said, quietly, by way of explanation. "The draught is very great when the study-door is opened as well as the outside door."

Madge felt the impulse to ask the question, "Did you take advantage of the friendly draught and master the contents of the letter?" almost irresistible. Her eyes and flushing cheeks asked it plainly enough; but Mr. Stubbs's pasty, expressionless features made no sign, and his eyes appeared fixed on nothing at all.

She had no more ideas to bestow on Sir Peter's correspondence. Everything in life had shrunk into insignificance beside the baleful tidings which those few sheets of closely written paper had brought.

XIV

Lance is a beggar!—a beggar!" Madge sat in her own room saying the ugly words over and over again. In good truth, for the moment she was incapable of any other thought. The news might be glad tidings enough to the childless Sir Peter, it might thrill other hearts with all sorts of pleasant possibilities. For her it had but one meaning: the man for whose happiness she would gladly, at any moment, lay down her life, was no longer to be the favourite of fortune which she had delighted to think him. His sun had set.

Once more she took up the letter, thinking that she would slowly and carefully read it from beginning to end, and see if she could find in it any excuse to doubt the veracity of the writer.

But the task was beyond her. Her hand shook so that she could scarcely hold the thin, crackling paper, and her eyes in sympathy with her hand got at the evil sentences in snatches only.

She read a string of names, at the end of the letter, of those persons who were willing to vouch for the credibility of the writer; the address of John Rutherford, the Scotch seaman; then her eyes glanced higher up the page to where the writer made an earnest appeal for an immediate reply. "For," he said, "the lad is strangely disturbed at the thought of having kith and kin of his own in the dear old mother-country, and is in a state of nervous tremor lest his father's people may not see fit to stretch out the hand of welcome to him." Then away from this her eyes darted to the signature at the foot of the page, "Joshua Parker," and then her hand dropt to her side, and her eyes refused to do farther work for the tears that blinded them.

Outside her room in the corridor sounded Lance's voice once more in its cheery and somewhat domineering baritone. What was he saying? Something about "my horses," "my dogs"? Evidently, he was giving to his servant a succession of orders to be transmitted to the stable, for presently there came, in reply to some question addressed to him by the man, a remark respecting last winter's sleighs. "They were not worth putting in order. I intend to have one—two, perhaps—made on quite another model. The sleigh of the period is far from being what it ought to be."

"A beggar! a beggar!" she repeated bitterly. This man, born and bred in the lap of luxury, was to be bidden to go forth and make his way in the world, or else be bidden to remain in his old home simply to play the steward, or live as a dependent on the bounty of others! Ah! would to Heaven the blow had fallen on her, not on him. She had been a born pauper; had known how to fill the role of *protégé*, at least not discontentedly! If all the Cohen wealth had disappeared in the night like so much fairy gold, she could have gone back to her early life as one "to the manner born."

And here Madge's conscience gave her as sharp a wound as any its barbed arrows had ever dealt. "Oh, you with your fine flourish of words," it seemed to say, "you, who would pray to fortune, 'give him my lot and give me his,' why didn't you put your pride and your vanity under a bushel six months ago when he asked you to marry him? If you had seen fit to do this, your wealth by now might have been his, and this blow, though heavy, would not have been a deadly one."

"If I could but have known! if I could but have known!" she moaned, beating her hands together once more.

Through the gloom of this thought there struggled a faint ray of hope. The "No" she had then spoken was not meant to be final, was not likely so to be unless something very unforeseen occurred between her and Lance—here a passing, a very passing thought was given to Miss Shore and her easel. Very well, then, her retraction of that "No" might be hastened somewhat or even might be volunteered—so in her impetuous longing to be of service to him it seemed to her—without loss of dignity or womanliness.

She and Lance were on the best and easiest of terms; it would be easy for her to say: "Lance, my pride and sensitiveness are ridiculous, and always have been ridiculous. I only wish I knew how to trample them under foot and be done with them forever." Lance, no doubt, would readily enough see the drift of her confession, and would speak over again the words that he had found so easy to speak before.

Till this was done she resolved that she would communicate to no one the contents of the Australian letter, and she thanked Heaven for the fortunate conjunction of circumstances which had made its hateful news known to her before anyone else in the house.

"If it were done when 'tis done, then 'twere well it were done quickly," was Madge's brief summing up of her long hour of painful thought as she nerved herself to the doing of a deed that had more than a spice of heroism in it.

She folded the letter, locked it up in her desk, and then still farther to ensure its safe keeping, slipped the key of the desk on to her watch-chain.

She had to pass a looking glass on her way downstairs. She carefully turned her head away from it. "No," she thought, "if I look in there my courage will be gone, and the words will never be said."

A self-congratulatory thought followed.

It was: "I have always said I would give all the Cohen wealth to be really beautiful. Now I would not give up the Cohen wealth for all the beauty under the sun."

And for one brief moment Madge felt as if she had turned the tables on her fortune.

She searched in vain for Lance in his usual haunts; library, study, smoking-room, gunroom, all were deserted. Then she went on to the billiard-room, hoping for better luck there; it was vacant like the other rooms, cool and pleasant, ruled with bars of light which filtered in through the half-turned Venetian shutters. Something else besides those bars of light filtered in through the shutters, the sound of voices from the outside verandah.

Lance's voice first caught her ear:

"Fate—believe in fate? Well, yes, in one way I do. I believe it is possible for a man once in his life to come upon his fate in the shape of a beautiful woman."

A beautiful woman! Madge had no doubt to whom he was speaking. For one brief moment she once more balanced the Cohen wealth against personal beauty. That woman outside there in the sunshine assuredly was what nine men out of every ten would call beautiful; and she here in this darkened room had the town and the country house, the diamonds, and the horses. If Lance were to hold the scales, which way would they incline? A dark cloud overshadowed her. She struggled with her jealousy and her prejudices once more. Of course, the words he had spoken as mere words were worth nothing. If he had said them to a man, or to a woman old enough to be his mother, they might have been taken as a simple statement of a simple fact. But spoken to a woman young enough to be his wife, and dowered with good looks into the bargain, they would—well, mean just whatever his eyes chose to put into them; and she knew well enough how Lance's blue eyes could double the meanings of his phrases at times.

Madge went back to her room with her heroic deed undone.

XV

Sir Peter had a relapse. He was sleeping so peacefully one evening, that nurse and doctor, growing confidential over their patient's idiosyncrasies, fell to congratulating themselves that the worst of the illness was over. Sir Peter was always a picture when he was asleep.

"He looks that smiling and child-like," said the nurse.

"It's such a blessing to see him at rest," sighed the doctor.

And lo! that very minute his head was off his pillow, and he was out of bed before anyone could stop him, vowing that he had the cramp in both legs, and must "walk it off."

"He has driven in the rash," said the doctor, trying to explain matters to Lady Judith, "and may think himself lucky if he gets about again in three weeks' time."

Lady Judith heard about one quarter of what the doctor had said. She only gathered that Sir Peter, as usual, had been lively and insubordinate, and wanted to take in hand.

"I'll go up and talk to him," she said, fanning herself and the doctor very hard.

"No, one knows how to manage him as I do—"

"No, no, no! "shouted the doctor at her. "He mustn't be worried; it'll put him into a fever—I mean," he corrected himself, "your fan would give him his death of cold."

Lady Judith fanned harder than ever. She only caught the word "fever."

"Fever!" she repeated. "You told me distinctly it was measles he had. You'll be telling me next it is small-pox, or rheumatic gout, or something else extraordinary."

The doctor tried in vain to explain. Being a short man, he got upon tiptoe in his eagerness to do so.

All in vain! Lady Judith fanned him out of the room, and through the hall, and out at the front door, all the while expressing her surprise, her "unqualified surprise, that he had not taken more pains to diagnose the case before he had pronounced so decided an opinion in the first instance. But I don't believe its fever—no. If the whole faculty of medicine were to swear it was fever, I wouldn't believe them. Do you think I don't know measles when I see it? There isn't a disease you could name that I don't know. So, I beg, doctor, if you've any respect for yourself or your profession, that you won't come near me again with the word 'fever' on your lips."

The doctor mentally registered a vow that he would not.

Before he could get out of earshot, however, he heard Lady Judith announce with great emphasis her intention of taking the sick-room under her own immediate supervision, and of keeping a steady eye alike on patient, nurse, and doctor.

There followed a rather bad fortnight for all three.

That fortnight came as a reprieve to Madge; it gave her breathing time. It was a weighty secret that she carried about with her. For two whole days she had felt herself almost crushed by and had only by dint of vigorous effort preserved an outward appearance of calm. Then she had awakened with a start, saying to herself that there was no time to be lost, and thanking Heaven that she was bound in honour not to communicate the evil news to living soul until Sir Peter had been put into possession of it and had resolved upon his course of action.

Possibly, by dint of vigorous entreaty, he might be induced to keep the secret from Lance till a certain definite provision had been made for him. This she knew, though it had often been talked about, had not as yet been done. Sir Peter always saying that her marriage with Lance should be the signal for setting the lawyers to work upon a handsome settlement for him, so that his income might be something on a par with hers. Madge, no longer anxious to repudiate Sir Peter's mediatorship, was beginning to feel now that this marriage and this settlement could, with a very good grace, be arranged by him before the contents of the Australian letter were proclaimed abroad. Once, however, let Lance know his changed position and she felt sure that his pride would stand in the way of both marriage and settlement.

In the meantime, all she could hope to do, while awaiting Sir Peter's recovery to health, was to try and keep matters between her and Lance on that easy, pleasant footing against which in her caprice she had rebelled as savouring too much of the familiar bond of a brother and sister.

A terror that can be proclaimed from the house-top sits lightly enough. It is the one that is locked up wordless within the heart that feeds "on the pith of life." Madge's secret told on her good looks. Even Lance, though he had seemed of late strangely self-absorbed, noticed it.

"What is it, Madge—headache?" he asked one morning over the breakfast-table, while Lady Judith, high over their heads, was delivering an oration on the degeneracy of the dairymaid of the period.

Madge flushed scarlet.

"That means am looking particularly ugly this morning," she thought, contrasting in her "mind's eye" her own sallow complexion with the ideally beautiful coloring of that "girl in gray."

To divert his eyes, as well as his thoughts, she made was sudden, abrupt announcement.

"I think shall open my house in Belgrave Square this year for the half-season."

Now, that "house in Belgrave Square" had been fruitful cause of squabbling between Lance and Madge.

Whenever she had been particularly bent on making herself disagreeable to him, by way of revenge for an unusual amount of teasing, she had been in the habit of tightening her lips, and saying, "I shall open my house in town this year and see a little society."

Whereupon Lance had never failed to reply: "There'll be the mischief to pay if you do, Madge, unless you set up a duenna at the same time. You'll get a mob of impecunious young idiots dangling after you, and I shall be called upon to administer a caning every other week."

To which Madge had never failed to retort, that "She adored boys—impecunious or otherwise—and that she had serious intentions of weeding from her visiting-list every family where the men were over two-and-twenty."

But there was to be no mimic skirmish over the town house now. Lance had drifted into dreamland and seemed to get his thoughts back from their travels with difficulty.

"It does seem a pity," he said, a little absently, "that that comfortable house should be shut up, and you have to stay at a hotel whenever you want to run up to town."

"They won't use their arms, my dear, that's what it comes to! And when the butter isn't what it ought to be it's the fault of the butter-worker, or the milk, or the cow, or the clover, or goodness knows what," flowed in the running stream of Lady Judith's talk between the two.

Madge, keeping a steady eye on Lance, saw that not she, nor her townhouse, nor yet Lady Judith's typical dairymaid, had a corner in his thoughts. His eyes were fixed on the garden-picture which the window facing him framed, with what seemed to her an expectant look in them.

"Shall we ride this morning?" she asked, suddenly-sharply; determined to awaken him to the fact of the existence of such a person as Madge Cohen, and that she sat at his elbow.

Lance jumped up from the table.

"So sorry, Madge—I have to be down at the kennels in half an hour—now Uncle Peter is laid by, I'm bound to see to everything; and when I get back I'm afraid you'll find it too hot for a canter."

But he did not get down to the kennels in half an hour's time, for Madge, compelled to a solitary ramble, and standing for a moment at the front door to call her dogs for company, heard his voice in conversation with Miss Shore, who was seated on the terrace at her easel.

Miss Shore's broken English reached her ear first:

"I can't do it," she was saying in a troubled tone. "When I look at these mountains, other mountains rise up before me and shut out these. Grander, gloomier mountains, with one bright evil star shining out of the purple clouds. I could paint those—not these."

"Well, then, why don't you paint them?" said Lance's voice in reply.

"They would be bound to be worth looking at. Paint out what is in your eyes, and then you'll be able to see what is outside them."

Then he caught sight of Madge under the stone porch, reiterated the necessity that existed for his presence at the kennels in half an hour's time, and departed in all but breathless taste.

This little incident, with a divergence of detail, repeated itself again and again. To her fancy he seemed to be perpetually leaving rooms as she entered them, going out of the house when she came in, and *vice versa*. When she wanted to talk he appeared to prefer silence, and when she grew thoughtful and reserved he would suddenly become loquacious and lively, or, worse still, would stimulate Lady Judith's powers of conversation to such an extent, that the room would become in tolerable to Madge with her distracting burden of thought.

It was no wonder that Madge, with wits sharpened by the necessity of the case, and prejudices stimulated by her jealousy, speedily fixed upon that "girl in gray" as the likely cause of Lance's eccentric conduct, and was ready to anathematise herself for finding pretext for prolonging the young woman's stay at the Castle, in weak compliance with Lance's wish.

It was no wonder, also, that with eyes once turned in that direction, that "girl in gray "grew to be an object of special attention to Madge. She found herself perpetually watching her, scrutinising her every action, look, speech, with eager, yet unsympathetic eyes. And the more closely she watched her the more of an enigma she grew to her.

Since the one memorable evening that Miss Shore had exchanged places with Madge at the dinner-table, she had not once sat down with the family to any of their meals. Her breakfast was taken to her in her own room with the morning paper as its invariable corollary. About luncheon-time she would appear outside on the terrace with her easel and painting accessories, and there she would sit until failing daylight put an end to her work, when she would go back straight to her room, where light supper of some sort was by her orders taken to her.

Madge, looking over Miss Shore's shoulder once, was surprised at the slow progress which the mountain picture was making, in spite of the evident ease and skill with which the artist handled her brushes and colours. Half her time she seemed to be washing off her colours, not washing them in.

That one occasion of looking over Miss Shore's shoulder was made memorable to Madge by the sudden start the girl gave, and the frightened, yet withal angry look which swept over her face.

"Why do you do it—you startle me? Come in front if you wish to speak to me!" she cried, vehemently. And there and then she removed her chair, placing it with its back to the house, and leaving no room for a passerby.

Madge related this circumstance to Lance, watching his face closely for tell-tale change of expression.

Lance seemed to feel her scrutiny, and tell-tale expression there was none.

"Much ado about nothing, as usual, Madge," he said, lightly. "Don't you remember the terrified jumps you used to give if ever I came behind you at your singing and joined in a bar or two?"

"Yes; but I never turned on you as furiously as she turned on me or sat with my chair with its back to the wall so that no one should ever get behind it again!"

"Miss Shore, I dare say, is of a very nervous temperament, and has—"

"A guilty conscience perhaps," interrupted Madge. Then the minute the words were out of her mouth she regretted them. They would just put another stone to the wall that seemed to be building between Lance and herself, and possibly make that "girl in gray" and her eccentric doings a sealed subject between them.

"Had a great deal of trouble, I was going to say," said Lance, walking away at his last word in order to prevent farther parley on the matter.

"She came into the house like a shadow, she falls between us like a shadow! Would to Heaven she would depart in the same shadowy fashion," Madge thought bitterly.

"I beg your pardon, Mrs. Cohen, for intruding," said Mr. Stubbs's voice at that moment at her elbow, "but I believe one of Sir Peter's letters, which I handed to you the other day, had an Australian postmark on it."

"Yes, what of it?" asked Madge, sharply, her looks at once betraying the fact that this letter was of vivid interest to her.

It was invariably difficult for this young woman to speak lightly and think heavily. To look tranquil when she felt like "a cauldron stirred by witches," was an impossibility to her.

"I merely wished to say," Mr. Stubbs went on respectfully, "that the Australian mail goes out in three days, and if a provisional answer is necessary—"

"A provisional answer is not necessary," said Madge without a moment's hesitation, giving not so much as a thought to the fragile, sensitive lad at the other end of the world, who was in "a state of tremor lest his own kith and kin should not hold out the hand of welcome to him."

XVI

One way or another, affairs seemed very much at sixes and sevens at the Castle just then.

For one thing, Sir Peter's illness upset all their autumn plans—a trip to Biarritz for Lady Judith and Madge, Lance's grouse shooting on the Scotch moors prior to a fortnight's fishing in Norway. For another, the spirit of Queen Mab herself seemed abroad in the house, and everyone appeared to be doing just exactly the particular thing that was to be least expected of them.

Madge, embroidery in hand, sat in her rocking-chair under the "dark-green layers of shade" of the old cedar on the lawn, watching a whole pageant of fantastic fleecy clouds sweeping across a deep-blue sky before a strong current.

"That's us to the life just now," she said to herself emphatically, though ungrammatically. "There's a mermaid—look at her fish-tail!—riding on a tiger! There's a big white cat with a Gains-borough hat on his head. Here I come! There's a huge four-wheeled triumphal-car with nothing but a stupid little swan to draw it. No, that isn't me either. A swan is a very beautiful creature; also, I'm not trying to drag anything along at the present moment; no, I only wish I could make one thing stand still-forever.

Here's a great snow mountain just toppling over, and there's a poor little bat stretching out its wings to protect something. What is it? A teacup? a pigeon's egg on end? That's me to the life-the bat, that is; ugly enough and trying to do impossibilities with its stupid little wings!"

Madge's train of thought had been set going by two little incidents of that day's occurrence, in which the chief actors had conducted themselves as uncharacteristically as could well be imagined.

Incident number one had been a little speech of Lance's, made a propose of nothing at all, so far as she could see.

"Madge," he had said, with a sudden energy which set her thoughts ranging upon wild possibilities, "what an unlucky beggar I am never to have had a profession given to me! Now, supposing I were ever to offend Uncle Peter in any way, and he were to cut me off with a shilling, how on earth could I get my bread and butter? I should have to turn either groom or gamekeeper! 'Pon my life I don't think I'm fit for anything else."

Incident number two had occurred during the reading of Sir Peter's correspondence, to which Madge devoted punctiliously two hours every morning. It cost her a huge effort to do this, and she never broke a seal now, without a chill quaking as to the news that seal might secure. Mr. Stubbs, as a rule, sat a model of respectful attention during the reading of those letters. He never uttered a syllable unless addressed, when his words in reply would be discreet and few. On this particular morning, however, Madge had no sooner taken her place in Sir Peter's chair than he began to talk, and the subject of his talk was himself and his family.

"I have had a letter this morning, Mrs. Cohen," he began, "which has greatly distressed me."

"Indeed!" exclaimed Madge, round-eyed with a sudden terror lest the subject of the Australian letter might be circulating from other quarters.

"I don't think I ever mentioned the fact to you that I have a son-Roger by name."

Madge drew a long breath of relief; her slight bow, however, in acknowledgment of the communication, expressed but the faintest interest in the "son—Roger by name."

Mr. Stubbs, however, felt sufficiently encouraged to proceed.

"This son, I grieve to say, has been one continual source of anxiety to me. He has had loss upon loss in his profession—that of a ship and insurance broker—and is now threatened with bankruptcy by his creditors unless I can get together a certain amount to meet his present difficulties."

Madge was not disposed to invite farther confidences.

"Will a cheque for twenty pounds be of any use to you?" she asked, by way of cutting the matter short.

"It would be of use, and I should be grateful for Mrs. Cohen," he replied, drooping his eyelids till the eyes beneath showed not as orbs but as slits. "But I hope you won't mind my saying that cheque for fifty pounds would be of much greater use, as the sum we have to get together is a rather large one."

If the armed warrior in bronze, who surmounted the clock on the mantelpiece, had suddenly descended from his pedestal and asked her to valse with him, Madge could not have felt more surprise than she did at this unexpected request. It was not made in Mr. Stubbs's usually obsequious fashion, but rather stated bluntly, as a matter of fact that must be patent to all.

She was always inclined to be free-handed with the Cohen gold, but she did not choose to have it demanded of her.

"I will think over your request," she said coldly, as she went back to her letter-reading.

And she did think over his request, as also over Lance's startling tirade on his incapacity for earning his bread and butter; but the only results to her thinking were the fantastic forms she evolved from the clouds—a sort of picture-poem of life at the Castle at the moment.

From where she sat beneath the cedar, she could catch a glimpse between the shining laurel leaves of an opaque patch of gray skirt, which at that distance represented Miss Shore at her easel.

That gray skirt was, as it were, a stumbling-block to the wheels of her thoughts every time it caught her eye; just, too, when she wanted those thoughts to be working at their hardest and smoothest. So, she turned her chair slantwise, shutting it out from her view.

It was too hot to finger her embroidery; her silks, a tangle of soft colours, slipped to her feet on the grass. A faint south wind blowing over the orchard, brought with it the scent of ripening fruits. Overhead, the great, golden, brooding clouds hung low.

Madge, with half-shut eyes, rocked herself backwards and forwards; now the tangled colours of the silks caught her eye, anon the golden, brooding clouds. Now the coloured silks were up in the sky, a many-tinted rainbow; now the full-breasted clouds were at her feet, blotting out the green earth, and transforming the whole garden-picture into a cloud-fresco in carnations and azure that Murillo might have painted as a background to his ascending Virgin.

Those clouds and the rocking-chair together sent her into dreamland. Her eyes, full of the sky, drooped.

She opened them, as she thought, in a beautiful garden; a garden scarcely to be realised out of fairy-fable, for the light poured down from the sky on it like some great falling rainbow, transfiguring trees, flowers, and green sward into all sorts of marvelous hues. Lance stood beside her.

"Is this Eden?" in her dream she thought she said to him. But even as she asked the question, a dense, gray cloud settled down upon the fairy garden like a great fog, and all the beautiful colours died under it. It came a misty bulk between her and Lance, and she saw him no more. Only his voice, far away from out the cloud, came, saying, "Madge, Madge, help me!"

Madge awoke with a great start. Yes, there was a voice at her elbow, not Lance's, however, but Mr. Stubbs's; and, instead of begging for her help, he was as usual making apologies for disturbing her.

"But old Donald, the grave-digger," he went on to say, "was here just now gossiping with the gardeners, and he gave me this, thinking it might belong: to some one in the house, for there's no such outlandish name as the one marked on it known in the village."

As he finished speaking he held out to her view a lady's pocket-handkerchief It was trimmed with lace and had the name "Etelka" embroidered in one corner.

Madge scrutinised the lace. It was unlike anything she had ever seen before—something of an old Greek pattern worked in Mechlin thread.

Mr. Stubbs's face said, "An I would I could!"

His lips said: "I told Donald that to the best of my knowledge no one at the Castle possessed such a name."

"Where did Donald find it?" queried Madge.

"He said under the yews in the churchyard."

"Leave it with me, I'll try to find its owner," said Madge, always inclined to abridge intercourse with Mr. Stubbs as much as possible.

He bowed and withdrew.

Madge sat staring at the handkerchief with the outlandish name in the corner.

"There's only one person here likely to own to that name," she thought. "And it suits her infinitely better than the plain English name she sees fit to mask under."

She looked towards the corner of the garden where Miss Shore had been seated at the easel. Now should she take the handkerchief to her at once, ask if it were hers, and what could be the object of her solitary rambles in the churchyard?

Miss Shore, however, together with her easel, had disappeared. Second thoughts assured Madge of the uselessness of such a course. A cold, expressionless "No," without change of feature, would, no doubt, be the only result to the plainly put question, "Is this yours?"

Better keep it awhile; find out a little more about it; ask Donald himself as to the exact "where" and "when" he had found it. She was not disposed to trust Mr. Stubbs implicitly in either small or great matters and had no wish to show him that the handkerchief had any special interest for her.

"I beg your pardon, Mrs. Cohen," said Mr. Stubbs's voice, at this very moment, "but may I ask if you have had time to think over my request of this morning?"

Madge's reply was a cold and repressive, "I have not."

Mr. Stubbs again bowed and withdrew.

He made half-a-dozen steps down the gravel path and came back again. "I beg your pardon, Mrs. Cohen," he said, respectfully as before, "but perhaps you have forgotten that the Australian mail goes out tomorrow. If the letter addressed to Sir Peter is of any importance, it might be as well to acknowledge it."

Madge had it in her heart to ask a string of questions, such as: "What is this letter to you? What do you know of its contents? How dare you keep thrusting yourself and your affairs upon my notice."

She controlled herself with difficulty, saying merely:

"The letter requires no acknowledgment whatever."

XVII

Madge had a lonely dinner that night. A message was brought to her that Lady Judith had gone to bed with a bad headache, and that Lance, who had gone out driving in the afternoon, had sent back his dog-cart with the intimation that he should most likely dine with Lady Brabazon—their nearest neighbor—and walk home afterwards.

Madge as much as possible curtailed her solitary meal. It was not a particularly cheerful one, eaten in that big dining-hall, with the "eight-and-twenty Critchetts looking down" on her.

After dinner she wandered out to her favourite twilight to haunt—the terrace, with its grand double landscape of sky and mountain, valley and plain.

The after-glow lingered yet in sheen of mother-o'-pearl athwart a limpid stretch of tender green sky. A veil of night-blue mist was slowly spreading itself over the valley, adding a mystery and poetry to it which in garish sunlight it never knew. Madge, without much stretch of imagination, could have fancied it some land of enchantment sinking slowly—slowly into the earth whence it had been evoked by magician's wand.

Her thoughts, however, in their restless turmoil soon brought her from the poem of shining sky and shadowy valley back to commonplace, hard-featured prose. Lance was the keynote, the beginning, end, and middle of those tumultuous thoughts.

The echo of the cry, "Madge, help me!" which she had heard in her dream, seemed to ring in her ears yet. Help him! Why, her heart was all one prayer to be allowed to do so. Years ago, she had stood on one side—had thrust herself out of his path, as it were—by marrying David Cohen, in order not to mar his future. Should she stand tamely by now, and see him blight that future with his own hands?

Here it was that Madge no longer beheld the fading glories of the afterglow, nor the mysterious valley under its night-blue veil seeming to sink slowly into the heart of the earth again. Her eyes instead, for their own torment, conjured up a picture-gallery in which Lance's face and form in? endless repetition did duty for a hundred. Now he was standing gazing with surprised admiration at a girl lifting a gray gossamer veil; anon he was seated facing that girl with an intense eager interest shining out of his eyes. After these came all sorts of scenes in which his face, together with its admiration and interest, had a kindly sympathy and pity written upon it.

At this point Madge's ears became filled with other voices than those of the thrushes among the sycamores, chanting their hallelujahs to the dying day. Lance's voice, in pitiful pleading for the forlorn stranger, rang in them instead.

And coming always as a refrain to these thoughts, persistent as the echo to the hammer on the anvil, was the bitter self-accusation that once, not so very long ago. Lance's fate had been in her hands, and she had had the privilege of making or marring it with a single word.

Here Madge's society became too much for her. A short sharp walk she felt before daylight closed in, would be the quickest way of putting an end to that hateful iteration in her ears of "Half your own doing, Madge Cohen, half your own doing."

The handkerchief with the foreign name on it afforded her a pretext for a ramble. Old Donald, the gravedigger, as a rule spent his summer evenings in St. Cuthbert's churchyard, trimming graves or sweeping paths. She would like to put to him direct a question or two as to the finding of this handkerchief. Old Donald had keen eyes and ears; perhaps in addition to answering her questions, he might be able to give her some little information as to when and for what purpose Miss Shore haunted the old burying-place.

It was a walk of about half an hour that Madge proposed to herself. She made that half-hour twice its length with the fancies she crowded into it. Like the old Indian, who painted a vivid picture of the little man who stole his venison, together with the bob-tail dog, merely from seeing a foot-print in a dusty road, Madge constructed a whole life history for Miss Shore out of the name embroidered on the pocket-handkerchief, which had not yet been identified as hers.

St. Cuthbert's church was built on a rocky headland about a mile and a half distant from the Castle. It commanded on its western side a magnificent view of the rolling Irish Sea; whose rough breezes had battered its gray walls for close upon two hundred winters. On its eastern side it was reached by a steep winding road direct from the valley. The larches, which drooped stately branches here and there over the stony path, had gone to a dusky olive tint as Madge wound her way upwards. At the end of the road the low, gray stone wall of the church showed bleak and bare from out the deeper gray of shadowy waving grass; above the stone tower rose dark square against the yellow zone which belted the horizon.

The place of tombs looked weird and desolate as Madge entered it. The sea-wind blew over ruffling the long grasses on one or two forgotten graves and setting group of aspens that over-shadowed the lych-gate whispering and shivering. There was no sign of old Donald anywhere. Madge wandered in vain down the by-walk which skirted the low, gray wall. An owl flew from out the tower with an old yew—black against harsh cry, white tombstone—creaked in the sea-breeze. Other sound there was none.

Madge felt that she had had her walk for nothing. Twilight was falling rapidly now; the gold had died out of the yellow zone which belted the horizon; a white ocean mist—itself a great silver sea—came surging up behind the church tower. Overhead here and there in the limpid gray of the sky, a star, like a tiny diamond spark, would catch the eye, twinkle—vanish—shine out again.

Madge turned her face towards the lynch gate, thinking the sooner she got back to the house now the better. She had walked a, little of the bitterness out of her thoughts, but somehow—she could not say exactly how—the sadness in them seemed to have deepened. She felt tired—chilled by the mist and the weird loneliness of the place.

"Good times, bad times, all times pass over," she could fancy those voiceless dead were preaching to her from under their grassy mounds.

How still the graveyard seemed to have grown! She could hear the twilt of the bats as they flitted in ghostly fashion round the belfry window. Even the light falls of her step on the gravel seemed to waken echoes from the other end of the long, dim walk.

But were those the echoes of her own tread? Madge asked herself, pausing under the shadow of a tall monument, white against the gray of the sky.

The sound of voices, which came nearer with the supposed echoes, answered her question in the negative.

Madge, prompted by impulse, rather than by any definite purpose, shrank behind the tall, white stone as two long, dark shadows, falling athwart her path, heralded the approach of a man and woman. Their voices came to her clear and distinct through the, stillness of the evening air. Madge's ears needed not to be told who the owners of those voices were.

"Lance and that girl in gray!" she said to herself. And after that the dead might have crawled from under their grassy mounds, and in their grave garments have preached their sermon to her; but she would not have heard one word of it.

Lance was evidently in as light-hearted a mood as usual. "We're early," he was saying as he came along. "'There's husbandry in heaven, their candles are'—not yet lighted. Last night we had better luck."

"Last night, last night!" repeated Madge, a great wave of jealous anger sweeping over her. "That was why, then, he did not come into the drawing-room last night I why he gave short, absent answers to my questions, and looked and walked like one in a dream."

For a moment the dim churchyard and ghostly white tombs grew misty to her.

Her ears even refused to perform their work, and Miss Shore's answer was a blank to her.

Not so Lance's next sentence. His voice in nearer approach rang like a clarion in her ear. It was:

"I haven't forgotten a word of what you taught me last night. I know which are the benefic planets and which the malefic ones, and I know that all the malefic planets are setting, and all the benefic ones are rising. And that means that those who have hitherto been unlucky will forthwith begin to have a real good time of and those who have been in luck before will be luckier than ever."

Miss Shore's voice in reply, by contrast with his light tones, sounded grave to absolute solemnity.

"Why do you laugh in the face of fate as you do? Evil stars are rising, not setting. You may be born to good luck—I do not know—bit others are born to ill-luck—to be evil, to do evil. It is no laughing matter.

There was one behind that tall tomb-stone, at any rate, who found it no laughing matter.

Lance's tones suddenly changed to an earnestness that sat strangely upon him.

"You are right," he replied, "there is a time to laugh, and a time to weep; and I'm confident if I knew one quarter of the ill-luck you've had to go through, I should feel far more inclined to weep than to laugh over it. But you won't give me the chance! You keep your lips sealed; you reject help; reject sympathy even."

He was standing still in the middle of the path now facing his companion. Madge could have stretched out her hand and touched him as he stood.

The words themselves expressed naught beyond the kindliest sympathy. Madge herself—any Sister of Charity—might have spoken them to any poor, forlorn outcast who came in their way. But they would not have sounded as they did on Lance's lips. He put another soul into them with his eager, heated, impassioned manner. That, not Madge nor any woman living could have so much as mimicked.

Miss Shore's pale face flushed into sudden animation under it. Her words came hurriedly, nervously, not with their usual cold, slow emphasis.

"You do not understand," she answered. "My ill-luck is not a thing past and done with, I take it with me wherever I go; it is written here," here she touched the palm of her hand. "An evil star is in the ascendant now, in three weeks' time—three weeks from tonight—it will be in opposition to my ruling planet." She broke off for a moment, then added in solemn, though still tremulous tones: "If that day passes over my head in peace, I will talk no more of fate, no more of ill-luck. I will look up at the stars and will laugh in their faces."

XVIII

"Lance, I'll undertake never to do it again. No—not if I live to be a hundred."

It was Sir Peter's first day downstairs. He was getting a breath of fresh air and "a little exercise," by walking up and down the big inner hall of the house, every one of whose long Gothic windows stood wide open.

Lance, on his way through the hall, had stopped to congratulate the old gentleman on his release from the sick-room.

"No, I dare say you won't do it again—catch the measles I suppose you mean. It would be rather difficult to have them a third time, wouldn't it?" he said, in response to Sir Peter's energetic assertion.

"No, no, no! That goes without saying. I mean get out of bed again in the middle of the night to walk off the cramp. I say. Lance?" this was added in a tone that signalled an interesting communication at hand.

"Yes, what is it?" answered Lance.

Sir Peter walked on tiptoes to the door, looking right and left, came back again and peered out of one of the windows.

"Down at the farm," said Lance, answering the action as well as the look on the old gentleman's face, which said plainly as words could, "Where is she?"

Sir Peter drew a breath of relief.

"Broughton has ordered me away—to 'complete the cure,' he says, and—and—and Lady Judith insists on carrying me off into Devonshire on a visit to some of her people!"

"Oh, well, if she insists, there's no more to be said. Submit, and be carried off."

"But—but I don't intend to be carried off, and, what's more, I won't be carried off. No, I won't—I won't," said Sir Peter, irritably, working himself into what Lance was generally pleased to call a "pucker."

"Well, then, I should say you won't, and stick to it if I were you."

"Yes, yes, of course, exactly. That's what I intend to do," said the old gentleman with dignity, as if it were his invariable custom to treat Lady Judith's behests without-spoken resistance. "And I was thinking, Lance, that a little trip to town with you—say for a week, or ten days—would be far more likely to do me good than a dreary fortnight in the wilds of Devon."

"Town in August! Heugh!"

Sir Peter read his own wishes into that shudder. "Well, of course it would be a little hard on you to ask you to lose a week, or ten days, of Madge's society," he began silly.

But Lance interrupted him. "Get that notion out of your head at once and forever, Uncle Peter," he said, peremptorily. "I've told you a dozen times over that Madge hasn't the faintest liking for me, and that I don't intend to worry her any more on the matter." He broke off for a moment to give time for the sly look to die on Sir Peter's face. Not a bit of remained as steadily fixed on his happy, infantine features as had been stereotyped there.

"Talk away, my boy," it seemed to say.

"But, for all that, know what I know."

Lance grew more and more exasperated.

"Look here, Uncle Peter, listen to reason." he began. Then he checked himself. As well talk logic to the eight-and-twenty Critchetts who smiled down on them from the walls as to Uncle Peter, with that wise look peeping from under his eyelids, and that sugary, benignant smile curving the corners of his mouth. Besides, a sudden idea had at that moment occurred to him. A few days in town alone with Uncle Peter would suit very well a plan that was hatching in his brain.

The notion that he was "an unlucky beggar," because he had never had the chance of a career in life offered him, had not died so soon as he had given utterance to it to Madge. On the contrary, it had been slowly gathering strength. What he had said to Madge he was in effect repeating to himself in one form or another all day long: "Suppose I were to offend Uncle Peter utterly, irretrievably, and he were to cut me off with a shilling, how on earth should I get my bread and butter?"

It would be a splendid idea to get Sir Peter all to himself for a day or two and have a little serious talk with him on one or two matters.

So, he mastered his inclination to combat Uncle Peter s wise look and sugary smile, and instead said, a little condescendingly, perhaps, "Make it three days in town, and possibly I may be able to manage it."

Sir Peter rubbed his hands gleefully. "I felt sure you would when you thought it over! You see at the longest we can't be away very long. My birthday, as you know, will be on the twenty-first. Well, I must be home at least a week before that to see that everything is going on all right—people want so much looking after—do you remember last year that tent suddenly giving way at one corner—that was the only one I hadn't given an eye to while they were driving the pegs in. It's wonderful to me, truly wonderful that—"

"Let's get back to ways and means," interrupted Lance, striding after Sir Peter, who was just completing his thirtieth measurement of the long room, and now stood in the doorway. "Look here, Uncle Peter, let's have a trot together, and arrange our affairs while we take our exercise. Now, then! what if Aunt Judy insists on accompanying us?"

But the mere suggestion of such a possibility brought Sir Peter to a stand-still at once.

"Not to be thought of for a moment," he said with a fine air of decision. "She would have to be reasoned with. You might do Lance—you have great influence, very great influence, I may say, with her. You might explain to her that—that she couldn't very well be away from Upton just now with so much to arrange for—for the ball on my birthday—that Madge would be lost without her—that her farm just at this time of year requires—"

"I have it!" interrupted Lance. "The farm's the thing! you write to that man in town who keeps her supplied with farm implements, and tell him to send down the latest sweet things in incubators or butter-workers. And then tell that other man at Carstairs to send over a dozen or two of Houdans and Creve-coeurs, and what's that other leggy sort—Brahmas? That'll do it. The poultry will have to be dieted, and the machines will have to be tested. We're all right now, Uncle Peter!"

Lance's suggestions, with modifications, were adopted. Lady Judith's eyes were gladdened one morning by the arrival of a small vanload of farming implements, and before the glow of pleasure caused by their unexpected appearance had time to subside, Lance and Sir Peter had packed their portmanteaus and departed.

"So thoughtful of Lance. Sir Peter tells me it was entirely his idea," said Lady Judith to Madge as she carried her off to the farm to inspect the new purchases.

"But there, he is a good fellow at heart—I've always said so—in spite of his heedlessness and want of respect for his elders!"

Madge was disposed to hail this trip of Sir Peter's as arranged by a special interposition of Providence. She had crept out of her hiding-place in the churchyard, and had made her way home through the twilight shadows with but one thought in her mind—that Miss Shore's visit at the Castle must be brought to an end with as little delay as possible. The absence from home of Sir Peter and Lance seemed to render this idea comparatively easy of accomplishment. She would take matters into her own bauds as soon as they were gone, tell the young lady that she had altered her mind as to the decoration of her boudoir, pay her handsomely for what pictures she had already done, and speed her heartily on her journey to "the North," whether it were to the region of the Arctic Pole or merely to that of North Britain.

Lance would come home and find that the mysterious guest had departed. "Out of sight out of mind," Madge reasoned hopefully with herself. No lovemaking so far as she knew had passed between the two, although a very fair prelude to lovemaking appeared to have been sounded. She stifled the angry jealousy that threatened to rise up in her heart with the thought that the occasion was not worth it. Once let this mysterious and attractive young woman disappear from the scene, and Lance would return to his former allegiance to herself, and things no doubt, by the help of Sir Peter, would be happily arranged between them.

She had concluded that, until Sir Peter's return, she would not hand to him the Australian letter. Among Sir Peter's numerous child-like propensities was that of proclaiming aloud in the marketplace every secret whispered into his ear. He might promise her a thousand times over that Lance should know nothing of this newly-found heir until matters were satisfactorily arranged, and the Cohen wealth as good as handed over to his keeping; but once give Sir Peter up to Lance's sole influence, as would be the case during a week's stay in town, and his promises would be as tow, or as the green withes wherewith Samson was bound. After Lance's future had been definitely arranged, she would, she said to herself, do penance for her subterfuge by making a full confession to Sir Peter, explaining to him the motives of her action.

So Sir Peter came downstairs, fingered his correspondence, sent the study carpet a little farther on its road to ruin, made the house lively with bell-ringing; in fact, effected generally a transformation-scene wherever he shed the light of his countenance, and finally departed in company with Lance. And the little key which represented a mighty secret hung still on Madge's watch-chain, and the burden of the untold tidings lay heavy on her heart.

"I hope your sketches are getting on satisfactorily, my dear," said Sir Peter to Madge, as be jumped into the dogcart and took his seat beside Lance. He glanced in the direction in which Miss Shore and her easel were generally established. "Nice young woman that! Nice to look at; nice to speak to! Wish she'd be a little more communicative though—

did my best yesterday to draw her out about herself and her people—she must have people of some sort you know—but couldn't succeed—"

"Chickabiddies all right, Aunt Judy?" interrupted Lance, catching sight of Lady Judith's advancing figure. But his eyes, to Madge's fancy, went wandering over "Aunt Judy's" head in the same direction as Sir Peter's.

Sir Peter had another "last word" to say. It was: "You'll see to my correspondence while I'm away, Madge, and it's bound to be all right. You've a capital head for business, though you won't acknowledge it."

The words stung Madge like so many hornets.

"Why should I be made to do an unworthy thing?" she had said to herself two nights before in St. Cuthbert's churchyard, as she resolutely trampled underfoot the burning desire to play the listener a little longer. Yet, as the echo of Sir Peter's words repeated itself in her ears, she felt herself to be doing a very unworthy thing in thus withholding his private correspondence from him.

"For Lance, for Lance," she said to herself, hiding her face in the thick fur of old Roy's tawny coat. "We'd die for him—you and I—wouldn't we, Roy?"

Roy, understanding perfectly, licked first her hand inside and out, then her cheek and behind her ear by way of response in the affirmative.

"And we hate her—both of us, don't we Roy?" she won't on. "And we'll do our best to get rid of her! But, oh dear, what if she won't go—cries and says she has no friends, or hangs about the place till Lance comes back, and then begins her wiles once more!"

Here Roy—like all well-bred dogs, a master of the art of thought-reading—once more expressed canine sympathy.

"Oh, for a counsellor!" she sighed. "If I could but turn you into Balaam's ass and get a word of advice out of you, you dear old thing!"

"Speak of an angel and you will hear its wings," says the proverb. Madge's sigh for a counsellor was answered so soon as it was out of her mouth, though not by the rustling of wings—by the slow, soft footsteps of obsequious Mr. Stubbs.

"I am so sorry to disturb you, Mrs. Cohen," he began, after carefully shutting the door behind him. "I merely wished to say that when I handed Sir Peter his letters yesterday morning, I did not say a word about the important letter you have to give to him."

An important letter! How did this man know it was important, and what did he know of her motives in keeping it back? Madge wondered, staring at him blankly.

"Yes, that was right," was all she dared to say, however, hoping that he would consider himself answered and depart.

Not so he. He stood in front of her, surveying her calmly through his half-closed eyes.

"I beg your pardon, Mrs. Cohen," he began, "but have you given a thought to my little request of the other day, respecting my poor boy and his embarrassments?"

Madge was no match for this man, with his effrontery and cunning. Partly from the wish to get rid of him, partly from fear lest he might betray her secret, she rang the bell and desired her maid to bring her cheque-book.

Mr. Stubbs was profuse in his thanks; they flowed in an unctuous stream, like oil from a pierced olive.

"Does he think I am going to give him a thousand pounds," thought Madge, contemptuously. Her pen paused at the figures it was about to write.

"You said?" she queried, looking up at him.

"I said fifty pounds," he replied without a moment's hesitation; "but if you would make it seventy, madam, I should be infinitely obliged to you."

Madge's pen, after a moment's pause, traced the words that transferred seventy pounds from her banking account to Mr. Stubbs's purse.

"There," she thought, "I'm paying him handsomely for keeping my secret for a few days. But I'll take good care that Sir Peter gets rid of him so soon as things are arranged a little."

Mr. Stubbs stood in front of her, cheque in hand, executing a series of profound bows.

"You may count on my deepest gratitude—my life-long gratitude, madam," he said again and again.

Madge's formal bow of acknowledgment was intended as a signal of dismissal. He did not so take it. From thanks he passed on to proffers of service.

"If I can at any moment be of the slightest service, you may rely on me, madam."

And then he suddenly dropped both thanks and proffers of service, came a step nearer to Madge, gave one furtive glance at the door, and said almost in a whisper:

"Does it not strike you as a very extraordinary thing, madam, that Miss Shore should be invariably so anxious to see the morning papers?"

Madge fixed contemptuous eyes on him.

It was easy to read his meaning. It was:

"I am willing enough to do any amount of dirty work for you provided you keep your cheque-book always handy."

"Why should I be made to do an unworthy thing?" was the indignant cry that once more rose up in her heart. Hard-pressed as she might be for counsellors, it was not to such a creature as this that she would apply for aid.

"I have never given the matter a thought," was her reply, in tones so frigid that Mr. Stubbs could not but feel himself dismissed and withdrew accordingly.

XIX

"Why should I be made to do an unworthy thing? Why cannot this thing, in itself right and expedient, be accomplished by honest, straightforward means?" reasoned Madge with herself on the day following Sir Peter's departure, as she thought over her emphatic rejection of Mr. Stubbs's obsequiously-offered services.

She had risen that morning strong in her resolve, not only to further what she conceived to be Lance's best interests in life, but to do so by means which consorted with her own honesty of purpose and integrity of heart. Miss Shore should be told simply and plainly that her services as an artist were no longer required, and that it would be esteemed a favour by herself and Lady Judith if she would as soon as possible continue her journey to the North.

Lady Judith must of course be previously consulted on the matter; so, Madge adverted to it across the breakfast-table.

Her remark, however, fell literally on deaf ears. Lady Judith had come down to breakfast with no less than five telegrams in her hand, and a tirade against Lance on her lips. She had quite forgotten that "he was a good fellow at heart, and that she had always said it," and now remembered only his "heedlessness and want of respect for his elders." Four out of the five telegrams had been despatched at different stages of Sir Peter's journey to town, and simply reported that he was "getting along all right;" the fifth had been sent the first thing that morning, just to show that he was up and doing. As, however, the first four had arrived at Lower Upton overnight too late for delivery, the whole five had been brought in a batch to the Castle the first thing that morning.

Lady Judith tossed them all contemptuously across the table to Madge.

"You may read just whichever you like first, my dear," she said. "It doesn't in the least matter which. One properly-worded telegram would have done for the whole lot. Will you tell me that that young man ever lifts his little finger to keep Sir Peter from making himself ridiculous! It's my belief if Sir Peter ever settles down quietly for ten minutes, he isn't happy till he has set him going again. And now that they're both away together, with no one to look after them, what will happen goodness only knows! "

And so forth.

Madge, so soon as a pause occurred, tried to bring the talk round to Miss Shore.

All in vain. Lady Judith, bent on Sir Peter's misdoings, continued her harangue.

"He'll be sixty-three on the twenty-first of this month, and will you tell me he has one whit more sense than a boy of sixteen? Philanthropy do you call it?" (Madge, by way of diversion, had remarked that the veal-and-ham pie on the table was particularly good.) "A nice sort of philanthropy that which lays burthens upon other people's shoulders, and straightaway forgets all about them! Now I wonder how many incapables he'll pick up in London streets this time to bring back with him. I can only hope that the wagonette will be big enough to seat them all."

And once upon the topic of *protégé*. Lady Judith did not let it go until the whole army of Sir Peter's waifs and strays had been passed in review. The squinting stable-boy, the bow-legged gardener's lad, the poultry-maid who would have been "in her right place picking oakum in a model prison, instead of tending prize-bred poultry on a model farm." And last, but not least, there was that young woman "who sits all day long in front of an easel doing, so far as anyone can see, just nothing at all, who occupies one of the best bedrooms—and I shall want every one of the bedrooms on the west side of the house for the twenty-first—and who won't condescend to give any account of herself or her belongings, but conducts herself as if she were an empress with her pedigree before the world. But I do think, my dear, now that Sir Peter is away and not likely to make a fuss on the matter, that you might just pat a question or two to the young lady as to the length of time her sketches will be likely to occupy. I would interrogate her myself, but she mumbles so I can't hear a word she says. Is she Irish or Welsh do you think?—ah, be so good as to open that window, the room is stifling!"

Madge rose with alacrity from the table. "I will go this very minute and speak to Miss Shore about her sketches, and if she is not down I will go to her room," she said, scarcely crediting the fortunate chance which made Lady Judith's wishes so thoroughly at one with her own.

At the door, however, leading into the hall, she was intercepted by Mr. Stubbs, who, instead of his usual look of carefully achieved expressionlessness, had "important information to give," plainly written upon his features.

"May I speak with you, madam?" he said. His manner emphasized his request; it seemed to add: "At once and in private?"

Madge led the way to Sir Peter's study.

Mr. Stubbs carefully shut the door behind him. "It's about Miss Shore," he began.

Madge slightly bowed but remained standings. "Whatever this man has to tell shall be told quickly and be done with it," she said to herself.

Mr. Stubbs noted her wish for conciseness and fell in with it. "One mustn't quarrel with the knife that spreads the butter on one's bread," was his way of looking at the matter.

"I drew your attention, madam, to Miss Shore's eagerness to get the morning papers so soon as they came into the house. Today I have discovered the reasons for this eagerness," he said.

"Stop," said Madge, "let me ask a question. Do these reasons in anyway concern me? If they do not, I must ask you to refrain from communicating to me whatever you may have discovered. I take no interest in Miss Shore or her private affairs."

Mr. Stubbs did not reply immediately.

It required a good deal of courage to answer this question point-blank, and no-thing but a point-blank answer would suit his purpose.

"It concerns you, madam, so far as the happiness of Mr. Clive concerns you. It is easy to see that he takes the deepest interest in Miss Shore."

Madge flushed scarlet. How she would have enjoyed ordering this man out of the room! But all she said was "Go on," in a low nervous tone.

Mr. Stubbs went on. "Since Miss Shore has taken to reading the papers so assiduously, I have taken care to have duplicates of everyone sent to the house. All the same I send up every morning to her for the preceding day's papers, telling her that I file them for reference. This morning the papers were sent down to me with one torn at the corners, together with the message that Miss Shore regretted very much that she had torn the paper accidentally. Naturally I refer to my copy of the paper that Miss Shore had torn 'accidentally' and in the torn column I find this paragraph."

Here he unfolded a newspaper which he held in his hand, and spread it before Madge on the table, indicating a paragraph.

Madge read as follows:

"The little fishing village of Santa Maura, on the coast of Corsica, has been thrown into a state of excitement by a singular attempt at murder. The intended victim was Count Palliardini, who was staying at a little chalet he owned among the mountains. The murder must have been attempts by some one well acquainted with the Count's habit of sleeping during the early part of the evening. While he thus slept, it seems the wine which stood beside him on a small table had poison put into it, and on awakening and drinking it he seized with all the symptoms of narcotic poisoning. Thanks, however, possibly to the insufficiency of the dose and to the promptness of the remedies administered, he recovered. The strangest part of the story remains to tell. The Countess Palliardini, the Count's mother, was seated just within the door of the house with her back to the light. She had not lighted the lamps, she stated at the judicial inquiry, because it was too hot to do anything but fan herself and eat sweetmeats. As she sat thus in the twilight, she chanced to lift her eyes to a mirror which hung over the stove-place facing the door. To her great surprise she saw reflected in it, not only the shadowy trees of the garden, but also the face and figure of a woman, who must have been standing immediately outside the door. For the moment she was too startled to move. When she recovered herself and went out into the garden the woman was gone. Up to the present moment the police have been unsuccessful in their endeavours to discover the perpetrator of this crime."

Madge drew long breath as she read the last word. That Miss Shore and this would-be murderess were one and the same person she did not for a moment doubt. In the light thrown upon it by this paragraph, the young lady's mysterious conduct since her coming to the Castle seemed easy enough to understand.

"It is monstrous! incredible!" she said, not addressing Mr. Stubbs, but uttering her own thoughts, and moving towards the door as she spoke with the newspaper in her hand.

Mr. Stubbs stood between her and the door.

"May I ask what you intend to do, madam?" he said.

"Do!" replied Madge, hotly, "there is only one thing to do. Go straight to her, tell her we have found out who she is, and advise her to get out of the house as quickly as possible."

Madge had fine reputation in the county for a kind heart and a generous temper; but if at that moment she could by *lettres de cachet* have consigned that "girl in gray" to a cellar-prison, there was little doubt but what she would gladly have exchanged that reputation of hers for that of the Pompadour.

"Pardon me, madam, if I suggest a more prudent course. We know who she is—you and I that is—but it would be difficult to impress other people with our convictions as matters stand at present!"

How the "You and I" grated upon Madge's ear even in that moment of excitement.

"What do you propose doing, then?" she asked, curtly.

"I propose to make the young lady convict herself, and of her own free will take flight from the house and keep out of our way—out of Mr. Clive's way," this was said with a furtive but keen look into Madge's face, which once more sent the blood mounting to her brow.

"You see it is just this," Mr. Stubbs went on after a moment's pause, "I have father evidence to produce; but all the same it is not evidence that cannot be disputed, and if we make a martyr of the young lady, and other perons"—here another keen look into Madge's face—"choose to constitute themselves her champions and contest that evidence, we simply put ourselves in an ugly light and young lady in a favourable one."

Again, that odious "We!"

"But there is no room for doubt on the matter," Madge cried. "She comes into the house under an assumed name; she refuses to give an account of herself; she dares not look into a mirror; she is eager for the daily papers; she tears out a paragraph that might criminate her. No one in their senses could refuse to believe such evidence!"

"Is a man in love ever in his senses?" said Mr. Stubbs, coolly, and now looking Madge full in the face.

Madge winced at his words but dared not grow furious at them. They might be true! Heaven only knew!

"My dear madam," Mr. Stubbs went on when he saw that his words and look combined had done satisfactory work, "every one of the circumstances you have mentioned could be explained, by any romantic, pitiful story the young lady might choose to concoct. You might suggest our handing her over to the police on the strength of our suspicions. That would be simply to make stronger still her claim to sympathy. It is more than likely that the police could not substantiate any charge against her, for there is nothing said in this paragraph as to the Countess Palliardini's power to identify the face she saw. No, no, my dear madam, take my advice; you want this young lady turned out of the house as soon as possible, as quietly as possible, as finally as possible. Let us make her eject herself. I have a plan to propose—"

Madge here cut short his sentences with the abruptly-put question: "What is the other evidence of which you spoke just now?"

Mr. Stubbs drew from his pocket a roll of cardboard, which he spread before Madge on the table. On it was sketched in watercolours, slightly and roughly, a mountain, at the base of which was a small country house. A gloomy sky had been lightly washed in, and high over one of the mountain peaks shone out a bright star. The foreground of the picture was unfinished.

Mr. Stubbs watched the changes in Madge's face as she looked at the sketch.

"Do you remember, madam," he asked, "that Mr. Clive on one occasion advised Miss Shore to paint out what was in her eyes so that she might be able to see what was outside them?"

Madge stared at him. "It was said in my presence," she answered, "but you were not there."

"I was just behind the Venetian blinds in the billiard-room and could not help hearing the remark."

Madge, remembering a certain occasion on which she had been an unwilling listener behind those self-same blinds, could say nothing; to this.

"Miss Shore followed Mr. Olive's advice. Two days afterwards I found this sketch among some others in a less advanced stage in a waste-paper basket which a housemaid was bringing across the gallery from Miss Shore's room."

"Across the gallery from Miss Shore's room! "repeated Madge, almost dumbfoundered at the deliberate system of espionage which, these words revealed.

"In the course of my chequered career, madam, I have occasionally found waste-paper baskets to be mines of hidden treasures," said Mr. Stubbs, answering the thought written on her face.

Madge wondered whether, "in the course of his chequered career," he had served his time in a private inquiry office but did not express the wonder.

"You will observe, madam," he went on to say, "that this sketch was torn in half, and that I have pieced it. together at the back. No doubt, after Miss Shore, in pursuance of Mr. Olive's advice, had made two or three such sketches, she found herself able to paint not what was in her mind, but what was before her. She had no other object than this in making these sketches, and consequently destroyed them when finished. Now, if you will be good enough to turn your attention once more to the paragraph we have just been reading, you will see that in it are mentioned mountains, ravines, and a small country house—all are in this picture. The time given for the attempt at murder is the early evening, in other words, the twilight. This is a twilight scene—look at the star fully painted out, though the picture in other parts is merely outlined."

"Yet," cried Madge, "in the face of all this you tell me we have not evidence sufficient to convict this young woman of an attempt at murder to the minds of people who have a fair amount of common sense."

"Has a young man of seven-and-twenty, supposing that he has eyes in his head, much common sense at command in the presence of a beautiful, mysterious, and forlorn young woman?"

Madge winced again; yet her common sense was forced to admit the truth of Mr. Stubbs's remark. Beauty, mystery, forlornness, had been the three-fold cord that had drawn Lance to the side of "that girl in gray."

"Let me repeat," said Mr. Stubbs, noting how the allusions to Lance hit the mark, "that the most effectual way of finally getting rid of this young lady will be to make her eject herself. If you can spare me another quarter of an hour, I will fully explain my plan to you. It is the result of careful thought, and I trust it may meet with your approval."

But Mr. Stubbs must have miscalculated the lengthiness of the project he had to unfold, or else he and Madge must have had other subjects of conversation, for not fifteen minutes, no, nor yet fifty, saw the end of their interview.

It was close upon luncheon-time when Madge came out of the study. She looked downcast and thoughtful. If Lady Judith, as they sat at luncheon together, had used her eyes with as much energy as she did her tongue, she might have seen that Madge ate next to nothing, and that she toyed incessantly with a small key that hung upon her watch-chain as if its presence there were an irritation to her.

At the end of the meal she had a communication to make which not a little surprised Lady Judith. It was:

"I have been thinking again over the matter; and, if you don't mind, I should like Miss Shore to finish the watercolours she has begun for my little room. She can't be much longer now over them; a fortnight, I should say, would see them finished."

XX

It was like a statue coming to life—a carven lump of marble suddenly kindling into human warmth and colour. Madge could at any moment as soon have pictured Old Cuddaw himself, descending from his height, walking up the garden-path and graciously bidding her "good-morning," as Miss Shore so far condescending. Yet that was what happened. And not only did the young lady condescend to the greeting of common life, but she absolutely displayed for Madge's inspection the water-colour drawing on which she had been so long occupied, asking for her opinion on it.

It was a spirited sketch. Miss Shore had caught the purple tone of the landscape together with the golden glow of summer sunlight. If it had been drawn by another hand, Madge would have gone into raptures over it.

"It is pretty," was all she said by way of praise. "I will, if you will allow me, see how it looks against the wall hangings of my room."

These wall hangings of the little room—an octagon, opening off the inner hall—were chrome silk. The landscape hung sideways to the light, which was strikingly effective.

"I suppose," said Madge, turning to Miss Shore, who held the sketch in its place, "I must give up the idea of more than one other, the same size. You are not quick with your brush."

She looked up at the girl's face and then for the first time noted the change that one clay had wrought. Ten years seemed to be effaced from the marmoreal hardness of the features had disappeared, faint flush of colour tinged the white cheeks, the gray eyes were shining. Madge's long look no doubt seemed to repeat the remark she had made as to Miss Shore's artistic capabilities.

"I am not always so slow," she replied, "but I was fit for nothing when I came here first."

"Fit for nothing!" repeated Madge, still eyeing the girl keenly.

"Yes. I was weak—I was ill. I could not eat—I could not sleep, naturally I could not paint"

Madge felt inclined to ask whether a certain paragraph in the preceding day's paper had not had something to do with the young lady's increased power of eating and sleeping; but restrained herself.

"I shall be glad to have a companion picture to this," she said. "A sketch of the valley if you will undertake it."

And then she looked and looked at her again, saying to herself: "A statue coming to life—marble glowing into flesh and blood—that's what it is."

But not alone in Miss Shore's face and manner was the change perceptible; Madge's maid, in her morning attendance, reported another wonder—that the looking-glasses in Miss Shore's room had been uncovered and appeared to be in use, and that the young lady had frequently of late asked her advice on the matter of hairdressing, and appeared to have suddenly awakened to the fact of the insufficiency of her wardrobe. This last statement was confirmed by Miss Shore expressing a wish one morning to be driven into the village, as she had sundry small purchases to make.

Madge watched her drive away in the little pony carriage, in and out among the shifting shadows of the larches and sycamores. She noted that the gray gossamer veil was tossed back, as if the wearer enjoyed the greeting of the bright sunlight and mountain breeze, and that the young lady, as she sat, was turning to the man who drove her, as if asking him questions.

"Would to Heaven she would never come back!" Madge prayed in the bitterness of her heart. The bitterness ended in a sigh. If Lance had been so fascinated with the ice-cold, shadowy maiden, what would he be in presence of such glowing flesh and blood loveliness as this!

"Weigh your wealth against her beauty, Madge Cohen, and see what it is worth," she cried aloud to herself, bitterly.

Sir Peter's stay in town had been prolonged beyond the three days to which Lance would fain have limited it. The old gentleman once on the wing was not to be easily persuaded to settle down again.

"I can't get him back," wrote Lance to Madge, "he's here, there, everywhere; I might as well try to catch ether or sal volatile and get it into a railway rain as Uncle Peter. Town is a wilderness; there's nothing on earth for a man to do, yet his hands are full of morning till night. I should run down to Cowes or to Exmoor for a day or two, only I daren't leave him lest he should get into mischief. For one thing, I'm confident I've kept him out of the mumps. I missed him suddenly the other morning and started in pursuit immediately. I traced him first to the telegraph office; I knew he had a lot to do there—off and on he has almost lived there lately—thence, I hunted him down to the bootmaker's—he's always wanting boots, you know—and finally, to my horror, found him down a blind alley attempting to adjudicate between two little dirty boys who were fighting over their marbles. Both of the little imps had their faces tied up and had a generally puffy appearance about the jaws. 'Uncle Peter,' I shouted, 'if there is anything to be caught, you'll catch it, depend upon it. Think of your birthday! Fancy receiving a deputation with your face tied up!' And so, I dragged him away.

With Sir Peter in so active frame of mind, Lance had found some difficulty in making an opportunity for the little serious talk with him, which he had planned. From morning; till night the old gentleman was never to be found alone. He received the secretaries of his pet charities at breakfast, the members of their committees at luncheon, and as rule dined with, or received at dinner, certain clerical magnates who chanced to be in town. At the odd moments which occurred between his meals he was either inspecting orphanages, or reformatories, or immersed in charity reports and subscription-lists.

Lance had rehearsed over and over again a little speech which ran somewhat as follows: "Uncle Peter you've always said that on the day Madge and I get married, you'll set aside a certain definite property from which I can draw a certain definite income. But supposing that match never comes off! What then?"

To get opportunity, however, to make this little speech was another matter.

He seized a chance that presented itself one morning when Sir Peter, suddenly looking up from his papers, said:

"I shall get Madge to put down handsome life-subscription to this 'working boys' refuge.' She might spend a couple of thousand yearly on charities and never miss it. Her income is princely."

Lance caught at the last words. "I don't believe there's a prince in England with half her fortune! Don't you think it's a trifle presumptuous, on my part, with no independent means of my own, to aspire to a marriage with her?"

Sir Peter smiled up at him benignantly.

"My dear boy, you're too modest! Your future is as assured as a man's can well be. You know—I've often told you—you stand in the position of an only son to me. And it strikes me, even if it were not so, that you'd stand comparison in Madge's eyes with the biggest millionaire in the kingdom. Ah, lend me your pencil a moment, I don't understand these figures—there's something wrong with this balance sheet—I'll tot it up again!"

Again, and again Lance beat about the bush, but all to no purpose.

"Supposing you'd had a son, what would you have done with me?" he asked abruptly on another occasion.

"Eh, what?" And Sir Peter pushed his spectacles high up on his forehead and said, "Eh, what?" again, before Lance's meaning dawned on him. "Well, my boy," he said at length, "I suppose you'd have followed your father's profession—been out in India by this time and have led much such a life as he did. By the way, Lance, it occurs to me, seeing that you belong to a service family, that your name ought to appear on the Military Asylum committee. I'll get you nominated, and you can—"

"No, I can't," interrupted Lance. "I'm not cut out for that sort of thing." And then he took his hat and made for his club, fearful lest, willy-nilly, Sir Peter would drag him into one of those stuffy committee-rooms, in which so large a portion of his own time was passed with entire pleasure.

It was not until the morning of their return to Upton that Lance contrived to put the momentous question, "What then?" after its due preamble of "supposing Madge does not feel inclined to marry again!" But it was absolutely out of the power of Sir Peter to realise such a possibility as this. "A young woman, at her age, to remain single all her life! Impossible, incredible! Tell me at once that she means to turn nun!" he exclaimed.

"Well, put it another way," said Lance, impetuously, speaking on the spur of the moment. Supposing that I was not inclined to settle down and marry just yet, what then?"

"What then!" cried Sir Peter, aghast, "My dear boy! My dear boy!" He jumped up from his chair and began walking up and down the room very fast. Then he stood in front of Lance, his eyes at first very bright, and then suddenly altogether as dim. "After all these years—my most cherished hope! Impossible!" He began his favourite heel and toe movement as if on rockers. "My dear boy! Don't say it again! Impossible!"

After this, Lance thought it prudent to let the matter drop for a time. Lady Judith had fidgeted a good deal over Sir Peter's prolonged absence.

"It's my belief, my dear, that Sir Peter has got into mischief of some sort, and Lance as usual has stood by and enjoyed the fun," she said to Madge.

But as the days slipped past, and Sir Peter's birthday approached, the note of complaint swelled to a louder tone.

"Most inconsiderate—most thoughtless of them both!" she exclaimed. "I don't like to say what I think of such conduct; but anyone who gives the matter a second thought must know how much their absence throws on my hands just now. The house will be full in a day or two—as many men as women to entertain. There are all sorts of final directions to give about the villagers' sports, and the tenants' dinner. I ask you, Madge—is it possible for one brain to undertake the arrangement of all these things, in addition—mind, I say in addition—to other subjects for thought?"

Madge did not pay much heed to Lady Judith's laments. She appeared at that moment to be wholly absorbed in the completion of the decoration of her little octagon sitting-room—an occupation in which, strange to say, Mr. Stubbs's assistance had been volunteered and accepted. He it was who supplied her with the name and address of a man at Carstairs—an "art-decorator" he styled himself—who came to the Castle to take Mrs. Cohen's orders.

They were very simple. A long, narrow looking glass was to be fixed in the wall facing the door, and a certain picture, which Mrs. Cohen had commissioned an artist to paint, was to hang immediately opposite. It was imperative that the room should be finished by the twenty-first, as it would be in use on the night of the ball.

XXI

Sir Peter and Lance returned to Upton three days before the old gentleman's birthday.

"Why a man at his time of life should insist on keeping his birthdays at all, passes my comprehension," Lady Judith was in the habit of saying, as the yearly festivity came around.

All things considered, however, the wonder was rather that Sir Peter, like the schoolboy intent on plum cake, did not insist on keeping his birthday twice over in the twelve months. The general racket and fussiness of the whole thing suited him amazingly. The deputations from the tenants, the village sports, bonfires and bellringing, were an inexhaustible source of delight to him; the constant demands for his personal presence, for his attention to a thousand and one things at the same moment, sent him into ecstasies, and gave colour to his inner conviction, that he was the life and soul of things generally.

He came back from his holiday trip with Lance, looking very radiant, and evidently prepared to enjoy everything. The wagonette was not required to bring the two from the station, as it had been on so many dire occasions when Sir Peter had paid flying visits to the metropolis and had returned encumbered with stable-boys or gardener's lads.

"No *protégés* this time," Lance telegraphed to Lady Judith on the morning of their return; but lots of luggage. We've spent a good deal of time in toy-shops lately."

Yes, there was a good deal of luggage. Even Madge, who was accustomed to travel about with a haystack of trunks and dress baskets, exclaimed at it as she saw it uncarted at the door.

"Presents of shawls for the old women, pipes for the old men, bushels of toys for the children, something for you, Madge, something for Aunt Judy—nobody forgotten!" exclaimed Lance.

Nobody had been forgotten; and there was one box in which Sir Peter showed a good deal of interest, and which, as the other boxes were carried to their destination, he desired to be placed for the moment in the hall.

"Madge will do it best—you ask her," he whispered to Lance.

"No, you ask her," whispered Lance. back again. "Madge thinks a great deal more of your requests than she does of mine."

Madge, a few yards off, heard this remark, and came forward, asking:

"What is expected of me?"

Sir Peter addressed Lance again:

"You explain; you know how it all came about."

"No, you do it," said Lance, "You've a much greater command of language than I have."

Sir Peter cleared his throat. "Well my dear," he said, addressing Madge, "you see this is a season of rejoicing for us all. I've got well through a very nasty illness, and—"

"Haven't caught anything fresh in town," suggested Lance.

"Exactly; have come back in excellent health—"

"Laden like Santa Claus at Christmas time," again suggested Lance.

"Exactly; shawls for the old women, pipes for the old men."

"Corals and gutta-percha toys for the babies—nobody forgotten," said Lance.

"No, nobody forgotten inside or outside the house," chimed Sir Peter, "And it occurred to us, for Lance, I may say, shared my feeling on the matter—" Here he looked at Lance, hoping that he would take up the thread of the narrative. Lance remained dumb, however; so, Sir Peter went on again:

"It occurred to use that—that at such a time of rejoicing, no one should be forgotten inside or outside the house—"

"You've said that before," said Lance.

"Ah, have I. Well, it occurred to—to us—"

"You've brought a present for Miss Shore?" asked Madge, jumping, as she so often did, at a possibility.

"Exactly, exactly, my dear," said Sir Peter, much relieved now that the truth was out. "Lance said to me—"

"No, you said to me," said Lance.

"Well, I said to Lance, 'I don't suppose, coming into the house in the unexpected way she did, that the young lady will have her any dress suitable for the twenty-first,' and Lance said to me, 'It would be a crying shame for a handsome young woman like that not to make her appearance at the ball.' And so, my dear, the long and short of the matter is, we went to your dressmaker in Bond Street, and left it in her hands to send down a dress fit for the occasion."

Had the choice been given him. Lance, in Madge's hearing, would sooner have had the former than the latter speech put into his mouth. For some reason, however, he did not attempt to modify Sir Peter's statement.

"The question is now," Sir Peter went on, cheerily, "how to present the dress to the young lady without hurting her feelings. Of course, it would come better as a gift from you than from me."

"I couldn't do it—it would be impossible—quiet, quite impossible," said Madge in a very low tone of voice, and with far more earnestness of manner than the occasion seemed to warrant.

"You always do that sort of thing so cleverly, Madge," put in Lance.

"You may be sure, my dear, the dress will be everything it ought to be," said Sir Peter, mistaking the cause of Madge's reluctance to present his gift. "I saw Madame Claire herself, and she said that nothing remained to be done to the dress that your maid couldn't do. It's a beautiful colour, a soft gray. Lance was very particular on this matter—"

"I couldn't do it. No, no, it would be quite impossible!" broke in Madge. Then, to avoid further discussion, she went back to the music room and opened her piano.

"It would be Judas-like," she said to herself, as she began to practise her singing with a great deal of energy in a very high key."

"May I speak with you, Mrs. Cohen?" said Mr. Stubbs's voice over her shoulder, before she had been three minutes at the instrument.

"What is it," asked Madge, letting her fingers glide into the quickest and loudest of Cramer's exercises.

"I merely wished to say that tomorrow the Australian mail will be delivered, and to ask for instructions in case a second letter may arrive for Sir Peter with the Rutland Bay postmark."

No answer from Madge. Only her fingers threatened to trip each other up with the speed at which they travelled over the keys.

Mr. Stubbs waited patiently.

"What have you to propose?" at length she asked in a low, nervous voice, but still not lifting her fingers from the keys.

"If you wished madam, I would put any such letter on one side, until after the twenty-first," he said, respectfully.

"Wait till one comes," was all Madge's reply, and then her fingers glided from Cramer's exercises into Weber's "Hilarité" which she executed at double-time, with the loud pedal down.

"Madge," said Sir Peter, coming into the room at that moment, "where is Miss Shore? I've been all over the garden in search of her. I want to know how your sketches are getting on."

Mr. Stubbs disappeared. Madge was all attention at once.

"The sketches have resolved themselves into a pair only, one of which is quite finished. I dare say Miss Shore is in the billiard-room, she has been at work there lately—the weather has been so wet. You know she gets the same view of the valley there as she does from the terrace."

All this she said with her eyes fixed on the piano keys. For the first time in her life she dared not look her benefactor in the face.

Sir Peter vanished but was back again in two minutes.

"There's not a soul in the billiard-room," he said as he came along. "And where is Lance? I have a hundred and one things to consult him about; everything, everyone seems all behindhand—"

Madge recollected that she had seen.

Lance pass outside the windows towards the conservatory. It occurred to her in a flash of painful thought that, where he was, it was possible Miss Shore might be.

A glass door at one end of the drawing-room commanded a view of this conservatory and gave admission to it. Madge led the way thither. Sir Peter followed her a step or two, then he remembered that he had forgotten to inquire after the health of his butler's mother, who suffered from rheumatic gout, and forthwith he flew off in an opposite direction, to set the library bell ringing, in order to have his mind set at rest on the matter.

The conservatory at the Castle was a large one and was arranged rather with a view to general effect than for the exhibition of choice flowering plants, as such. Seen from the drawing-room it was just a lovely tropical garden, where big flowering shrubs formed triumphal arches with palms and tree-ferns; and glowing cactuses wove a bowery ceiling with luxuriant passion-flower and the moon-convolvulus of Ceylon. A lemon and white macaw strutted majestically over the tesselated floor, scolding at the flies as it went along. A majolica fountain threw upward to the glass dome a sparkling jet of water, which caught the sunlight as it fell back into its basin among the broad-leaved Japanese lilies, and the flashing gold and silver fish. Beside this fountain stood the two of whom Madge was in search. Lance's fair, handsome face, though at one with the beauty of his surroundings, seemed to have its markedly Saxon type emphasized by them. Not so Miss Shore. Among roses in an English garden, she looked the foreigner she was; here among the palms and the cactuses she seemed to be in her own country. Those large, lustrous eyes of hers recalled the fire of the stars in a southern sky; that bandeau of jet-black hair seemed to demand magnolia or myrtle for its rightful crown.

Was that what Lance was thinking, for he had drawn downwards a heavy bough of a flowering myrtle-tree? Miss Shore's hand waved it on one side as if she would have none of it.

"You hate the scent!" Madge could hear him say, "from association, I suppose. It must recall some scene, some person you hate—that I can understand."

Madge, fearing to play the listener, opened the door and went in. Miss Shore turned with a start. Her face was flushed; her eyes brilliant. Madge, who had seen that same face look a cold, expressionless adieu to Lance and Sir Peter, as they set off for London, could only marvel over its transfiguration.

Lance did not start; there was evidently no intention on his part to hide his predilection for Miss Shore's society.

"Miss Shore has been telling me of her early days in—in—" he paused.

Miss Shore did not fill up the blank.

Madge felt disposed to suggest "Santa Maura," but forbore: "Norway, Greenland, Finland?" she said, sarcastically.

"Absurd," cried Lance. "Say the North Pole at once! 'In the South,' you said, didn't you, at any rate where magnolia—"

"Where 'the cypress and myrtle are emblems of deeds that are done in their clime,'" said Madge, to all appearance carelessly, but with keen eyes fixed on Miss Shore. "I hate that land. I would forget it," she said in low, nervous tones, halting and stumbling over her words. "My father was born in this country, and my father's people are living now up in the North."

"In the South." "In the North." Evidently the young lady did not choose to localise, with greater exactitude, either her own place of birth, or the home of her father's people.

"You will go to them when you leave here?" queried Madge, with a meaning hidden from the two who stood beside her.

"That is a far-away day at present I hope," interrupted Lance, hastily. His eyes also were fixed, though not with the expression in them that Madge's had, on Miss Shore's face.

Miss Shore answered his words, not his look, for her eyes were bent upon the water-lilies in the fountain. "Who knows?" she answered, absently. "If I say I will go here, go there, do this, do that, fate may say 'No' to me."

Lance gathered the water-lily on which her eyes were fixed. Look at him she should!

He presented the flower to her. "Fate is just another word for circumstances to my way of thinking," he said. "Some people rule them, some are ruled by them. Personally, I have found the second method an easy and agreeable way of getting through life."

Miss Shore toyed with the flower.

"Fate rules circumstances as well as people. There are some who from cradle to grave never have a chance given them—"

She broke off suddenly, turning her head away. Her voice had a wail in it.

Madge did not hear that wail. The only thought her senses brought home to her, was that the heart of the man she loved was being won by the woman she hated.

Her eyes blazed, her face grew pale, but words she had none.

The sudden opening of the conservatory door which led into the garden let in a rush of fresh, outside air. It let in something else besides—Lady Judith's voice in gradual approach.

"If he would but believe that the world could get on without him," she was saying as she came along; and there could be no doubt to whom the "him" referred. "Now, I ask you, can there be any necessity for him, so soon as his feet are inside the house, to set all the bells ringing, and messages flying in all directions, telling everybody that things are all behindhand, and must be hurried forward as fast as possible. Johnson" (the house-steward) "has been sent for and had a hundred and one directions given him. He even seized, upon Gordon" (the housekeeper) "as she was coming from my room, and told, her, 'he hoped she would see to the airing of the spare beds herself—'"

Here Miss Shore quietly slipped away.

Lady Judith followed her with her eyes out of the conservatory, and then went on again:

"A positive insult to a woman who has done her duty for twenty-five years in the house as Gordon has! Then he rings for the butler—"

"But—but," interrupted Madge, "has he done all that in something under ten minutes? He was with me just now."

Lady Judith turned to Lance.

"If only you could have kept him another day in town, it would have been another clay of peace for us all," she said, quite forgetting her former lament. Lance slipped his arm into hers.

"Aunt Judy, let's go down to the farm together; I want to see the latest sweet thing in cock-a-doodles you have on view." He said.

And Lady Judith was all smiles and complaisance at once.

Madge stood among the palms and myrtles, looking down into the clear basin of the fountain, with its floating lilies and flashing fish. "Her "heart to her heart was voluble." "Lance, Lance," she thought, "would you hate me could you know what I am doing for your sake?"

A shadow fell upon the sparkling water and gleaming fish. It was Mr. Stubbs approaching with a key in his hand.

"I have brought you the key of your sitting-room, madam," he said. "I thought you would wish it kept locked till the night of the ball. Everything is finished according to your orders."

Madge took the key. "Everything?" she queried.

"Everything, madam. And the door need not be unlocked until the morning of the twenty-first, when it will be unhinged and removed, and curtains substituted."

He turned to go. Madge called him back.

"One moment," she said. "You are confident that this is the best, the most effectual way of—of doing this thing?"

"I can see none better, madam."

"And you charge yourself with her departure—that with seeing her out of the house, and on her road to her people 'in the North,' wherever that maybe?"

"I do, madam."

"Stay moment. You may want money. It had better be in gold. If I write you a cheque for—for—?"

"A hundred pounds, madam?"

"Yes, a hundred pounds; can you get it cashed without exciting suspicion?"

"I will do my best, madam," said Mr. Stubbs, as he bowed and departed.

Later on, that day Madge was to have another glimpse of Miss Shore.

Dinner was over. Lady Judith had as usual fanned herself to sleep on a couch in the drawing-room; Sir Peter and Lance had gone to one of the farm meadows to inspect the arrangements that had been made for the villagers' sports on the day following the ball; Madge, a little wearily, was crossing the gallery on the upper floor on her way to her room. A cool current of air, meeting her half-way thither, told her that one of the gallery-windows was open. Outside this window the stone parapet formed a narrow turreted balcony, and, kneeling there in the dim twilight, was a woman's figure. It was easy enough to identify her long, graceful outline. Her hands were clasped, her face was upturned to the night sky with an eager, questioning look on it.

The Cuddaws stood out in defined gloomy grandeur against the deep translucent blue of the summer sky, one sharp, jutting crag cutting a segment off a great, golden harvest moon that was slowly sinking behind it.

High above both mountain and moon there shone out, among the legions of stars, one glittering planet. On this the kneeling girl's eyes seemed fixed. Her lips moved. "Have mercy, have mercy, she said, piteously, as if she were addressing a living human being.

Madge's heart at that moment must either have been of marble coldness or one quick fire of jealous love, for she went on her way with her purpose unshaken.

XXII

How I'm to get into my dear, don't know," said Lady Judith to Madge, as together they inspected an elaborate arrangement of crimson satin and lace sent down by her London milliner.

"They've absolutely squeezed me into yard at the waist, as we're trying to make myself into girl in her teens, when they know perfectly well that I've been yard and an inch for the past fifteen years!"

It was the morning of Sir Peter's birthday bells were ringing from St. Cuthbert's old tower the district generally had broken out into flags, triumphal arches, best clothes, and a whole holiday. A delightful air of liveliness and bustle pervaded the Castle; guests were arriving by every train, the well-trained servants went about with a more animated tread, as if their minutes were of value to them. As for Sir Peter, rosy and radiant, he was here, there, and everywhere, now at the front of the house, now at the back; yet, strange to say, whenever he was wanted, he was nowhere to be found. Servants seemed to be perpetually running after him—in at doors, out of windows—his movements being so rapid that it was rather a difficult matter to overtake them.

"If he'd only keep in one room for half an hour, we should all know what we're about," sighed Lady Judith, when she had finished her lament over her dress.

"Madge, is it going to rain, do you think?" said Sir Peter, at that moment putting his head inside the dressing-room door.

"Good gracious! You were in the garden half a minute ago. I saw you myself superintending the rolling of the gravel paths, or the lawn-mowing, or perhaps it was the stoning of the flower beds!" cried Lady Judith, sarcastically.

The weather appeared to be very much on Sir Peter's mind that day. It was among the few things utterly beyond his superintendence, and he was proportionately anxious on the matter.

"Uncle Peter, Uncle Peter," sounded Lance's voice at that moment outside the door. "Are you anywhere to be found? You are as difficult to catch as the fluff off a dandelion; I've sent half-a-dozen servants hunting all over the grounds for you, and now I hear your voice up here!"

"Wanted again! Another deputation?" said Sir Peter, gleefully. "Dear me, dear me! What with one thing and another, I shall be worn to fiddle-strings before the day's over! The end of it will be I shall have to give up keeping my birthdays, they'll be too much for me—eh, Madge?"

Give up keeping his birthday! There was but little fear of Sir Peter doing that till he gave up himself and went into his grave.

Madge had come downstairs in the morning with such a white, tired look on her face that everyone had overwhelmed her with inquiries as to headache, neuralgia, or such possible ailments. Later on, in the day, however, as the demands on her time increased with the arrival of the guests, her cheeks grew so flushed and her eyes so bright, that people altered their minds and complimented her on her good looks.

Between thirty and forty of the invited guests were to be accommodated at the Castle on a two- or three-days' visit. Lady Brabazon and other near neighbors had filled their houses in anticipation of the yearly festivity. The inn at Lower Upton had been hired from top to bottom by Sir Peter, and special trains were to run throughout the night from Carstairs for late arriving or early departing guests.

Young Mrs. Cohen was always greatly in request at this annual festivity. Naturally enough she was looked upon as Lady Judith's representative, and as it was a much less fatiguing matter to carry on conversation with her than with the elder lady, she frequently found herself over-burthened with confidences intended for Lady Judith's ear.

Even Miss Shore followed suit in this matter.

"Will you tell Lady Judith how grateful I am to her for her handsome present?" said that young lady's voice suddenly over Madge's shoulder. "I never can make her understand me—she asks me always 'Are you Scotch or Welsh?'"

Madge was having a brief five minutes' rest in the cool, darkened library, where she knew she would be within call if wanted, and where was her only chance of quiet if such were to be had that day.

She started at the sound of Miss Shore's voice, shrinking from the young girl as heretofore Miss Shore had shrunk from her.

Miss Shore repeated her request:

"Will you thank Lady Judith for the beautiful dress she sent me yesterday by her maid, and for the help she allowed her maid to give me in arranging it?"

Madge immediately guessed the truth of the matter, and giving honour to whom honour was due, saw Sir Peter's ministering hand alike in the manner as in the matter of the gift.

"It is Sir Peter who should be thanked, I think," she said, coldly.

A sudden idea occurred to her.

"Now that I have the opportunity of asking, will you tell me how much I am in your debt for the picture you have been good enough to paint?" she asked, a little formally.

Miss Shore coloured slightly.

"The pictures are not finished; one is only half done," she answered.

"If you do not mind, I would like to pay for the one that is finished—for the two if you like. It makes no difference to me."

Again, Miss Shore flushed. Madge, in her own mind, could not help contrasting this with a former conversation she had had with this young lady on the subject of pictures. Then she had been warmth, and Miss Shore had been ice. Now, the cases seemed reversed.

"It is as you like," she began, hesitatingly.

"Twenty, thirty, forty pounds?" queried Madge.

"Oh no, no," exclaimed the girl. "I could not—would not—"

"I dare say you would like it in gold." interrupted Madge. "I haven't so much lost money now. I will ask Sir Peter to lend me some. Wait here, please, till I return."

But to find Sir Peter was a thing not easy to accomplish, although not a minute before he had put his head inside the door, and had told her that, "The wind was getting around to the south-west." Madge, however, appeared to have strong reasons for wishing to discharge her debt. She hunted high, and she hunted low, and eventually lighted on Mr. Stubbs, who, it may be inferred, from the ready manner with which he supplied her with gold, had already cashed her cheque for a hundred pounds.

Miss Shore was not alone when Madge returned to the library. A screen shut the door off from the rest of the room. As she entered behind this screen Madge heard Miss Shore's voice concluding a sentence:

"I will thank Heaven when the evening is ended!"

To which Lance's voice replied, laughingly:

"Have you been looking at the stars again? I would like to tell them to mind their own business, and not trouble themselves with our affairs. But it's the beginning, not the end, of the evening I want to talk about—the first valse, don't forget—you've promised to give it to me."

The last sentence was said, not whispered, as Madge crossed the room towards them.

"Miss Shore believes in the ruling of the planets, Madge, in these days of steam engines and electric-lightning! Can such a thing be credited?"

Madge did not reply. Instead, she began counting her sovereigns on a table in front of Miss Shore.

"Ten, twenty, twenty-five," she said.

Miss Shore laid her hands over the gold. They were trembling; her face was flushing; her eyes seemed—could it be possible?—swimming.

"No, I will only take ten. I would not take that only—" She broke off abruptly.

"I do believe the older one gets the younger one feels," said Sir Peter's voice, gradually approaching from behind the screen. "Now, isn't this sweet—isn't this touching, I ask you?—'Presented, by the children of the infant-school of St. Cuthbert's, to Sir Peter Critchett, as an expression of their love and duty.' That's what the label attached says. Now, I ask you all, isn't it worth being sixty-three years of age to receive such a tribute as this?"

He stood in the middle of the room with an enormous nosegay in his hand. It was entirely composed of cottage-garden flowers, such as orange-lilies, columbines, marigolds, and in size was about the circumference of a small umbrella.

He had evidently been repeatedly enjoying the fragrance of the flowers, for a portion of the pollen of the lilies was transferred to the tip of his nose.

Sir Peter could scarcely have expected an affirmative answer to his question from any one of those three young people assembled there. He rarely, however, expected answers of any sort. He walked up and down the room about half-a-dozen times; asked Miss Shore a variety of questions concerning her sketches; catechised Lance as to the dancing capabilities of certain of the younger men who had arrived that morning; finally directed Madge's attention to the generally cloudy appearance of the heavens; and then vanished.

All this in about a minute and a half.

Madge recommenced counting her sovereigns.

Lance made an impatient movement and walked away to the window.

Miss Shore stood for a moment looking from the gold to Madge's face, from Madge's face to the gold.

Madge grew restless under those furtive yet questioning glances.

"Shall I take this gold from you?" they seemed to ask. "Do you wish me well? Can I trust you?"

"There goes Lancelot Clive, but for the special interposition of Providence," said Lance, suddenly, from the window recess where he stood looking out into the grounds.

Madge's eyes followed his and rested upon a groom coming up to the house in company with a gamekeeper.

"Where, who, which?" she asked, a little bewildered.

"Whichever of the two you like. Upon my life, Madge, if I were turned out into the world tomorrow to get my own living, I don't know how I should do it except by grooming or gamekeeping!" he answered as he left the room.

Could it have been the sight of Miss Shore being paid for her pictures that had aroused in him the thought that he had even less capacity for earning a decent livelihood than she; or had he been suddenly seized with an altogether inexplicable wish to be independent of Sir Peter's bounty and patronage?

But whatever might have given rise to the thought, Madge felt that there was no gainsaying the truth of it.

XXIII

"I feel like a camel threading a needle," said Lady Judith in her voluminous crimson draperies, entering the drawing-room where Madge was already seated. "Madge, my dear, are you going to throw open your little sitting-room tonight? I suppose your wall decorations are finished by this time?"

Dinner—on this particular night was a stupendous affair—was over; guests had retired to their rooms to put finishing touches to their ball toilettes. Lance and sundry other of the younger men lounged on the terrace outside in the soft early night, waiting for the dancing to begin.

Sir Peter, as usual, was everywhere that he was not wanted to be, nowhere that he ought to have been. Madge and Lady Judith, ready to do the honours of the evening, were having a little chat together, or, in other words, Lady Judith was turning to the best account a quiet five minutes that gave her all to herself a silent if not an attentive listener.

Dancing was to be in the big inner hall where "the eight-and-twenty Critchetts looked down," with glazed eyes and varnished smiles, on banks of exotics and ferns specially arranged to grace the evening's festivities.

Madge's octagon sitting room was little more than a big recess opening off this hall. She replied, at the top of her voice, to Lady Judith's query, that, "When the hall grew unbearably hot, she would throw open her boudoir for fans and flirtation."

Not a word did Lady Judith hear; she had fallen upon another subject now!

"Sir Peter tells me that Lance and he went to Claire's and ordered a smart ball-dress for Miss Shore," she said, wielding with great energy a fan that might have suited Titanic fingers.

Madge had to unfold her own fan in self-defense and hold it as a screen sideways to her forehead, for her curls were flying hither and thither in all directions.

"It seems to me a far-fetched idea," Lady Judith went on, "to expect the young lady to make her appearance at all tonight! But then everyone knows that Sir Peter's ideas are—"

"Madge," said Sir Peter, at that moment appearing at one of the long French windows, "I don't believe it will rain after all! But will there be a moon tonight—that's what I want to know—is there an almanack anywhere handy?"

"Uncle Peter!" said Lance, appearing behind the old gentleman with the big nosegay of cottage flowers in his hand, "you've left your buttonhole behind you!" Then he turned to Madge, "Isn't it time the fiddlers struck up! Lovely visions in clouds of tulle and lace are beginning to descend the stairs! "

Madge, on her way to the ballroom, stopped a moment to give an order to a servant. It was to see that the candelabra in her octagon boudoir were lighted, and that the curtains which overhung the doorway were kept closely drawn.

Sir Peter, as might have been expected, considered it incumbent on him to open the ball. He chose for his partner in the first quadrille a Dowager Countess, about half-a-dozen years younger than himself.

"Now," he said, with a deprecating air, as he led the lady to her place at the top of the room, "I'm sure if the choice had been given us, you and I would much sooner have been in our beds than footing it here with the young people."

But to Madge he whispered when, in the course of "flirtation figure," it fell to his lot to guide her through the dance, "If the choice had been given to me I would have had you for a partner, my dear—and isn't the music horribly slow? I must speak to the bandmaster."

Lance and Madge were partners in this quadrille.

"A duty dances!" said Madge to herself, bitterly, as she thought of dances in days gone by when his eyes had looked into hers their tale of boyish first love.

"That'll be a match, not a doubt," she heard one elderly chaperon whisper to another. The whisper came inopportunely enough on the heels of her thought. She glanced furtively with flushing cheeks at Lance, wondering if he had heard it. His face, however, told no tale save that of eager expectancy as, turned towards the door, it watched the stream of guests flow in.

That long, low-ceiled hall presented a gay pageant. "A wind-waved tulip bed" it seemed, brilliant with swaying colours under soft, bright light.

Madge, looking up and down the ranks of young, happy faces there, thought that her own face must have shown strangely haggard and wan among them all, if one quarter of her thoughts were written upon it. But a casual glance into a mirror un-deceived her, and she started back amazed at her own presentment.

It seemed as if for the evening a certain wild bizarre beauty had been granted to her. Her eyes were brilliant, her cheeks glowed, a reckless, defiant gaiety seemed to have taken possession of her. In her dress of pale green, all ablaze with rubies and diamonds, one might almost have fancied her

> "A cross between
> A gypsy and a fairy queen."

who for the evening had condescended to quit the woodland and don ball-room attire? She danced, she talked, she laughed incessantly, till every one of her partners began to think that young Mrs. Cohen had suddenly developed into a most fascinating creature, and to speculate on his individual chance of winning her affections. But though Madge proved herself a very mistress of the fine art of ball-room fascination, it was her lips that did the work, not her eyes. They were fixed as steadfastly and expectantly on the door as Lance's were, though not with quite the same look in them.

The first valse, the second, the third had been danced out by the swift young feet. The fourth had begun; Madge, in the midst of the swaying dancers, was saying to herself: "She will not come, she has changed her mind, and perhaps gone to bed," when suddenly she felt rather than saw a gray figure silently glide into the room. If her eyes had been shut, she knew she would have felt that gray, cool presence, just as one standing in full sunlight with closed eyes is conscious of a cloud passing athwart the sun. In the brilliant, moving throng the shadowy gray draperies and still white face seemed to show like a patch of moonlight falling cool, clear, apart, into a heated, gas-lighted room.

"Who is that distinguished-looking young lady?" asked Madge's partner, a stalwart young fellow, who seemed to think that the whole art of dancing consisted in letting his partner's feet touch the ground as seldom as possible.

Madge did not answer—did not even hear the question.

"I am tired; I must sit down," she said, abruptly. Her partner found a seat for her at once. She speedily, however, found another for herself, a low settee placed immediately beside the dark tapestry curtains which covered the entrance to her octagon boudoir. There she leaned back against the cushions, watching the dancers as they whirled past. Or, rather, watching one pair of dancers from out of the motley throng, for Miss Shore had no sooner entered the hall than Lance had claimed her for his partner, and together they floated along the soft stream of valse melody.

They made a distinguished and handsome couple. Nature had put some of her best workmanship into Lance—had not left him to be fashioned hap-hazard by any of her journeymen. Lithe, and full of grace, he guided his partner as only the lithe and graceful can through the crush of the dancers. The misty gray of the girl's filmy dress floated lightly around them like so much vaporous cloud, out of which looked their two face—the man's with an unmistakable look of admiration for his partner in his blue eyes—the woman's with a look of wild, mournful spirituality in her dark-gray ones such as is rarely seen out of a picture.

"How cool and comfortable Miss Shore looks when everyone else is so remarkably red in the face! "said Sir Peter, bustling up to Madge with a very red face himself, and his right-hand glove split up the back through the energy wherewith he had been shaking hands with everyone. Then his voice changed to a confidential whisper, "Madge," he said, "I have just a polka—a nice quick one—substituted for the dancers; you and I will dance it together, eh?"

Madge pleaded fatigue. Her last partner had danced on castors instead of feet, she said, and she had had to run after him all round the room at six-eight time.

Sir Peter opened his eyes very wide.

"Tired! tired!" he repeated, blankly. "Why, I've only just begun to feel alive, and to enter into the spirit of the thing!"

"The breeding of young ladies of the present generation is something to wonder at!" said Lady Judith, bearing down upon them at that moment, like a sou'-wester incarnate. "Miss Lottie Brabazon absolutely answers a remark I address to her on her fingers! On her fingers, my dear, if you'll believe such a thing, as if I were as deaf as a post! If young ladies were only taught to speak as I was taught when I was a girl—to take hold of their consonants properly, and to open their mouths wide enough to get their vowels out, their elders would have no difficulty in understanding them!"

All this with her fan going at double speed. She fanned Sir Peter away from Madore's side, as one might fan a moth from the wall, and then fanned him on a little farther into the ball-room, following him up with a string of vigorous questions as to whether another pair of gloves could not be found for him, was it not possible for him to renew his button-hole, and so forth.

But Madge had not heard a syllable of all this. Lance and Miss Shore were at that moment floating past, and their words, like so many sharp stabs, pierced her ear.

"You said this morning," said Lance's voice, deep and clear below the waves of valse melody, "'Would to Heaven tonight were over!' Do you say the same now?"

To which Miss Shore replied in soft tremulous tones:

"I say now, would to Heaven this night could last for ever—this valse, at least, for anything more like heaven I never knew!"

Madge leaned back on her cushions, her breath coming in short, quick gasps. For a moment all was confusion to her. The room dissolved into a whirling chaos of colour, light, and tuneless music. She pressed her hand over her eyeballs. It was easy enough to shut out the zigzagging light and colour, but not so easy to muffle the sound of that discordant, jarring valse. On and on, on and on it seemed to beat against her very ears in hateful regular rise and fall. Would the feet of those dancers never tire? Had fate conspired with the infernal powers to render Miss Shore's wish a reality, and would this valse go on aimlessly, endlessly, through eternity?

One after another the dancers yielded to fatigue and sat down, till Lance and Miss Shore had the floor to themselves.

Still the musicians played on. A fascinating sight some would have said that handsome man and beautiful young woman rivalling the waves of the sea in rhythm and grace of motion.

One there was, leaning back on her cushions, who felt her eyeballs scorched by and she had been called upon to describe an eleventh circle to Dante's Inferno, would have said, "Here it is;" for she could have pictured no worse form of torture than to behold eternally the sight which confronted her at that moment.

"It must be now or never, Mrs. Cohen," said Mr. Tubb's voice suddenly, stealthily, right in her ear.

The music had ceased, and Lance was leading Miss Shore up the room, towards the settee on which Madge was seated.

Madge's eyes, in answer to his whisper, said: "Keep back! Don't dare to come near me tonight! "

Her lips said nothing. She rose from her seat, steadying herself with one hand against the arm of the settee; with her other hand she pulled the cord of the tapestry curtains, laying bare to view the cool, dark little room, just as Lance and Miss Shore reached her side.

"Here is a tempting little nook!" she said, addressing the two. "What a glorious valse you have had!"

A tempting little nook indeed it looked. The light from the brilliant hall caught the dark sheen of its polished oak floor, the bright sheen of its yellow silk walls. A large deep sofa and some luxurious low chairs showed in solid outline in the dimness.

"What a jolly room you've made of it!" said Lance, standing back in the doorway to allow the two ladies to pass in before him.

A long, narrow mirror nearly faced the door. On the wall immediately opposite to it hung a picture, lighted on either side by candelabra, and necessarily reflected in all its details in the mirror.

And this is what Miss Shore saw in that mirror, as she stood in the middle of the room, a little in advance of Madge.

A gaunt mountain, standing out in black outline against a stormily purple sky, with a stone-built chalet in a bowery garden at its base. And high over the mountain there shone out one star of intense and fiery brightness.

XXIV

One after another the dancers began to stream into the little room, attracted by its look of cool dimness. Madge found herself overwhelmed with compliments on the taste she had displayed in the decoration of her boudoir.

"There is such a delightful air of mystery through the arrangement of the light," said one.

"And the position of the mirror is most effective," said another.

Madge gave back but short and absent answers in acknowledgment of the compliments; her eyes were fixed on the white, startled face of the girl who stood with clasped hands staring blankly into the dim mirror.

"Take me out of this room," Madge heard her say to Lance, in low, unnatural tones. "I am tired, I have danced too long."

Lance was startled by the tone in which these words were uttered. It brought back to him the stony, tuneless voice in which, in the midst of the crashing storm, she had told him that "it" must be by poison or fire or flood.

He made way for her through the crush, thence through the ballroom into the outer hall. Here there was of necessity more air and space; save for an occasional servant passing, they had it all to themselves.

"You are feeling faint with the heat?" he asked, anxiously. "Come outside on the terrace for a few minutes, it's a glorious night—stay, let me get you a cloak."

All sorts of cross lights met here in this vestibule; a stream of light poured forth from the inner hall, where the strains of the inspiriting military band proclaimed that dancing had recommenced; yellow and pink light from the lamps on the staircase in a bewildering stream met this and crossed and through the high windows, one on either side of the hall-door, little beyond this glare, there fell on the tesselated floor patches of faint moonlight, just discernible, nothing more, telling of glorious golden moon on high.

If had not been for those coloured lamps and cross lights, Lance must have seen how ashen-white and rigid Miss Shore's face had grown. As was, though her voice had startled him for the moment, did not occur to him that anything ailed her more serious than a passing faintness, caused by the heat of the rooms and the prolonged valse.

He opened the hall door. It showed an outside picture of a garden drenched with moonlight, which set the seal of tawdriness at once upon the dazzling and illusive light indoors. He turned to take a cloak from a stand.

"It's a night to tempt even Midsummer fairies out of their acorn-cups," he said. "I don't believe that in your sunny South you'd outshine such a moon as this."

There came no answer; he turned sharply to see if she were following.

There was at this end of the hall a narrow archway, half-draped by a curtain, which led to a second staircase leading to the upper floor. Neither this staircase nor the passage to it was lighted, and the archway showed a dark oblong in the light of the hall. Just within it stood Miss Shore, her gray draperies fading into the shadowy dimness behind her. She was turning from him as if she wished to leave him without so much as a word of excuse or regret.

He sprang towards her. "You are not coming!" he cried in a disappointed tone.

"I am going to my room," she answered in the same stony, tuneless voice as before.

"You will come down again in a few minutes?" he pleaded.

With one foot on the first step of the staircase at the end of the passage, she waved her hand to him.

"Go back and dance," was all that she said.

If Eurydice, as she faded into the shadows whence, she had emerged, had bidden Orpheus "go tune his lyre," it might have been in much such a voice, with much such a look in her eyes.

XXV

Lance went back to the ballroom; but not to dance. He made straight for Madge.

"Miss Shore is ill, I fear; will you go to her?" he whispered.

"I will send my maid at once," said Madge, promptly giving an order to that effect.

It was not far off midnight now. The doors of the supper room were at that moment thrown open, and Madge was called upon to assist Lady Judith in the marshalling of her guests.

The dowager, who was placed under Lance's charge during what seemed to him an interminable repast, vowed that in all her experience of ball-suppers she had never before sat side by side with so singularly taciturn a young man.

Within an hour after supper Lady Brabazon and her party departed. This relieved Lady Judith of a large number of the more distinguished of her guests and gave her leisure to discover how terribly she felt the heat, and how deliciously tempting was the thought of a featherbed.

"I shall creep away quietly," she informed the lady by whose side she was sitting, in a voice that reached to the other end of the room. "I shan't be missed, Madge does the honours so well."

After the departure of the Brabazon party, the roll of carriage wheels in the drive continued at intervals till daybreak But long before the "orange light of widening morn" set the birds thinking of their matins, Madge found her appearance of feverish gaiety very hard to maintain. She fought her increasing lassitude vigorously, however, and did her best to keep up the brilliancy of the ball to its end.

Not so Lance, he played his part of a "son of the house" very badly indeed. Restless and ill at ease, he wandered aimlessly from room to room with so absent and discontented a look on his handsome face, that some of the young ladies who knew his dancing capabilities began to say hard things of him.

Madge caught sight of him once, as she flitted across the outer hall, speaking to her maid. She guessed in a moment what the subject of the inquiry must be.

"Is Miss Shore better?" she asked him, as the girl disappeared, her own curiosity on the matter not one whit less intense than his.

"She said she was all right, and desired the girl not to disturb her again," was Lance's reply; but, for all that, he appeared far from satisfied on the matter, and he took no pains to hide the fact from anyone.

The last hour of the ball tried Madge the most. As a rule, she took her balls very easily, danced but little, and vanished from the scene early with her dress nearly as fresh as when she put it on. But tonight, mental and bodily fatigue had come hand in hand, and now at the eleventh hour the double strain became all but insupportable.

Sir Peter, blithe as a cricket, insisted on leading off "Sir Roger de Coverley" with her.

"Forty years difference between us, my dear," he said, gaily. "But for all that I don't feel like going out of the world yet!"

No, nor yet like going out of the ball-room, if that meant going to bed, for when Madge, at the bottom of the line of dancers, whispered to him, "I simply must go; I can't put one foot before another," he chose immediately the youngest partner he could find. And he kept the dance going with such spirit, that as one by one the couples, yielding to fatigue, disappeared to their rooms or to their carriages, the tired musicians whispered to each other that the old gentleman left bowing to the last young lady on the floor must be strung on wires, not muscles, for he seemed as fresh at the end of the evening as he did at the beginning.

Madge, as she entered her dressing room, dismissed her sleepy maid. Then she went on to her bedroom, and, too tired even to lift her hand to her head to remove the jewels from her hair, flung herself in her ball-dress on the bed. Her head ached and burned; her ears were filled with the twanging of the band, her eyes with pink light and dancing colours. But not the loudest of twanging music could shut out from her ears the echo of a startled voice with a piteous note in nor the most dazzling of light and colour shut out from her sight rigid, ashen-white face, with the look of terror in its eyes.

The candles on the toilet table had burned low; long straight lines of gray light came through the half-turned Venetian blinds; the chill air of early morning swept in through a half-open window at the father end of the room. Something seemed to stir and rustle in a large easy chair, which was placed near this window with its back to the room.

What was it? Madge wondered, raising herself on one elbow and looking around her. Was it a breeze springing up and foretelling a storm, or had old Roy taken refuge in the room from the racket of the ball and curled himself up to sleep in the easy chair?

She peered into the dimness curiously. It is wonderful how unlike itself in its noonday prettiness a sleeping-room will show in the half-light of dwindling candles and growing dawn. Shadows flickered across the ceiling and seemed caught back again by invisible hands into the dark corners whence they had emerged. Thence they seemed to creep out once more to play hide-and-seek round the tables, and among the high-backed chairs.

Madge shaded her eyes with one hand. Was that a shadow rising slowly from the big easy chair beside the window and approaching, not flickeringly, but with easy, gliding motion? Then a sudden chill fell upon her, as, in that graceful, gliding shape, she recognised Miss Shore, clad, not in her ball dress, but in the gray travelling dress and beaver hat in which Madge had first seen her. Her heart failed her; she would have liked to shout aloud for help, but voice she had none.

Her hand failed her, too, it was powerless even to ring the bell beside the bed. Nerveless and helpless, she sank back on her pillows, hiding her face in her hands. Miss Shore's voice, low, clear, cold, told her that she stood beside her, leaned over her in fact.

"I have been waiting here to say goodbye to you," it said, "I have also a word to say beside goodbye if you will listen."

If she would listen! Madge felt that choice she had none, her feet would not have carried her across the floor had she essayed flight. This strange, wild girl who had failed in an attempt at murder through chance, not want of purpose, must work her will now whatever it might be.

"You took me in a stranger; you gave me shelter, and food—for that I thank you," she went on in the same low, cold monotone, "You turn me out into the night, into the darkness and loneliness—for that I thank you not—no, for that I hate you—I wish you evil."

"Bring me here presently John Baptist's head in a charger." Those words, like these, were nonetheless terrible because spoken by beautiful lips in a tranquil voice.

Madge shrank farther back in her pillows.

Miss Shore resumed.

"When I am gone you will say, 'I have won! I have saved that man I love from an evil woman!'"

She broke off from a moment; then suddenly raised her voice to a passionate cry:

"Oh, you with your hold and your jewels, your home and your friends, are you the one to say, 'This is evil, that is good?' You are what you are made to be, you call that good; I am what I was made to be, you call that evil!"

Again, she broke off, and now her voice sank to its former low, cold monotone.

"But I did not come here to tell you this. No; I came to say to you, 'You have won so far!' I go back into the darkness and loneliness whence I came; you will stay here in the light and the happiness. You will win back the love you have lost; you will say, 'I have conquered.' Wait! At the moment of your victory I will stand between you and your joy as you have stood between me and mine."

Madge heard no more. Worn out with the heavy mental and physical strain of the past twenty-four hours, her senses left her.

And outside, the gray expanse of heaven was broken up into a hundred massive, rugged clouds, to let out the rainbow glories of the morning; the great plumed trees waved in the summer breeze, and a whole orchestra of wild birds broke into their hallelujah chorus, as if desolation, despair, and death were words without meaning in so fair a scheme of creation!

XXVI

Very few of the guests made their appearance at the breakfast table on the morning after the ball. Sir Peter and one or two of the most youthful of the party had things very much to themselves until close upon the luncheon hour. Madge sent down a message that she had a very bad headache and was reserving her strength for the villagers' sports in the afternoon and tenants' supper in the evening.

These sports and the supper formed the staple topic of talk among the house party until another item of news was announced, which altogether put these into the shade—nothing less than the sudden disappearance of Miss Shore. It was not until nearly noon that her flight was discovered.

The discovery was made through Lance's instrumentality. He had sent Madge's maid, about breakfast time, to make inquiries as to the young lady's health, and to present on his part a nosegay of freshly-gathered forget-me-nots. The maid came back with her flowers, saying that Miss Shore was sleeping and did not wish to be disturbed.

This was her version of the fact that her repeated knockings brought no response.

Lance waited awhile impatiently, grew discontented with his fading forget-me-nots, and, gathering a nosegay of exotics, went himself to the housekeeper—a somewhat important personage in the establishment—and commissioned her to present them herself to Miss Shore, with inquiries from him as to whether she felt rested from her fatigues of overnight. Evidently, he had not the slightest wish to conceal his anxiety on the young lady's behalf.

The housekeeper came back in a few minutes looking rather scared, and bringing the startling news that, not receiving any response to her rappings at Miss Shore's door, she had ventured to turn the handle and look in, when, to her great surprise, she had found that the room was empty, and that the bed had not been slept in.

Lance, for a few seconds, refused to trust his own powers of hearing. Then, after desiring the housekeeper to go to Sir Peter and report the fact to him, he made straight for Madge's room.

Madge, in her loose *peignoir*, opened her door to his summons. She knew well enough what lay behind and he, he had not been so preoccupied with his own thoughts, must have seen how white and haggard she looked.

Ten words told her the story.

"Do you know anything I don't know, Madge?" he queried, impatiently; "did you see her after you left the ballroom, or did she send you a message?"

Madge evaded his questions.

"Let us go to her room. She may have left a letter or written message," she said, herself trembling at the bare thought of the possibility of such a hang.

At the door of Miss Shore's room, they were met by Sir Peter, bent on a like errand. The three entered the room together.

They found that the bed, as the housekeeper had stated, had not been slept in. On it was flung carelessly the ball dress of overnight, strewn with sundry faded sprig of stephanotis, which had been worn with it.

A small portmanteau stood open beside the bed, with its contents tossed about as if some things had been hastily abstracted. On the toilet table glittered the gold—to its last half-sovereign—which Madge had paid on the previous morning for the pictures; but never note or written message of any sort with all their searching could they discover.

The gold caught Sir Peter's eye.

"Ah, that's a good sign. She must have had plenty of money in her purse or she wouldn't have left it behind," he said cheerily. "Depend upon it we shall get a letter from her in the course of the day explaining—"

"Madge," interrupted Lance in an odd, quiet tone, "do you mind looking through that portmanteau and seeing if there are any letters there, or anything that will give us a clue to her people or friends?"

Madge immediately complied. One by one she carefully turned over the contents of the portmanteau. They searched it thoroughly for secret places where letters might be hidden, turned it upside down and sounded its sides and bottom for false partitions.

It was a fruitless search. The box contained nothing save articles of clothing, most of them unmarked; but one or two embroidered with the name "Etelka."

Madge related the circumstance of a handkerchief being found with the same name upon it.

Sir Peter's eyes grew round and rounder.

"Most extraordinary—" he began.

Lance interrupted him:

"Of course, you will at once communicate with police and offer a reward for information of any sort?"

A sudden impulse seized Madge. "Don't let that be done," she said in low, nervous tones, addressing Lance. "Whatever else you do, don't do that."

Lance stared at her blankly.

"Why not? What else on earth are we to do? Of course, I shall start for Lower Upton at once, and follow up any clue I may get there; but the police would do more in a day than I should do in a week."

"My dear boy," cried Sir Peter, aghast, "you mustn't dream of such a thing. Let Stubbs go." He broke off for a moment. "Ah, by the way, he can't, he's off already to Carstairs—had a telegram late last night—so he told me this morning."

Here he turned to Madge: "A very dear friend of his at Carstairs had been suddenly taken seriously ill and wished to see him."

Madge said nothing; only she grew white and whiter, and her eyes drooped.

"But it is easy enough to send someone else to make inquiries." Here he turned to Lance: Your servant is a trusty fellow, send him—but I couldn't get on without you today at all—you'll have to be umpire in all the races and the vaulting and jumping—"

Lance gave him one look. It said:

"Talk of such things to a man whose soul is on the rack!"

But his lips said only:

"I'm afraid you'll have to get someone else to act umpire. I start for Lower Upton at once!" and he left the room as he spoke.

Madge followed him hastily into the outside gallery.

"Lance," she said, in the same low, earnest tones as before, "let her go! Be advised! Don't set the police on her track; don't hunt her down yourself."

He stared at her stonily.

"For her sake, if not for your own," she implored.

His face grew pale as death. This was clothing with a body a spectre of dread that more than once before had stood in his path.

"For her sake!" he repeated, hoarsely, "Made, if you know anything about her that I don't know, tell me at once—do you hear?—at once right out, and be done with it."

Madge was silent. When she had laid her plot, she had not taken thought for such a contingency as this, so was unprepared to meet it. After all, she was a bad plotter, and was acting very much on the spur of the moment now.

"Come, Madge, speak out," he said: and now his voice grew stern and peremptory.

Still Madge was silent.

If she were to tell him the story the newspaper paragraph told, he might be quick enough to discover the source of her inspiration for the mirror-picture and might hate her forever for the deed she had done.

He stood still, waiting for her answer.

She clasped her hands together once more. "I beg—I entreat—" she began.

"No, not that," he interrupted. "Give me a reason—a simple, straightforward reason why I am not to go in search of this young lady—a guest in our house, with every claim to our courtesy."

A reason, a simple, straightforward reason! She could have given him one had she dared. "My love; is that not reason enough?" she would have liked to cry out of her full, breaking heart. "The love that led me to sacrifice myself in a hateful marriage; the love that is making me do unworthy things now; the love that will send me to my grave should you choose this young woman or any other but me for your wife!"

A hot rush of tears came to her eyes. She stumbled forward and clung to his arm.

"Lance, Lance," she cried, passionately. "I can't give you a reason. There is one—a strong one—"

"Give it to me," he interrupted, doggedly. "It is all I ask of you."

"It would be impossible!" she cried, her tears almost choking her. She broke off for a moment, and hen her voice rose to a loud, passionate cry, "Oh, Lance, Lance, will you not trust me after all these years of—of—companionship? It is not of myself I am thinking of now—not of Miss Shore even—only of you. I beg—I implore you, let her go, or your life, your whole life, may be wrecked."

Something in her tone startled him. If his heart had not been full of the thoughts of another woman, he must have heard the cry of wounded love in this one's voice.

As it was, he only thought that she was strangely excited, and was using language which she was not warranted in using.

He tried to disengage his arm from her clasp. "You are talking wildly, Madge; be reasonable."

His words stung her. Yet she clung to his arm.

"Is it unreasonable to implore you to think of your life in the future—to try to save you from the wiles of an evil woman—"

Here he coldly and firmly released his arm from her clasp.

"That will do, Madge—you've said enough for one day," he said, sternly.

As if struck by a sudden thought, he went back to the room they had just quitted and came out again in a few seconds with one or two of the sprays of the dead stephanotis in his hand. Then, without another word to or look at Madge, he went.

She stood staring after him through her blinding tears. This was the man whom she had accused of treating life as a big jest, and of never being in earnest, from year's end to year's end. Well, he was desperately—it might be fatally—in earnest now, not a doubt.

XXVII

Sir Peter's birthday festivities had never before so nearly approached a failure as they did on this, his sixty-third anniversary. No one had ever before realised how much they owed their success to Lance's buoyancy and high spirits. Even Lady Judith—impervious though she generally was to outside influences—was conscious of a limpness and want of spirit in the day's proceedings. She put her finger at once upon Lance as the sole cause of the dejection that prevailed generally.

"If that young man, my dear," she said to everyone she could get to. listen to her and occasionally to the same person twice over, "if that young man would only consult his elders a little more and his own inclinations a little less, it would be much better for him and for those about him."

She took Miss Shore's disappearance—in due course made known to her—very lightly indeed. It was what she had expected from the very first, she averred. She had always been opposed to the admission of another *protégé* into the house—the *protégés* Sir Peter had already been but little credit to him. From this she rambled on to similar instances of flight which the records of Sir Peter's benevolence afforded.

"There was that little imp of a page, in town, my dear—really nothing better than a street Arab, but Sir Peter would have him dressed in blue cloth and buttons—well, he had no sooner got some decent clothes for himself, the little thief, than he disappeared, and to this day he has never been heard of! And there was that housemaid—a girl taken out of a union—she seized the very first opportunity—"

But at this point her listeners, as a rule, would themselves seize the very first opportunity to disappear, and Lady Judith had to begin all over again to the next person who approached:

"There was that little imp of a page, my dear," and so forth.

It was entirely owing to Sir Peter's energy that things went even so well as they did. He surpassed himself in activity that day. One or two of the younger guests, who had volunteered to act as umpires in the villagers' sports in Lance's stead, declared that their office was sinecure, for Sir Peter saw the beginning, and end, and middle of every race himself.

The marvel was that he didn't enter himself as competitor in every one of the "events" of the day, the greasy-pole business and all.

"If I were only half-a-dozen things ought to be done," he said in confidence to one of the ladies of the party.

"Gracious Heavens!" thought the lady to herself, "it's a blessing he isn't, or he'd want a keeper!"

No one wondered that Madge was pale and silent throughout the day. It had been a generally received notion among Sir Peter's and Lady Judith's friends that young Mrs. Cohen and Mr. Clive would make a match of it. Everyone had remarked his unmistakable admiration for and attention to stranger-guest overnight, and now his sudden flight in search of her excited considerable comment.

Every one decided that Sir Peter's conduct in thus introducing an utter stranger to his home-circle had been reprehensible in the extreme, although of a piece with his usual eccentric benevolence, and confidentially stated their conviction that the reason for the young lady's flight would no doubt be speedily enough discovered in the loss of one of Mrs. Cohen's jewel caskets.

It was more or less a relief when the last health had been drunk by the farmer tenants with "three times three," and the lights in the tents had begun to be put out.

Madge lingered last and latest in the grounds, pleading headache and need of fresh air. Indoors there was no one to extemporize a dance, or *tableaux vivants*, so the guests dispersed to their rooms sooner than they otherwise would have done. Had they lifted their blinds somewhere between ten and eleven at night, they might have seen Mrs. Cohen walking up and down the terrace in the moonlight. But not alone; her companion was Mr. Stubbs, and their talk was of his hurried journey to Carstairs.

His voice was low and apologetic, hers low and vehement.

"I thought it the best thing to do, madam, under the circumstances," he said. "My friend at Carstairs, Mr. Symons, is in a private inquiry office; I have commissioned him to take the matter in hand and communicate at once anything that comes to light."

"I gave you no authority to commission any one to act in the matter. My orders to you were plain enough—to chare yourself with her departure, to supply her with money, to ascertain exactly where she was going, what she would do," was Madge's answer.

"I am very sorry, madam; I can only repeat that I am very sorry. How she got away without my seeing her I don't know. I stood outside the Lodge close to the gates till morning—looked into every carriage as I thought. You see there was almost an incessant roll of carriages between two and four. There were so many hired ones, too—she must have gone away in one of these—and stayed at the station till the first train left for Carstairs. I cross-questioned every one of the men at the Lower Upton—in general terms, that is, not mentioning any special guest from the Castle—and they told me that a large party went on by the first train to Carstairs."

"From Carstairs possibly she had gone on to the North."

"Or she may have gone South—say to Liverpool."

Madge turned sharply upon him. "What makes you say that?" she asked, suspiciously.

He shrugged his shoulders. "It would be the most reasonable thing to do if one wanted to get on board a steamer quickly."

"What makes you think that she wanted to get on board a steamer?" she asked.

"I have not the slightest reason for thinking she wished to do so, madam. It was only an idea that occurred to me, and I uttered it on the spur of the moment."

They made one turn up and down the terrace in silence.

Mr. Stubbs was the first to break it.

"About that hundred pounds, madam," he began.

Madge got her thoughts back from their wanderings with difficulty. "Yes?" she said, absently.

"I've been thinking that as you may possibly require my services again—"

"How do you know I may he likely to require your services?" she queried, sharply, but perhaps a little nervously also.

"I am only suggesting the possibility of such a thing madam. Unforeseen circumstances might arise necessitating a sudden journey on my part or the expenditure of money—"

"Keep it," said Madge, contemptuously, and suddenly bringing their interview to a close. The look on her face, as she said this, might have been interpreted by a thin-skinned listener to convey the intimation: "Consider yourself paid and dismissed."

But Mr. Stubbs was not thin-skinned, so he rubbed his hands together and chuckled to himself: "There's more fish in the sea than I've landed at present."

XXVIII

"When once that girl is out of the house things will be all right between Lance and me," Madge had said to herself over and over again, as she had worked out the details of her plan for ejecting Miss Shore.

Well, the girl was out of the house now, and there was little likelihood of her ever returning to it; yet "things" were as far off as ever from being "right" between Lance and herself.

Sir Peter's birthday guests had departed, and the household at the Castle had resumed the even tenor of its way. A week had passed since Miss Shore's disappearance, and not a scrap of intelligence had been received concerning her. From Lance there had come a hurried half-dozen lines—addressed to Sir Peter, not Madge—giving a brief account of his movements: his visit to Carstairs had been without result so far as Miss Shore was concerned: he was now on his way to Edinburgh. He had ascertained that the first train leaving Carstairs, after the Lower Upton special train had arrived, had been the Edinburgh Express; he had, therefore, determined to start at once for that city, and intended stopping at all intermediate stations to make further inquiries. He gave an address at Edinburgh, to which letters during the ensuing week might be addressed and begged that any news that might reach the Castle concerning Miss Shore should be at once telegraphed to him. He said nothing whatever of having called the police to his aid in his search, so Madge concluded that in this respect her entreaties had carried more weight than she had dared to hope they would.

Sir Peter as usual took an optimistic view of the situation.

"It's very good of him to take all this trouble for an utter stranger—eh, Madge?" he said, doing his utmost to dissipate any slight cloud of jealousy which he fancied might have arisen in Madge's mind. "It's real goodness of heart, that's what it and has saved me world of trouble."

Then suddenly occurred to him that the "world of trouble" would have been world of delight to him, since involved journey to the North with license to get out at all intermediate stations—a dozen times of getting in and out, say, for once.

So, he added, after a moment's pause:

"Not but what I think Lance might just as well have put off his journey for a day or two, so that I might have gone with him. I took a great interest in Miss Shore, and nothing would please me better than to hear good news of her."

Madge, according to all showing, ought to have been exultant and jubilant now that her little plot had so far come to a successful issue; instead, after one day of wild energy, she relapsed into a nervous and ill-at-ease frame of mind, shunned the mere sight of Mr. Stubbs, and seemed ever on the watch for the arrival of ill-omened telegrams.

During that one day of wild energy she did her best to sweep all traces of Miss Shore out of the house.

The beautiful gray ball dress, left lying on the bed, seemed to tell all over again the story of its wearer's triumph and defeat; the small portmanteau seemed like an evil omen of its owner's return to claim her property. Madge gave orders that both should be locked up safely in a store cupboard, in case, she said, Miss Shore might write for them.

Then she fell to work on her little boudoir; had the mirror and the picture which faced it removed from the walls, and, together with Miss Shore's watercolour drawings, carried to a lumber-room, alleging to Lady Judith, as her reason for so doing, that she had another plan in her head for the decoration of her boudoir; and, finally, she changed her bedroom—the one she had occupied from the first day of her coming to Upton Castle—for another on the other side of the house; and gave orders that a certain high-backed easy-chair, which she was in the habit of occupying, should on no account follow her to her new quarters.

These things done, she drew a long breath, as it were, and tried to look ahead at the dangers that were threatening.

Time was getting precious—any day, any moment a second Australian letter might arrive, and Mr. Stubbs would need to have explicit instructions on the matter.

Evidently the same thought was in Mr. Stubbs's mind also.

"I suppose you know, madam, that the Australian mail is delivered fortnightly?" he said to her on one of the rare occasions that he chanced to be alone in the same room with her.

Madge's only answer was an angry frown, and the sudden stretching out of her hand to reach a book which lay on the table beside her.

She might, however, as well have tried the effect of a frown on a spider about to net a fly, as on Mr. Stubbs at that moment.

"Time is pressing," he went on, eyeing her stealthily from beneath his half-closed lids. "The great thing now, it seems to me, is to get Mr. Clive back—"

But here Madge, with her book in her hand, cut his sentence in half by leaving the room.

How she hated and despised herself for the alliance which she had formed with this man. Sometimes she felt herself almost driven to wish that instead of calling in his aid she had had the courage to tell Lance outright her own suspicions respecting Miss Shore, and the foundation on which they rested. Second thoughts, however, seemed to show her at one glance the danger and the uselessness of such a course. The story of a Corsican vendetta—after all it might be nothing more—might be alluring, not repelling, when confessed to by beautiful lips, and might have supplied a young man, chivalrous and hot- headed to the last degree, with an excuse, rather than otherwise, for his chivalry and hot-headedness.

Her brain grew chaotic with its pressure of thought; she felt herself incapable of deciding upon any settled course of action. Sometimes she could almost persuade herself that the whole thing; from first to last had been a dream. With Miss Shore's pictures, easel, and portmanteau safely locked up out of sight, the romance seemed to be swept out of the house, so to speak. It would have been almost possible to have forgotten the episode of the coming and going of that "girl in gray," in the leisurely comfortableness of every-day life at Upton, if only Lance would return his old, cheery, light-hearted self, and Mr. Stubbs could at once and for ever be dismissed to that low stratum of society whence he had emerged.

She grew to hate the sight of that man; she shunned him on every possible occasion and did her best to make him understand that his presence was distasteful to her. This was a lesson, however, he seemed incapable of learning. Let her snub him as she pleased, morning, noon, and night, he never failed to seize every opportunity of endeavouring to make himself agreeable to her. He even went so far as to send up, nightly by her maid, little notes reporting, as a rule, that there was nothing to report.

"Through my friend at Carstairs, I am still making inquiries, but can learn nothing," sometimes these notes would run.

At other times it would be, "Nothing fresh from Australia," or "Correspondence this morning satisfactory."

Madge used to tear these notes into a thousand pieces when she had read them and would stamp her foot at herself literally as well as metaphorically for having soiled her hands with such a tool. But one night there came a note which she did not tear into morsels, but sat staring at stonily instead, with thoughts all in a wild whirl of dread.

"Important and terrible news," it ran.

"Can I see you at once? Sir Peter has gone to bed—the study is empty."

Dreading she knew not what, Madge hastily made her way down the darkened staircase to the study, at whose door stood Mr. Stubbs in the patch of light made by the single lamp on the writing-table.

He closed the door behind her as she entered and began a profuse series of apologies for the untimeliness of his message, but he had only just had time to open and attend to his correspondence which had arrived by the morning's mail—

Madge interrupted his apologies. "Tell me your news at once," she said, feeling that another moment of suspense would be intolerable.

He spread on the writing-table before her, a newspaper; and just as he had done on a former occasion, laid his finger on a paragraph.

The newspaper this time was a Liverpool daily journal. The paragraph ran as follows:

"The body of a young woman was taken out of the Mersey yesterday at daybreak. It was dressed in gray travelling-dress, gray cloak, gray beaver-hat, with feather. In the pocket of the dress was an empty purse, and an envelope which bore the name 'Jane Shore.'"

Madge started back with a low cry.

"The newspaper is four days old," began Mr. Stubbs. Then he broke off, startled by the sudden change which had swept over Madge's face.

"It's my doing—mine," she said, in a voice that sounded strained and unnatural. She clutched at the table for support. At the moment it seemed as if her senses must leave her.

"I entreat you to calm yourself, Mrs. Cohen," said Mr. Stubbs, venturing to approach her.

Madge's senses came back in full force.

"Stand back!" she cried, passionately. "Do not dare to come near me—you who urged me to this—this deed of murder."

He drew back, a curious expression flitting over his face. "Wait," it seemed to say, "you'll be glad enough of my help before long."

But his lips said respectfully:

"After a night's rest, madam, you may be able, possibly, to see the matter in another light, and to discuss with me the advisability of conveying the tidings at once to Mr. Clive."

Madge did not hear him. She raised her hands on high, clasped convulsively together.

"I call Heaven to witness," she cried in the same reckless, passionate tone as before, "that I thought not of this when I drove her from the house."

Then she bowed her head, and, with feet that stumbled as they went, left the room.

XXIX

No one saw Madge's face for more than a week from that day. Lady Judith paid a daily visit to her room, and her maid brought her meals to her bedside; but the room was kept darkened, and, when anyone approached her, she hid her eyes with her hands, complaining of racking pain in her head.

Lady Judith in her daily visits reported the household news with the minuteness of a *Daily Chronicle*. The golden opportunity of a listener, who, perforce, must remain a listener, was one to be made the most of. "Sir Peter actually advised me to keep out of the room," she said, sweeping in in her voluminous draperies. "He said perfect quiet would bring you round sooner than anything. I told him perfect quiet had a very nice sound on his lips. It was not I who came in at doors and went out at windows every five minutes in the day."

The curtains fluttered in response to her vigorous fan, the floor creaked under her weight, and her long skirt turned up the corners of every rug that lay in her path, and eventually carried along in its folds a footstool or two, wrong side uppermost. Madge said never a word, but lay still with covered face, listening to the high-pitched voice, as one in a subterranean passage beneath a big city might hear without heeding the hum and rush of busy feet and voices overhead.

Of all Lady Judith's flow of oratory during the first day's visit, Madge heard naught save that Sir Peter and Mr. Stubbs had "been closeted together the whole morning and were closeted together now. Goodness only knows what they can find to talk about. I should call it a sinful waste of time to shut myself up for half a day in a study to chatter about nothing at all."

Lady Judith's voice on the second day seemed to come a little nearer to Madge's muffled ears. It recounted how that Sir Peter had laid before her a newspaper paragraph recording the terrible fate of Miss Shore, and how she had reminded him that on the very first day that the young lady set foot in the house, she had said that she had a most repulsive manner in spite of her good looks, and was bound, sooner or later, to come to an unfortunate end. Lady Judith further added—with comments—that Sir Peter and Mr. Stubbs had started off at once for Liverpool, to state to the authorities there all that they knew of the unfortunate young lady, and to see that decent, not pauper, burial was given to her.

On the third day Lady Judith's chronicle of events grew more distinct by a great deal to Madge's dulled senses.

She came into Madge's room about noon with no less than seven telegrams in her hand, all from Sir Peter.

Telegram No. 1—stated that on his arrival at Carstairs he had changed his mind, and instead of continuing his journey to Liver-pool with Mr. Stubbs, had thought it better to take train for the North in order to see Lance and apprise him of the sad news.

The telegram did not add what in reality had been the case that this change in Sir Peter's intentions owed its origin to a suggestion from Mr. Stubbs.

Telegram No. 2—reported that he had reached the first station on his journey to Edinburgh.

Telegram No. 3—reported that he was getting on all right.

Telegram No.4—reported another step on the journey.

Telegram No.5—stated that he had crossed the Border.

Telegram No. 6—announced that he had arrived at Edinburgh, but that Lance was not there.

Telegram No. 7—stated that he had started on a return journey, trusting to find Lance at a little village in North-umberland, to which orders had been given that his Edinburgh letters should be sent.

After this day's report, Madge found her ears thirsting for the news which Lady Judith's next day's visit would bring.

But the next day was a blank. It brought no news whatever.

On the day following came the tidings by telegram that Sir Peter and Lance had joined Mr. Stubbs at Liverpool; and the day after that Lady Judith paid Madge a second—an evening—visit to her room, on purpose to report the fact that the three gentlemen had returned to the Castle.

"But in a very extraordinary state of mind, my dear—two of them, at least; for Sir Peter I've scarcely seen—certainly have had no opportunity of conversing with. He has been in and out of the stables, through the greenhouses—to see that the plants are growing right end uppermost, I suppose—but no, not for five minutes at a time has he been in the same room with me. Well, as I was saying, Mr. Stubbs is going about on tip-toes with his eyes half-shut and speaking in a solemn whisper, for all the world as if the terrible affair had happened in this house—as it very well might, considering the sort of people Sir Peter brings into it—instead of miles away. And as for Lance, my dear! well, you must see him to know what he looks like—a perfect wreck of himself, with a white face and sunken eyes, as if he had had no sleep for a week! and as for talk! there's not a word to be got out of him! Say what I will, I can't get him to tell me what they've all been doing at Liverpool, and not even did he open his lips when I remarked what a mercy it was that the young lady didn't commit suicide here, and jump out of her bedroom window on the very night of the ball."

"Must see him to know what he looks like!" Madge felt at that moment as if she never dared meet him face to face again. "For Lance, for Lance," she had said to herself over and over again, as she had sought to stifle the voice of her conscience. But now, as she hid her face lower still among her pillows, came the voice of her own heart echoing, not stifling, the whispers of conscience, with the terrible question: "What if this thing done 'for Lance' shall have wrecked, not saved his future for him?

Sir Peter had not been twenty-four hours in the house before a doctor was sent for to see Madge, and she had to sit up and face him.

He came down from his interview with her with a very grave face. She was in a terribly weak state, he said, and must have run down a good deal without anyone noticing it. He recommended change of air and scene so soon as it was practicable.

Sir Peter felt his hands very fall just then.

"Really, Stubbs," he said, confidentially, to his secretary, "what with one thing and another, I hardly know which way to turn. Mr. Clive, the first thing this morning, announced to me that he intended joining an exploring expedition into Africa—or was it the Spice Island?—really, I'm not sure which—and now Mrs. Cohen to break down in this way! And there's that letter from her lawyers about her property at Redes-dale. They say they've written to her again and again, and can't get any answers to their letters, and now they're obliged to apply to me. It's a matter of first importance."

Mr. Stubbs proffered his services immediately.

"Would it be any use. Sir Peter, if I took the lawyers' letter to Mrs. Cohen and offered to write a reply to her dictating?" he asked.

Sir Peter caught at the idea. A message was at once despatched to Mrs. Cohen, which elicited the reply that she would see Mr. Stubbs in her own room.

Mr. Stubbs found her seated as far from the window as possible. The room was much darkened; she leaned back in her chair, shading her eyes with her hand, so that he could scarcely see her face. He took the chair which she indicated; it was a long way from her own, considering how confidential their talk was likely to be. He placed it by a yard nearer. Madge immediately drew in front of her a small table, as if to set up a distinct barrier between them.

Her movement left him free to note how much her few days' illness had told upon her.

Her voice sounded weak and unlike her own as she asked the question: "Did you see her?" in a low, agitated tone.

"I grieve to say I did not, madam," he replied. "I was too late—the paper sent to me was four days old. The body had lain for identification at the mortuary for a day, but no one coming forward, an inquest had been held, and it had been buried in the paupers' burial ground."

Madge, with a low cry, leaned forward on the table before her, hiding her face in her hands. There seemed to come a sudden rush of some soft valse music into her ears, a graceful figure in misty gray draperies seemed to float before her eyes. It vanished; in its stead there lay a still and silent form, swathed in graveclothes, in a pauper's coffin.

Mr. Stubbs went on composedly:

"I went to the local authorities and stated that although, the young lady was an entire stranger to Sir Peter, she had been staying for some little time at the Castle. I further requested them to hand to me the purse, and the envelope on which her name was written. This they did. Mr. Clive took possession of both."

The slight tremor which thrilled Madge's hands showed that she had heard his last words.

"I also requested them to point out to me her place of burial, as I knew it would be Sir Peter's wish to place a stone over it. They could not do so with exactitude. It was a big cemetery; there had been a good many pauper buried that day; two in one grave, three in another, and they were not certain in which grave the drowned young lady had been buried."

He waited for Madge to speak, but never a word came from her lips. Her head bent lower and lower, till at length, covered still with her white, tremulous hands, it rested on the table.

"I did my best, madam," he said at length.

Still not a word from Madge.

He was determined to make her speak. "Mr. Clive was in a terrible state of mind. Sir Peter didn't know what to do with him. He was half-frantic at first. He was going to do all sorts of wild things, vowed he'd have the whole cemetery dug up to find her body, he must see her once again and say his 'goodbye' to her, he said, or he should know no rest in this world. I asked him if he remembered the face of the girl who was taken out of the river at Lower Upton? After that he said no more about searching the graves for her."

Madge's fingers clutched each other convulsively.

Mr. Stubbs had no pity.

"Unless something is done promptly, he will be doing something desperate, and may ruin his life for himself," he said.

Madge drew her hands from her white, tear-stained face.

"Listen," she said, "I shall do something promptly—before this day is out—go to Mr. Clive and tell him the whole truth, from beginning to end."

"My dear madam—"

"Be silent," she said, sharply, peremptorily. "After this—this—shall I go to you for advice?"

She pushed back her chair and rose from the table. So long as she sat facing this man, she felt all that was good in her dwindling, all that was evil in her growing apace.

She pressed her hands to her forehead.

"I cannot keep it to myself, it will drive me mad—mad!" she said, desperately.

Mr. Stubbs rose also; he looked at her in silence for a few moments, then he drew his letter case from his pocket.

"What about the Australian letter, madam?" he queried.

Madge started.

The second terrible catastrophe had for the time thrown the other into the shade.

"Shall you, when you make your full confession to Mr. Clive, tell him also the story of Sir Peter's nephew and heir?"

Madge drew a long, weary breath.

"It will help him a little further along the road to ruin, that's all. Pardon my speaking plainly, madam, but this is a crisis—forgive my saying so, in Mr. Clive's life as well as in your own."

"My own life may go," she said, recklessly. "One way or another I have ruined it for myself—it is not worth taking into account now." She made one step towards the door, then abruptly paused.

Was her resolution wavering or gathering strength, Mr. Stubbs wondered.

"Will you be good enough to read this, madam?" he said, opening his letter-case and spreading a letter before her.

Madge, with a hasty eye, read as follows:

Liverpool, *August 22nd*

"The Rev. Joshua Parker regrets that he is unexpectedly prevented from calling upon Sir Peter Critchett, a he had intended to do on his way to the North. He hopes, however, that the pleasure may be only deferred for a month or six weeks."

Madge was prompt enough to recognise the name and handwriting of the writer of the letter which lay locked in her desk. It was startling news this, that the man who knew the story of Gervase Critchett was in England and would shortly make his appearance at the Castle. She had taken it for granted that all communications on this matter would be by pen and ink across fifteen thousand miles of ocean, and had formed her plans accordingly; it had never for a moment occurred to her that Gervase's guardian would follow in this fashion on the heels of his letter.

"It came this morning, madam," said Mr. Stubbs, watching her face as she read it; "I recognised the handwriting, and, of course, would not lay it before Sir Peter until I had your instructions on the matter."

"How dared you—" Madge began, but broke off sharply, her words of reproach dying on her lips before they could be uttered. How dared she in very truth even frame them in thought?

She stood with one hand resting on the table, the other she pressed against her hot eyeballs. After all, this announcement of the Rev. Mr. Parker's intentions savoured somewhat of the nature of a reprieve, in so far as it assured to her definite space wherein to arrange her plans.

It seemed as if Mr. Stubbs read her thoughts. "It seems to me, there is no time to be lost, madam," he said, "a month soon slips past."

Madge made an impatient movement with her hand.

"It is a crisis in Mr. Clive's life," he went on, insinuatingly, "He is reckless, broken-hearted; a second blow might drive him headlong to desperation—I only suggest—"

Madge threw back her head. She pointed to the door. "Go," she said, in a voice in which hatred and fear strove for mastery. "Go, and never dare to come near me again."

Mr. Stubbs went immediately. He, however, carefully left the Rev. Joshua Parker's letter behind him on the table.

Madge stood staring at it blankly for a few minutes, then she deposited it under lock and key beside the Rev. Joshua Parker's former communication. She had now the responsibility of two purloined letters resting on her shoulders.

XXX

"My dear boy, my dear boy," said Sir Peter, now at one end of the study, now at the other, "think it over. Africa, did you say? For years? No, on you don't mean it. Make it months—and—and—wouldn't Vienna, or Paris, or Rome, or—or—New York even do as well?"

"They might do every whit as well—or as ill," answered Lance, slowly. "But I think it will be Africa."

Nevertheless, it didn't look as if it would "be Africa"—that is to say supposed to be the case, a journey to Africa implied a little energy on the part of the would-be traveler. He was leaning heavily against the study mantelpiece, while Sir Peter pursued his peregrinations. Lady Judith had in no wise exaggerated in her portraiture of Lance, when she had described him as looking "the wreck of himself." He had all the appearance of a man stunned by a heavy blow; whom instinct sends crawling: out of sight while he gets his breath back again.

Sir Peter paused in front of the young man, executing his favourite heel and toe movement, his eyebrows going up and down with the motion. One terrible half-hour passed in Lance's company at Liverpool had revealed to him the true state of his feelings towards Miss Shore. He was afraid of raising even the ghost of that terrible half-hour now, yet he knew that Lance must be reasoned with, and not allowed in a sudden rash moment to ruin his whole future.

The situation seemed to him to require diplomatic treatment, and he felt that he had a great many threads to manipulate at that moment.

He racked his brains to think of the strongest argument he could bring to bear, and after tip-toeing and going back on his heels for about a minute and a half, brought out the remark, "Africa is a long way off," and then he set off round the room again.

"Yes," was all Lance's reply.

"And—and, my dear boy, how do you mean to get there?" said the old gentleman, from the farther end of the room.

"Upon my life, I don't care two pence-halfpenny about that. All I care about is to go somewhere—do something, or else I shall go out of my mind."

Sir Peter caught at the word "do." It brought him back in a trice from the farther end of the room.

"Do! yes, that's it, that's it, Lance—it's something to do that you're wanting—occupation to do that you're wanting—occupation; your time hangs heavily. Occupation, my dear boy, the unacknowledged necessity of existence. It means contentment—a mind at rest."

Here he stood at Lance's side. "It means quiet, peacefulness, tranquility." The last word found him at the other end of the room.

Lance did not seem to hear him. He had walked away to the window, and now stood looking out at the cedar tree, under which he had more than once established Miss Shore and her easel at the sloping garden-path which led down to the river-bank, where he had caught sight of her in hiding among the reeds and osiers; at the winding mountain road, up which he had followed her in his effort to arrest her death daring footsteps.

Once upon the topic of occupation, Sir Peter's eloquence grew apace. He drew a touching picture of the general deficiency in funds and workers of the larger portion of benevolent societies—to hear him speak one would think that every one of the charitable institutions of England was on the verge of bankruptcy—mourned over his own inability to devote a larger portion of his time to their good work.

"But—there, what with the management of his own estate and Madge's—"

But here he broke off abruptly. Madge's name came to him like an inspiration.

"The truth of it is," he said, "Madge ought to get married, and then her husband could look after her affairs. I'm always at work, and yet I can't keep things under. Redesdale alone would take the whole of a man's time; and Madge never takes the slightest interest in anything connected with it. A most important question has arisen. The lawyers have written again and again telling Madge that the estate adjoining Redesdale has come into the market, and unless she buys it up the speculative builder will get hold of it and Redesdale will be ruined; but no, they can't get her to give them her attention—"

But Redesdale, and Madge's neglect of it, evidently had no attraction for Lance.

He left his stand at the window and crossed the room towards the door.

Sir Peter stood in his way, tiptoeing very hard.

"Don't you agree with me that she ought to get married? It's dreadful to think of that young woman left all alone with that immense property on her hands and her own health not what it was. She's far from strong, Broughton tells me, and ought to go away at once."

"Well, what's to prevent her getting married? Heaps of men would jump at the chance of marrying her," said Lance, absently.

"My dear boy!" cried Sir Peter, aghast, "you wouldn't like to see Madge fall into the hands of a needy adventurer!"

"I should hope she'd have too much sense ever to do such a tiling," said Lance, making another effort to get to the door.

Sir Peter laid his hand on his arm.

"My dear boy, can you put two and two together and find that they make four?" he asked, energetically. "You want something to do? Well, I've told you the management of Madge's property would take the whole of man's time. You want to start all in a hurry for a journey—to—to—Well, say to the moon. Madge has been ordered by her doctor to take a trip in precisely the same direction. Now, do you understand?"

But if Lance did understand he did not say so. He stared blankly at Sir Peter, then the door opening at that moment from the other side, he took the opportunity and made his escape.

The door had opened to admit Mr. Stubbs. Sir Peter, with energy and a little touch of irritability, related the heads of his talk with Lance, and demanded his sympathy for Madge and the Redesdale property.

Mr. Stubbs knew all about Redesdale and the adjoining land. He had a suggestion to make, and he made it with a great show of diffidence. It took the form of a question:

"Was the estate adjoining Redesdale a good paying property, and of the kind that Sir Peter had had in his mind when he had talked the other day of buying one to settle upon Mr. Clive?"

Sir Peter caught at the suggestion. "It shall be seen into, Stubbs; capital idea!" he cried, gleefully. Then he started off at once to confide the notion to someone else—Lance, if he could find him—if not to Madge.

Madge had come downstairs for the first time that day. She and Lance had met at the luncheon-table but had scarcely exchanged a word. His listless, frowning face had set her shivering, she had felt as if some vast ocean had suddenly rolled in between them, and as if she and he would never again stand side by side on the same shore. Then she had become suddenly conscious that Mr. Stubbs's sleepy eyes were fixed on her own face, and she had made a huge effort and had into commonplace talk, complaining of the cold east wind which had set in, and had vowed that winter must be beginning; it was like a November day.

Lady Judith had recommended her to have a fire made in her little boudoir, and to sit there all the afternoon. Whereupon Madge had kindled into sudden vehemence, had declared that she hated the room and would like to have it bricked up. Then she had risen hastily from the table and had thrown at Mr. Stubbs one angry, furtive look which had said: "I hate you, I defy you, I mean to assert myself and to get back a clear conscience."

Mr. Stubbs's acknowledgment for this courtesy was to say in a low voice as he held open the door for her to pass out:

"Be cautious, madam, this is a crisis."

After luncheon, Lance had followed Sir Peter into his study to announce his intended journey to Africa, and Madge had wrapped a thick shawl about her and had gone wandering out into the garden.

A chill air was blowing; winter assuredly was not yet setting in, but the most golden of the golden days were over. Madge, weak still from her short, sharp illness, felt the bracing wind too strong for her; she turned down a sheltered alley—a little bit of shrubbery leading off the flower garden—where the larches entwined their feathery boughs overhead, and the dappled blue sky showed here and there in patches.

She walked up and down with quick yet weak footsteps, the echo of Mr. Stubbs's warning still in her ears. A crisis in Lance's life was it? She knew that just as well as he did. Why, his future positively trembled in the balance. Now did it behove her, who had dared to take his future in hand and to say, "It is for his happiness that my wealth and my love should be given to him," to finish the work she had begun, to continue to steep her soul in deceit in order to assure to him this wealth and love? Or, on the other hand, should she go to him and say:

"Lance, hear my confession; I have done my best to break your heart with my supreme folly, do now what one had better have let you do at the first, choose your future for yourself."

A stupendous effort, a courage all but heroic, this latter course would demand. She stood still in the middle of the path, asking herself if it were in her power to do this thing—lose forever the chance of winning his love, see him, perhaps, in hot haste and desperation, fling himself head-long into poverty and ruin.

As she stood thus asking herself these momentous questions, Lance passed along slowly at the end of her shady path. A sudden rush of courage seemed to come to her. "Now or never it must be," she said to herself. She waved her hand to him. He caught sight of her among the shadows of the larches and went to meet her.

"I was going to the stables to give some special directions about my hunters—I want them well looked after while I'm away," he said, intent on breaking the news of his intended departure to her.

Madge for the moment could not speak. She looked up into his face as they stood there in the breezy sunlight, he looked down into hers. Each felt thrilled with a sudden sharp pity for the other's changed, white face.

Madge was conscience-smitten and silent.

Lance, not being conscience-smitten, had words to express his pity. "What has pulled you down in this way, Madge?" he asked. "Come indoors, the breeze is too strong for you."

Madge laid her hand upon his arm.

"One moment, Lance, I want to speak to you," she said, in a low, tremulous tone.

More than this her lips were absolutely incapable of.

Lance looked a little surprised at her flushing, downcast face. "What is Madge?" he asked, kindly; and Madge's lips parted as to speak, but still the words would not come. But though her lips were silent, her thoughts were clamorous. "It must be now or never, Madge Cohen," those thoughts seemed to say, "Make up your mind at once which must be, full confession, or lips for evermore to be sealed."

She was trembling from head to foot.

"Lance, when are you going away?" she asked, presently, in the same low, nervous tone as before.

Paraphrased, her question would have been: "Will you give me another chance of making my confession?—the words won't come to my lips today."

"Tomorrow morning, before you are down," he answered, "I shall go straight away to Paris, and make up my mind when I get there what I shall do with myself. I've prepared Uncle Peter for my being away a long time—but of course I shall write."

The mingled hopelessness and recklessness in his tone frightened her. She seized his hands impetuously in hers.

"Oh, don't go—don't go, "she implored.

"Lance, Lance, if you do, you will break my heart."

Every other thought was swamped now in the fear lest this might be a final parting.

Lance looked at her wonderingly. This was Madge in a new light.

"I don't think you know—I don't think you understand," he began after a moment's pause.

"Yes, I do know, I do understand," she interrupted, impetuously and nervously as before. "I know how you—pitied her—" she could not bring the word "loved" to her lips.

"Madge," he interrupted, sharply, "pity doesn't crush a man into the dust and take all the life out of him."

Madge grew whiter and whiter.

She let go of his hands suddenly, as if they stung her. But still she cried despairingly: "Don't go, don't go; oh, why should you let this—this sorrow ruins your whole life?"

"A man must fight through his troubles in his own fashion, Madge; this is my way of fighting through mine," he answered, gravely, "But come indoors—this east wind is too strong for you—and tell me what you have to tell me there."

In silence they went back to the house together, Madge nerving herself as best she could for what lay before her. "In half an hour it must, it will be, all over," she said to herself, "and he will either hate me and curse me to my face, or he will forgive me and help me to tell Sir Peter of my other deceit."

She led the way to the smallest and sunniest of the drawing-rooms, but still kept her thick shawl wrapped around her. He shut the door as they entered. Madge stood before him flushing and trembling. "Lance, Lance," she said in a voice half-choked with tears, "the words will not come."

He took her hands in his. "Why, what can there be that you should be afraid to tell me, Madge?" he asked in kindly astonishment.

The door-handle turned at this moment, and Mr. Stubbs entered the room. Madge started but did not attempt to withdraw her hands from Lance's grasp. Mr. Stubbs's face had possibly never before been seen with so ominous a look on it. His lips said respectfully enough, "Sir Peter is looking everywhere for you, Mrs. Cohen," but his narrowing eyes said: "Take care, only half your secret is yours to confess, the other half is mine."

Madge felt that he had played the spy on her. She lost her self-control utterly, her tears came in a flood now, her head bowed on Lance's hands, which she grasped convulsively in her own.

"Don't go, don't go," was all that she could say. "Don't go, Lance, or it will break my heart."

And Lance, looking down on her wonderingly and remembering old love passages in days gone by, thought he read the meaning of her passionate tears and halting words, and felt his own purpose falter.

"Capital idea! capital idea!" said Sir Peter, coming into the room as Mr. Stubbs backed out of it. "They're in here together, did you say—the very thing! Capital fellow Stubbs is—knew he was, though Lady Judith had so much to say about him. Well, I've got something special to say to you two young people. You know how you've been bothered lately, Madge, with letters from the lawyers about the land adjoining Redesdale? Well, Mr. Stubbs suggests that instead of you buying it and getting more responsibilities and anxieties on your shoulders, I should buy it for Lance—eh, do you see now, and settle it on him! Eh, do you understand, Madge—and—and then—then, don't you see, don't you understand—it's all in the nutshell? Well! if I must speak out—"

But Lance interrupted him here. It was his hands that held Madge's now, not Madge's that held his, and he answered Sir Peter with his eyes bent on her bowed head, "I understand you, at any rate, Uncle Peter, and it shall be as you wish."

XXXI

So, Madge's confession remained unspoken; she fixed the date of her wedding-day instead. She caught up the burthen of Miss Shore's song and said: "It is fate, my lips must be sealed eternally now." And she set herself to stifle the voice of her conscience, to banish every thought but the one that Lance so far was saved, and to look ahead at naught but the dangers which had yet to be faced and conquered for his sake.

Sir Peter did not say it was fate. He put himself in the place of "the sisters three," and went about telling everybody that "if it had not been for him these young people would have made a nice mess of their love affairs; one would have been off to Africa, and the other to goodness only knew where."

He surpassed himself in activity during the week following the announcement of the engagement. Nothing went fast enough to please him. One way or another he anticipated everything that had to be done in the way of business arrangements. The estate to be purchased for Lance must not be allowed to come into the market, so his solicitors were commissioned to negotiate for it privately. Before, however, they had time to despatch one offer for the property, Sir Peter had sent off no less than three. And so on throughout the transaction. The price of the estate went up proportionately.

He pushed forward the date of the wedding-day in much the same fashion. A three weeks' engagement was the utmost he would hear of. "Why, you've been engaged from childhood, and ought to have been married ages ago," he said, anticipating any possible demur Madge might make, and skipping lightly over the Cohen episode in her history.

Lady Judith thought the hurried manner in which the wedding was arranged typical of Sir Peter's general method of conducting affairs, and off and on she had a good deal to say about it.

On the whole, the two persons most deeply interested said the least.

Lance a little listlessly accepted the fact, telling himself a hundred times a day how grateful he was to Madge for her love, and that to the end of his days his one aim would be to put as much happiness as possible into her life. But of lovemaking, so far as he was concerned, there was not one jot.

Miss Shore's name never passed his lips, and it was quickly evident to Madge that they two would have to begin their life together with a sealed subject between them.

As the days went by that sealed subject seemed to her less like a sepulchre, with a stone decently rolled to its mouth, than an open grave whose proper occupant wandered at will, a restless shade, among the scenes and people to which it was supposed to have said goodbye.

If, when they sat side by side, a sudden silence fell upon him, Madge would say to herself: "He is thinking of that girl in gray, wondering over the mystery of her life, and what sudden terror drove her to her death."

Or, if in the course of conversation, he gave an absent answer, or let his gaze rest longer than usual on her face, she would think bitterly: "He is comparing the beauty of that girl with my sallow face. Oh, Madge Cohen, what have you beyond your wealth to give him?"

Her thoughts travelled back to the bright summer's afternoon when, as she and Lance stood facing each other in the sunlight, the chill, cold shadow of that desolate girl had seemed to fall between them. Well, she might be buried six feet below the earth in her pauper's coffin, but she had left her shadow behind her; Madge might lock up easels and ball dress and change her room a hundred times over, but all the same the shadow was there.

As the days went by, Madge, instead of rallying from her short, sharp illness, grew whiter and thinner. Cold weather setting in at the beginning of September, brought with it for her a series of severe colds; whereupon, the old doctor once more lifted up a warning voice, advising that his patient should get away to the south before the Cumbrian mists and east winds set in continuously; in fact, as soon as possible, or he would not answer for the consequences.

Sir Peter would have liked the wedding to be not as soon as, but sooner than possible. He redoubled energy over the business arrangements. Letter-writing became far too slow a process for him now; he took to telegraphing two or three times a day to his lawyers, also to the trustees of the property for which he was negotiating.

This property was in Durham, and promised to yield a good income if judiciously managed in connection with the Redesdale estate; it occurred to Sir Peter that it might expedite matters if Lance, in person, were to survey the property and discuss matters generally with the trustees of the estate, and the land-steward of Redesdale.

Then he took Madge vigorously in hand, and just as in the old days he had hurried her into her marriage with old David Cohen, so now he hastened forward her wedding-day by another seven days.

One of Lady Brabazon's sons was to be married only the morning before the day now fixed for Lance's and Madge's wedding. Lance was to act as his best man. It was therefore arranged that Lance should go straight from Durham to this wedding, which was to take place at York; spend the night of that day with the Brabazons, coming back to Upton in the morning to receive his bride from Sir Peter's hands at St. Cuthbert's church.

Lance did not throw much spirit into the part of "best man," which he was to perform for his friend. He characterised the Brabazon wedding as a headstrong, foolish affair. On the day on which he set off for Durham, Madge rose at six o'clock in the morning to have breakfast with him, and to "see him off." He spoke his mind freely to her about his friend's "infatuation" as he called and vowed that the choice had been given him he would sooner have followed Eric Brabazon to his grave; "a man had far better lie down in his coffin than make suck marriage as that."

Madge knew the history of Eric Brabazon's courtship the lady of his choice had as good as jilted him, but friends had interfered, and the wedding had eventually been arranged.

Madge was standing outside in the bright morning: sunshine caressing Lance's horses as he said this. She had been saying soft, sweet things to him with her goodbyes, wondering whether the Redesdale fishing was as good as that at Upton, whether the stables there would need enlarging, and so forth; when, however, he spoke of choosing rather to follow Eric Brabazon to the grave than go to his wedding, her soft speeches came to a halt. She bent her face till her curly brown hair seemed one with the horse's mane. "He may be happy; he may make up his mind to forget the past," she said, in a low voice.

"What, forget lies and deceit?"Lance cried, hotly.

"And it doesn't follow because she has deceived him once that she will attempt to do so a second time," she continued after a moment's pause.

"If I had been in Eric's place, I wouldn't have given her a chance. The first deliberate piece of deception would have put an eternal barrier between us," said Lance, vehemently.

Madge felt herself frozen into silence. She walked with him to the park gates, the groom following slowly with the dog-cart; but she had no more sweet speeches to make.

"An eternal barrier, an eternal barrier," her thoughts kept repeating. She watched him drive away down the steep road, shading her eyes with her hand to catch a last glimpse of him. He waved his hat in farewell, then his hand; then a bend in the road hid him from her sight.

"When next we meet it will be before the altar rails of St. Cuthbert's," she said to herself, but with none of that rush of joy in her heart which the words might be supposed to bring with them. "Would it be so if I had spoken out the truth and told him what I have done for his sake?"

"I beg your pardon, madam," said Mr. Stubbs's voice at that moment. "I saw you walking through the park with Mr. Clive, and, as I particularly wanted to speak to you, I ventured to follow." Madge was startled; this man, like an emissary of darkness, seemed perpetually hovering over her path.

"What is it?" she asked, coldly. "Will it take long to tell?"

"There is nothing specially to tell, madam, it is merely a suggestion I have to make; it can be made easily enough as we walk back to the house together."

That "we" was a perpetual torture to Madge. It seemed the outward and visible sign of the evil bond between her and this man. She never heard it without feeling as she felt on the day when old David Cohen clasped her first diamond necklace round her throat.

Nevertheless, she did not refuse Mr. Stubbs's company on her way back through the park, nor did she attempt to cut his communications short, for her steps slackened as they neared the house.

Mr. Stubbs's last words as they parted at the front door were:

"Everything is going on satisfactorily, madam; just exactly as we could wish."

To this Madge made a sharp, impatient movement with her hand.

"And the second letter, of which you spoke just now, gives me no anxiety whatever. If allusion is made to it when the Rev. Mr. Parker arrives, I simply say I read it to Sir Peter with some half-dozen others of a similar kind—there are always a lot of people writing to make or to break appointments with him, and half the letters of that sort which I read to him he pays no attention to—he is either walking about the room, or thinking of something else. The first letter is also now a very simple affair, and the sooner it is in my hands the better, for really there is no time to be lost."

XXXII

One or two things happened during Lance's stay in Durham.

Madge suddenly grew what the French call *devote*. She developed a fondness for saints' days and early services. St. Cuthbert's old church, off and on, saw a good deal of her just then. Her friends in the neighbourhood shared with St. Cuthbert's church the honour of her society, for she balanced her devotion in the early part of the day with an increase of gaiety towards its close. She accepted every invitation to entertainments given in honour of her approaching marriage; seemed to enter warmly into the local enthusiasm that was growing on the matter and talked freely of the preliminary arrangements that were being made for the wedding.

Once, however, when so chatting with Lottie Brabazon, she was suddenly frozen into silence by a remark made by that light-hearted young lady.

It was:

"Of course, you will be married in gray—it's the only colour widows can wear."

Madge felt that she would as soon be married in her shroud as have to face Lance at the altar in gray garments.

Something else noteworthy occurred while Lance was away inspecting the Durham property. A sudden remarkable increase of intimacy seemed to spring up between Mrs. Cohen and Mr. Stubbs, and they were frequently to be seen in each other's company. Sir Peter noted the fact and rubbed his hands over it with delight.

"Capital fellow that!" he said to Madge.

"I'm glad to see you appreciate him. I think I've an eye for character, eh, Madge? although Lady Judith, at first, hadn't a good word to say for him. Now, if you could get just such a man as that for your land-steward at Redesdale, he'd double the value of your property in less than ten years."

Madge, standing with her back to the light, and speaking in a hurried voice, gave an answer which almost took Sir Peter's breath away.

"I was thinking of pensioning off the present steward at Redesdale. He's very old and not very active—and I was wondering if—if you thought—if you would like, I mean—Mr. Stubbs to take the post. I mean if you were thinking of getting a new secretary, Mr. Stubbs might like to undertake the steward's duties at Redesdale."

She had stammered a great deal over this speech. In truth, it was a speech not easy to make gracefully.

Sir Peter was fairly taken aback. "My dear child, my dear child!" was all he could say at first. Then he walked up and down the room once or twice very fast. Then he stood still in front of her, and tip-toed and lifted his eyebrows at her till she felt quite giddy.

"I wasn't thinking of making a change, Madge," he said; "but now you speak of it, I think Stubbs exactly the man for the post you could give him. He's getting on in life—a younger man could write my letters and do all I should require. His remuneration as your steward would be twice what should give him as secretary. He would have a nice house, servants, and horses of his own. Yes, capital idea! I won't stand in his light. Think it over! No, there's no need to do that. Consider it settled, my dear. I'm delighted."

After this arrangement was made, it was only natural that Mr. Stubbs and Madge should be still more in each other's society. It seemed reasonable to suppose that there were many matters in connection with the stewardship at Redesdale that required discussion and arrangement.

Thanks to Sir Peter's telegrams and the general energy which he displayed on the matter, the purchase of the Durham property, and the deeds conveying it to Lance, were much less lengthy businesses than such things generally are. Two days after Lance's departure to Durham, and three before the day fixed for the wedding, saw the purchase as good as concluded by the payment of an instalment of the purchase-money by Sir Peter to seal the bargain. Final legal forms, it was arranged, should be gone through on Lance's return with Madge from their wedding tour.

"And they talk about the interminable length of law processes," said Sir Peter triumphantly, to Mr. Stubbs. "Why, how long have we had this matter in hand, eh? Park, woods, river, farms, in all about one thousand eight hundred acres; rent-roll about five thousand a year; and we've as good as pulled it through in three weeks' time! Now we've just a few telegram to send off this morning to the Durham people, and then we'll set to work on the day's correspondence."

If Mr. Stubbs had had two pairs of hands, one for the day's telegrams, the other for its letters, he might have been able to satisfy the demands of Sir Peter's energy. As it was, long before the telegrams were despatched, Sir Peter was asking the question, "Anything of importance today, Stubbs?" and had begun his usual quick march, which betokened that replies were ready to ooze out of his fingers' tips.

Mr. Stubbs laid aside his telegrams and read in succession one or two unimportant letters which the morning's post had brought. Then he laid his hand upon a packet of three letters, and his face grew long and serious.

"These, Sir Peter," he said, "I grieve to tell you, were, by Mr. Clive's orders, placed on one side unopened in an inner compartment of your writing-table, and, I am sorry to say, have been forgotten. If you remember when you had the—"

"When I was ill," interrupted Sir Peter.

Of late he had grown sensitive on the score of the juvenile ailment and had repudiated asserting that Broughton had made a mistake, and it had been nothing but a nettle rash after all.

Stubbs bowed. "When you were ill, Sir Peter, if you remember, for one day Mr. Clive undertook your correspondence. He dictated a general answer to a few letters and told me to put the rest on one side, as no doubt they'd answer themselves if left alone."

"Just like him! Read them out Stubbs."

"I'm sorry to say that afterwards they were forgotten."

"Ah Madge, I remember, undertook my correspondence the next day—so she forgot them eh?"

"I fear I must own to the neglect, Sir Peter. Mrs. Cohen attended to everything that I put before her."

"Ah, well, open and read them; I don't suppose it matters much."

The first letter opened and read was the prospectus of a mining company in the adjoining county. It had no date attached. It received a scanty attention and was forthwith tossed into the wastepaper basket.

The second letter shared a similar fate. It was an intimation from a brewing firm that they were about to convert themselves into a chartered company. There was no date to this communication also.

The third letter Mr. Stubbs opened with a little preamble.

"It has an Australian postmark. I trust its contents did not require immediate acknowledgment," he said, in a concerned voice.

And then he began to read the story of Gervase Critchett, as told by the Rev. Joshua Parker.

But long before he had got halfway through it, Sir Peter had cried to him in a hoarse voice: "Stop! Stop! For Heaven's sake, stop!" and had got up from his seat, and had taken the letter into his own hands to read.

His hands, however, trembled so violently that he was perforce obliged to spread the paper before him on the table. And then there had come a mist before his eyes, so that the lines danced backwards and forwards, and reading become an impossibility; so, he handed the letter back to Mr. Stubbs.

"Go on," he said. "Read quickly."

He leaned back in his chair for good five minutes, still and silent, his brain possibly overweighted, not only by the startling news that letter brought, but by the memories of years long gone by, which the startling news conjured up from the land of shadows.

But that five minutes at an end, Sir Peter was himself again. He jumped up from his chair, seized the Australian letter, and rang the bell violently.

"Ask Lady Judith to come here to me at once—important news," was the order he gave to the servant who answered his summons. "And—Mrs. Cohen also." And then as soon as the servant had disappeared, he rang the bell again to countermand the order. Four walls couldn't contain him at that moment, and before the servant could answer his second summons, he had set off to scour the house and grounds in search of Lady Judith and Madge.

Lady Judith, in her morning room, studying with deep interest a catalogue of patent farming appliances, was suddenly startled by having the pricelist shut out from her view by a letter in strange handwriting spread athwart it by Sir Peter.

"Read it," he shouted into her ear, "and tell me what you think of it."

Before, however, she had time to realise the fact that it was something other than a written recommendation of the barrel churns which she was contemplating so lovingly in her picture-catalogue, Sir Peter had disappeared through the window, having caught sight of Madge coming up the drive towards the house.

Madge was wrapt in furs and had on the thickest of Shetland veils; she had complained a good deal of the cold of late and had taken to muffling herself up as if it were mid-winter. When Sir Peter had breathlessly told his startling news, she had a sharp fit of coughing which for the moment prevented her making any comment thereon, and Sir Peter, while executing a quick march up and down the gravel path, discoursed upon Gervase, his manners and doings from boyhood upwards.

"A handsome fellow he was! My poor mother used to say whenever I put her out that it was a thousand pities Gervase hadn't come into the world first, he would have carried the title with so much more dignity than I should. Poor Gervase! Poor Gervase! I remember he had a good opinion of himself—never would take advice—restless, too, he was—always wanting to do half-a-dozen things at once—used to have a hundred and one schemes in hand at the same moment, but never brought any of them to maturity! Poor Gervase, a sad ending! I wonder if his boy is like him in any way!"

By the time he had got to Gervase's boy, Madge had recovered her voice, and was ready to ask a few questions.

"What will you do about the boy—send for him, I suppose, to Upton?" was the first.

"Of course, of course; what else in life could I do? I shall telegraph to him this very day, sending the message from 'your uncle at Upton.' Poor little lad! And he's in a state of anxiety for fear we shouldn't give him a welcome! Gervase's only boy not to feel sure of a welcome! Thank Heaven for the cablegram, Madge. Fancy that poor boy having to wait three months for the news that his father's people would hold out their hand to him! And that letter already has been most unfortunately delayed. Ah, you don't know about that—never mind, I haven't time to tell you now!" Here Sir Peter in a great hurry pulled out his watch. "Haven't a minute to spare, Madge, I'm off at once to Durham to tell Lance the good news. You explain everything to Lady Judith. I shall just save a train at Lower Upton if I'm quick about it."

Madge demurred vigorously to his hot haste to carry his news everywhere. She felt that her lips—by right of her love and sacrifice for him—should have been the ones to tell this tale to Lance.

But Sir Peter was resolute, and Madge had to realise the truth of Lance's saying, that, "If once Uncle Peter took a thing into his head, not the Lords, nor the Commons, nor the whole bench of Bishops combined could get it out."

Lance was seated in his quiet little country inn writing a few lines to Madge, when the startling announcement was made to him that Sir Peter was below waiting to see him.

Lance had arranged to be at York on the morrow, in order to be present at Eric Brabazon's wedding. He had spent the day in taking a final survey of his newly-acquired property, planning alterations and improvements.

From the window where he Sat, writing his letter to Madge, he could see the exact point where his estate met the Redesdale land. Redesdale itself, with its park, woods, and meadows, formed the larger portion of the landscape of which the window commanded a view. Between the trees he could catch a glimpse of the house: a handsome, modern structure of palatial dimensions.

Most men in Lance's position, with such a prospect as this facing them, would have owned to thoughts of a decidedly roseate hue.

"A11 to be mine so soon, and a loving wife into the bargain! And youth and health mine also! Lance Clive, you're a lucky fellow!" If thoughts such as these, with a touch of pride and triumph in them, had found expression in the letter he was penning, it might have been pardoned him.

There was, however, no necessity to plead extenuating circumstances for the letter that lay before him. It was soberly worded to the last degree! The sort of letter which a brother might have written to a loving sister with an eye to its perusal by the whole family afterwards.

And, soberly worded though it was, once or twice his pen had slackened in its task, and his left hand had pressed his eyes as if to shut out a vision, that night and day seemed ever before them, of a girl, with wan, white face, waving a farewell to him from out a shadowy darkness, while her lips, as if in mockery of the farewell she waved, bade him—

"Go back and dance."

The announcement of Sir Peter's arrival sent his thoughts running in all sorts of channels; something must have happened. Illness? Death? His fears flew to the worst.

But Sir Peter's beaming face reassured him quickly enough, and the old gentleman had not been five minutes in the room before the story of the two Gervases had been begun and ended.

Lance listened in silent astonishment. Many a time when the story of Gervase Critchett's erratic ways had been told him, he had felt disposed to envy the man his life of adventure in spite of the ill luck which had seemed to attend it. Now the awfulness of the ending of that life—the hopelessness and desperation of the man, with death facing him and those dearest to him—was the thing that touched him most.

"He must Lave died a thousand times over that night," he said, pitifully, and then there fell a silence between the two which Sir Peter broke by forcing a cheerful voice, and reading over again the story of Gervase Critchett, the younger.

Then other thoughts began to come to Lance. He rose from his chair and laid his hand on Sir Peter's shoulder.

"Uncle Peter," he said, gravely, "the estate you have been buying for me is so much robbery to Gervase—it must be his, not mine."

Sir Peter's amazement was boundless. Such a notion as this had not for a moment entered his brain. It took him a long time to grasp it.

That "he might do what he liked with his own, he had enough and to spare for Gervase," was the first argument wherewith he endeavoured to rebut it—and argument, however, which fell pointless before Lance's vigorous reasoning on the matter.

Lance, to his own fancy, stood pictured as an interloper who had somehow crept up the backstairs to good luck, while the one who had the right to enter it by the front door had been barred out in the cold.

"Poor boy; poor little fellow," he said, "to be knocking about in the world in that way, and a stranger here to step into his rights!"

Sir Peter tried his hardest to make him see the matter in another light. But logic had never been Sir Peter's strong point. His arguments were mostly interjections, spoken now at Lance's elbow, anon at the further end of the room.

The sun went down, the moon rose; the inmates of the quiet little inn put out their lights and went to bed; but still Lance and Sir Peter talked on, Lance getting firmer in his reasoning, Sir Peter's interjections gaining in vehemence and intensity.

"My dear boy, my dear boy," he had said over and over again, "I have brought you up to no profession. It would be like sending a soldier out to battle without weapons, to turn you out into the world to get your own living."

To which Lance had replied, also over and over again:

"I have a head and I have hands; if I can't use one, I can use the other; and no man with both at command can be said to be without weapons."

At last, one of Sir Peter's interjections struck a keynote not to be silenced by argument. It was:

"The tie between you and me, my boy, is as strong as any blood could be."

Lance faltered a little at this.

"If you don't choose to be looked upon as my eldest son, take the place of second and best loved," Sir Peter went on, seeing what words of his had told most.

Whereupon Lance had felt himself driven farther back in the field.

Finally, and this was when the night had nearly ended and both men were a little wearied with the strain of feeling they had undergone. Sir Peter had brought out three words:

"Think of Madge!"

And then Lance, paraphrasing the words somewhat thus: "If you refuse this property, how dare you, a pauper, offer marriage to Madge with her wealth?" struck his colours and gave up the contest, on the condition that Sir Peter would commission his solicitors to settle the estate on him for life only, and that on his death it was to revert to Gervase and his heirs.

XXXIII

Just before Lance had started for Durham, a terrible storm had swept the Cumberland coast; boats had been dashed to pieces on the rocks, some fishing-smacks, which, as a last chance had bravely put out to sea in the teeth of the gale, had been swamped, and not a soul on board had been saved.

In all, eight men and one boy had perished; four bodies only, however, had been washed ashore, together with remnants of the boats.

With Sir Peter and Madge in the immediate neighbourhood, it was not likely that destitution would be added to the grief of the bereaved families.

Madge was an angel of goodness to them; in spite of her own increasing inability to face the keen, rough air of the coast, every morning found her in the cottages of these poor souls, doing her utmost to assuage their grief and to meet their necessities. It was she who paid all funeral expenses as body after body was washed in by the tide; and finally, when hope failed of the recovery of the other bodies, she requested the Vicar of St. Cuthbert's to hold a memorial service that should be a fitting tribute to those whose resting-place could be marked by neither mound nor tablet. This service, by her special request, was to take place on the evening before the day fixed for her wedding.

All the arrangements for the wedding were now completed. It had been decided that it should be as quiet as wedding could well be. Eight o'clock in the morning was the time fixed for the ceremony. Madge was to be married in her travelling dress and was to drive straight from the church to the railway station, *en route* for Italy, by way of London.

Lady Judith had uttered her last lament over the unseemly haste with which the wedding had been urged forward. After saying, in her most scathing manner, right into Sir Peter's face, that "There were some people who would like to live out their lives in half an hour, and would send twenty minutes of that time in winding up the clock and greasing its wheels to make it go faster," she turned her attention to Sir Peter's newly found nephew and heir, taking for her text the misdoings of Gervase' the elder, and old Lady Critchett's foolish indulgence of him.

Madge had lived through one terrible night of suspense—the night after Sir Peter's departure for Durham—wondering with a wonder akin to agony how Lance had borne the news which cut him off from his former brilliant social position. Sir Peter, returning radiant on the following morning with triumphant accounts of the manner in which he had vanquished Lance's Quixotic notions—as he called them—relieved her of this distress.

Naught now remained for her to do, she assured herself, but to forget the past and live for the future only.

"'Past cure should be past care,'" she said to herself, from morning till night of the two days that remained to her before her wedding day. "The past is dead and should be buried; the future is mine. I have saved Lance from folly and beggary. I may well cry 'Victory!' now."

She looked at herself in the glass on the day before the one that was to make her Lance's wife and vowed that she had never looked so young and happy in her life before. She went so far as to scold her maid vigorously; first, for not echoing her assertion; secondly, for venturing to suggest that the memorial service for the poor, drowned fishermen was scarcely one that a bride-elect should be expected to attend on the eve of her wedding day.

That memorial service was one of the saddest and most solemn that had ever taken place in St. Cuthbert's old church. Certainly, a bride-elect seemed a little out of place in a church draped with black? and filled with mourners.

The minute bell tolled unceasingly during the service. Part of the funeral service was read, then followed Luther's judgment hymn, and finally St. Paul's grand resurrection chapter.

And through it all, with never a pause, the waves on the outside shore beat their own monotonous requiem for the dead, outsounding in the pauses of the service the sobs of the women in the church; the voice of the preacher even, as he flung down the gauntlet to death, with the cry, "O death, where is thy sting? O grave, where is thy victory?"

Madge felt her self-control giving way. Again and again she essayed to keep her mind fixed on those poor, drowned men, over whom the words "earth to earth" were never to be spoken; the ghost of another drowned soul, as with human voice, seemed to put in its claim to a share in this memorial tribute: "Was not I even more desolate than they, and was not my ending every whit as tragic? You gave me but scant kindness in my lifetime, is it too much to ask a tear of you now!"

Madge abruptly rose from her seat, and, letting her veil fall over her face, left the church.

She had given orders that the carriage should meet her at the foot of the steep pathway leading up from the valley. It wanted fully half an hour of the time she had fixed for it to be there, so she wandered slowly round the church, to its western side, to catch all she could of the sea breeze.

Outside in the growing dark the scene was as drear as within the church. The sky was one broad expanse of gray, unbroken save where a pale moon, travelling down to the horizon, showed faintly through some jagged clouds. Beneath, the sea stretched a still more somber expanse of gray, from out which the dirge of the waves rose unceasingly with its hopeless "break, break, break." Behind her lay the dim churchyard, where the chill ocean breeze seemed to wander, "soughing under its breath," as if it had somehow lost its way among the ghostly white tombstones which accentuated the gloom.

Madge drew her cloak more closely round her and shrank under the shelter afforded by the projecting corner of the church porch. The days in which she used to rejoice in the wash of the waves and the rush of the sea breeze were past forever now.

A light shone in one of the church windows above the organ, and presently the tones of Chopin's sublime funeral march sounded. To Madge's fancy, those grand strains had ever seemed less like music evoked by mortal fingers from an instrument made by mortal hands than a story of human agony, desolation, and death acted out before her "mind's eye." There were the dull, monotonous beats as of heavy hearts, heavy feet conveying a heavy burthen; suddenly athwart this there seemed to come a triumphant outburst of resurrection joy as from a church towards which the mourners were journeying with their heavy burthen. Then there began once more the dull, monotonous beat of heavy footsteps, heavy hearts returning with half of themselves left behind.

But, tonight, the wizardry of the music conjured up another scene to her fancy. Those dull, heavy, monotonous chords were not human footsteps journeying to a church, but the weary feet of cattle being driven along a heavy road—a slow herd going with lagging tread from the market to the slaughterhouse. What had seemed to her a burst of resurrection joy came now as a wail, with the echo of words in it which she had somewhere heard before:

"There are some who from cradle to grave never have a chance given them."

Suddenly a hand was laid on her shoulder. She turned to find Lance bending over her. She thanked Heaven for the shelter of her black veil.

"I knew your figure at once," he said. "I've been home—they told me where I should find you. Madge, come around this corner—the people are leaving the church now—and I will tell you why I have come here tonight."

Madge followed him to the side of the church which she had just quitted, where the dull, dark-gray stretch of sky hung above the duller, darker, grayer stretch of sea.

His words did not seem to come easily. They stood there in silence for a few minutes, a silence broken by the tread of the congregation leaving the church, by the dying strains of the solemn funeral march, by the slow "break, break" of the waves.

When at last he spoke, his voice was very unlike that of the light-hearted young fellow with whom at one time she had delighted to fence and to squabble.

"I don't think, Madge, the funeral service you've been attending tonight is one quarter so sad as the wedding I was at this morning!" he said, "If you could have seen Eric's face! Depend upon there'll be a tragedy in his home before the year is out."

Madge said nothing.

The words, "Why should there be?" trembled on her lips, but she dared not speak them.

He went on:

"He loves the girl he has married to distraction; but he doesn't trust her—it was on his face as he led her out of the church. I said to myself, 'Thank Heaven, it won't be thus between Madge and me! Whatever there is not between us, there will at least be perfect truth and trust.' And then I started back aghast at my own effrontery, asking myself what right I had to expect any woman to trust me all in all, when I had trusted her not at all—when, in fact, half my heart was hidden away from her. So there and then I made up my mind, dear, that before I met you at the church in the morning I would go to you and lay my heart bare to you that as we are to be husband and wife in name, so should we be in deed and in truth—that there should be no past, no present, no future to come between us."

His voice had kindled with his last sentence. He paused, evidently expecting a word from Madge.

None came, so he repeated:

"No past to separate us, do you see, Madge?"

Madge's lips parted, but instead of a gently murmured assent there came a low, half-stifled sob.

He drew her towards him.

"Don't be frightened, Madge," he said, gently. "I have no confession to make that need part us, unless you so will it. You know half my secret already—it concerns Jane Shore."

Madge shuddered, and shrank from his touch.

"Does it pain you?" he asked. "Shall I stop? Don't you see, dear, I am raising the ghost of this past, so as to set it at rest forever."

"Go on," was all she could bring her lips to utter in low, all but inaudible tone.

"It is soon told, Madge," he went on. "You may have thought that I only pitied this girl and wanted to help her out of kindness. It was not that—I loved her, truly, honestly, passionately; and once here, on this very spot, as we stood together looking at the stars, I made her an offer of marriage."

Madge started and began to tremble violently.

"She would not listen to me," Lance went on, speaking hurriedly now. "She said there was ill fortune hanging over her head—"

He stopped abruptly; his voice grew unsteady. "Madge," he said, brokenly, "do you know sometimes I think that she ended her life solely to prevent me from linking mine to hers."

But here his words failed him.

It was a minute or more before he could go on.

"And now that you know everything, dear, will you forgive me if I say I can't bear the thought of her out of my heart? Will you think that such a thought as this ought to separate us one from the other, or will you share it with me—the tenderness and pity for her I mean?"

Again, he broke off.

Madge's veiled face and solemn silence made him wonder.

The chill breeze swept past. The leaden clouds overhead parted and let the pale moonlight filter through. It threw a gaunt shadow here and there; one, that of a tall white cross, which stood out from the ranks of square tombstones, fell in clear outline at Madge's very feet.

"Lift your veil, dear," he said. "Put your hands in mine; look up in my face! Let us say to each other that as we join hands so will we join hearts, with never a thought to divide us."

Madge's trembling hand lifted her veil from her white face, but she dared not lift her eyes to meet his.

He held her hands fast, her head bowed over them.

"Look up, Madge," he said, "speak to me. Let me hear from your lips that not this nor anything else can come between us now."

Madge's lips moved, but with the shadow of that cross lying at her feet, she dared not speak the words he craved.

Another shadow fell, at that moment, athwart her hands as Lance held them, and thence to the ground at her feet, a shadow rounded, shaped as of a woman's figure.

Madge started and turned to see who stood behind them.

On the topmost of the steps leading up to the porch and well clear of its shadowy arch, there seemed to stand the tall, slight figure of a woman, clad in gray draperies, with white face upturned to the faint moon.

Madge gave a low, terrified cry. Only Lance's arms prevented her from foiling senseless to the ground.

XXXIV

I saw nothing—absolutely nothing," said Lance. "All I know is that Madge gave a startled cry and fell forward fainting. Her nerves, I should say, were overstrung—she has been far from well lately, you know—and she fancied she saw something. It was a thousand pities she attempted the funeral service."

The Vicar had come to Lance's aid in the churchyard, and between them they had got Madge down to her carriage, and thence home. Arrived at home, she had gone from one fainting fit into another during the early part of the night, and now, weak and exhausted, lay upon her bed while Sir Peter and Lance together discussed the strange occurrence.

Sir Peter echoed Lance's regret. "Yes, a thousand pities," he said, pushing back his chair and indulging in a brisk trot round the room, "but I've no doubt she'll be all right again by the morning; a good night's rest works wonders"—this was said at Lance's elbow. "And the little trip to Italy is just the very thing she's needing"—this was said at the door. "I say, Lance!"—here he came back at a run to Lance's elbow once more, with a look on his face which proclaimed a serious subject for thought on hand now.

Lance looked at him absently. He was leaning forward as he sat gazing dreamily into the fire. His appearance was scarcely that of a happy hearted bridegroom who expected to have his happiness crowned on the morrow.

Sir Peter was determined to have the whole of his attention.

"I say, Lance," he said again, raising his voice, "I do hope they'll remember to unmuffle that bell at the church; it would be dreadful if they started your wedding peal tomorrow with a muffled C."

Then he set off on tramp again once more.

"Oh, they'll think of it right enough. The men are supposed to have an idea or two about their work."

"I think I had better send down a message in the morning to make sure—or two, perhaps; one to the Vicar, and one to the verger?"

Here he paused in his quick march for a moment in front of his writing table, as if intending there and then to despatch his notes to Vicar and verger. He took up a pen, felt its nib, then laid it down and rubbed his eyes.

"The truth of it is I'm horribly sleepy," he said, deprecatingly, as if the fact called for an apology. "I've had, on the whole, a busy day—a busy and exciting day, I might say."

Lance roused himself from his reverie.

"If I were you, I should go to bed. You'll have lots to do tomorrow, you know."

Sir Peter rubbed his eyes again.

"Yes, I suppose, off and on, there will be a good deal on my hands," he said, complacently, "and one can't do without sleep altogether."

"I wouldn't try if I were you. It's past two—"

"Yes, and I must be up early. I've told Simmonds to call me at five. And, by the way, Lance, don't you think an awning should be put up from the church to the gate?—it might rain, you know. By the way, I wonder if it will rain; I'll just tap the barometer again."

"The one outside your bedroom door is more dependable than this, and here's your lamp, Uncle Peter," said Lance, facilitating as far as possible the old gentleman's departure.

Halfway up the stairs he paused, calling to Lance over the balusters "I say, Lance, I suppose there really is nothing to keep me up any longer? Madge is really coming around all right, isn't she?"

"Lady Judith said she left her asleep half an hour ago, and her maid has gone to bed in the next room—there can be nothing to keep you up. Goodnight."

Sir Peter went a step or two higher, then came to a standstill again. "And you may set your mind at rest about that bell, Lance," lie said. "I shall go to sleep with it on my mind and think of it the very first thing in the morning, so don't you trouble about it."

But Lance made no reply this time.

He had gone back to the study, and his gloomy thoughts swooping down upon him once more, his ears were shut to Sir Peter's voice.

He leaned moodily against the mantel piece, staring into the live coals—his thoughts a turmoil so far as the present was concerned, and a blank as to the future.

What was it that had changed Madge so much of late? What was the reason of her extraordinary terror in the church-yard, and, above all, why was it that she had failed, in response to his direct appeal, to give pledge for pledge, and reciprocate trust with trust? These were the uppermost of the doubts which presented themselves for solution. But below these, sounding a deeper note, were other doubts and questions equally difficult to answer. Did this marriage that he was about to contract with Madge really promise happiness in the future for her, for him, or, to put it on a lower ground, contentment and satisfaction? Had he been wise in thus yielding to Uncle Peter's wishes? Was not the past too real, too living for it to be hurried in this way into its grave of oblivion?

The fire burned low; the lamp on the table grew dim while these thoughts, in slow procession, trooped across his brain. The room was a large one; it seemed all shadows at the farther end, save where the half-open door admitted a faint patch of lamplight from the dimly lighted, outer hall.

Across this faint patch of light there suddenly fell a stronger gleam as from a lamp carried by hand. A tremulous hand, too, it must have been, for the gleam wavered; now high, now low, it fell upon the floor.

"It's Uncle Peter back again," thought Lance, leaving his leaning posture at the fireplace and going to the door.

But in the doorway he paused, astonished to see not Sir Peter but Madge descending the broad flight of stairs, in some long, trailing, white gown.

His first thought was that she was walking in her sleep; a second look undeceived him. Her steps were too rapid and unsteady for those of a sleep-walker, also her eyes had not the fixed, staring expression of a dreamer, but were bright and dancing. The light of her lamp, thrown upward on her face, emphasized its pallid wanness, framed in a cloudy halo of short, dusky, dishevelled hair.

"Why, Madge, what is it?" he cried, advancing to meet her and taking the lamp from her hand.

"I have something to say to you—something I must say at once—tonight, for I cannot live through another night with it unsaid," answered Madge, in low, unsteady tones, as she passed in front of him into the library.

He followed her in simple, blank astonishment. He set down her lamp on a side table and laid his hand on her shoulder.

"Say on, dear, if it must be said," he answered, kindly.

And standing thus facing her, and looking down into her troubled face, he was struck with the havoc which sleepless nights and anxious days had wrought in her. Madge, at her best, would never have been a beauty; but he had been accustomed to see her piquante, radiant, full of animation and spirits. It seemed impossible that aught but years of actual bodily suffering could have sharpened her features in this fashion, traced such rings round her eyes, and lines of care about her mouth.

Her eyes did not meet his as they stood thus. They went wandering hither and thither, now to the dark corners at the farther end of the room, anon to the half-opened door with a searching, terrified look in them.

'What is it, Madge?" he asked. "What do you think you see there?

And then another fear took possession of him. This might be the first stage of some delirious fever. The right course would be to get her as quickly as possible back to her room.

He took her hands in his.

"Wouldn't it be better to get back to your room, Madge, and try for some sleep?" he asked. "Tomorrow you can tell me anything you like, you know."

Madge did not seem to hear him, though he could feel her thrill to his touch. Her eyes were still wandering from corner to corner, the terror in them deepening.

"Do you see anything?" she asked, presently, in a frightened whisper.

"Nothing—absolutely," he answered, the impression that she was suffering from delirium growing upon him. "Come, Madge, let me see you up the stairs again to your room. It'll soon be morning; try and get an hour or two of sleep."

She drew a long breath and looked up in his face.

"Sleep!" she repeated. "I tell you there will be no sleep for me till I've told you the truth—the whole truth from beginning to end!"

She looked down on his hands which still clasped her cold, trembling ones in a warm grasp, and suddenly bowed her head over them, kissing them passionately.

"Oh dear, dear hands!" she cried, brokenly, "how can I speak words which will make them grow cold as death to me!"

Lance grew alarmed.

"I don't think anything you could tell me would bring that about, Madge," he answered, gravely; but for all that his heart quaked for what her tale might be.

She looked up in his face piteously.

"Not if I were to tell you—that it was I who drove Jane Shore out of the house and sent her to her death?" she asked, bringing out the words with difficulty, and with many a pause between them.

His hands let go at once.

"Wh—at!" he cried hoarsely, and he recoiled a step, staring at her blankly.

Madge's breath came in gasps.

"It's true! It's true!" she cried, bringing out her words now in a rush. "I found out her secret, and flashed it out on her, on the night of the ball, in the picture placed opposite the mirror in my boudoir; and—and—and—you know the rest."

And the confession made now, she sank, trembling, into a chair which stood near, covering her face with her hands.

Lance drew a step nearer. His face had suddenly grown hard, white, rigid.

"Will you be good enough to tell me what that secret was, and how you found it out?" he asked, in a voice that matched his face.

Madge drew her hands from her face, looking up at him wonderingly. Was this Lance's voice, with a ring of iron in it, in place of its usual mellow kindliness.

His set face repeated his question.

Then Madge, with trembling lips, and in tone so low that sank at times to whisper, repeated the story which the newspaper paragraph had told. Once or twice she nearly broke down was hard story to tell to the man standing there facing her, with arms folded on his chest, and white, set face.

Only once he interrupted her to ask the question who had possession of the newspaper now. But that one interruption nearly brought her story to an abrupt ending, and was with many halt and voice that threatened to fail her altogether, that she resumed and told the finish of that ill-fated night of the ball—Jane Shore's visit to her room, and her farewell threat.

Lance drew a deep breath as she finished speaking, but said never a word.

She clasped her hands together, looking up piteously into his face. "Oh, Lance!" she cried, "do not look at me like that—speak to me, tell me you forgive me now that I have told you the whole truth!"

His face grew harder still. "Will your telling me the whole truth raise her from the dead and give her back to me? He asked in harsh, cold tones. Then he turned his back on her and went towards the door.

She sprang after him and laid one hand on his arm. "Lance, Lance," she cried passionately, "do not leave me like this! We must not part in this way!"

It was easy to read her sentence in his eyes. They said plainly enough: "Everything is at an end between us! All I ask of you now is to keep out of my sight to the last hour of my life!"

"Speak to me, speak to me," she implored, "one word, just one word of kindness or pity!"

"Kindness! Pity!" he repeated.

Madge's head drooped. "I know—I know," she said, "what would say, that I had neither kindness nor pity for her. But if you did know what I have suffered, what I do suffer—"

Her voice gave way, though her eyes were dry. She bowed her head on the hand which clutched his arm.

"You could not help forgiving me if you only knew how I have been—how I am punished," she went on, piteously. "She has kept her word; she stood behind me in the churchyard tonight; she followed me home and sat behind my bed; she came down the stairs with me."

She broke off for a moment, then suddenly lifted her face to his once more. "Look in my face," she said humbly, pleadingly. "You can see what I have suffered."

His words came stern and wrathful now.

"You looked in her face and saw what she had suffered; but did that teach you pity?" he asked, striving as he spoke to release his arm from her clasp.

But there had come to her fingers a strength twice their own, and their clasp did not loosen. There rose up in her mind some faint sense of injustice. It seemed as if her great love for him, as well as her suffering, must be written on her face, and plead for her.

"You do not know—you do not understand," she faltered, then broke off.

The story of this great, passionate love of hers would be even harder to tell than had been the story of her mercilessness to the woman who had threatened to frustrate that love.

"After all these years," she began, then broke off again.

All his reply was the endeavour once more to unloosen her fingers.

She could bear it no longer.

"Oh, Lance, Lance, it was for you, because I loved you," she cried passionately.

And then tears came to her at last, and she bowed her head once more on his arm.

But it was to be neither a rest nor hiding place for her now. He released himself from her clasping, trembling hands. For once he raised his voice, "Then I would to Heaven that you had hated me," he said, hotly, turning away from her towards the door once more.

She put herself between him and the door.

"Oh, Lance, Lance," she implored, "don't leave me thus; only say you'll forgive me, or, if you cannot do that, say you will try to in the years to come—some day, some long way off perhaps."

Then she threw herself on her knees at his feet, crying brokenly:

"Oh, Lance, Lance, kill me, punish me, do anything cruel you please to me, but only tell me you'll try to forgive me in the years to come. We must not part in this way. In this life we may never set eyes on each other again."

He put her clasped hands stretched upward to his face away, and passed on to the door. He turned and gave her one last farewell look as she crouched on the floor in her tumbled white draperies, her weeping face hidden now in her hands.

"I pray Heaven," he said in low constrained tones that emphasized his prayer, "that in this life I may never set eyes on your face again."

XXXV

Madge crouched on that floor till day-break, hiding her face in her hands. Not till the cold gray light of early dawn began to find its way in through the chinks of the shutters did she dare to withdraw those hands, lest from out some dark corner there should loom forth a white face and shadowy form.

Her limbs were stiffened, her brain felt dazed, and all power of weeping seemed to have left her, when, at length, she made her way back to her room. All power of feeling seemed to have left her also. Had Lance stood before her once more she could not have raised the feeblest plea pity and forgiveness for the Madge Cohen who had sinned and suffered. The reaction from the overstrain of passion was so complete as to seem a positive lull of pain. Over and over again she said to herself, as she threw herself face downwards on her pillows, "He prayed Heaven that he might never see my face again," but the bitter words touched no answering chord now. An odd feeling of drowsiness was beginning to creep over her, and she seemed to feel, think, see, and hear, as it were, through a haze.

As the day grew, sounds of movement about the house began. She heard Lance's footsteps pass along the gallery outside her room.

"Dear footsteps," she said to herself, softly; "I should know them among a thousand."

Then in a dim far off sort of way she heard his voice outside below her windows giving some order, and presently the sound of wheels and horses' feet told that his dog cart was being brought round. She knew in the same dim far off way that this meant departure; he was going away—for how long she knew not—and she lacked power—and will, too, it seemed now—to prevent him.

For one moment there came to her a sudden wild longing to look her last at him. To see him, as she had seen him so many times before, strong, and beautiful in his strength, driving those strong, beautiful horses would be a sight to thank Heaven for. She made one great effort, gathering together all the strength that was left in her. It was inadequate, however, to carry her to the window. She succeeded in lifting herself from the bed only to fall helplessly into a chair, on whose high back she had rested her hand for support. And seated there with face turned towards the window, through which the rosy light of morning was now streaming, she heard the crack of Lance's whip, the plunge of his horses, and presently the sound of wheels dying in the distance.

Then drowsiness like a thick cloud seemed to enfold her once more, and thought became a blank to her. And one coming into that room and seeing her seated thus facing the window with head thrown back, and the bright morning sunshine falling on her pale face, might have exclaimed: "One could fancy that sleeping woman was dead!" or another gazing down on her might have said, "Hush, one could fancy that dead woman was sleeping!"

The hour which Madge had passed crouching on the study floor, had been a busy one for Lance. It was in a white heat of passion that lie had shaken her touch from his arm, and turned his back on her; but it was a white heat that had method and purpose in it. As he had stood listening to her confession, that purpose had formed. The woman he had loved had been surrounded with mystery from the first day he had known her, and the cloud of a terrible suspicion rested on her grave. To clear that mystery, to lift that cloud, should henceforth be the purpose of his life; till this was accomplished everything else in creation would be as naught to him.

His heart was very bitter against Madge.

At that moment it was simply out of his power to form any—even the most shadowy—conception of her great, passionate love for him. He realised only that she had failed in what seemed to him one of woman's best qualities—pity for the forlorn and desolate, and had, by an act of unexampled cruelty, wrecked his whole life for him. If she had been a man, he had said to himself, he would have known how to deal with her; as it was, her conscience would punish her; and so he dismissed her from his thoughts.

He left the study with the intention of making immediate preparations for a journey to Corsica, where he purposed fully investigating the attempt at murder with which Madge had associated Miss Shore. Before he started, however, he would see and explain matters to Sir Peter; also, he would put a few questions to Mr. Stubbs and demand of him the newspaper containing the paragraph from which Madge had drawn inspiration for her picture.

Both interviews, he judged, must wait till a later hour. Meantime, he roused his servant, gave sundry directions as to his packing, and transmitted orders to the stable for his cart to be brought round in time for him to save the first train from Lower Upton.

On his way back from the servants' quarters he had occasion to pass a small room where Madge was accustomed to write her letters, and where had been placed a small davenport for her sole use. A light shining under the door of this room attracted his attention; it seemed to be extinguished at the approach of his footsteps. A suspicion of burglars for one moment flashed across his mind, and he at once opened the door, to find, not burglars, but Mr. Stubbs immediately behind it. This was the same room in which Madge had, upon one occasion, discovered the self-same individual in a listening posture.

Lance stared at the man uncompromisingly; he looked disturbed and flurried.

"What, in the name of fortune, are you doing here at this hour?" cried the young man; and now, for the first time, it occurred to him that, possibly, this man, whom he had been wont to describe as a "harmless old fellow, who did what he was told, and never got in anybody's way," was not quite what he had imagined him to be.

"I was just on the point of going to bed, sir; I've had a heavy night's work—I've been going through some of Mrs.Cohen's papers," here he glanced at the davenport, "at her request, sir."

Lance still stared hard at the man. He did not see written on his face that the fact that Madge's sudden illness had filled him with consternation, and had sent him listening about the house in the dead of night; that, from what he had heard, he had drawn the inevitable conclusion that women were undependable allies, and that it as high time he looked to himself, and made provision for the future. All Lance saw in the low brow and narrowing eyes which fronted him was a look of mingled cunning and servility, that filled him with an unutterable contempt, not alone for this miserable specimen of humanity, but also for the woman who could stoop to such a confederate.

"I believe," he said, keeping his eyes fixed contemptuously on the evidently disconcerted Mr.Stubbs, "that Mrs.Cohen has employed you in more than one confidential capacity?"

Mr.Stubbs plucked up courage.

"I am proud to say, sir, I have enjoyed Mrs.Cohen's entire confidence, of late," he replied.

"Very well then, be so good as to fetch me a newspaper which on one occasion you took the trouble to lay before Mrs.Cohen—it contains the account of an attempt at murder at Santa Maura."

Mr.Stubb's face turned to an ashy whiteness. So, then, he conjectures had been correct. Madge had snapped the alliance between them by making full confession of the part she played. The question was now, how far had she betrayed his complicity in the matter?

"Did you hear what I said?" asked Lance, his face taking an expression which seemed to Mr.Stubbs a remarkably unpleasant one.

"It's here, sir; here, sir," he said, going to the davenport and taking thence a newspaper, which Lance at once took possession of, "Mrs. Cohen has kept it here ever since I gave it to her. And, sir, will you be so good as to remember that in this matter, from first to last, I have acted entirely under Mrs.Cohen's orders?"

"I congratulate you on the fidelity with which you have carried them out. May I ask your motive for placing a paragraph of this sort in Mrs. Cohen's hand, instead of in Sir Peter's or mine?"

"I knew Mrs.Cohen's anxiety on the matter, sir; we have been on a very confidential footing, as I've already told you, sir, for some time past. Mrs.Cohen's orders were imperative—I did my best, sir, to carry them out."

Lance, with his wrath against Madge still at white heat, began to see a sufficient reason for the appointment of this wretched being to the lucrative post of land steward at Redesdale.

What Mr.Stubbs considered an unpleasant expression of countenance deepened on his face.

"I have only this to say," he said, contemptuously, as he folded the newspaper and put it in his pocket, "I shall advise Sir Peter to send you about your business as quickly as possible, and you may thank your stars that you are an old man instead of a young one, otherwise I should send you out of the house a little quicker than Sir Peter could." Then he turned on his heel and left the man to his own reflections.

Five o'clock was striking as Lance went along the gallery towards his own room. With the last stroke of the clock, Sir Peter's door opened and Sir Peter, fully dressed, came out.

"What, you there, Lance?" he cried. "Now, isn't it a good thing I can wake myself at any hour I choose? If I had depended upon Simmonds I should be sound asleep still, and there's that churchbell and a hundred other things to see before breakfast—"

Lance laid his hand on the old gentleman's shoulder.

"Come into my room for a few minutes, Uncle Peter, I've something to say to you," he said.

"Eh?" said Sir Peter, blithely, "no doubt you have, my boy! I dare say, like me, you've a good many thing on your mind just now—not to be wondered at in a bridegroom elect."

He, a bridegroom elect! From his haggard look and disordered appearance it would have been easier to believe that he had been making preparations for his funeral rather than his wedding.

Lance lost not time in preamble.

"There'll be no wedding today, nor any other day, so far as I am concerned," he said, as he shut the door behind Sir Peter; "I am going away, at once, to Corsica."

"At once! to Corsica!" repeated Sir Peter, utterly unable to credit his senses.

"Yes, I shall start in about half an hour's time. I have something to do there—read this"—here he handed the newspaper to Sir Peter—"I have just heard, for the first time, that Miss Shore is supposed to be the person who made the attempt at murder there related. I shall make it my business to prove the supposition false."

But Sit Peter's senses were still beclouded.

"Miss Shore—attempt at murder—I don't understand," he repeated, blankly.

Lance grew impatient. "If you'll read that paragraph, you will understand—I've no time to go into details; I tell you, simply, I'm off to Corsica at once, to do my utmost to clear the reputation of a young lady who was once a guest in this house."

Sir Peter, recollecting a certain half-hour he had spent with Lance at Liverpool, began to understand. "But, my dear boy, what will Madge say—"

"Madge has said all she has to say on the matter—to me," interrupted Lance, sharply; "and I may as well tell you at once that everything is at an end between Madge and me."

"No, no, no! my dear boy," cried Sir Peter, "no, no, not possible! You don't mean to say—you can't—that there's to be no wedding this morning?"

Lance cross the room and stood in front of Sir Peter.

"Uncle Peter," he said, "look in my face and see that I mean every word I say. I would put a bullet through my brain sooner than marry Madge Cohen."

But Uncle Peter could not look steadily in the young man's face, his eyes were beginning to blink very hard, and for the moment he dared not trust his voice.

There came a rap at the door, and a servant announced that the cart was brought round.

Lance hailed thankfully an excuse for cutting his farewell short. "I'll write to you from Dover," he said; "I shall most likely have an hour or two to wait there. Shake hands, Uncle Peter, there's nothing for you to break your heart over." This was added a little bitterly, with emphasis on the pronoun.

Uncle Peter held out his hand; once, twice he cleared his throat very loudly, but still words would not come.

Lance's hard, even voice was curious contrast to the old gentleman's want of self control. "I would suggest that you should take the blame of the broken engagement on yourself," said the young man; "it will be easy for you to say that you did not consider that I, in my changed position, was a suitable match for Madge, with her wealth—it might save any feeling of wounded pride on her part."

There was a touch of sarcasm in his voice as he said the last words. But, for all that, there was no doubt that he meant them. He might, in his wrath, have prayed for the right to kill her, as she stood confessing the deed she had done; he would never have prayed for the right to confer an insult on her.

The words "In my changed position" brought back Sir Peter's voice, though but a quaking, tremulous voice.

"Lance," he said, huskily, holding the young man's hand in a tight grip, "whereever you go, whatever you do, don't forget what I said to you a little while ago, that if you do not take the place of my eldest son now, you take that of my youngest and best loved—best loved, do you hear Lance?"

"Thank you, Uncle Peter. At present the future is blank to me; but I shall always be glad to remember your farewell words."

"And, Lance," the old gentleman went on, still holding Lance's hands in his, "you'll draw your supplies as usual; you won't let this—this make any difference?"

Lance's reply was short and all but inaudible.

Then he wrenched his hand away and was gone.

And Sir Peter, after gazing blankly at the closed door for a moment or two, sat down and cried like a child over his broken toys.

XXXVI

That was to be a day of departures. Sir Peter had scarcely time to dry his eyes and reflect on what a harassing day's work he would have to get through, before Mr. Stubbs, equipped for travelling, presented himself.

If Sir Peter had not been so occupied with his own depressing subjects of thought he would have noticed the anxious look on the man's face, the nervous twitching of the corners of his mouth.

"I've come to say good-bye. Sir Peter. I suppose I had better start at once," he said, looking this way, that way, all ways; but never once at Sir Peter.

"Eh! what! You going, too, Stubbs?" exclaimed Sir Peter, trying all in a moment to collect his thoughts and arrange some settled plan for meeting the day's difficulties. The warmth of Sir Peter's greeting reassured Mr. Stubbs. Things had happened then as he had surmised they might—Mr. Clive had been so occupied with his own affairs that he had forgotten to give Sir Peter the warning he had threatened respecting the rascality of the man he employed to open his letters.

"I think the sooner I start the better, if you've no objection, Sir Peter," he replied. "You see, I enter upon my duties at Redesdale, in ten days' time. You were good enough to tell me I might take a ten days' holiday before I got to work there—"

"Yes, yes; I remember, my good friend. Take a holiday, and welcome; but—"

Here he broke off, and began what, compared with his usual quick tramp back- wards and forwards, was a veritable funeral march from end to end of the room.

"I will make it my business, before anything else," Mr. Stubbs went on, "to inquire fully into the antecedents of the gentleman who has been recommended as my successor here, and, meantime, there is the lad the Vicar spoke of."

"Yes, yes, I know; but I was thinking whether I could do without you today. I've a very great deal to see to and arrange."

Sir Peter paused abruptly in his walk. Now, how far should he take Mr. Stubbs into his confidence on this very delicate matter"

"Do you refer to the wedding arrangements?" asked Mr.Stubbs, scanning furtively Sir Peter's anxious features.

"No, no. I fear—a—h'm—I greatly fear, Stubbs, the wedding will have to be put off—for a time, that is."

"Put off, sir!" This was said with a great show of surprise. "May I ask if anything unforeseen has occurred?"

Sir Peter thought for a moment. The only way he could see out of his difficulties that day was by the juvenile course of fibbing. He must fib prodigiously all day long, he said to himself, so he might as well begin at once.

"No, no; nothing unforeseen has happened. I'm sorry to say I've noticed for some time past, that Mrs.Cohen's health has been failing, and by my express advice—my advice, do you see, Mr.Stubbs?—the wedding will be deferred till she pulls round a little."

"I see, Sir Peter. And Mr. Clive has started off, I suppose, for Carstairs, to get further medical advice?" asked Mr. Stubbs, still furtively regarding Sir Peter.

"Exactly, exactly," exclaimed Sir Peter.

"Splendid idea, that," he thought to himself, "I'll enlarge upon it."

"At least," he went on, "I advised that course; but Mr. Clive said: 'No, there's not a man in Carstairs I'd trust in a case like this; I shall go straight to London and consult a man there who makes fainting fits a specialty.'"

And then the old gentleman sighed and thought to himself:

"Dear me, I wonder if I shall forget all that, and say something quite different before the day's out!"

Mr. Stubbs was all sympathy.

"I fear it will be a harassing time for you. Sir Peter; I would willingly stay on a day or two longer, but I've some pressing private affairs of my own—"

"Ah yes, that boy of yours; I remember you told me all about him, and I promised you a cheque, didn't I, in addition to your pay?"

"I should be very grateful for it, Sir Peter I'm outfitting him now for the Colonies, and, as I told you, should like to give him a little capital to start with."

"Ah, yes I remember. Come into the study a minute, you shall have your cheque at once and don't forget, any one asks you about the wedding being put off, it's all my doing, on account of Mrs. Cohen's health, and Mr. Clive has gone to Carstairs—no, to London, I mean, to consult leading doctor about her."

So Mr. Stubbs departed with a handsome cheque in addition to his handsome quarterly salary. And if any one had taken the trouble to watch his movements on his arrival at Carstairs, they might have seen that, instead of taking a ticket direct for London as he had told Sir Peter he intended to do, he made Liverpool his destination.

Sir Peter's fibs grew in number and variety as the day went on. Lady Judith unintentionally gave an impetus to them.

About seven o'clock she rustled downstairs in an extra allowance of skirt and floating lace lappets, expecting to find arrangements for the wedding in a satisfactory state of progress. The hints which her maid had let fall during the process of dressing as to a troubled condition of the household atmosphere, had been uttered so timorously that they had not arrested her attention.

Sir Peter met her at the foot of the stairs, feeling that the sooner she was put into possession of the leading facts of the matter the better.

"Madge is not down—she is no better," he shouted into her ears. "Wedding must be put off—I've sent for the Vicar."

Lady Judith was all startled attention in a moment.

"This comes of doing thing in a hurry—" she began.

Sir Peter knew that a sermon would follow on this text, but did not feel in the mood to personate an audience.

"Lance has gone to London to consult doctor—bring back one with him," he shouted again.

"Lance gone—where? Bring back whom?" questioned the lady, only catching half his sentence.

"Stubbs has gone off, too—to London," Sir Peter went on, anxious to put her in possession of all the facts necessary for her to know in as short a space of time as possible.

"What, Stubbs and Lance are gone off together?"

"No, not together, one after the other."

"What, Lance has gone off after Stubbs! Another *protégé* has disappeared! They do you credit, Sir Peter, I must say, these *protégés* of yours! First one, then another! They make themselves at home in the house, and get all they can out of you, and then they disappear and commit suicide, or do something; else disgraceful. And as for Lance going in pursuit of the man, I do think—"

"No, no, no," shouted Sir Peter, "Stubbs is right enough—Lance—too." Then he tip-toed, and with a stentorian voice, added—"Gone—after—doctors."

And it was not until Lady Judith had commenced an oration on the folly of two men starting in quest of one doctor—before which he beat a hasty retreat—that he realised the fact that his story had already slightly deviated from its original form.

But later on in the day when he began seriously to consider the state of affairs, the reality of the estrangement between Lance and Madge, and the difficulties which might lie in the way of putting things once more on an amicable footing between them, it occurred to him that an even greater modification of his original statement was necessary.

The Vicar, who was to have performed the wedding ceremony, was looked upon as the fountain head of gossip in the neighbourhood; to him, therefore, it would be necessary to tell a story which the county would be expected to credit, as a true statement of affairs.

So when the worthy clergyman, in response to a hurried note from Sir Peter, presented himself at the Castle, the story to which he was asked to give credence was that Sir Peter had taken advantage of the weak state of Mrs. Cohen's health to defer a marriage, which, since the change in Mr.Clive's position, was scarcely so desirable a match for her as it had at one time seemed.

"Heaven help me!" sighed the old gentleman, buttoning up his coat and going for a weary little trot by himself in the Park.

"How I'm to remember all these different stories and stick to the right one to the right person, is more than I know!"

Before, however, that day came to an end, Sir Peter had ceased to trouble about the number and variety of his fibs, in fact, had no heart left in him for fibs of any sort.

About noon a message was brought to him from Madge that she wished to see him at once and alone. Sir Peter went up to her room to find her seated in the same high-backed chair into which she had fallen in her endeavour to get a last glimpse of Lance. There her maid had found her on resuming her attendance at seven o'clock in the morning, and seated thus she had endured a disturbing quarter of an hour of Lady Judith's society. Neither the maid nor Lady Judith, however, had read in Madge's face the story of her utterly broken physical health; to both she had protested a little feebly, it might be, that she felt better and would be quite herself before the day was over. Sir Peter was not a sharp sighted man, and as a rule nothing was easier than to persuade him into taking an optimistic view of the gloomiest situation. On this occasion, however, his first look into Madge's face put all optimistic views to flight, and sent him to her side with a pained, startled cry on his lips:

"My child, my child, what is it—what has pulled you down in this way?"

Madge was still in the long, white gown she had worn overnight. Her hair strayed in loose disorder about her white face. Her head leaned wearily on one hand, the other rested on the arm of the chair.

"Hasn't Broughton been to see you, my child? He must be sent for at once!" pursued Sir Peter, making for the bell there and then to give orders for the immediate attendance of the doctor.

Madge's voice arrested him; it sounded weak, and far away—so far away, indeed, that he could almost have fancied that she was speaking to him from the other side of a wall.

"Not now, not yet. Will you sit down a moment? I have something to say to you—to you," she added, correctingly.

"I know all, my child; Lance has told me," said Sir Peter, hurriedly, thinking that he knew to what she referred.

Then as he looked down into her haggard face with something written on it which he had never seen there before, he uttered his first and only reproach against Lance.

"Why is not Lance here?" he cried.

"It's disgraceful that with you in this state he should start off on a wild fancy of his own!"

Madge sighed. "Lance was right to go; if he had not gone I must—"

She broke off for a moment. Then she took Sir Peter's hand in hers. "Will you sit down and listen to me?" she said, faintly. "It isn't the story I told Lance—it won't take long to tell."

Sir Peter, with a scared look on his face, sat down. And Madge, in a voice scarcely above a whisper, and in a monotone like that of a child repeating a weary lesson, told the story of how she had tampered with the old gentleman's correspondence, and had kept back the tidings of Gervase Critchett's only boy.

Straightforwardly and simply she told the tale. On Mr. Stubbs's share in the matter she touched but lightly—she had no wish to claim palliation for her offence by magnifying his share in it.

"He would have done anything I told him to do for money," she said, simply, in reply to Sir Peter's astonished exclamation, "Stubbs did that!"

Her last word left her without voice wherein to plead for forgiveness. And Sir Peter had no voice wherewith to utter it; but all the same she knew that it lay in his heart for her. And he knew that she knew it was there without any telling on his part.

XXXVII

The other half of a great love is a great humility. Great love knows nothing of self-seeking, self-justification, nor of that miserable plea which little love is so apt to set up, "half my transgression must lie at your door."

Madge's love for Lance, measured by her humility, must have been great indeed. No word of self-justification, from first to last, ever escaped her lips. Not once did she set up, as she very well might have done, the plea, "I did it for Lance." In good truth she felt she had done so badly for the man she loved, that the less she said about it the better. Even what she had purposed she had failed to perform, either through too little courage, or too much conscience. She had put out her hand, as it were, to stop the wheels of fate, with this only result—that her fingers had been crushed in her weak endeavour.

For a day or two she kept her room, dispensing, however, with the doctor's attendance and seeing not a soul but her maid. When she once more joined the family circle she looked literally the ghost of her old bright self. She had never learned the art of the economy of the emotions, and sooner or later her sensitive, passionate nature seemed bound to wear out the slight frame that held it. Sir Peter stood looking at her aghast as she sat under multitudinous wraps shivering beside a huge fire. Her voice, too, as she answered his greeting, thrilled him as the touch of a dead hand might; it was cold, tuneless, far-away, the sort of voice that one lying at the gates of death, and only saved by a miracle from passing through them, might be supposed to bring back to life with him.

Sir Peter fussed a good deal over her that day, suggested all sorts of plans for bringing back the roses to her cheeks, ran over a list of German 'Bads and Swiss Spas as desirable places for her to winter in. Madge listened to him quietly.

"I have made up my mind where to go," she answered, "it will be to Seville—I hope to get away next week."

Sir Peter was all astonishment; his questions came in a string.

Madge put them on one side, unanswered. It would have been difficult to make him see, in the fact of there being at Seville a convent ruled by an Abbess with whom Madge had some slight acquaintance, a sufficient reason for her choice of that city as a place of abode. Yet such was the case. In that convent Madge saw a refuge from the terrors of her conscience which conjured out of every dark corner the face or the form of the woman she believed she had driven to her death. Atonement for this was denied her; but penance still lay in her power, and penance she eagerly grasped at, even though it might involve the necessity for the abandonment of the faith of her childhood.

This Spanish convent was one of the strictest of its order, and Madge knew well enough what rigorous discipline would be included in a life of penitence within its walls. But what matter, if it did hurry her a little faster out of the world than she felt herself going already? Her purpose was fixed, never again in this life to meet the look of Lance's wrathful eyes.

The greatest kindness she could confer on him, and on all her friends, now, it seemed to her, would be, without any fuss of leave-taking, to creep quietly out of life. And as she made her way towards the dark valley, she could lose the sense of that pursuing shape which filled her days with terror and rendered her nights so many waking nightmares, she would feel that Heaven had bestowed blessing upon her such as she had no right to demand.

Madge did something else besides expedite her departure for Spain—sent for lawyer from Carstairs, and gave to him full instructions for the making of will which assigned to Lance the whole of the property she had right to leave away from the Cohen family.

Sir Peter had to be let into the secret of this will, in order that his consent to act as executor to might be obtained.

He fussed a good deal over the affair; there seemed a gloom and a mystery about Madge's doings just then, which acted like a douche of cold water on the bright little fire of hope, that he was perpetually trying to stir into a flame. It was not easy for him to discard his lifelong habit of looking at the cheerful side of things; at the same time, he was bound to admit that there seemed little enough just then, upon which to build his cheerfulness.

Wet, wintry weather set in, and the old gentleman felt that little by little his cheerfulness was, as it were, slipping through his fingers.

"If I could but smoke, it would be something to do," he sighed, looking out drearily from successive windows at the dismal landscape of mountains, half-hidden in mist, leaden sky pouring down rain' in sheets, woods already half-stripped of their foliage. He furtively repeated his juvenile efforts to master the mysteries of tobacco; was compelled to abandon them for reasons which had obtained in his youthful days; and was driven to find other outlets for his energies.

He went about the house ordering big fires to be made wherever there chanced to be a vacant fireplace; sent for a man from Carstairs, and another from Edinburgh, to supply him with plans for increasing the heating apparatus of the corridors and larger rooms. Lady Judith, debarred from her outdoor pastoral amusements, added not a little to his discomfiture by generally superintending his occupations. She complained loudly of the extra warmth he was putting into the bouse, armed herself with a huge fire screen in lieu of a fan, and informed everybody on every possible opportunity that she "suffered so from the heat."

The letter received from Lance, written in a railway carriage on his way to Marseilles, did not mend matters. Madge's name was not so much as mentioned in it; in fact, it seemed written for the whole and sole purpose of saying that he had forgotten to say what a rascal Stubbs was, and that he hoped Sir Peter would get rid of him as soon as possible; the man he was certain had been playing a double game, and he would "stake his life"—these were Lance's words—"that there was no foundation in fact for the evil suspicion he had chosen to fasten upon a young lady who was an utter stranger to him."

Lance in this letter said not a word as to his plans, so Sir Peter naturally concluded that they remained unaltered. A second letter, however, which arrived two days after—when they imagined him to be tossing about on the Mediterranean—showed that these plans had been completely reversed. It was a hasty line, written in pencil, during the railway journey back from Marseilles. In it Lance explained the reason for this return journey. The conviction of Stubbs's rascality had been gradually gaining ground in his mind, he said, and now had taken such hold of him, that, before setting off for Corsica, he thought it wiser to run over to Liverpool and thoroughly test the man's statements as to what had taken place there.

He would himself see and question the local authorities, whose names Stubbs had used so freely; and he could now only wonder over his own and Sir Peter's simplicity in not having adopted such a course before.

It was possible that Stubbs's elaborate accounts of his interview with the municipal and cemetery authorities at Liverpool might be equally unworthy of belief; no one had been at pains to verify them. As for the empty purse, the envelope with the name, Jane Shore, upon and the handkerchief, any one might produce the two first and assign them to any one he pleased and the last, the handkerchief, could be easily obtainable by man who would hunt through waste paper baskets, and listen at keyholes.

If in any way, he added, he found his suspicions of Stubbs verified, he would at once place the matter in the hands of the police. He supposed Sir Peter would have no objection to his doing this. In conclusion, he gave an address to which letters might be sent, and begged Sir Peter to consider his communication as strictly confidential, "for," he added, "if the rascal gets an idea that he is suspected, no doubt he will be off at once."

Sir Peter felt his head go round. The man he had trusted with his private correspondence, his cashbook, his chequebook, to turn out a rascal! In his heart, the old gentleman did not object to a spice of roguery in his *protégés*—it added, so to speak, a piquancy to the exercise of his benevolence. This that Lance charged Stubbs with, however, was downright villainy, which, instead of adding piquancy to his benevolence, took the flavour out of it altogether.

It seemed past belief, yet it was not easy to shake off the impression which Lance's strongly expressed opinions had made upon him. It was altogether bewildering. The worst part was having to keep the whole thing a secret. He would do his best; but still, if it should ooze out that his faith in his late secretary had had a severe shock—well, he dared say no very great harm would be done after all.

He could not resist the temptation of hinting to Madge that possibly it might be as well to reconsider the appointment of Stubbs to the land stewardship at Redesdale.

Madge turned away wearily from the subject.

"The lawyers will see after that," she said. "Let him go. I don't want even to think of him."

In good truth to her—with the thoughts she had in her at the moment—Stubbs and his rascality seemed to be of colossal insignificance.

It may reasonably be doubted whether Sir Peter's power of keeping a secret would have stood the strain put upon it had not a second letter arrived which, for the moment, threw Lance's communication into the shade.

It was received two days before the day which Madge had fixed for her departure to the South. She had spent the morning with Sir Peter at his writing table, going through various matters connected with her Durham property, in the management of which Sir Peter had promised to be her representative during her absence.

"Of course, my dear, I'll do my best in your affairs," he said, "but my hands, as you know, are very full just now!"

They were literally very full at the moment with the unopened letters which the morning's post had brought him.

To emphasize his statement, he. began breaking seals and opening envelopes very fast, keeping up a light flow of talk as he did so.

"Better open this first," he soliloquised, fingering a black edged envelope; "dare say it's from a widow with six or seven children, whom she wants to place out in life or get into schools."

Madge, looking down at the envelope which he threw on the table, recognised the handwriting of the Rev. Joshua Parker.

"Eh! What's this?" cried Sir Peter, dropping his letter and turned a startled, white face toward Madge. "Read it, my dear, read it—I don't seem able to take it in."

Madge picked up the letter and read a few short lines from the Rev. Joshua Parker, enclosing, with many regrets, a letter which the Australian mail had just brought to him. It was from the Wesleyan minister who had succeeded him in his charge at Rutland Bay, and after a brief preamble on the duty of resignation to the will of Heaven, told the said news of the death of Gervase Critchett, of colonial fever, within a month of the departure of the Rev. Joshua Parker from the colony. Full details, the writer stated, would be sent by the next mail.

Sir Peter rubbed his forehead, "I'm all in a maze," he said; "I get a nephew one mail, I lose him the next! I can't realise it, eh, Madge."

Madge said nothing. She realised it sharply enough, and with it realised something else also, that all her careful thought for Lance, her plotting and subterfuges had been after all but so much winnowing of the wind and ploughing of the ocean.

XXXVIII

"I've told you all I can remember of the clear boy—you shall see any subsequent accounts that may come to me from Rutland Bay detailing his illness," said the Rev. Joshua Parker, addressing Sir Peter. "He was always fragile and delicate—that picture, though a little roughly done, is as like him as could be."

The Rev. Joshua Parker had followed his letter to the Castle within twenty-four hours, and now sat narrating to Sir Peter the story of Gervase Critchett's brief life.

The minister's tall, thin figure presented a striking contrast to Sir Peter's short, stout one. He had large features and solemn gray eyes. There was one point of resemblance between the two men—a bald patch on the top of the head in the region of the organ of benevolence, which suggested the idea that the excessive use of that organ had destroyed the roots of the hair.

Sir Peter took up the roughly executed photograph once more. It was that of a boy of a Greek type of beauty, with large, dreamy eyes, and an abundance of curly hair.

"Poor Gervase!" he sighed. "The image of his father! He would have brought back my young days to me!" And then he sighed again.

The minister sighed too. "It is a mysterious dispensation of Providence; a grievous blow to you. Sir Peter, no doubt, and to me also. When I passed this way a month ago and looked up at your Castle, high among the Fells, I said to myself, 'I shall soon be bringing glad tidings to the master of that house;' and lo, instead—" he broke off abruptly. There could be no doubt as to the strength of the bond which had existed between him and the orphan boy.

"You passed this way a month ago?" queried Sir Peter, feeling the necessity of a brief respite from the sad subject. Then, as the recollection of Madge's pitiful confession of a second abstracted letter crossed his mind, he added, hurriedly: "Ah, yes! yes, I remember; it must have been just about the time of my birthday festivities."

"It was just after, Sir Peter. I arrived at Liverpool, on my way to Upton, on the morning of the twenty-second. I remember, during the ensuing week, reading an account of your birthday festivities in a Cumberland paper."

"Ah, you should have been here and taken part in them; we kept things going merrily for nearly a week."

"I should have been at Upton during that week had not my plans been entirely change by an extraordinary occurrence."

"An extraordinary occurrence!" repeated Sir Peter, all eager curiosity in a moment.

But instead of attempting to satisfy that curiosity, Mr. Parker leaned forward in his chair, fixed his solemn eyes full upon Sir Peter, and said, sententiously:

"Once I was a gardener's boy!"

Sir Peter jumped to his feet with a spring, and laid his hand on the minister's shoulder. "Ah," he said, delightedly, "and some benevolent person rescued you from that position, educated you, and sent you forth to teach and to preach?"

Mr. Parker shook his head. "Not a bit of have only myself to thank for the choice of a calling with which I am thoroughly in harmony."

Sir Peter walked away to the window.

Mr. Parker's next words brought him back at a run. They were:

"Have you ever studied the theory of transplanting, Sir Peter?"

"Transplanting, transplanting!" repeated Sir Peter. "That's one of the many thing I have not yet, through pressure of occupation, been able to give thought to."

"Transplanting, transplanting!"

As he said this, it flashed into the old gentleman's mind that the "theory of transplanting," as propounded by the Rev. Joshua Parker, might be a thoroughly congenial one; and instantly there rose up before him a vision of backgrounds of shrubs, and foregrounds of flowers, removed from one corner of the Castle grounds to another, and if they didn't do there, to somewhere else.

"People frequently," the minister continued, "carry out the principles of an art without giving much thought to them. I in my young days not only carried out the principles of the art of transplanting, but thought about them and built a theory on them."

"Ah, an ingenious, thoughtful lad!" said Sir Peter, thinking what a *protégé* this gardener's boy would have made.

"One of the wisest of our statesmen made a noteworthy remark about the uselessness of 'matter in its wrong place.' I never saw a. shrub or flower that needed sunshine pining in the shade, or *vice versa*, without thinking of it. The thing that in its right place would have been a joy and a beauty, and so have played the part it was meant to play in the scheme of creation, was, in its wrong place, simply so much inert, useless matter."

"Ah," murmured Sir Peter, "I'll get you to make the round of my flower garden while you're here. You might make a few suggestions."

The minister went on.

"After a time my eye, trained to detect matter in its wrong place, wandered from plants to the men and women about me. As with the plants, so I found it with my fellow creatures; and I came to the conclusion that half the sins and the miseries of the human race arose from the fact of people being planted amid unsuitable surroundings."

"And you tried your hand at transplanting men and women," cried Sir Peter, excitedly, now thoroughly convinced that the subject was a congenial one.

"I did my best, Sir Peter, but that was little enough. My eye, trained to detect want of harmony between person and place, suggested more work than my feeble hands could accomplish. In fact, to have accomplished one quarter of must have played the part of Providence to the community generally."

"And very good part to play, too, my dear sir," said Sir Peter, sympathetically.

"But so much beyond my capabilities," replied the minister, "that, after adopted my sacred calling, was almost driven to regret the power my eye had acquired of detecting matter in its wrong place I was perpetually tormented with desire to set things straight." Sir Peter's face here became aglow. "There were peers of the realm should like to have transplanted from their grand houses to costermongers' cellars, and there were hewers of wood and drawers of water whom would have made peers of the realm. It was this sense of the fitness of things that made me say, so soon as I set eyes on Gervase Critchett: 'That boy is out of place among working men.' And on the very evening that I was starting for Upton—what's the matter, my dear sir; do you suffer from cramp?"

"A trifle now and then," said Sir Peter, giving one or two vigorous stamps; "I've been sitting still a good bit this morning—ever since I've been listening to you. How would it be to take a turn outside on the terrace? The wind has lulled a bit. After all, it's only a sou-wester."

Only a sou'-wester! But that sou'wester had done its work well during the night, as the stripped trees and battered flower-beds in the garden testified. The damaged sea-wall also below St. Cuthbert's church had a tale to tell, of the combined fury of wind and wave, and the fishing boats, drawn up high on the beach, showed that the weather-wise fishermen knew well enough that that fury was as yet but half spent.

Just now, however, as Sir Peter had said, the sou'wester was taking a rest, and the terrace, under a fitful noon-day sun, looked a fairly tempting promenade.

Mr. Parker made a brief exclamation as to the wind swept clearness and beauty of the surrounding landscape.

"You were saying an unusual occurrence took place at Liverpool," said Sir Peter, eager as a child to get the finish of what promised to be an interesting story.

"Ah, yes! I was saying that just as I had detected the want of harmony between Gervase Critchett and his surroundings, so did I, on the night of my arrival at Liverpool, detect the incongruity of another person—this time a young woman—with her surroundings."

"Ah, a young woman!"

"I had been spending the evening with a brother minister, and, as I was going back rather late to my hotel, I met a policeman with a young woman in his charge. Now there are some people who look in their right place on their road to a police station in charge of the police, and one is delighted to leave them to the surroundings that so admirably become them. But a single glance at this young woman's face showed me that whatever might be her right place, assuredly it was not within the walls of a prison."

"Ah! Good looking girl, eh?"

"It was not her good looks, but the utter forlornness and hopelessness of her expression that at first attracted me. I caught sight of her face beneath a gas lamp—it was haggard, death like it its pallor; a quantity of jet black hair hung about it. She was dressed entirely in a long, limp gray garments. I could have fancied some poor soul bidden against its will to come forth from the tomb, looking much as she looked."

Sir Peter stopped abruptly in his walk.

"Forlorn-looking, pallid, with jet black hair," he repeated thoughtfully. "Dressed all in gray too, and on the night after my birthday!"

All Lance's ugly suspicions of Stubbs's double dealing at Liverpool seemed suddenly to have substance given to them.

On some one else's ear beside Sir Peter's the minister's narrative had fallen with startling effect. Madge, wrapped in her furs, was standing in the parapet balcony where once Miss Shore had knelt, addressing her piteous prayer for mercy to the star-lit heavens. Preparations for the journey to Spain were now complete, and on that very afternoon, Madge, accompanied only by her maid, intended to set forth. She was standing now in that balcony of painful memories looking her farewell to the beautiful landscape tricked by the fitful sunshine into a transient semblance of a summer smile.

"Goodbye, you dear lanes, where Lance and I have had so many canters together! Goodbye, dear stream, where we used to fish and boat through the summer mornings! Goodbye, dear woods; goodbye, dear hills," she was saying to herself.

Spain, it is true, might own to landscapes far more magnificent than this; but only between the bars of a convent window would she catch glimpses of them, and—this it was that would take the colour and glory out of them all—there would be nothing of Lance in them.

Thus her thoughts ran, when suddenly the minister's story, summed up by Sir Peter, reached her ears, and forthwith the landscape became a blank to her, and her heart seemed to stand still, as she leaned over the parapet above the speakers in intense, painful eagerness to catch what was to follow.

Sir Peter was eager for the sequel also.

"What was she charged with, tell me—you did not let her go to prison?" he asked.

"I put the first of your questions to a man—a dock labourer, who followed them," answered Mr. Parker. "He told me that she had made a most determined attempt to commit suicide from the deck of a steamer under repair in one of the docks. That it was only by the merest chance that the attempt had been frustrated. He had remained behind on this steamer till late in the evening, in order to finish some work, and by main force had held the girl back from her attempt to jump over its side into the basin—"

There came a low, startled cry from the balcony at this moment; and, before Sir Peter had time to realise who it was that stood there, Madge was beside him with clasped hands praying for the finish of the story. "She is alive, only tell me that," she prayed, with blanched checks and quivering lips.

Mr. Parker looked astonished. "Did you know her—Etelka McIvor?" he asked. "She said that she had not a friend in the world."

"She is alive, only tell me that!" implored Madge.

"Yes, she is alive and in safe keeping. I attended the next day at the police court when she was charged with the attempt at suicide. No friends came forward to claim her, so I made myself known to the magistrate and volunteered to charge myself with her safe keeping."

Madge leaned against the stone balustrade of the terrace. This sudden reprieve from the sentence of her condemning conscience was almost more than she could bear.

Stubbs's story then from beginning to end was a fabrication! The chances were that the man or his confederate had traced the girl to Liverpool, and had there lost sight of her. With an eye to a comfortable provision for himself in the future, and taking it for granted that Jane Shore would never again make her appearance at Upton, he had then fabricated what seemed to him a fitting end to the tragic story, and one most likely to conduce to the fulfilment of Madge's wishes—a necessary condition this in order to the bringing about of the aforesaid comfortable provision for himself.

The insertion of the false statement in the Liverpool newspaper would be a matter of easy accomplishment to him, for the double reason that such sad stories were of daily occurrence in the place, and that his former connection with the Liverpool Press made ways and means ready to his hand. All this in quick succession passing through Madge's brain, and coming hand in hand with her sudden revulsion of feeling, for the moment deprived her of the power of speech.

It was not so with Sir Peter; his ready exclamations and questions flowed in a stream.

"My dear sir, this is good news—I've not had better for many a day past! Lance will be overjoyed—"

Here he broke off, and looked at Madge.

"But you found a home for her, of course?" he went on, cheerily, after a moment, "Now tell us everything that happened—all you found out about her from beginning to end."

"Yes, I found a home for her. I took her first of all to the wife of the Wesleyan minister whom I knew intimately in Liverpool. A worthy woman she was, with eleven small children, and neither nurse nor maid-servant in the house. Now here there will be plenty of occupation, I thought, for the young lady. If she has a kind heart, and is grateful for her rescue from death, she will set to work with a will to help this poor Christian mother with her many burthens."

Sir Peter fumbled in his pocket, and presently produced from a letter case an indelible pencil and a telegraph-form, two things, it may be remarked, which went as regularly into his pocket every morning as his purse or pocket handkerchief.

"If you'll give me the address of that worthy woman, I think I'll send Miss Shore—ah, Miss McIvor, I mean—a few words of—of congratulation on—"

"She is not there now," interrupted Mr. Parker; "and if you'll allow me to make the suggestion, she is not in the frame of mind at the present moment to appreciate congratulations, however kindly intentioned they may be."

Sir Peter looked disappointed as he put away his pencil; then a bright idea came to him, and he took it out again and began scribbling on his telegraph form, making a writing pad of his letter case.

"Lance will be glad to know," he muttered half to himself.

Madge thought her ears must have played her false.

"Lance is on the Mediterranean?" she exclaimed.

"No, no, my dear; at Liverpool. Ah, you didn't know—there, I've let it out—it doesn't matter. He altered his mind to say—came back from Marseilles, and is now at Liverpool investigating—ah well, investigating—something!"

Madge needed no farther telling. In a flash of thought she pictured Lance at his dreary work at Liverpool—searching grave records, hearing perhaps a hundred sad stories in order to prove one false. She pictured the rush of joy which Sir Peter s telegram would bring him at his hopeless task.

"Let me send it," she pleaded, laying her hand on the old gentleman's arm. "I should like it to go signed with my name."

It seemed to her that the one who had so nearly wrecked the man's happiness for him, might well be the one to send to him the glad tidings that her endeavours had been futile as well as misguided. Her message was a brief one:

"She is not dead. Come back at once.—
MADGE."

XXXIX

Later on in the day, Madge and Sir Peter were to hear the story of Etelka McIvor, otherwise Jane Shore, so far as it had been confided to the Wesleyan minister.

It was a testimony to the aptitude of the Rev. Joshua Parker for winning the confidence of his fellow creatures that he should have succeeded in drawing from lips so reserved a story fraught with such bitter memories.

Possibly, however, the supposition that she was lying on her death bed, and the natural wish not to pass all unknown into the land of shadows, should by rights share with the minister's persuasive powers the credit of opening those hitherto obstinately-closed lips.

Scared, stunned, with shattered nerves and enfeebled bodily powers, Etelka followed her rescuer from the police court, which figured to her bewildered fancy as a veritable bar of justice. A fortnight's serious illness followed, during which she was nursed with assiduity by "the Christian woman with many burthens." It was during that fortnight—when she believed herself to be lying at the gates of death—that she gave, in fragments, as her strength permitted, the story of her life.

It was a pitiful story enough. Her parentage was a curious one. Her father was a McIvor of Inverness-shire, who, when cruising in his yacht in the Mediterranean, fell in love with a beautiful peasant girl, whom he chanced to see dancing in the streets of Ajaccio, to the music of a mandoline, played by her old grandfather. The girl was of gipsy extraction, and the old grandfather gained his livelihood partly by his mandoline playing, partly by the practice of magic and occult arts, which had come down to him from his ancestry.

Hector McIvor must have been madly in love with this girl, for when she refused to leave her native mountains and return with him to Scotland, he spent nearly the whole of his patrimony in the purchase of an estate on the island, married her, and settled down there as a fruit-grower and sheep-breeder.

In spite, however, of her great beauty, the Corsican girl could not have made a pleasant companion. She owned to a gloomy temperament, was endowed with all the passions and prejudices of her race, and, among other superstitions, had a fixed belief in the ruling of the planets. It was possibly a matter of congratulation to her husband that the whole of her kindred in the island was represented by her aged grandfather, who died shortly after the marriage.

But though Hector McIvor gave up his Highland home, he did not forget it When Etelka was born, he sent for his own faithful old nurse and committed the little one to her 'care. No doubt, in due course, Etelka would have been taken over the seas to make the acquaintance of her Scotch kinsfolk if a bad form of fever visiting the island had not ended her father's life. Etelka was barely four years old when this happened. The father left no will, and his property fell unreservedly into the hands of his wife. Less competent hands could scarcely be imagined. It was not only that she lacked the most elementary knowledge concerning fruit-growing or sheep-breeding, but that her superstitions and prejudices interfered on all sides with those who had practical knowledge of these matters, and had filled positions of trust in her husband's time. Unlucky days were marked by her in the calendar, and on those days nothing must be done. Only when the moon was propitious must fruit be gathered; only when Jupiter was in the sixth house must sheep be bought or sold. Before she engaged even a labourer on the estate she must cast his nativity and read the lines on his hand.

The result can be imagined; both farm and orchard speedily became unproductive and unprofitable, and a yearly decreasing income was the result.

It was providential for the child that her Scotch nurse was a fairly educated woman, otherwise she would have grown up in ail-but heathen ignorance; the mother never attempted to teach her daughter save astrological lore and the beautiful dances in which she herself was so proficient; and this, she openly avowed, was merely by way of amusement in order to bring back in memory the happy days of her own girlhood.

"For where was the use to fight fate?" she would ask. "Save in recollection, happiness and prosperity could never more visit their home." Life, so far as she was concerned, was at an end; the stars had said and the stars could not lie. As for Etelka, the malefic planets were in the ascendant when she was born, and there was nothing before her but life of misery and an early and violent death.

"Look," she would say, opening the child's hand. "Her line of life breaks here, before she is twenty and at her birth the moon was in opposition to Mars in the eighth house. Any one who reads the stars knows what that means."

So the mother cut herself off from all companionship and sympathy with the ill-fated little one, and Etelka was left to the charge of the Scotch nurse, to be instructed by her in such lore as the old body had at command. Naturally, the child was taught by her to speak her father's as well as her mother's tongue. They were sadly at a loss for books, however. Etelka's mother took no interest in procuring any for her child; and the old nurse was intent upon saving every penny she could scrape together in order, some day, to take flight with the little girl to her father's people in Inverness. She kept alive the memory of the father in the child's heart by endless stories of his early days. A Scotch newspaper, occasionally received, was a mine of wealth and enjoyment to the nurse and child. Etelka would have all sort's of strange stories read to her by the old body, who, with finger travelling down the columns, would try to bring before the child the geography of the places whose doings were there recorded.

Honestly enough the nurse tried to do her duty by the neglected child. She racked her brain for tales from English and Scottish history that would amuse and instruct the little one. The stories of the "Queen's Maries," "Fair Rosamond in her Bower," and of "Jane Shore," were as well-known to the child as if she had been English-born. The story of the last named ill-fated beauty who "bewitched a King and died a vagrant," made a deep impression on her; and the fact of the name being easy of recollection and pronunciation, no doubt led her later on, under changed conditions, to adopt it for her own, when a sudden request for her name was made to her which she was unprepared to meet.

It was the nurse who, when the child began to develop a rare talent for landscape painting, supplied her with colours and brushes, wherewith she taught herself to paint the wonderful skies and grand mountains of her Corsican home. It was she also who gave the little one her first faint notions of religion.

Calvinistic teaching of from the nurse, partial initiation into the mysteries of astrology by the mother, wrought in the little Etelka's mind a curious habit of thought. "My mother," she said, as she related this portion of her history to the minister, "believed in fate, and called her belief astrology; my nurse believed in fate, and called her belief by a long Scotch name—predestination."

Lying awake at nights and gazing up at the stars, the little one used to wonder in quaint, childish fashion which was the star with the long Scotch name, which no doubt had ruled her father's destiny.

Debarred from playthings and all childish playfellows, it was no wonder that Etelka turned for companionship to the only young human being who ever came in her way, a boy—Giovanni by name—who kept her mother's goats on the mountains. Giovanni was about her own age, and speedily became devoted to the little girl. He taught her to climb the mountains, he made rods for her to fish with in the mountain streams, and showed her how to peel the young cork trees and make canoes of the bark, which together they floated out to sea.

In return, Etelka taught him all she knew of the lore of the planets, and tried to read his destiny for him in the heavens.

So things went on till Etelka was about twelve years of age, when her aged nurse died. On her death-bed she handed to Etelka the whole of her savings in English gold and Italian silver, bidding her keep the money safely, as sooner or later she might want it in order to make her way to her father's people, who, she assured the girl, would receive her with open arms. She also gave Etelka many and minute directions—which she made her taken down in writing—as to the route she would have to follow in order to get to her Scotch home.

No doubt the faithful servant, taking into account the young girl's rapidly developing beauty, saw dangers ahead of which Etelka had no conception.

After the nurse's death, things grew gloomier than ever. The house and the estate by this time had fallen into utter ruin, and if it had not been for Giovanni and his mother, Elmina—who took the place of the Scotch nurse in the house—Etelka, at times, would have wanted food, and also would have been compelled to perform the commonest household duties.

Her mother she rarely saw. All absorbed in her occult arts, she was shut in one room nearly the whole day, and only wandered out at nights to lonely heights to study the positions of the planets. At rare intervals she would take Etelka with her on these midnight wanderings, show her her ruling planet, and talk to her of sextile, trine and square aspects, and the passage of the planets through the signs of the zodiac.

Etelka, thirsting for sympathy and companionship, prized these rare opportunities of intercourse with her mother beyond measure; she stood greatly in awe of her, and treasured her words as the inspired utterances of a prophetess. The words "Fate wills it," so often on the mother's lips, were slowly but surely exercising a baleful influence on the young girl's daily habit of thought; and when one day the mother took her by the hand and pointing out one planet, told her that an evil star was rising for her, and a crisis in her life was at hand, Etelka trembled for what was coming.

Etelka carried her fears to Giovanni, who had by this time grown into a fine, handsome youth. Giovanni, for the first time in his life, only gave her half his attention.

He had a great piece of news to tell. A chalet on the coast which had long been empty, had been rented by a Neapolitan gentleman and his mother; the mother was an invalid, and came for the sea air; the son—the Count Palliardini—was a sportsman, and he came for sport. The Count had met Giovanni as he was driving his goats along the mountain road, and had offered him good pay if he would act as his guide during his stay at Santa Maura.

Etelka, describing this Count Palliardini to the minister, admitted that he was handsome in person, courtly and polished in manner. He was cosmopolitan in his tastes, a first-rate linguist, speaking with ease three or four languages; he was also a wonderful improvisator, and skilled mandolinist; last, but not least, he was so formidable a duellist, that to cross swords with him meant certain death.

The first time that this man saw and spoke with Etelka, he fell desperately in love with her, and, young as she was, wished to make her his wife.

Etelka shrank from him with what seemed an unaccountable repugnance. She distrusted his courtly suavity, and suspected that his obtrusively-displayed, effeminate tastes covered a coarse and brutal nature. Man of the world as he was, he laughed at her girlish dislike, and referred the matter to her mother. The mother as usual declined to take an active interest in her daughter's affairs. "What fate ruled would be," she said. "That year was a portentous one to Etelka; before it ended an evil planet would be at the square aspect of the place of the sun at her birth." And then she shut herself up once more in her lonely observatory at the top of the house and abandoned herself to her mystic studies.

It is possible that Etelka, in spite of her dislike to the Count, might have yielded to his importunities if Giovanni had not at this time begun to make his influence felt. He brought to her strange stories of Count Palliardini's life in the outer world of which they knew so little.

He had gathered from talk which he had overheard between the Count and his mother, that neither the Countess's ill health, nor the Count's love of sport, had been their real reason for coming to Corsica;

but that the Count was "under a cloud" for a duel which he had fought in Naples under suspicious circumstances, his adversary being his own cousin, by whose death from his sword thrust he had greatly benefited.

People in Naples had raised a hue-and-cry over the business, saying that the Count had purposely picked a quarrel with his young cousin; and, hence, the Count and his mother had found it expedient to retire for a time from Neapolitan society before attempting to take possession of the dead man's inheritance.

Giovanni further went on to say that the Count in his own home drank freely of wine, was hard and tyrannical to his servants, cruel to dumb animals, and boasted freely of the women's hearts he had broken, and the men whom he had killed in duels.

Etelka, with her mother's prophecy of approaching evil ringing still in her ears, was seized with a sudden terror lest that prophecy might have its fulfilment in her marriage with this man whom she hated and feared. She resolved to do her best to flee from her evil destiny, and, together with Giovanni, laid a plan for taking flight from Santa Maura to her father's people in Scotland.

They took Giovanni's mother into their confidence; and she, no doubt stimulated by ambitious views for her son, helped forward their plans. The three joined over the old nurse's directions which Etelka had taken down in writing, and again and again they counted up the legacy of English gold and Corsican silver which Etelka had kept in a safe hiding-place. They decided that Giovanni should accompany Etelka to Ajaccio (whence she would take boat for Marseilles), and remain there until Etelka sent money for him to follow her, as their store of gold was inadequate for the travelling expenses of two persons. The early twilight was fixed for the time of their departure, when Etelka's mother would be shut up in her observatory, and Giovanni's master would be enjoying his evening siesta.

Their councils were held, and arrangements were "made with the greatest care and secrecy they imagined. Some incautious act, however, must have betrayed them.

On the day they had fixed, and at the twilight hour, Etelka crept out of her home and made her way over the mountains to the edge of the forest, where she and Giovanni had arranged to meet. She kept her eyes downcast; she would not look up to the skies, for there she knew shone out the bright planet she had learned to hate.

But it was not Giovanni who stepped from out the shadows of the big plane tree and took her by the hand, but Count Palliardini himself.

"Might he have the pleasure of being her escort? Was she expecting to meet the boy Giovanni? Ah, yes, he had met with an accident that day. Well, there were enough and to spare of such canaille as he, and one less would be so much to the good."

These were the words with which he greeted her.

Giovanni's accident, when it came to be told, proved to be "that last dread accident which men call death." The Count's statement was that he and Giovanni had gone fishing in the early morning in one of the mountain streams; he had gone higher up the stream than the lad, and when he came back had found him lying face downwards in the river bed with his rod floating downstream. He conjectured that the lad had dropped his rod into the water, and trying to recover had fallen in, and been carried out of his depth. The Count had called to some shepherds for help, but when between them they had got the boy out of the stream, life was extinct.

Etelka went back to her home dazed and stunned she and Elmina suspected foul play on the part of the Count, but there was no evidence to support their suspicions. Before Etelka had time to rally from the shock of this calamity, another followed on its heels. Her mother, in attempting to cure herself of ague, from which she suffered through exposure to clamp and night air, took an overdose of some vegetable poison that she was in the habit of employing as a medicine, and in a few hours was dead.

Her last words, as she lay with dying eyes fixed on Etelka's face, were: "Poison for me; poison, or fire, or flood for you—the stars have spoken."

After the mother's death the Count pressed his suit more hotly than ever. Then it was that Etelka, driven to desperation, looked up at the evil glittering planet high in the heavens and defied it. She resolved to fight her destiny. She had tried to flee from it and had failed, now she would fight it.

But of the means by which she endeavoured to do this the minister knew nothing for certain, although, possibly, his suspicions went near to hitting the mark.

"At this point in her story," he said, "the girl had turned her face to the wall, and her lips had once more been obstinately sealed." Of her attempt upon Count Palliardini's life, her hurried flight to England, and her stay at Upton, she had told him nothing.

From this point, however, Madge found it easy enough, in imagination, to take up and finish the pitiful story. She could picture

Etelka, in the gloom of her desolate home, handling her mother's poison bottles, while the lamentations of Elmina over her only son rang in her ears, together with the woman's cries for vengeance on his murderer.

She could picture the girl laying her plans, step by step, up to and after her terrible attempt at crime; her hurried flight to Marseilles; her brief stay there to provide herself with less remarkable clothing than that her island village could supply; her arrival, half-dazed and bewildered, in England; her attempt to reach her father's home in Inverness; and her recognition of the hand of fate in the railway accident, and the arrival of Lance and Sir Peter on the scene of disaster.

After this, there had come, no doubt, a partial awakening of conscience, a sense of remorse intensified by the thought of a relentless pursuing Nemesis.

With the light of her luckless history thrown upon became easy to understand her attempts upon her own life; her terror of what was hanging over her head as each attempt failed and, finally, her revulsion to joy and gratitude, and her tremulous snatchings at better things when the newspaper brought the tidings that she was not the murderess she had supposed herself to be, and the proffer of Lance's love made her judgment subordinate to the voice of her heart, which suggested that possibly her mother had misread her future, and that after all happier days were in store for her.

XL

Sir Peter's handkerchief had gone very often to his eyes during this recital. "If we had only known, eh, Madge?" he said again and again, picturing to himself the benefits he would have showered upon the friendless girl had he known one quarter of her friendlessness.

His heart was divided in two. It seemed to him that so much misery should by rights be crowned by the happy storybook ending:

"And she lived for ever afterwards happy and comfortable."

Under the influence of this thought he was disposed to bid Lance God speed in his wooing. Yet there was another side to the question; there was Madge looking every, whit as white and forlorn as ever that friendless young girl had looked. Really, it was hard to say which way his sympathies should be allowed to incline.

But something else beside sympathy must surely be required of him. They had been sitting still a long time, it would be a positive relief to set the wheels of life going in one direction or another. "Did you ascertain from Miss McIvor the name of her father's family place in Inverness—McIvor is a very general name in the Highlands?" he presently asked with a passing vision of a delightful little trip to the Highland capital to make the acquaintance of the young lady's kindred.

"Miss McIvor refused to give me any information on the matter," replied the minister. "'It was not to be,' she said, in reply to my inquiries. From this I concluded that she imagined that fate had spoken against her joining her father's people, and she had given up all idea of doing so. I confess I did not urge her on the matter. I could not see her in her right place among the followers of John Calvin, getting the seal set, as it were, to her fatalism. It also occurred to me that supposing Count Palliardini saw fit to pursue the poor girl to England, he would naturally, in the first instance, trace out these relatives of hers."

Sir Peter suddenly seemed to see a way to a benevolent interference in Miss McIvor's affairs.

"It occurs to me," he said, taking a little trot round the room and coming to a stand still at the minister's side, "that if any one had taken the trouble to put the matter in the right light to Count Palliardini—I mean had represented to him the impropriety of persecuting a young girl with his addresses, he might have been induced to offer her friendship instead. Now I should amazingly like to have a good talk with the man; I'm sure I should do something with him."

And now the old gentleman's brain was filled with the vision of a pleasant little trip to Corsica, and a delightful *téte-a-téte* with the Neapolitan Count.

"My dear sir! my dear good sir!" exclaimed the minister.

"Where is Miss McIvor now—at Liverpool?" interrupted Madge.

The minister resumed his story. "I quickly found out that she was out of place in the busy home in which I had placed her; but where would she be in her right place? I asked myself again and again. I tried to picture her in a modern fashionable drawing room, on the boards of a theatre, in a convent even. No; I could see her nowhere in her right place. Then one day I had a letter from my sister Jenny—"

"Ah, Jenny! Who was she; what was her occupation in life?" interrupted Sir Peter; to his fancy the minister was not telling his story half fast enough.

"I was about to say. I left Jenny a child when I went off to the colonies, I returned to find here—well—say mature. Jenny is a capital housewife, stout, handsome, healthy, and active. And she had been condemned, by circumstances, for years to lead the life of a student; to be eyes, in fact, to a blind astronomer; to read science to him, and act as his amanuensis by day, and at nights to gaze through his telescope at the stars."

"Capital!" cried Sir Peter. "And you made sister Jenny and Miss McIvor change places!

"I did so. I could see Miss McIvor—mentally that is—in her right place in a lonely observatory, with face upturned to a night sky! "

Madge started. There came back to her the vision of a white face upturned to the stars with a prayer for mercy on its lips. The minister went on. "I knew, too, that her astronomical knowledge and habit of close observance of the heavens would be most useful in an observatory. Poor Jenny used to get such severe scoldings at times for inaccuracy and carelessness. 'Deliver me from this if you possibly can,' she had written to me on my arrival. 'I'm losing my hand for short crust, and as for stockings, I couldn't turn a heel now to save my life!' So I asked Miss McIvor if she would allow herself to be guided by me in this emergency. 'It is written,' was all her reply. On her lips it meant 'Kismet! I bow to that.'"

Here Sir Peter's handkerchief went to his eyes again. "Ah, that Count," he murmured. "I would like to get hold of him for five minutes!"

Mr. Parker continued his story. "I knew something of this astronomer, or I would not have suggested such a thing. He is of Norwegian descent, Harold Svenson by name, a man between seventy and eighty years of age, whose eyesight failed him ten years ago. He knows that his life is drawing to a close, and he is bent on verifying and classifying his observations of the past fifty years of his life. He is very poor; has spent nearly all his fortune in buying the finest astronomical instruments that can be had, and consequently he cannot afford to engage a scientific assistant in his work. His wife, a woman of about sixty years of age, does his housekeeping for him; and, because Jenny wanted next to no salary, he engaged her to act as his amanuensis, and, under his direction, to survey the heavens. He is a good man; all who come in contact with him are the better for it."

"Ah! poor, learned, good!" summed up Sir Peter. "We must get him here, Madge? Bring him back with Miss McIvor, build him an observatory on one of the hills, and set him up in instruments. What's the name of the place where he's to be found?"

"It's not far off. There is a bleak rock on the Cumberland coast, about five-and-twenty miles from here—at high tide it is cut off from the land; on it stands a round tower, that, some years ago, was used as a lighthouse. Svenson has been allowed to locate himself in it for a small yearly rental, and the roof-room, which formerly held the light, he has adapted to the exigencies of his telescope."

"Father circumscribed for space though," exclaimed Sir Peter, thinking of the difficulty of getting "a little exercise" under such conditions. "It strikes me Miss McIvor will be uncommonly glad to get a little more breathing room. We must get her back as soon as possible, eh, Madge?"

"If you'll take my advice. Sir Peter," said the minister, preventing Madge's reply, "you'll leave her where she is as long as possible. To be under the same roof with a man like Svenson is an education to a person of Miss McIvor's temperament. He is a man of a high order of intellect, and though untrammelled by religious conventionalities, religion is the life and soul of his being. I wrote to him fully of Miss McIvor's sad career, and begged him to do his utmost to bring her to a happier frame of mind. 'Make her, if possible, see I wrote, 'that her astrological notions, to be worth anything at all, must be pushed to their widest limits, and then they will be found to contain truths bigger than any she wots of.'"

"To their widest limits!" echoed Sir Peter, enthusiastically, more than ever convinced that the Rev. Joshua Parker was a man after his own heart. "I heartily endorse, I entirely concur in all you say, my dear sir! But—but," here he stammered and hesitated somewhat, "it's a little puzzling—a little bewildering. Do you mind explaining slightly what you do mean?"

"Not in the least; my meaning is very simple. I look upon astrology as a praiseworthy endeavour, by thinkers of a certain order, to account for the mystery of our three-fold nature, and to embody, classify, and time the apparently arbitrary and resistless influences which compel men to certain courses of action. Now, if these thinkers had thought a little harder, they would have found that this three-fold nature exists, not only in humanity, but in all creation; and that these apparently arbitrary and resistless influences prevail, not alone in this world, but throughout the universe, and antedate the planets which mark time for us by as much as eternity antedates time. In other words, they would have found that we are in harmony with the planets only because the planets, like us, are in harmony with the grand and eternal laws which govern the universe, and that these planets can no more give a law to man, woman, or child on the earth than the dial plate of a clock can give a law to the mechanism which moves its hands."

Sir Peter passed his hand over his forehead. "Eh! it's a little puzzling. Did Svenson understand all that, do you think?"

"Undoubtedly; his reply to me showed he did. 'My telescope will make her see this better than my words could,' he wrote. 'Before she leaves my roof I guarantee she will see, that to make the stars spell out the decrees of fate when she might read in them the laws which govern fate, is like persisting in reading nursery rhymes when one might revel in the enjoyment and education of Homer, Milton, or Shakespeare.'"

Madge, who had sat a silent listener throughout this conversation, was impatient to bring back the talk to Miss McIvor's more immediate doings. She had a question, to ask, which held for her a painful interest.

"When did Miss McIvor go to this observatory?" she said in a low, eager tone.

"About ten days since we left Liverpool—'we' means Jenny, Miss McIvor, and I," answered the minister; "I had written to Jenny to arrange matters with Mr. Svenson and to come to Liverpool in case I might not be able to escort Miss McIvor on her journey North. We reached Carstairs; there I received a telegram recalling me to Liverpool on matters connected, with my ministerial duties, so I commissioned Jenny to continue the journey alone. She had an anxious time with

Miss McIvor after I left them. The young lady refused to continue her journey, and took to gazing at the stars again. There was another crisis in her life at hand, she said, as also a crisis in some other person's. She kept her room all day long, and wandered out at nights. Jenny was scarcely so vigilant as she ought to have been, and Miss McIvor disappeared one afternoon, and did not return till early the following day."

"Did she give any account of her doings during her absence?" queried Sir Peter.

"She came back saying that she had taken train to a place that was memorable to her, and had seen what she had expected to see—'the stars had not lied to her.' Those were her words."

Madge drew a long breath. She felt that the gray, shadowy form in the churchyard was accounted for now.

XLI

All Madge's plans seemed turned, upside down; her preparations for her journey to Spain came to a halt. The startling revelations of a brief twenty-four hours had seemed to put the Spanish convent into the far distance. Now that what had appeared to her as a sin, almost beyond the hope of Heaven's pardon, no longer brought a tragedy in its train, all thought of penance for it vanished. Her mind began to recover its balance, and, unconsciously to herself, other duties in life began to assert their claims. At the present moment, however, her future was blank. Till Lance's fate was decided, she could give no thought to her own.

Although she no longer harboured enmity against the woman who had supplanted her in Lance's love, she had no wish ever again to stand face to face with her. Also, from the bottom of her heart, she prayed that she might never again in this life meet the look of Lance's wrathful eyes. All she desired now was to know that the happiness of this man, for whom she had risked so much, was assured to him. Gervase Critchett's death had given back to him wealth and worldly prosperity. Her one desire was that love and happiness might crown both for him.

She waited impatiently for telegram from him acknowledging hers. When, however, one day had ended and another had begun, and there had not come back the swift "Thank Heaven" on which she counted she grew vaguely uneasy, and consulted Sir Peter on the matter.

His face, as he listened, implied a secret to be kept; and his lips disclosed that secret on the spot. He even fetched Lance's letter, and, skimming it with his eye, read portions aloud. He seemed to feel considerably relieved when he had got rid of his secret, and she knew as much about Lance's movements as he did. He hazarded the conjecture that Lance's investigations might have taken him out of Liverpool—to London, perhaps; but suggested that work might be found for the telegraph wires in the shape of a kindly message to Miss McIvor.

Madge demurred vigorously to this.

By a painful effort of self-abnegation she put herself for one moment in Miss McIvor's place, and swiftly decided that overtures for a renewal of friendly intercourse must, in the first instance, come from Lance. If Miss McIvor were inclined to accept him as a, future husband, she might be willing, for his sake, to pardon the slights put upon her by his people. If such a far away possibility as her rejection of Lance's suit came to be realised, then the wider the gulf between her and Upton the better.

Before that day ended, Sir Peter's conjecture as to the reason of Lance's silence was confirmed.

A stranger arrived at the Castle stating that his business was urgent, and that he wished without delay to see both Mrs. Cohen and Sir Peter. He was a detective from Liverpool; for Sir Peter he had a question; for Mrs. Cohen an important communication. The question to Sir Peter was: What was the latest news received of or from his late secretary, Mr. Stubbs? The communication to Mrs. Cohen conveyed the intelligence that cheques for various large sums, bearing her signature, had lately been paid into the county bank at Liverpool by persons who had had dealings with Mr. Stubbs, and it was important to know if these signatures were forgeries.

The detective went on to say that suspicion in the first instance had been aroused against Mr. Stubbs by inquiries made by Mr. Clive of local magistrates, and, subsequently, of the police authorities. It had so chanced, also, that, on the very day on which Mr. Clive's inquiries were made of the police authorities, a man, who gave himself out to be a clerk in a private inquiry office at Carstairs, in which Mr. Stubbs had at one time been employed, made an important communication to the chief inspector. It was to the effect that he had reason to believe that Stubbs had stolen Mrs. Cohen's chequebook, and that certain cheques which he had been dealing out rather freely of late, had forged signatures attached to them.

The detective furthermore added that there was little room for doubting that the informer had at one time been an accomplice of Mr. Stubbs's in certain shady transactions which had recently come to light, and it was possible that Stubbs's greed in keeping his spoils to himself in his latest peccadillo had severed the bond between the two rogues.

Madge had also but little doubt on the matter, when she recollected Mr. Stubbs's ready talk of a friend at Carstairs, who had acted as his agent from time to time.

A search through the davenport, in which Mrs. Cohen had been wont to keep her cheque-book, confirmed the surmise as to its abstraction.

Sir Peter's grief and bewilderment at these revelations took in turns a comic and a tragic form. He vowed—walking up and down the room very fast—that he would have no more *protégé* if he lived to the age of Methuselah; that he would withdraw his name from every charity list on which it figured, except that of the asylum for lunatics and idiots, who, after all, were the only reliably honest people in the world. Finally, he "got upon rockers" in front of the detective, and, raising his eyebrows very high, and tip-toeing very fast, asked a series of surprising questions: "Why should he not withdraw his charity subscriptions if he felt so disposed? Was not his money his own, his name and his time also at his own disposal? Was he to stand still, and allow himself to be cheated by every rogue who came along?"

The worthy detective, never before having had the pleasure of meeting Sir Peter, was a little inclined to doubt the old, gentleman's sanity. His doubts grew upon him when, the next moment, Sir Peter suddenly sank into a chair, supplemented his series of questions with a series of apologies—"He wasn't himself at all; his head was going round with the startling news he had received during the past twenty-four hours"—and then as suddenly started up again, vowing that he had had no exercise that morning; and there and then set off for a promenade in a gale that fell little short of a hurricane.

Madge, left alone with the detective, put the question which she had with difficulty kept back:

"Did he know where Mr. Clive was at the present moment?"

The detective replied that when Mr. Clive had called at the police office on the previous day, he was on his way to London to institute an investigation into the disappearance of a young lady who, Mr. Stubbs had stated, had committed suicide at Liverpool, but who it was possible might not have been near Liverpool at all. Mr.Clive, however, had said that he would be back at Liverpool the next day in order to follow up a certain clue which he had in hand there. He had given in writing a description of this young lady to the chief inspector of police, who had forthwith set inquiries on foot.

Then the detective drifted back to Mr. Stubbs and his roguery. There was every reason to believe that the man under another name had taken passage to America with his stolen property; the cable, however, had been set going, and there was little doubt but that as soon as he landed he would be arrested and sent back again.

But Madge had too many deeper interests at heart at the moment to be much concerned by Mr. Stubbs's chances of detection or escape.

"Did Mr. Clive give any address in London to which a telegram could be sent?" she asked.

"He did not, madam," replied the man, astonished at the lady's want of interest in her banking account. "He won't dare attempt to pass another cheque now—he'll guess that by this time the affair has got wind—Stubbs, I mean," he added, getting back to the subject which had the greatest professional attraction for him.

Sir Peter came back, scarlet and breathless from his battle with the elements, but in a decidedly more cheerful frame of mind. It was to be a busy day for him. He had no sooner got back to the house than Mr. Parker presented himself, great coated and with bag in hand, ready to depart. His time was not his own, he said. He was but a paid servant after all, and was bound to go about his business, not his pleasure, without further delay.

Sir Peter was vastly disappointed. He had conceived a strong liking for the worthy minister, whose theories on matters of benevolence were, from one point of view, strangely in accordance with his own.

"If I had only known you earlier in life. I could have accomplished so much more in my sixty years," he sighed.

He forgot his outburst of a moment ago against philanthropy in all its branches, and pictured regretfully what a wonderful partnership in benevolence might have been set up if his active mind and liberal purse had seconded the minister's keen eye for matter in the wrong place.

"We'll build you a chapel in the valley, and find you lots to do if you'll pitch your tent here," he said, utterly oblivious of the fact that he had always announced himself to be "a staunch supporter of Church and State, sir."

The minister shook his head.

"I must go where I'm sent. I can't see myself here among your educated respectful farmers and peasants; but I can see myself where I'm ordered to go—among the rough-and-ready miners in the Durham coal pits. "Sir Peter's hopes revived when he found that the minister's destination was not far from Redesdale. He knew that he must of necessity see a good deal of Redesdale now that Madge's interest in her property there had grown so languid, and hence there was a chance that he and the worthy minister might often meet.

A large amount of hand-shaking and a very hearty farewell followed.

The minister's last words were an entreaty that news of Miss McIvor might be sent to him so soon as there should be any to send, for he would never cease to take the deepest interest in her, although he felt himself to be supplanted in his guardianship of the young lady by these influential friends of hers.

The arrival of a second visitor, before the wheels which conveyed the minister on his road had died in the distance, thoroughly restored Sir Peter's equanimity.

"Dear me," he said to the servant who announced the fact to him, "first one thing, then another. Wanted everywhere; can't get a minute to myself! What name did you say? Palli-ar-di-ni! Count Palliardini! Ah! Show the gentleman in at once, and see that we're not disturbed." It seemed to the old gentleman that this unlooked for event must have been arranged by special intervention of Providence, in order to give him scope for his benevolent intentions.

"He has come to make inquiries after Miss McIvor, of course," he said to himself. "Now I shall have the opportunity of reasoning with him and setting matters before him in a right light. Shouldn't wonder if I make a different man of him altogether before I've done with him."

His sense of importance grew upon him. He wheeled a big chair up to a big table, and pictured himself seated there lecturing the Count.

"But I must be discreet—very," he said to himself as he heard the Count's steps approaching. "What am I to say when he asks where the young lady is? Well, I'm not obliged to tell him, am I? I flatter myself I can keep a secret if I set my mind to it."

XLII

"Ah, a fine, handsome young fellow! doesn't look the villain we've given him credit for—perhaps things have been a trifle exaggerated. But I must be discreet—very!" said Sir Peter to himself, as Count. Palliardini crossed the room, and gave him for greeting the most courtly of bows.

The Count was tall, and slight in figure. His carriage was good, his dress was faultless. He had driven nine miles across country in a blustering gale, yet not a hair of his head seemed blown astray. The solution of this mystery lay in the fact that on arriving at the Castle, he had stopped for a good five minutes in front of a mirror in the hall to arrange his hair with a pocket comb.

"Of the lazy, effeminate, Italian type," was Sir Peter's second thouought as he noted the young man's slow and languid movements.

And "his hand is the hand for the guitar, not the sword; depend upon it his prowess has been exaggerated," was his third and last thought as he looked at the slender, white hand which, for a moment, touched his in response to his essentially English acknowledgment of the courtly bow.

Count Palliardini summed up Sir Peter in a very few words.

"A very small picture with a very large margin," he said to himself, as he took a leisurely survey of the small, plump, old gentleman seated in the lofty room, which could with ease have accommodated the congregation of a village church.

"Now, how shall I begin? I've a good deal to say," Sir Peter thought. Then a sudden fear seized him: "What if he doesn't understand English! The idea never struck me before."

The Count speedily set his mind at rest by saying in excellent English that he must beg Sir Peter to accept his apologies for his sudden and unceremonious arrival. He could only plead the extreme urgency of his business as his excuse.

Save for the roll of his R's, and the distinctness with which he spoke his final syllables, one might have set down English as his mother tongue.

"No excuse is necessary, my dear sir," said Sir Peter, immensely relieved at the Count's linguistic capabilities. "Your name is not unknown to me. Only yesterday I was expressing a wish to make your acquaintance."

The Count for a moment let his large, black eyes rest on Sir Peter's face. "Now, what is behind all this?" those eyes seemed to say.

He would have been greatly surprised if he had been, told that nothing beyond a benevolent wish to deliver a homily on the duty of kindliness and unselfishness lay behind the old gentleman's friendly speeches.

He acknowledged the friendliness with another courtly bow. Then he went on to explain the object of his visit, mentioning Miss McIvor by name, and speaking of her dead mother as a valued friend of his own.

"I have had some little difficulty in tracing the young lady to your house," he added. "If it had not been for her striking personal appearance, I do not suppose I should have succeeded in doing so through the many breaks in her journey."

"Ah, what made you fancy she had come to England?" queried Sir Peter, desirous to get a little time for himself in which to arrange the opening sentences of his lecture.

"I knew that Miss McIvor had relatives in Scotland, and when she suddenly disappeared from her home I naturally concluded that she had gone on a visit to them. I had some little difficulty in discovering to which of the McIvors her father had belonged—there are so many of that name in Scotland. When, however, I succeeded in finding his people, and heard that she had not been near them, I set the police in Edinburgh and in London to work. It is thanks to their efforts that I am here."

Sir Peter was perplexed. He knew well enough what the Count's next question would be. He wished he had had time to consult Madge on the matter before rushing into so momentous an interview.

"Miss McIvor left us some little time back," he said, presently. "There, that tells him nothing," he added to himself.

"Yes, I know," answered the Count. "It was the stir which her sudden departure from your house caused in the neighbourhood which enabled the police to trace her to Upton. But you have had news of her since she left?"

"Ah, yes—very satisfactory news, I'm glad to say."

"There, that tells him nothing," once more he added to himself.

The Count looked at the old gentleman steadily. "I shall be much obliged if you will tell me where she is at the present moment, and the quickest way of getting to the place," he said, after a moment's pause.

Sir Peter pushed back his chair, rose from the table, and commenced a quick march round the room. Now or never for his homily, he thought;

but really his ideas wanted a little arranging. "Let me see," he said to himself. "First, there's this gentleman to be reconciled to Miss McIvor. No, by-the-bye, he's in love with her already; it's the other way! Miss McIvor is to be reconciled to the Count. Ah, but we don't want her to fall in love with him; there's Lance to be thought of. Well, I must put in a good word for Lance somehow—I can't have these two young men quarrelling over the girl—and I must give this young man a little bit of good advice. What a blessing it is he speaks and understands English! Yes, I've a good deal to say, and, before anything else, I must be discreet-very!"

The Count kept his seat, his eyes following Sir Peter in his quick march.

"Is he a lunatic," he thought, "or does he suffer from rheumatism? He seems a little jerky about the joints."

Sir Peter came to a stand still in front of the Count's chair. He laid his hand kindly on the young man's shoulder.

"My young friend, look at me. I'm an old man—old enough to be your father," he said.

The Count turned and looked at him. "No, it is not rheumatism; flighty—but harmless—that's what he is!" he thought.

He bowed acquiescence in Sir Peter's remark.

Sir Peter went on briskly:

"I'm sure you'll agree with me that young men are sometimes the better for a little fatherly advice."

"A little fatherly advice!" repeated the Count, slowly, with just the faintest curl of his upper lip.

"Exactly. A little fatherly advice. Now, I have an adopted son of my own. He is about your own age; a fine young fellow like you; and what I say to you this morning, I am going to say to him. 'Lance,' I shall say to him, 'the only way to get happily through life is to give and take.'"

"Ah, and this Signer Lance, this fine young fellow,' will listen to you, and do as you tell him—'Give and take'?"

Sir Peter shirked the question.

"I've a great deal to say," he began.

The Count pulled out his watch.

"Pardon me," he said, "if I say that my business is urgent, and I have a train to save. I shall be greatly obliged to you if you will tell me where Miss McIvor is at the present moment, and allow me as quickly as possible to continue my journey."

Sir Peter was disconcerted.

"What I have to say is of great importance. It concerns you, it concerns Miss McIvor, and it concerns my adopted son, Lance."

There came a sudden change of expression to the Count's face.

"How can what concerns Miss McIvor and me concern also this Signor Lance?" he asked.

He was prepared to listen now, not a doubt, to what Sir Peter had to say.

Sir Peter shirked this question also. He made an apparently irrelevant remark.

"If we would be happy we must make others happy."

"Must we?"

"Now—pardon my saying so—it occurs to me that it is in your power to make two people very happy. Those two people are Miss McIvor and my boy Lance."

All the languor, in a moment, had gone out of those large Southern eyes upturned to Sir Peter's face.

"Miss McIvor's happiness is of importance to me. Your boy, Lance, I do not know."

"I shall be delighted to introduce you; we're expecting him back by every train. I ought to have told you that when Miss McIvor left us so suddenly, he went in search of her. Then, when he heard—ah! well, it's a long story. At any rate, he returned, and then set off again, intending to go to Corsica."

"Ah, I would have welcomed him, this Signor Lance, if I had been there," murmured the Count.

"I'm sure you would," said Sir Peter, heartily. "Now where was I?—I've lost myself, somehow, I was going to say—ah, what was it?"

The old gentleman looked "very much mixed," and once more set off on a trot to the farther end of the room. A question from the Count, asked in a voice which Sir Peter had not heard before, brought him back.

"Tell me," he said, "this Signor Lance, did he take a very great interest in Miss McIvor?"

"A very great interest is no name for it, my dear sir; he fell desperately in love with her," answered the guileless Sir Peter; "and I'm bound to say that at first I was a little disconcerted at it—I had other views for him—"

"You had other views for him?"

"Yes—all this is in strict confidence, my dear sir—a marriage was as good as arranged between him and a lady—my ward, Mrs.Cohen—But bless me, I'm running on; this can't interest you in the slightest degree."

"I am deeply interested," said the Count, in the same voice as before. "The lady whom you wished the Signor Lance to marry, did she take a deep interest in Miss McIvor?"

"She did not at first; in fact, I'm sorry to say she took a most unaccountable dislike to the young lady; but afterwards, in a most noble and unselfish way, she gave up all thought of her own happiness—"

He broke off abruptly.

"Ah, that's it," he cried, delightedly, "that brings me back to what I was going to say—"

"Such sad news from the coast," said Madge, coming into the room at that moment, all unconscious of Sir Peter's visitor. "A barque ran ashore last night, about three miles below St. Cuthbert's church Oh, I beg your pardon, I thought you were alone."

"A barque ashore!" cried Sir Peter, excitedly. Then he bethought him of the courtesies of life. "Madge, may I introduce to you the Count Palliardini?" He turned to the Count. "This is my ward, Mrs. Cohen."

Madge almost started in her amazement. She knew in a flash of thought that here was a crisis to be faced. She looked at the Count's slender white hand, and thought of the stain of blood on it; she looked at his dark, handsome face, and said to herself: "An Iago with the face of an Adonis." And the Count, as he bowed in acknowledgment of the introduction, took a slow, steady survey of Madge, and said to himself:

"She has no beauty; it is her lot to love better than she is loved. She is white and worn to a shadow; she has suffered. The little Marietta who broke her heart for me had much such a look in her eyes when I said to her: 'My child, we must part.'"

XLIII

The news of the stranded barque set Sir Peter ringing the bell and ordering his dog cart to be brought round immediately. He was equipped and out of the house in a little over five minutes. During that five minutes, however, he managed to get through a good deal.

Madge wandered after him into the hall, trying to whisper a question as to what information he had or had not imparted to Count Palliardini, for it was of first importance to her to know on what footing affairs stood now. But no! before she had time to get her question to her lips, Sir Peter was back again in the library, going through a series of polite apologies and explanations to the Count.

"So sorry to have to run away like this; but I'm sure you'll understand my anxiety to be at the scene of disaster. Now, may I have the pleasure of putting you up for the night?"

The Count rose from his chair. "I would rather you should have the pleasure of dismissing me," he said. "I am anxious to continue my journey, and if you will be good enough to tell me where Miss McIvor is to be found, and how to get to the place, I will start at once."

Sir Peter waved his hand towards Madge, who stood in the hall just outside the library door.

"Mrs. Cohen will answer all your questions, I am sure, with a great deal of pleasure."

Then he flitted into the hall again.

"Madge, my dear," he whispered, "I leave the matter in your hands; you will know exactly what to do for the best."

"What have you told him?" asked Madge, anxiously.

"Nothing, my dear, absolutely nothing; I have used the utmost discretion."

Then he was back again in the library, ringing the bell to countermand some order already transmitted to the stables.

"Now, you won't hurry away; you'll have some refreshment before you go? It seems so uncourteous for me to start off in this fashion; but I'm sure you'll understand. I've a big scheme in my head—"

This was said to the Count.

"Ah, yes!"—this to the servant—"have Leah put to, she gets along faster in the wind than Havelock—"

Then again to the Count:

"A big scheme, yes—I shall telegraph to the Mayor of Carstairs and some of the clergy to meet me this afternoon, so that we can at once form a Vigilance Committee to watch this part of the coast while the gale lasts. Now I'm off!"

Naturally, very little of this information was of the slightest interest to the Count. He slightly smiled.

"Mrs. Cohen, you say, will answer my questions?" he asked.

But Sir Peter was now in the hall, talking to Mrs. Cohen. "Madge, my dear, he was saying, "you have before you a grand opportunity! By the exercise of a little tact and discretion, you may succeed in effecting a vast amount of good. You must speak plainly to the Count—The cart's at the door!"—this to a servant who approached at the moment. "Ah by the way, I must get some more telegraph forms," and back into the library he went, to provide himself with these from one of the writing tables.

The Count had another "passing word" from him.

It was:

"I'm delighted to have had this opportunity of speaking to you in my boy Lance's interests—as I said before, 'give and take' is a golden rule."

Madge started aghast. Had he absolutely flourished in the face of this man the fact that Lance wished to figure as his rival?

"Madge, my dear," said the old gentleman, hurrying towards the door, and stuffing telegraph forms into his pocket as he went along, "don't forget there lies before you the grand opportunity of making two people very happy; that of course, you can manage to make the Count see matters in the right light. I've paved the way for you. Between ourselves, I don't think he's half such a bad fellow as has been made out; but be discreet above everything else—remember I've told him nothing. Now I'm off!"

Madge knew by experience that he wasn't yet!

He got his foot on the step of his dog-cart, then ran up the hall steps in a great hurry to give an order that blankets were to be sent after him in bundles, all that could be got together, as quickly as possible—and brandy—and rum—also as quickly as possible.

Then Madge had another word whispered into her ear: "Not half such a bad fellow; but be discreet, my dear. Now I'm off!"

And this time he really was "off." With his foot once more on the step of the dog cart, he waved his hand to her; the wind carried his voice away, but she could see that his lips formed to the words:

"Be discreet!"

The old gentleman's anxiety to escape from what threatened to be an embarrassing situation was easy enough to read, and at any other time Madge would have laughed at it. The crisis, however, which this anxiety of his compelled her to face without a moment's preparation, was no laughing matter.

She strove to collect her thoughts. One thing only seemed clear to her—that there was no use in attempting to shirk an interview with Count Palliardini; whatever danger threatened must be met and faced, alike in Lance's interests and in Miss McIvor's.

Of course the Count's one and only object in coming to the house was to discover Miss McIvor's hiding place. Supposing that she refused to give him any information concerning two dangers seemed to threaten one that he would stimulate the energies of the police on the matter by pressing the criminal charge against the girl, the other that he would seek an interview with Lance, or dog and follow his footsteps, and in this way obtain the information which he sought.

Now how was she to face two such momentous difficulties as these?

She might have studied this question for days and not have arrived at any satisfactory conclusion on the matter. To arrive at any conclusion, satisfactory or otherwise, in mere flash of thought was an impossibility. She could only hope that as she met or parried the inevitable questions, her good angel might whisper suggestion in her ear.

She went back to the library to find the Count standing in the window recess, looking after Sir Peters vanishing dog cart.

"Is he always like this?" he queried, a little contemptuously Madge thought.

To gain time for herself, she began a series of apologies for Sir Peter's sudden departure.

"It is an amazing benevolence," he answered, the contemptuousness of his manner becoming even more pronounced.

"A few fishermen, more or less! A few more or less of the *canaille* to annoy and get in one's way! What does it matter?"

The words unpleasantly recalled the story of the boy Giovanni's death.

He gave her no time, however, to express her indignation, but went straight to the object of his visit.

"Sir Peter has referred me to you, madame, for an answer to my inquiries respecting Miss McIvor."

Madge seated herself in the window recess, thereby turning her back to the light. He took a chair facing her, the full light falling upon his handsome, well-cut features, and bold, black eyes.

He went on:

"Miss McIvor, I believe, was staying some little time in this house. Will you be good enough to tell me where she is at the present moment?"

Madge felt that she must speak.

"I scarcely think I am justified in doing so," she answered, slowly.

The Count smiled, and looked handsomer than ever. His smile, however, was not a genial one, but was caused by the thought at how great a disadvantage these English women were whose consciences would not let them tell lies. Now, an Italian woman, if she had not felt inclined to answer his questions, would have vowed readily enough that she knew nothing whatever on the matter.

But he said only:

"Will you be good enough to tell me why you hesitate to give me this young lady's address?"

And Madge answered slowly, as before:

"I do not know that I am justified in doing even that."

For a moment he let his black eyes rest full on her face.

"She is not so much like Marietta as I fancied about the eyes," he thought to himself. "She is lovelorn; yes, but she is something else beside. Ah, it is that stupid thing called conscience which makes, her unlike Marietta. Marietta knew nothing about that."

Again he smiled, and said lightly:

"You have scruples! Ah! Englishwomen are always scrupulous—it is their charm. But to whom shall I go if you will not answer my question? Sir Peter has departed; the Signor Lance is not here. Shall I wait till the Signor Lance comes back, and put my question to him?"

And the way in which he spoke those words, "the Signor Lance," told Madge that her worst fears were realised, and that Sir Peter had surpassed himself in indiscretion.

In addition, it sounded a note of alarm. Lance, most probably, was at that very moment on his way back to Upton. At any cost, a meeting between the two men must be prevented, or at least deferred.

She answered calmly, although she felt that her face betrayed her:

"I suppose you mean Mr. Clive. I do not know that he would feel any more inclined than I do to answer your question."

But, so soon as she had said the words, it occurred to her that there was in them an undertone of defiance which, in the circumstances, was scarcely prudent. So she added, in a more conciliatory tone:

"You will understand, I am sure, that the fact of a person staying in one's house, and eating at one's table, lays obligations of friendship upon one."

"Ah, you and Miss McIvor were the greatest of friends while she stayed in your house," he said, in a tone that to Madge's fancy bordered on the insolent.

She flushed scarlet. What did he, or did he not know? Had Sir Peter revealed her feelings as well as Lance's towards Miss McIvor?

"I did not say that," she cried, indignantly, then broke off abruptly, fearing where her candour might lead her.

She took a moment or two to recover herself.

"Why should I say anything at all?" she began, and stopped herself again, feeling as one might feel on boggy ground, when every step lands one farther in the mire.

"Why should you, indeed," he answered, calmly; "and why should I ask questions which make you speak against your will, when I can so easily get them answered in another quarter?

Madge guessed in a moment which was that other quarter.

"You would not—could not surely—" she began.

"I would—I could surely," he answered, "apply to the police for information I want if I could procure it from no other quarter. Your English police are immaculate. I should simply say to them: 'This young lady, whom you have traced for me so far, once attempted to take my life by poison,' and before a week was over my head, her hiding place would be found out."

Madge rose to her feet impetuously. The words she had dreaded to hear were spoken now.

"I will not believe it," she cried. "I do not believe there lives a man who would—could act in so despicable a manner!"

He rose also and bowed low. "Madame," he said, "you see that man before you now."

For a moment neither spoke; they simply stood facing each other.

Madge, with her weakened health, her want of confidence in her own powers of persuasion or argument, dreaded to open her lips; the words, "It would be cruel—atrociously cruel!" escaped her against her will.

He bowed again. "I do not contradict you, madame; do you not know that men are often cruel—'atrociously cruel'—to the women they love? They will kill a woman rather than let a rival win her."

And as he said this his dark eyes flashed with an evil light, which made her once more look at his slender white hand and say to herself: "It ought to be red—red as the blood it has shed."

The Count suddenly changed his tone to his former courtly suavity.

"Why do I tell you this?" he said, softly. "Why do I distress a tenderhearted Englishwoman with stories of what men can, or cannot do, when they love or hate?—let us sit down, madame, and talk this matter over. This young lady is a friend of yours?"

The sudden, upward look which Madge gave him might have been taken to express dissent, but her lips said nothing.

"Well, at least," he went on, "she is a friend of a friend of yours!" Here, to Madge's fancy, his insolence in suavity surpassed his former unmasked insolence.

"And being a friend of this friend of yours you wish her well," he continued. "Now tell me, do you not think the young lady would be happier in Corsica, in her own home, among her own people, than among strangers in a foreign land, hiding in terror from your police? Sit down, madame, let us talk the matter over!"

But Madge would not sit down. She stood leaning; her elbow against the window recess, looking far away over the Castle grounds and the valley beyond, to the road along which Lance would come riding on his way home.

Suddenly she turned and faced the Count with the question:

"Why must it be one thing or the other? Why will you pursue her in this way? Why will you not let her alone to live in England, or in Corsica, as she pleases?"

He laughed a low, scornful laugh.

"Ask the rivers why they flow to the sea; ask the sea why it follows the moon," he answered, "before you ask a man, who loves, why he follows the woman he means to get possession of." Here he broke off a moment, then added, with a sudden, furious energy: "I tell you, madame, if that girl, Etelka, were shut up in the heart of the earth, I would dig her out of it, although I had nothing but these hands to do it with!" Here he extended towards her his slender, white hands. "And I tell you, moreover"—his voice lost its fury, and fell to a low, sullen, resolute tone, that held even more of menace in it—"I tell you that if I were lying on my death bed, and I felt that that girl were slipping away from my grasp, I would take a knife and shed her blood, drop by drop, rather than let another man win her."

All the lazy effeminacy which Sir Peter had fancied he had detected in the man, had disappeared now. His eyes flashed, he set his teeth over his last word.

Madge, as she stood silently facing him, took the measure of a man, relentless, cruel, and of iron purpose, and said to herself that he might well figure as the embodiment of the forlorn girl's pursuing destiny.

Her indignation would find voice for itself.

"You call that love!" she cried. "A selfish, cruel passion, that would sacrifice everything to the desire of possession!"

He bowed low. "In England you may call it by another name; but, believe me, in Italy it is what is known by the name of love."

"And you think that such love as that would bring happiness to you—to Miss McIvor?" she queried, impetuously.

He eyed her keenly for a moment. Then a slight smile curled his lip, and he met her question with another:

"Tell me, madame, are you very much interested in procuring happiness for Miss McIvor, or is it the happiness of the Signor Lance you are thinking of, that you thus refuse to tell me where the young lady is to be found?"

Madge was staggered by this directly personal appeal; also, she did not feel inclined to admit his right to make it.

"I decline to answer that question," she replied, coldly.

He was in no way disconcerted.

"If you wish the Signor Lance to marry Miss McIvor," he went on, "no doubt you do well to keep her hiding place a secret from me. But supposing"—here his voice sank to an insinuating tone—"that you did not wish the Signor Lance to marry this young lady, all you would have to do would be to tell me where she is to be found, and the Signor Lance would never hear of her more."

He said the last words with a slow emphasis.

Madge felt as if the pulses of her heart for a moment ceased beating. So, then, she was to be called upon to fight all over again the battle which had nearly cost her her life and Lance his happiness.

The continued gaze of his bold, black eyes became insupportable. She pressed her hand to her forehead, shutting it out; shutting out everything, in fact, except the voice of her own heart, which seemed to tell once more from beginning to end, the story of her shattered hopes and deathless love.

It seemed as if he read the turmoil of her thoughts. He went on mercilessly:

"But of course, since you wish the Signor Lance to marry her—the woman I love—you will not do this. No; you say to yourself: 'The Signor Lance is my friend; I will do my best to give him the wish of his heart.'"

He broke off for a moment, then added, contemptuously:

"Ah, these cold-blooded fools of Englishmen, who will marry with the hot-blooded daughters of the South! Let them catch a wild bird on the wing, and make it what they call 'respectable' before they try to tame a Corsican girl with a wedding ring! "

Madge felt as if she must go down on her knees, and pray to be delivered from evil. Was this Count Palliardini speaking? she wondered. In very truth, she could have believed that that poor, reckless, passionate Madge, who had loved and hated so desperately, had suddenly taken separate bodily form, and stood whispering her evil suggestions with the Count's voice.

She withdrew her hands from her eyes. In the brief moment that she had hidden them, she had fought as mighty a battle with her own heart as ever saint had fought in cloistered cell.

She looked him full in the face.

"I have given you my answer," she said, slowly, decisively. "I cannot—will not give you the information you ask for."

He bowed low.

"Then I must seek it elsewhere," he said. "If you will allow me, I will ring your bell and have that thing—'fly' do you call it?—which carried me here from your station, brought to the door."

Madge laid her hand impetuously on his arm.

"Oh, why—why will you do this?" she cried, passionately. "Why are you so hard-hearted and cruel? If you hunt her down in this way, persecute her, make her miserable for life, you will be none the better for it; it won't bring happiness to you."

The look in his cruel, relentless eyes had convinced her that the only plea likely to prevail with him must be based upon purely personal, selfish grounds.

"Madame," he answered, again bowing low, "I have the honour to wish you good morning. If you will allow me, I will continue my journey at once. I will prefer to discuss my chances of happiness with the Signer Lance."

XLIV

Madge for a moment stood like one stupefied, listening to the sound of the wheels which carried the Count away, dying in the distance. Then she drew a long breath. Yes, he was gone, not a doubt, and there could be no fear that he would ever return to trouble her with his insolent questions and black temptations; but what, she asked herself, would be his next step, what piece of wickedness would he endeavour to set in motion now?

She began to reproach herself, not for what she had done, but for what she had left undone. She had trampled under foot his hideous temptations, she had' given him a negative to his request—a negative, indeed, so calm and so decisive that any one who heard it might have fancied that she was acting upon a settled plan of action, instead of being at her wits' ends to know what to do for the best. But was the doing one of these two things an adequate way of meeting so serious a crisis? Looking back upon her half hour's interview with the Count, it seemed to her that her pleadings for Etelka had lacked fire and earnestness, and that she had been terribly wanting in common sense to have let him thus depart without getting from, him—as she possibly might have done by adroitly put questions—some definite clue to his movements and destination.

He had threatened to stimulate the energies of the police by the revelation of Etelka's crime; he had said as a parting word that "he would discuss his chances of happiness with the Signor Lance," and this, of course, was tantamount to a threat of waylaying Lance with hostile intentions. But which of these two threats did he intend to put into execution first? If the former, then he would no doubt go straight from Upton to London or Liverpool—or it might be to Edinburgh—to one of the chief centres of police inquiry, in fact. If the latter, then he would assuredly remain within a short distance of the Castle, on the look-out for Lance.

She rang the bell, thinking that possibly the servant who had shown the Count out of the house might be able to throw some light upon his movements, or, at least, upon his present destination.

"Did Count Palliardini make any inquiries as to trains when he left the house?" was her question when the servant made his appearance.

"None whatever, ma'am," was the reply.

"He told the man to drive him back to Lower Upton. He asked me as he went out if visitors to the Castle from London or Liverpool must all pass through Lower Upton? Of course I told him 'yes.'"

"If visitors to the Castle from London or Liverpool must all pass through Lower Upton," Madge repeated to herself.

The question seemed to point to the fact that the Count intended to await Lance's arrival at Lower Upton, either to pick a quarrel with him or to dog his footsteps thence, taking it for granted that by so doing he would come upon Etelka's hiding place.

Madge felt that her course lay plain before her now.

She was willing enough to admit that sooner or later Lance and the Count, as rival candidates for Etelka's favour, must meet face to face, and that no endeavours of hers could prevent such a meeting. She could only hope that when it took place, Lance's cool courage and common sense might carry the day over the Count's bravado and insolence. It was, however, manifestly to Lance's interest that this meeting should be retarded as long: as possible, or at least until after he had seen and pleaded his cause with Etelka.

The one who was first in the field there would be the one likely to win the day—the Count by threats of a criminal prosecution. Lance by the pleadings of his passionate love. Madge knew little enough of the penalty which English law attached to attempts at murder: of the Corsican law on the matter she knew nothing at all.

It seemed to her, however, that when the circumstances under which Etelka's crime had been attempted were taken into consideration, together with the Count's object in instituting a prosecution, but a light sentence would be passed on the girl, more especially if weighty influence were brought to bear on her behalf as Lance's affianced wife.

All these thoughts in quick succession passed through Madge's brain. Self was dead in her heart now; all selfish aspirations, hopes, and longings had had their death-blow dealt to them over again, as it were, in that brief moment when, with hand covering her eyes, she had stood listening to the Count's evil whisperings. All her energies were concentrated now on the endeavour to win for Lance the desire of his heart, just as one on a death-bed does his utmost to ensure the happiness of his dear ones in a future in which he himself can never play a part.

Her plan was quickly arranged. She wrote a brief line to Lance, telling him of Etelka's hiding place, and bidding him go there direct instead of returning first to the Castle. There were strong reasons, she added, why he should do this. It would be easy enough, she knew, for him to get to Cregan's Head from Carstairs by posting direct to Elstree, a bleak little village distant about two miles from the headland below which, on a ridge of low rocks, stood the disused lighthouse.

She said nothing of Count Palliardini's unexpected visit, nor of any one of the bewildering events which had occurred in such rapid succession during Lance's short absence from Upton. The great thing she felt now was to defeat the Count's evident intention of either delaying him on his way to Etelka, or of acting the spy and following on his steps.

Her letter written, she cast about in her own mind for a trusty messenger. Passing over Sir Peter's *protégés*, one and all, she fixed upon Lance's groom as being not only a discreet person, but also a good rider—a consideration this.

She sent for the man and herself committed the letter to his charge, bidding him to take the swiftest horse out of the stables for the nine miles of rocky road which lay between the Castle and Lower Upton. At Lower Upton he was to put up his horse, and take the train to Carstairs; he could just save it by hard riding. At Carstairs he was simply to remain at the station, await Lance, and immediately on his arrival there, place the letter in his hands. Whether Lance came on from Liverpool or direct from London, he must change trains at Carstairs for Upton, and the man had orders to watch all trains arriving from both places.

Madge took the man so far into her confidence as to caution him not in anyway to attract the attention of Count Palliardini, who might be waiting about at Lower Upton station; and still further to prevent such a misadventure, she desired him to change his livery for his plain clothes.

After she had despatched her messenger, she wandered about from room to room, restless, nervous, and ill at ease, occupation of any sort being an impossibility to her.

There was not a soul in the house to whom she could apply for a word of sympathy or counsel. Sir Peter was not likely to get back from his errand of mercy much before nightfall, and Lady Judith, as usual, was down at her farm. The gale of over night had unroofed a cattle shed, and had sent down a chimney pot into one of the poultry yards, so she had deemed her presence at the scene of disaster a necessity, in order to the safe housing of her short-horns and Houdans.

Madge racked her brains to think whether she could better have expedited Lance's meeting with Etelka. At the time that she had despatched the groom on his errand, it had seemed to her that he could not fail of intercepting Lance on his return journey; but now, as she thought over things, all sorts of mischances began to suggest themselves. The fact that Lance had not acknowledged her telegram of the previous day pointed to one of two things: either that he had not yet returned to Liverpool, and consequently had not received it; or else, that he had decided upon acknowledging it in person by an immediate return.

If the first supposition were correct, he as yet knew nothing of the good tidings concerning Etelka; but most likely, with a heavy heart, was pursuing in London some supposed clue that might lead him far afield, and Liverpool might not see him for days.

If the second supposition were correct, he might have started on his return journey before she had despatched her messenger; in which case it was possible that he and Count Palliardini had already met at Lower Upton.

She scarcely dared to think of the latter possibility; it seemed a catastrophe whose evil consequences she was powerless to avert. But the first difficulty, looked fairly in the face, did not seem insurmountable.

It might be that Lance, in the course of his investigations in London respecting Etelka's supposed death, or Mr. Stubbs's false statements, had consulted Sir Peter's solicitors on certain points on which, perhaps, he dared not trust his own unaided judgment. If that were the case, they would no doubt be kept informed of his movements, and would have his latest address. Why not telegraph to them for this, and then forthwith send a second telegram to Lance, repeating the message she had already sent by his groom to Carstairs?

She caught at this idea so soon as it presented itself, wondering over her own dullness in not having thought of it before. To ensure secrecy in the despatch of her telegrams, she resolved that she herself would send them from Lower Upton station. It might be that Count Palliardini, if he waited there, had decided upon watching the wires as well as the rails as a possible source of information.

Also of necessity time would be economised by her being on the spot to receive the reply from the London solicitors, and Lance would get his message, at the lowest computation, about two hours the sooner for it.

Madge, at her best, was not a good horse woman, and her recent failure in health had still further unfitted her for a sharp ride along a rough road. According to all showing, she ought to have been ready to collapse from fatigue before she had accomplished five out of the nine miles which lay between the Castle and Lower Upton. The exact contrary, however, was the case.

"When the soul is strong, the body is strong." With every step her horse took along that steep road, a fresh rush of strength seemed to come to her. Even the keen breeze, from which of late she had shrunk, seemed to bring life and energy to her. By-and-by, no doubt, the inevitable reaction would set in; but for the moment she was in the mood in which great things can be dared and done.

"Oh, you," she said to herself as she rode along, "who once before made it your business to part these two, make it your business to bring them together again, and thank Heaven that the chance of atonement is given to you!"

The afternoon was beginning to wear away. She timed herself for her nine miles' ride.

"Five o'clock," she said, "it must be when I ride past the knoll at the corner of the station road." And five o'clock it was. At this knoll she dismounted, gave her horse to the groom, and bade him wait for her there. It seemed to her that she would attract less attention by slipping into the station by a side door than she would if she rode up to the front.

The wind, which had lulled throughout the day, was beginning to rise now, whistling among the stripped trees and whirling the dry leaves before her in a cloud. The knoll, at which she had pulled up, was crowned with some straggling young hazel trees; the sun had just sunk behind these, leaving a great golden glare which shone through the delicate tracery of slender rods and leafless branchlets, like some pale fire from behind a wrought iron screen.

Madge had brought with her a long cloak and thick veil. Before she attempted to enter the station, she shortened her habit and donned both cloak and veil.

The telegraph office was on the other side of the lines. The ringing of the bell and a slight bustle on the ordinarily quiet platform announced the arrival of a train from Carstairs, and that consequently the other side could not be reached at present.

She judged it best to slip into the ladies' waiting room till the confusion subsided. This waiting room, small in dimensions, owned to a good-sized window, which, looked directly on to the platform; through this she could see all that was going on without running any risk of recognition.

Naturally, as she took her stand at this window, her first thought was: "Where is the Count? A single glance answered her question. There, in the very middle of the platform, he stood, in a line with, but with his back towards her window. Among the sturdy country-folk, with their baskets and bundles, his tall, well-moulded figure showed somewhat as a giraffe might show among a herd of bullocks. He addressed a question to a porter who stood near him; the man appeared to answer it in the affirmative; so Madge conjectured that the question might have been whether the incoming train brought passengers from Liverpool.

There followed the usual bustle of arrival and departure. Madge thanked Heaven, as the train glided out of the station, that it had not landed Lance at the very feet of his unknown foe.

There seemed to be a good deal of luggage to be disposed of; some had to be labelled for transit to outlying hamlets by later trains. Evidently for this purpose a small box was placed temporarily immediately beneath the window at which Madge stood.

And now a circumstance occurred which sent telegrams out of her head, which, in fact, reversed all her plans, and sent her in hot haste upon another quest.

The Count came close outside her window and addressed another question to the man whom he had before interrogated.

Madge could not catch the question, but she distinctly heard the man's reply, "No, sir, he has not come by this train," so she naturally concluded that the Count had commissioned the porter to watch for, and report to him Lance's arrival.

She drew further back into the room, for the Count's large black eyes to her fancy seemed to be piercing and searching in all directions. Once she could have vowed that they rested on her window, and she trembled lest her thick veil might be an insufficient disguise. It was not upon her, however, that his eyes were fixed, but upon the box which had been deposited beneath the window, and upon which an address card had been nailed in rough and ready fashion. The name on that card had evidently attracted his attention.

Madge, closely watching his face, saw a sudden change of expression sweep over it. Then he took from his pocket a notebook and pencil, and carefully copied the entire card.

A terrible suspicion flashed across her mind. As the Count moved away to the farther end of the platform, she crept out of her hiding place. A single glance at the box confirmed her worst fears; it was addressed to

Miss Etelka McIvor,
Cregan's Head,
Near Elstree,
Cumberland.

The writing was big and bold; the label on the box showed that it had come from Liverpool. Madge conjectured that possibly it was some friendly package from Jenny, the minister's sister, to whose duties at the observatory Miss McIvor had succeeded, and who, knowing the scanty supplies Cregan's Head could command, bad done her best to remedy local deficiencies by kindly gifts from the big city.

For a moment Madge stood as one transfixed. All her elaborate plans and precautions had been defeated by blind chance.

The Count's voice immediately behind her recalled her to herself. He was asking in his slow, mellow tones, which was the most direct way to get to Cregan's Head.

The man so questioned replied that in about an hour's time a train would start for Elstree, a little hamlet about two miles and a half distant from Cregan's Head. There might be the chance of a horse or a conveyance to Elstree, but people generally walked the two miles. The railway journey from Lower Upton to Elstree occupied about an hour and ten minutes. The Count had evidently changed his plans, and instead of lying in wait at the station for Lance, he intended to set off for Etelka's hidingplace with as little delay as possible.

Madge, in one flash of thought, seemed to see alike Etelka's extremity and her own opportunity.

Etelka suddenly confronted by the Count would most likely say, "It is fate," and yield to his combined threats and entreaties; more especially as she was unaware of the fact that Lance's love for her had not wavered, and that Lance's people were ready to welcome her among them.

The only way by which this danger could be averted, it seemed to Madge, would be for her to reach Cregan's Head before the Count, plead Lance's cause with Etelka, and make light of the Count and his threats—hold the ground, in foot, for Lance, till he could take it and hold it for himself.

In pursuance of this plan there was evidently not a moment to be lost.

She made a swift reckoning of the time that would elapse before the Count could arrive at Cregan's Head. There would be an hour before the train would start for Elstree, then an hour and ten minutes in the train, then two miles to walk in the darkness in a country he knew nothing at all about. She felt that close upon three hours was scarcely too much time to allow for all this, and that a pair of good post horses might cover the distance in about two.

She threw a furtive glance in the direction of the Count. Gas lamps were being lighted on the platform now; beneath one of these he stood rolling up a tiny cigarette in leisurely fashion. His easy attitude, and the half-scornful, half-triumphant smile which lit up his handsome features, seemed to say: "The road before me is plain and easy now."

With swift feet she made her way out of the station straight to the one inn that Lower Upton could boast.

She lifted her veil and made herself known to the landlord.

"Yes, I am Mrs. Cohen," she said, in answer to the man's look of surprise. "I want to get to Cregan's Head—posting it—within two hours from now. Can it be done?"

The man's face began to lengthen to a demur.

Madge would not let him utter it. "It must be done—it is of first importance," she said, peremptorily. "You know I do not spare my gold when I am in earnest about anything."

Yes, he knew that well enough, as did the whole country round for miles.

"Very well," Madge went on, watching the demur die rapidly out of the man's face. "I will give you twenty pounds for every mile of the road your man takes me over if he will get me to Cregan's Head within—mind, I say within—two hours from now; and in addition I will give him twenty pounds for himself. And you must not let a soul in the place know that I am here, or that any one has started for Cregan's Head. I will wait for your horses outside the village, at the knoll beyond the station."

There were of necessity no objections that were worth weighing against such golden inducements. Madge went back to the little knoll outside the station to dismiss her groom, and to send back a message of excuse to Lady Judith. Within ten minutes from the time that she had given the order at the inn, she was being whirled along the country road that led to Elstree at an altogether unconscionable speed.

There was no golden glare to be seen in the sky now, it was one expanse of leaden gray, splashed here and there—as if by an angry hand—with sullen red. The wind was steadily increasing in strength.

And it so chanced that at the very moment that Madge was setting off behind her two sturdy, yet swift-footed hacks, Lance, arrived at Carstairs, was reading the letter put into his hands by his groom.

It took him about a minute and a half to debate with himself which was the best line of route to be followed, and then he, too, was on the road to the same destination, mounted on the best horse that he could hire in the place.

So here was Etelka's destiny hastening to her that night by three several roads.

XLV

That swift drive in the windy darkness along the steep road was one to be remembered. The wind seemed to increase in strength with every half-mile they covered. It was not a mighty wind, but a strong rushing one that filled Madge's ears with all sorts of strange, wild cries, and seemed to bring the rush of the ocean to the very road-side long before they neared the coast. There was a moon, nearly at its full, a cold, white, ghastly thing which showed now and again, when a gust of wind swept away an inky mountain of cloud. Madge held her watch in her hand the whole distance in order to take advantage of every such passing gust. It had been half-past five as a turn in the road had hidden the slate roofs and gray walls of Lower Upton from view, and seven o'clock chimed from the village church as the sturdy chestnuts clattered along the stony street of bleak little Elstree.

Here at the little inn which vaunted itself as a "railway hotel," Madge dismissed her postboy with his tired horses, and took possession of the only two which the stables of the small hostelry could supply, thereby cutting off from the Count all means of transit to Cregan's Head from this place, save that which his legs afforded.

She reckoned that by this time he must have accomplished about half of his short railway journey from Lower Upton to Elstree, and that consequently in half an hour's time he would be exactly at this point in his road. To this half hour she thankfully added another for the two miles' walk along the steep dark road which lay between Elstree and Cregan's Head.

Madge knew Elstree very well, but, as it chanced, had never been to Cregan's Head, in spite of its short distance from Upton. Although she had frequently heard it described as "the other end of nowhere," or "a God-forgotten place, where gulls were plentiful and Christians few," she was totally unprepared for the scene of utter desolation which met her view, as the man pulled up his steaming horses at the foot of a narrow pathway, which seemed cut out of a mass of black rock.

"It's as near as I can take you, ma'am," he said in reply to Madge's astonished exclamation:

"But surely this is not Cregan's Head!"

She strained her eyes, peering into the surrounding darkness.

"Which way lies the coastguard station?" she asked. "Where is the little fishing hamlet, and where the old lighthouse?"

Behind her the bare gray road, along which they had driven, wound away into gloom; before her stood the dark mass of rock, cleft by the narrow, upward-winding pathway; on her left hand lay a dim waste of country, with stunted trees showing black out of the whitish ocean mist which overhung it; on her right hand stretched the expanse of ocean miles upon miles of moving, rushing, noisy darkness.

The man answered her questions in succession.

"The coastguard station is two miles distant, ma'am, on the other side of these rocks, and the fishing hamlet is half a mile beyond that. This pathway, after winding upwards a little way, descends to a sandy hollow, in which, so far as I know, are only two cottages. A ridge of low rocks stretches out from this hollow, and on these rocks stands the old lighthouse."

It was not a tempting prospect, this, of having to follow this steep, narrow pathway without lantern or guide.

"If I could leave my horses, ma'am," began the man.

But at this moment a light shone in gradual approach along the road they had just quitted. It suggested to Madge the cheering possibility of a local guide.

To save time, she advanced to meet the light, and found it to be a big lantern carried by a man of about sixty years of age, clad in the rough serge of a fisherman.

In addition to his lantern he carried a basket and sundry bundles, which seemed to suggest the likelihood that he was returning from a day's marketing in a neighbouring village.

He stopped at the unwonted sight of a lady and post horses.

Madge accosted him, and stated her business in a breath.

"I want to get to the other side of these rocks," she said. "Is there any one called Harold Svenson living there? Does he live in the old lighthouse, or at one of the two cottages which I am told are in the hollow below here?"

Fortunately the man was able to give her the information she wanted. He lived in one of those two cottages, he said, and Harold Svenson lived in the other, using the old lighthouse simply as an observatory.

"And a mighty lot of queer things he has put i' the lightroom, ma'am," he went on to say. "Telescopes—Lord ha' mercy on us!—that show what's going on i' the moon, an' clocks that ha' insides to them big enuff to lie down in; and tell the time, they do, in such outlandish fashion that naebody can understan' them."

It was easy to secure the services of the old man as guide, so Madge at once dismissed the post boy and his horses, exacting from him the promise that, in consideration of the handsome fee she had paid him, he would not take his horses back to Elstree that night, but would put up at the village on the farther side of Cregan's Head.

A fitful gleam of moonlight enabled her to look at her watch once more. It was just three minutes past the half-hour. The Count must be getting dangerously near to Elstree now.

The old fisherman grew loquacious as they trudged along the rocky path. He took the weather side, putting Madge under shelter of the rocks. Every now and then the rush of the wind carried his voice away, and she could only get at his long speeches in snatches.

He had been a fisherman all his life, he said; his name was Thomas Cundy—he pronounced it "Tammas Coondy"—he hadn't a big boat now, but just a little cockle shell of a thing that he had made for himself. He lived all alone in his little cottage; his wife was dead; his daughters were married. He "did" for himself; made his own clothes—

But here Madge interrupted him, her impatience refusing to be longer restrained.

"Had Harold Svenson lately had a young lady—a foreigner—as a visitor?"

"A young leddie, yes. Some fouk wud ha' called her a witch." Here a prolonged shake of the head did duty for a sentence.

"No one scarce had heard her open her lips, and he was told she had come from they outlandish foreign parts where people didn't know decent English ways."

As they had talked, their path had been sloping downwards. A black chasm of a hollow lay at their feet, out of which a curl of red smoke, puffed this way and that way by the wind, showed where a human habitation stood. Cundy nodded to it.

"That's fro' my chimney," he said. "Svenson an' his wife ha' been abed the last half hour."

"In bed," repeated Madge, dismayed at the possibility of having to arouse the old couple before she could get speech with Etelka.

They were standing on a ledge just over Cundy's hut. On the other side of the hollow, at about the same level, a dark square blot indicated Svenson's cottage.

From top to bottom of it not a glimmer of light was to be seen. Looking seawards, Madge could make out a black line about sixty yards out at sea—a ridge of sunken rocks, no doubt, for there, out of a mist of dashing spray, arose the gaunt outline of the disused lighthouse.

The old man nodded towards it.

"She's there—the strange young woman," he said, "she's not gone to bed, like other Christian fouk."

"What!" cried Madge, aghast, "she's alone there this terrible night!"

"It's her own doing—naebody could keep her indoors. You see Svenson had her here to help him wi' his books and look up at the stars for him—he's gone blind you know—but directly he set her there to look through his telescope, he couldn't get her awa' fro' it. She crouches over the fire i' the day time i' the lower room, and so soon as the sun sets, she goes up to the light-room and stares at the stars and says her prayers to them as if they were living things. Svenson won't get his book done if he waits for her help I'm thinking. Here we are, ma'am, at Svenson's door. Shall I knock the old people up?

Madge thought awhile. Why disturb them? Her mission was to Etelka and Etelka only.

She pointed to the gaunt tower with the white-crested waves dashing furiously against it.

"Can I get there tonight, will your boat take me?" she asked.

Cundy shook his head. "Better wait till mornen, ma'am," he said. "The wind is gay bad. There are some nasty sharp rocks between this an' the lighthouse; you might walk across to it in fair weather scarce wetting your feet; but i' the dark with this sea!" and again he shook his head.

But Madge had not come all these miles to be turned back by the first glimpse of danger. She determined to be lavish with her gold again.

"Listen," she said. "I am a rich woman. I'll give you twenty—thirty pounds if you'll take me across to that lighthouse in your little boat."

The man hesitated a moment, then he shook his head again. "Na, na," he said. "I'm a Christian man, and I've a soul to be savit. I would na risk your life, my leddie, for thirty pounds. If it were only my ain—" here he broke off.

"It will be at my own risk," said Madge, "not yours. See, I will give you forty—fifty—sixty pounds if you'll just row me across that little bit of water!"

"That little bit of water!" The phrase but ill represented the sixty yards of wild sea which lay between them and the lighthouse.

Possibly the prospect of so large a recompense made the old man feel a little less like "a Christian man with a soul to be savit," for after muttering something which the racket of wind and wave prevented Madge hearing, he bade her wait there in a sheltered corner of the beach while he ran his boat out and saw what he could do.

Minutes seemed to prolong themselves to hours while Madge stood there with that gloomy lighthouse facing her. Once more she pulled out her watch—the hands pointed to five minutes to eight; the Count by this time, most likely, had covered three parts of the road which lay between Elstree and Cregan's Head. Heaven grant that he might miss his way in the dark, and again and again have to retrace his steps!

And it so chanced that exactly at the moment that the dark figure of old Cundy, dragging his boat behind him, appeared on the beach, Lance, with a heavy heart, was pulling up at a road-side inn, half-way between Carstairs and Cregan's Head, with his horse hopelessly lamed by a big boulder lying in the dark road.

XLVI

Before she got into that boat, Madge had a request to make.

"After you've taken me across that little bit of water," she said, trying to keep up her grand show of courage, "shall you come back here With your boat, or will you stay all night at the lighthouse?"

The old man jerked his head towards his hut, where the dull light of a peat fire showed through one window.

"I've just put a bit o' bacon on th' peat for my supper; it'll want turnen by the time I get back," he said, deeming that an all-sufficient answer.

Madge again thanked Heaven for her gold. "Listen," she said. "As I told you before, I am a rich woman, and. I don't mind spending my money when I want a thing done. I am Mrs. Cohen from Upton Castle; do you know me by name?"

Cundy nodded. Madge's name, as local benefactress, was known all over the county.

"Very well. Do you wish to earn a hundred pounds by this night's work?"

"A hundred pounds!"

"Yes, I will give you that, so soon as you get back here, you will stave in your boat—before you turn your bacon even."

The old man gave a sorrowful look at his boat.

"I've had un a long time, it's like a living thing to me—but still-a hundred pounds 's a goodish bit of money—yes, I'll do it, never fear, my leddie."

"And," Madge went on, "soon after you get back, a man—a gentleman—will possibly find his way to your hut and want you to help him get across to the lighthouse. You must give him no help whatever. Remember, I have bought your services until the morning. Promise me that not a soul shall cross after me to the lighthouse before then."

The old man was profuse in his promises and protestations.

Directly he had taken his old boat to pieces, he said, he would turn in, put out his fire and all lights, and then not a soul would find out his hut under the shadow of the shelving rocks. As for Svenson, supposing the gentleman succeeded in finding him out, he would be unable to afford any help, for he owned to nothing in the shape of a boat.

Madge's courage nearly gave way when she and Cundy were fairly launched on "that little bit of water." She could never, at her best, boast of much physical courage, and now what with her rapid travelling, and the excitement she had gone through that day, she was beginning to feel far from her best. She hid her eyes with her hand, and sat shivering in the stern of the little boat as it bravely mounted crest after crest of the furious waves. Every moment she expected they would be dashed to pieces against some sharp, jutting crag of that low ridge of rocks, which stretched away from the beach to the lighthouse.

The old man, however, knew his ground, and kept as straight a course as wind and wave would let him. He had not battled with the elements on that coast for fifty years for nothing.

As they neared the lighthouse, the dull, red glare of a fire showed through a high narrow slit which served for a window. The old man directed Madge's attention to exclaiming that, "they furriners were nowt without fire."

Madge drew her hands from her eyes to find that the boat had reached the foot of flight of steps, which had been let down from another window below the narrow slit to meet the exigencies of the high tide ingress and egress being no longer possible through the door of the lowest room. The boat tossed now high on top of wave, now low in its trough. Drenched to the skin and half-blinded with spray, was with difficulty, and many misgiving, that Madge scrambled out of the boat and gained the topmost of that flight of steps.

"Push the wooden flap—it opens on th' inside—it's now but shutter," shouted the old man; and then his boat was tossed away in the darkness, and the rest of his words were lost to her.

Madge, in haste, pushed back the flap and crept in, fearful lest the next puff of wind might whirl her away like a leaf into the blackness beyond.

For a moment, as she stood within, she could hear nothing—see nothing—for the outside racket of the gale still filled her ears, and she had brought into the light tower with her a rush of breeze which sent the smoke from the peat fire that burned upon the hearth, whirling in all directions, and obscured the sullen gleam of the firelight. Other light there was none.

Presently those clouds of smoke parted, and Madge could make out that the room in which she stood was. lofty, but circumscribed at the farther end by a flight of steps, which wound away upward into darkness. The lowest steps also were begirt with shadows and whirling wreaths of smoke. Out of those cloudy wreaths a pair of large, luminous eyes seemed for a moment to look out at her and then disappeared. The haze of the smoke made everything uncertain; but she could feel the silent presence of Etelka McIvor, though her eyes failed to assure her of the fact. Madge thought of the last time that she had seen those large, desolate eyes, and her courage began to fail her. She felt that she must speak or succumb as to a spell.

"Are you there, Miss McIvor? I am Mrs. Cohen. I have come to speak to you on an urgent matter," she said, in a voice which even to her own ears sounded strangely.

Then, from out the smoke wreaths and shadows at the farther end of the room the tall, slender figure of Etelka slowly advanced and came to a standstill within two yards of Madge.

Madge stretched out her hands by way of greeting.

"Forgive me if I am abrupt," she said; "but time is precious tonight."

Etelka did not speak, did not take the proffered hands, and Madge bethought her of other things beside abruptness for which she ought to beg forgiveness.

She let her hands fall to her side.

"I do not wonder that you will not shake hands with me," she said, sadly. "I did you a grievous wrong once—I have come travelling to you tonight, in the dark and in the storm, to try and undo that wrong—to make amends for it, if amends are possible."

Etelka drew step nearer. The smoke, carried the current, was making its way now for the aperture which served as chimney. The red gleam of the fire threw a fitful light across the gloom, and Madge could get a clearer view of the girl's face. Madge thought that she had learnt to know that face; she had seen it rigid and white as carven marble; she had seen it soften and glow as might a carven marble statue flushing into warm life; she had seen it brilliantly beautiful, radiant with hope, as on the night of the ball; and she had seen it darkened with its forlornness and despair before that night had come to an end.

But the face which confronted her now was none of these.

"Jael, who drove the tent peg into the tired Sisera's forehead, might have had much such a face," Madge had said to herself on the first day that she and Etelka had met. Now, if time had been given her to put her thoughts into words, she would have said:

"Jael, with a deed of blood in her past, turned prophetess, priestess, seer, might have much such a look as that in her eyes. Is she looking at me or at things in the room which I do not see? Is she talking to me now or answering voices which I do not hear?"

The last thought was caused by Etelka saying in slow, low tones:

"I knew it would come tonight. I said to myself: 'I may shut myself up here alone, and the winds may make the waves my jailors; all the same, my fate will find me out.' And lo, it comes travelling to me in the darkness and storm!"

Madge's heart sank. This was the woman she wished to inspire with energy to fight a pursuing evil in the strength of an encompassing love!

"If fate is finding you out tonight," she said, trying her utmost to speak out bravely, "it must be a glad and happy fate, for I come as a messenger of glad tidings. Listen, I bring you news of Lance. He will be here tomorrow morning—the very first thing I hope—to tell you all over again how truly he loves you, and how that it was only in seeming that he gave you up, when he thought—as we all did—that you had—died—at Liverpool."

She faltered over the concluding words. But it was impossible to avoid abruptness. Necessity was laid upon her to say all that she had to say rapidly. In truth, she thought little of the manner of her speech in her eagerness to unfold to Etelka's view the bright things the future might have in store for her, before she told the evil tidings of Count Palliardini, his threats and pursuit.

But it seemed as if Madge might as well have shouted her good tidings to the stone walls which shut them in, as into Etelka's ears, for, still as a statue the girl stood, with her large, dreamy eyes looking beyond, not at, the flushed, eager face which confronted hers.

Madge lost her self-control. She sprang forward, seizing both Etelka's hands in hers, and crying out impetuously:

"Oh, if one came to me, bringing the glad news I bring to you, I would not stand as you do, saying never a word! I would go down into the very dust and kiss the feet of the messenger, and then I would jump up and clap my hands and shout for joy! Do you not understand me? I come from Lance, as Lance's messenger."

Something of animation shone in the cold, pale face.

"You come as Lance's messenger, do you say?" she said, in the same slow tones as before; "then take a message back from me to him. Tell him that since I saw him last a revelation has come to me—the stars have taught me things that they never taught me before."

"Oh, do not talk of the stars now," broke in Madge, impetuously.

Etelka held up her hand.

"Hush," she said, "you are a messenger, you say, therefore you must take as well as bring a message. Promise me you will."

"I promise," answered Madge, strangely impressed with the solemnity of Etelka's manner. It might have been that of a person, who, about to depart on a very long journey, gives minute and special directions as to what is to be done during his absence.

"Say to him," Etelka went on, "that, since I have been here in this lonely place, I have spent hours looking up at the stars through a grand telescope, and things have changed to me. Tell him I have seen the houses of life in the heavens, and I have seen the house of death; but I have seen something else which has made life and death fade into nothingness. I have seen Eternity there—immeasurable time, immeasurable space. Tell him that—promise me!"

"I promise," answered Madge, a sense of awe creeping over her, for Etelka's manner recalled now less that of a person about to depart on a long journey, than that of one about to undertake the longest journey of all—that journey from which there is no return.

There fell a pause. Outside sounded the solemn antiphony of wind, calling to wave, wave answering to wind; within, those two women might have heard each breath the other drew as they stood silently facing each other in the dim light.

Madge felt that she had succumbed to Etelka's strange powers of fascination, as well as to the weirdness of the scene, and had but ill done her work. Why should she, indeed, consent to carry Etelka's messages to Lance, when—as she hoped—he would be here on the morrow, and receive them for himself? One half, also, of her mission remained unfulfilled; her bad news had yet to be told—perhaps it might make a deeper impression than her good appeared to have done—so, making a great effort, she broke the silence, and said:

"There is some one else I must speak to you about besides Lance; for he, also, is on his way to you tonight—some one whom you have no reason to love."

Etelka started, a change of expression passing over her face.

"Count Palliardini?" she exclaimed, under her breath.

Madge's reply was cut off by a heavy and prolonged puff of wind, which must have sent the sea dashing over the top of the lighthouse; it set the wooden flap, which served at once as window and shutter, rattling as if it were being shaken on the outside by a human hand.

Madge's fancy instantly conjured up a vision of Count Palliardini having succeeded somehow in obtaining a boat, and now standing outside on the steps seeking means of entry. She bethought her of the possibility of fastening down that wooden flap.

"Is there bolt or fastening: to it?" she asked, at the same time crossing to the window to ascertain for herself what means of securing it could be improvised.

Etelka followed her. Madge pushed back the flap, and looked out into the darkness, in order to assure herself that her fears were groundless.

The salt spray dashed in her face; the wind sang in her ears. Clouds were scudding rapidly over the face of the wan moon. Not a light was to be seen on the shore in either cottage, and the red curl of smoke from Cundy's fire had disappeared; so Madge dismissed her fears, concluding that the old man had kept and meant to keep his promise to her.

A dark mass of cloud at that moment separating, a fuller stream of light poured down from' the faint moon; a receding wave also for a brief space left the air free from spray, and Madge could get a clearer view of the beach. In that brief space she saw something else beside the black outlines of coast and cliff—the figure of a man standing just where she had stood waiting for Cundy to bring his boat round. Then clouds swept over the moon once more, and sea and shore became again one dark expanse.

Madge knew that Etelka must have seen that man's figure as clearly as she had. She let fall the wooden shutter, and turned impetuously to the girl, taking both her hands in her own.

"Do not fear," she cried, "he can't get to us tonight. Cundy, at my request, has stayed in his boat, and there is no other. And tomorrow Lance will be—must be here!"

Etelka's hands were cold and trembling; her breathing came thick and fast.

"He will come—he will be here presently," she said, in low, hurried tones.

"I know that man; he will lose his life—his soul—but let go his purpose—never!"

Madge noted with thankfulness that the girl did not say now, as she had so often before, "It is fate—I bow to it."

"I tell you it is impossible—impossible," Madge repeated, "for him to get here till the tide runs out, which will not be till morning. Oh, Etelka, have you no courage? How can you be so faint-hearted, when you have true and strong friends to take care of you, and such a bright future before you!"

All Etelka's reply was to free her hands from Madge's clasp, lift the wooden shutter, and peer out into the darkness once more.

And this is what they saw when, after a moment's waiting, the faint moonlight again filtered through the drifting clouds—the man standing on precisely the same spot on the beach, throwing off his heavy overcoat and boots, and tightening and drawing together his other garments. He meant to swim.

He, the dandy who carried a pocket comb, who had hands whiter than a woman's, and fit for no rougher work than the twanging of a guitar, was going to dare death in the darkness rather than defer his purpose by even a few hours.

A low cry escaped Etelka's lips.

Madge threw her arms around her.

"Promise me," she cried, "that you will not be frightened by his threats; that you will say 'No' to his entreaties! Think of Lance now on his road to you! Think of all the happiness that lies waiting for you!"

Etelka freed herself from Madge's arms.

"He will drown!" she said, in a strained, unnatural tone. "He will be dashed to pieces against the low ridge of rocks in the darkness!"

Even as she spoke black masses of clouds rolled up from the horizon, and the moon was gone.

She walked away to the fire, which still burned low on the hearth.

Madge wondered if she were going to take away the man's one chance by quenching that fire—it still threw a fitful gleam, which must have shone in the outside darkness through the glazed slit in the wall.

But the next moment showed her that Etelka had another purpose. With her foot she stirred the embers together, then, picking up a short pine bough which lay on the hearth, she ignited and carried blazing torch, to the window at which Madge still stood, and passed through on to the outside wooden steps.

The life which she had once before attempted to destroy she would now do her utmost to save.

To the last hour of her life Madge never lost the vision of that tall, slender figure in shadowy, gray garments standing out there in the windy darkness, with flaming torch held high above her head. The wind tossed her black hair in disorder about her shoulders: the torch threw fitful light on the beautiful white face, with wide-open, desolate eyes, and mouth slowly settling into hard, rigid lines.

Not a second Hero assuredly! For the priestess of Venus lighted the man she loved across the dark waters, but this woman the man she hated.

And as Madge stood dumbly gazing at her, there came a sudden terrific blast which seemed to shake the lighthouse to its very foundations, and turned the solemn antiphony of wind and wave into one wild turmoil of rushing, dashing sound and fury, as of some fiend-orchestra let loose upon creation.

The wooden shutter was wrenched from Madge's hand, the embers of the peat fire were swept from the hearth, and the room for a moment seemed filled with whirling clouds of smoke and salt spray, which came rushing in through the now unshuttered window.

Something else fell upon Madge's ear beside the roar of the gale and the dash of the waves—a human cry, a crash, and then a great stillness, which seemed something other than the sudden lulling of the wind. And when, half-blinded with smoke and spray, and with a great terror at her heart, Madge ventured once more to peer out into the darkness, no slender figure holding high a flaring torch was to be seen, nor dark form battling with the angry waves; all that met her eye was the great, black, desolate expanse of furious ocean; nothing else.

"I did my best. Lance, for you—for her," said Madge, as she ended the terrible story which, with quivering lips and many a halt, she told him on the morrow.

But Lance stood looking at her, saying never a word, struck into silence, not only by the greatness of the tragedy, but by the magnitude of Madge's love for him, which, until that moment, he had never measured.

Epilogue

Six telegrams from Sir Peter Critchett:

No. 1.—To the Rev. Joshua Parker, Chadwick Coal Pits, Durham:

"I know you will be glad to hear that the marriage of my adopted son and Mrs. Cohen—delayed a year ago—took place this morning. Excuse haste; my hands are very full."

No. 2.—To Mrs. Lancelot Clive, Hotel des Anglais, Nice:

"So glad you remembered to send Lady Judith the patent incubators from Paris. I start at once for Redesdale to see that things are going on all right there."

No. 3.—To same:

"Arrived safely at Redesdale. Lovely weather."

No. 4—To same:

"Glad I came here. Lots of things want seeing to. The weather-cock on the top of the village church has stuck at north-east."

No. 5—To Lancelot Clive, Esq., Hotel de Anglais, Nice:

"Forgot to tell you I went to see Stubbs, at Millbank, the other day. Poor fellow—truly penitent—must look after him when he comes out."

No. 6—To same:

"Don't let Madge worry about the weather-cock, I'll have it set going before you get back. Will telegraph again tomorrow."

The End

A Note About the Author

Catherine Louisa Pirkis (1839–1910) was a British author known for her detective fiction. Pirkis wrote fourteen novels and contributed to many magazines and journals, sometimes publishing under her initials, C.L Pirkis, to avoid gender discrimination. Later in her life, Pirkis transitioned away from her writing career to join her husband, Frederick Pirkis, in his fight for animals' rights. Together, the couple founded an activist organization to save animals from cruel conditions. Their organization continues their advocacy today, and now goes by the name "Dogs Trust".

A Note from the Publisher

Spanning many genres, from non-fiction essays to literature classics to children's books and lyric poetry, Mint Edition books showcase the master works of our time in a modern new package. The text is freshly typeset, is clean and easy to read, and features a new note about the author in each volume. Many books also include exclusive new introductory material. Every book boasts a striking new cover, which makes it as appropriate for collecting as it is for gift giving. Mint Edition books are only printed when a reader orders them, so natural resources are not wasted. We're proud that our books are never manufactured in excess and exist only in the exact quantity they need to be read and enjoyed.